D1489950

✪ THE BLACKSMITH'S BRAVERY ✪

Susan Page Davis

JAMAICA MEMORIAL LIBRARY
P.O. Box 266
17 Depot Street
Jamaica, VT 05343

BARBOUR
PUBLISHING

© 2010 by Susan Page Davis

ISBN 978-1-60260-796-5

All rights reserved. No part of this publication may be reproduced or transmitted in any form or by any means without written permission of the publisher.

This book is a work of fiction. Names, characters, places, and incidents are either products of the author's imagination or used fictitiously. Any similarity to actual people, organizations, and/or events is purely coincidental.

For more information about Susan Page Davis, please access the author's Web site at the following Internet address: www.susanpagedavis.com

Cover design: Müllerhaus Publishing Arts, Inc., www.Mullerhaus.net

Special thanks to Woolaroc Museum, Bartlesville, OK, for use of facility and props

Published by Barbour Publishing, Inc., P.O. Box 719, Uhrichsville, OH 44683, www.barbourbooks.com

Our mission is to publish and distribute inspirational products offering exceptional value and biblical encouragement to the masses.

 Member of the
Evangelical Christian
Publishers Association

Printed in the United States of America.

DEDICATION

For all the women who dream big—
and for those who wish they dared.

★ CHAPTER 1 ★

Fergus, Idaho
October 1887

Griffin Bane picked up the big bay's foot. He stretched the gelding's hind leg back and rested the hoof on his leather-aproned knee. Reaching with his long arm, he pulled a rasp from his toolbox. The horse had chipped its hoof so badly that the nails had come loose. As he filed away at the remaining clinches on the nails, a shadow blocked his light.

"Morning, Griff."

"Ethan." Griffin didn't have to look up to recognize the sheriff's voice.

"Scout lost a shoe. I wondered if you could tend to him."

"Did you find the shoe?"

"Yeah, got it right here."

Griffin glanced up at the worn shoe Ethan held. Bent nails dangled from the half-dozen holes on each side.

"Front foot," Griffin noted.

"Yep. There's some bad footing out Silver City way. I rode up there yesterday."

Griffin grunted, placed the rasp in his toolbox, and pulled out the shoe pullers. "Reckon I can do it after this one." As he fitted the pincher ends under the edge of the horseshoe he was removing, he added, "Got to do the coach horses first."

"That's all right. I plan to stay in town this morning."

"Is his foot all right?"

"I think so. He's not limping."

Hurried footsteps echoed on the boardwalk that ran up the street from the feed store. They pattered softly on the ground after they reached the spot where the walkway ended. Griffin looked up. The dark-haired girl from the Spur & Saddle—Vashti—scurried toward them.

"Morning, Mr. Bane. Morning, Sheriff." She stopped a couple of yards away.

"Miss Edwards," said Ethan, tipping his hat.

Griffin grunted. Odd green eyes she had, almost like aspen leaves.

"Miss Bitsy wanted me to buy her a ticket to Boise. She's got business there and wants to take the afternoon stage, but you weren't at the office."

Griffin clenched his teeth and twisted the pullers, prying the remaining nails out of the bay's hoof. The shoe came off, and he tossed it on the ground near Vashti's feet. He reached for the hoof nippers and began clipping off the ragged horn around the edge of the hoof. "Tell her I'll be up to the office in a couple of hours. I've got two horses to shoe, but I'll be there in plenty of time before the stage leaves."

"All right." Vashti didn't move.

Griffin clipped all the way around the hoof and exchanged the nippers for a rasp so he could smooth the surface of the hoof wall before he put a new shoe on. "You want something else?" he growled.

"No, sir. I'll tell her." Vashti turned away and hurried back up the street.

"Pretty thing," Ethan said.

"I'm surprised at you, Sheriff, you being married and all."

Ethan grinned. "I said that on your behalf."

"Ha." Griffin finished smoothing the horse's hoof and set it down. He straightened and tossed the rasp into the toolbox, then pressed both hands to the small of his back.

"You getting the rheumatiz, Griff? A young fella like you?"

Griffin grunted. At thirty-five, he didn't think he ought to be having old folks' ailments. "Reckon it's all the hours I spend bent over."

Around the corner of the smithy from the livery stable came Marty Hoffstead, who had lately been working for Griffin, though he never had much to show for the hours he claimed he put in.

"Kin you come look at the brown wheel horse? I think he's favoring his off forefoot."

Griffin sighed. "I hope you're wrong, because I don't have a replacement for him today for the stagecoach team. I'll come look when I finish this job, but then I've got to reset the shoes on the sheriff's paint."

Marty nodded. "Oh, and Ned came over from the boardinghouse. Says Bill's got the heaves and he's shaking all over. Doesn't know if he can make the run to Boise this afternoon."

"Wonderful." Griffin lifted his eyes skyward and shook his head. "I'll probably end up driving myself. Again." He frowned at Marty. "You tell Bill if he's not dead, he'd better be on the box of that coach at two o'clock."

"I'll tell him, but I wouldn't count on it." Marty walked away.

"Looks like you could use more help around here," Ethan noted.

"You're telling me. Ever since I took over the stage line, I've been running nonstop. Can't get anyone to work the forge, and I can't get enough help running the livery. And keeping good drivers? Let's not even get started on that."

"Maybe you should advertise for help."

"Maybe so." Griffin scooped up the horseshoe he'd just removed from the coach horse and stalked into the smithy.

At half past eleven, Vashti scurried about the dining room of the Spur & Saddle with a wet dishrag, making sure all the tables were clean. Already a few folks had come in for lunch and seated themselves. Bitsy Moore, who owned the establishment with her husband, sauntered over to the table where Mayor Peter Nash and his wife, Ellie, sat.

"Good morning, folks. What'll it be?"

Bitsy could charm anyone with her sunny smile. Though Vashti reckoned Bitsy was twice her own age—approaching fifty—she still showed signs of the pretty woman she'd been. Her reddish hair had faded, but she no longer dyed it. She wore one of the satin gowns she'd purchased back when the Spur & Saddle was a saloon, but she'd recently added a creamy lace insert across the top of the bodice. Bitsy had gone more modest since she got religion, and she insisted the hired help adjust their fashions, too. She kept her bright lip color and rouge and her flamboyant jewelry. Bitsy did enjoy decking herself out.

"What's Augie cooking today?" Ellie asked.

"Thought I smelled fried chicken." Peter smiled hopefully at Bitsy.

"Oh yeah, he's got fried chicken. Venison stew, too. Biscuits and sourdough bread. And we've got us some carrots and Hubbard squash."

"I fancy the squash, myself." Ellie smiled across at her husband. "Of course, Peter never cared for winter squash."

"Bring me the fried chicken. You got potatoes with that?"

"Yes, sir, Mr. Mayor."

"Good. And the carrots."

Vashti scurried behind the serving counter that had been made out of the old bar. She poured two glasses of water. Bitsy paused beside her on her way into the kitchen to give Augie the Nashes' order.

"Before it gets busy, could you run across and see if Griffin's got the ticket office open yet? I don't want to get there at the last minute and not have my ticket."

"Yes'm." Vashti delivered the water glasses with a smile to the Nashes and ducked out the door and across the street.

She hiked up her skirt and ran past the emporium and across the alley to the stagecoach office. The big blacksmith had shed his apron and was tacking a notice to the wall beside the door.

"Mr. Bane, Miss Bitsy sent me for her ticket to Boise." Vashti halted beside him, panting.

He looked up. "Oh sure. Just a second." He hammered a final tack into the poster and went inside. "You got the money?"

"Yes." Vashti stared at the notice he'd posted:

HELP WANTED
STAGECOACH DRIVERS
BLACKSMITH
LIVERY STABLE HANDS
INQUIRE WITHIN

She pulled in a deep breath, squared her shoulders, and stepped inside. Griffin sat at the desk, fumbling at the ticket book with his big hands.

"You said she's going through to Boise?"

"That's right. On business. Taking the two o'clock."

Griffin wrote in the book and tore out the ticket. "Three dollars and six bits."

Vashti handed over the money Bitsy had given her that morning. "I noticed that poster you put up."

"Uh-huh." Griffin gave her the ticket. He put the ticket book in a drawer and, in the process, knocked his pen off the desk. He bent to retrieve it.

"It says you're hiring."

He sat up and squinted at her. "That's right. I need some more manpower."

She ignored the *man* part and plunged on. "Mr. Bane, I'd love the chance to drive. I learned how when I was a kid, and I've always been good with horses. I know I could do the job."

His jaw dropped.

"If you'll give me a chance, I can take the stage through. I know I can, easy as pie."

Griffin stood and stared down at her with such a thunderous expression that Vashti faltered to a stop and waited.

"You want to *drive*?"

"Yes, sir."

"Stagecoaches?"

"Yes, sir."

He threw back his head and laughed.

★ CHAPTER 2 ★

Something must be funny."

Griffin Bane looked past the saloon girl. Ned Harmon, one of his shotgun messengers for the stage line, stood in the doorway to his office.

His office. Griffin still found it hard to believe he had one. But since the former division manager of the Wells Fargo branch line had died, he'd taken over running the coaches, office and all.

"It's downright balderdash, Ned. This here gal thinks she can drive a stage."

Ned's eyes narrowed, and he looked Vashti up and down. The girl had enough decency to blush.

"Mr. Bane, I really can drive." She turned to him, clutching the pasteboard ticket. "I used to drive my daddy's team when I was eight or ten years old. Sometimes I even drove a four-in-hand. I haven't had much chance to work with horses these last ten years or so, but—"

Griffin held up one hand in protest. "Gal, you can't be more than—what?—seventeen? Eighteen?"

Vashti stopped short and eyed him cautiously. A gentleman never asked a woman her age, but Griff had never counted himself a gentleman, and he didn't reckon Ned was one, either.

She clenched her teeth. "I'm twenty-four, and if you two spread that around town, you'll live to regret it, but not much longer."

Ned howled with laughter. "Maybe you'd best hire her, Griff."

The blacksmith shook his head. No way was he going to hire a girl, even if she was older than she looked. He'd be the laughingstock of the Idaho Territory if people saw her driving one of his stagecoaches. Passengers would refuse to ride with her, and the shotgun riders would want to start a flirtation. She was pretty enough, after all. And if they knew she used to work in a saloon. . .

Nope, he wasn't going to think about that. He put on a firm face and said, "No."

He strode past her and Ned, ducked his head, and escaped out into the sunlight. Behind him, Ned was still laughing. He was halfway to Walker's Feed when he realized light footsteps pattered after him down the boardwalk. He swung around, and the girl almost plowed into him. She stopped so short, her earrings swayed.

"You followin' me?"

"Yes, sir."

Well, she had spunk. "I thought you were still working for Bitsy and Augie."

"I am."

"Then you don't need a job."

"Well, sir, it's like this." She glanced over her shoulder.

Ned had come out of the Wells Fargo office and ambled off across the street toward the boardinghouse. Griffin wondered vaguely what he'd wanted. He'd better not have come to tell him Bill couldn't drive today.

"Bitsy and Augie aren't doing so good," Vashti said. "This is just between you and me. Bitsy would have a conniption if she knew I'd told anyone. But they're not making nearly the profit they were when they sold liquor. Goldie's started clerking at the emporium, and I figured to look around for another job myself. Miss Bitsy says we're welcome to board with them as long as we want to, but it wouldn't hurt to look for another position. She figures she and Augie can support themselves but not much more than that unless we get more people in this town to patronize the restaurant."

Griffin frowned. He didn't like to hear his friends were having trouble. "That right? Augie came by the smithy day before yesterday, and he didn't say anything."

"He wouldn't. They're proud, both of 'em."

"Reckon that's so. But I can't let a girl drive a stagecoach. It wouldn't be fittin'."

She sighed. "Please, Mr. Bane. I really do know how to drive."

"Maybe so, but driving six is a whole lot different from driving two. Or even four. It takes drivers years to master it."

"Then let me start."

He shook his head. "I can't. I might find something else for you, though."

"Well, I can't shoe horses."

"Could you work at the livery?"

She wrinkled her nose. "I suppose I *could*, but. ..."

"What? You're too dainty to shovel manure?"

"I wasn't going to say that. I don't know as I'd want to work with Marty Hoffstead. I heard he goes over to the Nugget every night and puts back a few, and when he's got a brick in his hat, he treats those girls over there shamefully."

"That right?"

"Yes, sir, and I wouldn't make up stuff like that."

"I don't imagine you would." Griffin had heard Marty tell some coarse stories, and he'd seen him stagger out of the Nugget on a few occasions, but lately he couldn't be fussy about whom he hired. He scratched his chin through his beard. It was getting long—he ought to trim it, or soon it would be catching sparks from the forge. As if he had time. He didn't even get a minute to work with the colt he'd hoped to start training this fall. "Well, it'd help me some if you could sit in the office for a couple of hours every morning, say ten to noon, when folks want to buy tickets. I'd give you two bits for every ticket you sold."

"Well. . .I usually help Bitsy set up for lunch, but if she can spare me—how many tickets do you think I'd sell?"

"Maybe none. Maybe two or three."

"Hmm."

He could see she didn't think much of the idea. "You think about it. I've got to make sure the team's ready for the afternoon stage. If you want to try it, come see me later."

Without waiting for a response, he turned and walked swiftly toward the livery. All he needed was a pretty girl flitting about, getting in the way. The thought of that little bit of a thing handling a stagecoach made him laugh again. As if she could hold down six horses.

Of course, she was part of that shooting club Trudy Dooley—that is, Trudy Chapman now, since she married the sheriff—had started for the ladies. Unless he misremembered, Vashti had placed pretty well in the shooting match at the last town picnic. If someone could take Ned Harmon's place riding shotgun, then Ned could drive—he wasn't half bad in a pinch, though he needed more finesse to become a really good driver. Why, then Griffin might get by with the drivers he had. Provided Bill recovered from whatever ailed him.

He shook his head. What was he thinking? A girl for a shotgun messenger. He must be mad-brained. He stomped into the stable. Marty was just bringing in the two wheelers. They'd never have the team ready in time. Griffin dashed out back to get the swing horses from the corral.

Loco. That's what he was to even think of hiring a woman for this business. Crackbrained.

The next day, Vashti served lunch to three patrons. Bitsy wouldn't be back until the following afternoon, but there was barely enough work to keep Vashti busy, even though Augie had cooked a scrumptious roast beef dinner. The restaurant business was mighty slow now that the days were getting shorter. People were trying to get things ready for the coming winter and not thinking about eating in town.

When Oscar Runnels, Doc Kincaid, and Parnell Oxley had finished their meals and sauntered out of the Spur & Saddle, Vashti whisked their dishes into the kitchen and had them washed, dried, and put away before Augie had covered the stew pot and put the leftover lemon meringue in the pie safe. Augie walked over to the corner shelf where he and Bitsy kept the cash box. He opened the cover and stared down into it.

"Things are getting tight, aren't they?" Vashti asked.

"A mite." Augie slapped the lid shut. "We've been through hard times before."

"Still, you have to buy enough food for twenty, in case they come, and if nobody shows up, it goes to waste."

"Mrs. Thistle wants four pies for the boardinghouse." Augie pulled his sifter out of the flour barrel. "Guess I'll get started."

The boardinghouse down the street, owned by schoolmarm Isabel Fennel, was feeding more people than the Spur & Saddle. Terrence and Rilla Thistle, who ran the place, could count on their boarders. The stagecoach drivers and messengers usually slept and ate at the Fennel House, and sometimes passengers from the stagecoaches did, too. A few would wander out in the evening for dinner at the Spur & Saddle, but most of the Moores' customers were townsfolk who wanted a change of pace. Some of them probably came to help Augie and Bitsy. The Sunday chicken dinner was still the big event of the week at the Spur & Saddle, but that didn't generate enough to support the Moores and their two hired girls.

"I'm going out for a minute." Vashti took off her apron and hung it up. "Do you need anything?"

"No, I don't think so."

Augie sounded so glum that Vashti reached the decision she'd been chewing on for twenty-four hours. She'd take Griff Bane up on his offer and sit in his office two hours a day. If she sold eight tickets a week, she could give Bitsy two dollars for her board. And she could still help out at the supper hour, when the Spur & Saddle generally got more traffic than at noon. That would square what she should be paying for her room. Right now, she was living for free with the Moores, but her friend Goldie had started paying them every week for room and board when she began working at the Paragon Emporium. Vashti hoped in time she could do the same.

She went up to her room and put on a hat and shawl. She didn't want Griffin to think she wasn't proper enough to deal with his customers. Since she'd trusted in Christ, she'd stopped serving drinks to cowboys and poker players. Bitsy's decision last summer to turn her saloon into a family restaurant had made that part easy. Vashti felt cleaner now—almost decent again. But she knew some folks still pegged her as a barmaid. As a last thought, she wiped off most of the lip rouge she'd put on that morning.

She hurried down the stairs and across the empty dining room. Outside, the sun felt good on her shoulders, and the shawl was almost too much. She slowed down and took ladylike steps as she crossed the street and headed for the Wells Fargo. Reaching the office, she stopped and pulled in a deep breath. The door was closed. She knocked and then tried the latch. Locked. That figured. Griffin was probably down at the livery stable or the smithy. She'd go find him.

She held the ends of her shawl close as she turned. The poster on the wall caught her eye again, and she gasped. That man. That exasperating lunk of a man!

After HELP WANTED, Griffin had scrawled, MEN ONLY NEED APPLY.

She turned on her heel and marched up the street toward the smithy. No smoke came from the chimney, and she didn't hear the clang of Bane's hammer. He mustn't be working at the forge. A quick glance inside confirmed her conclusion. She strode around the corner toward the livery stable.

Marty Hoffstead was bringing in two big geldings from the back paddock. He walked between them, holding one halter with each hand.

"Whoa now." He stopped them in the middle of the barn floor. He let go of one, and the horse immediately put its head down, snuffling the floor. It walked along, picking up stray wisps of hay with its lips.

"Whoa, you!" Marty spotted Vashti standing in the door and waved his arm. "Can you get that nag and hook him up? There's a rope tied to the ring over there." He nodded toward the side wall.

Vashti stepped smoothly into the dim barn, without any sudden moves, and stooped to catch a leather strap that ran along the horse's cheek. "Come on, big fella." The gelding raised his head. She pushed gently on his nose. He backed up, and she was able to lean over and snatch the end of the dangling rope. How Marty had expected to get it and hitch the two big horses without help, she didn't know.

"Thanks," he said. "This is a two-person job, for sure." He hooked the other horse to a rope on the other side of the barn floor.

"Where's Mr. Bane?" Vashti asked.

"Gone to Silver City on the morning stage."

She arched her eyebrows. "Oh?"

"Yup. Ned Harmon caught whatever Bill Stout had yesterday and was too sick to go, so Griff had to ride shotgun for Bill this morning."

"Why didn't he send you?"

"Me? I'm not a good enough shot to hold off road agents. But I don't know as I can hitch up the six for the Boise coach alone." Marty eyed her speculatively. "Guess you're too scrawny. Would you step across to the Nugget and see if anyone over there can help me?"

Vashti scowled. She didn't especially want to get her good clothes smelling like a stable. On the other hand, she resented the implication that she couldn't hitch a horse or two. And while she disliked Marty and didn't trust him farther than she could throw an anvil, a little voice inside her egged her to show him just what *he* knew.

"I can do it. You want me to harness these two, or to bring in the next two?"

Marty's eyes narrowed. "Well, missy, the harness for the two wheelers is hanging yonder." He nodded toward the barn wall. "Iffen you want to try to sort that out, I'll go bring in the swing team."

By the time he'd brought in the next pair, Vashti had the first harness over the near wheeler's back and was buckling the belly band. Marty somehow managed to get the two new horses into place and came to survey her work. He grunted and went out the back again.

She had two horses done before he had the team all lined up. Marty grabbed the next harness off the wall and went to work. They labored without speaking. Occasionally Marty said, "Get over, you," to a horse or swore quietly. Vashti scratched each horse's forelock as she slipped on their bridles. They were good horses. Cyrus Fennel had always bought good stock for the line, and Griffin seemed to be keeping up the standard. Vashti loved to watch the coaches come thundering into town. The drivers always had them run up the main street while they cracked their whips, just for looks.

The lead horses didn't have breech straps, and the harnesses went on quickly. Marty was still messing with a buckle on his side. Vashti took an extra moment to caress the two leaders' silky noses.

"Guess you're all set," she said.

Marty came around and cast a critical eye over the work she had done. "It appears I am." He nodded at her grudgingly. "Thank you, missy."

"You're welcome. Do you expect Mr. Bane back today?"

"Nope. Not until the stage comes in tomorrow. I've got to get up to the office and see if anyone wants tickets for the two o'clock. When the next coach comes in, someone has to be there to meet the passengers. Then the driver will bring the coach around here to switch the teams, so I'll have to run back over here. . . ." He pushed his hat back and sighed. "Best get going."

"I can tend the office," Vashti said.

Marty's brow furrowed.

"I can," she said. "Mr. Bane offered me a position to sell tickets for him. That's why I came here this afternoon. Wanted to tell him I'd do it. So if you want, I can start now. Give me the key, and I'll open the office and meet the incoming coach."

"You know how to make out the tickets?"

"Well. . ." She gritted her teeth. "Not especially, but it can't be too hard."

Marty shook his head. "Griff's got a table telling the prices for all the stops. It changes every now and again, and Wells Fargo sends him a new one. You have to look up the destination and put the price on the ticket."

"I can do that."

"You sure?"

"Sure as sunup."

Still he hesitated. "I'd best go over there with you. Griff didn't say nothing to me about a gal getting to have the key to the office. I'll unlock for you. Most likely there won't be any tickets sold, anyhow. We hardly get any passengers going out on Thursday."

At a quarter past ten the next morning, the stagecoach rattled up Fergus's main street. Driver Bill Stout flourished his cowhide whip, and the horses obliged by stepping along smartly. On the box next to Bill, Griffin dug in his pocket for the watch that had once been Cyrus Fennel's.

Griff squinted down at the hands. It always took him a minute to work it out. He'd learned to tell time as a kid but hadn't practiced in more than twenty years. After Cyrus died, his daughter gave Griff the watch when he took over her father's Wells Fargo contract.

The coach was late. He'd known that since before they pulled out of the stop at Dewey. Bill was a good driver, but last night's rain had left the roads a little sloppy, so the delay had increased.

If he was figuring the time right, they were twenty minutes late. Griff sighed and closed the watchcase. Could be worse. Of course, if Cy Fennel were alive, he'd threaten to fire Bill for being late.

They pulled up hard in front of the office. Griff climbed down carefully to open the door for the three passengers—a rancher's wife returning home and two miners coming into town to dispose of their meager findings. Ned Harmon would have jumped down from the box like a monkey, but Griff was too big and too old—yes, he was feeling his age after hours of jolting along on the hard box—to do that.

When he reached the ground and turned around, a vision in blue satin skirts stood on the boardwalk. Vashti Edwards again, complete with a ridiculous feathered bonnet that must have come from that Caplinger woman's millinery shop. She may have quit wearing knee-high skirts and plunging bodices, but she hadn't parked her vanity at the church door when she found her faith, had she?

"Morning, Mr. Bane," she said. "I hope you had a nice trip down from Silver City."

He grunted and turned to open the door. Mrs. Tinen grabbed his hand, gingerly climbed down, and stepped toward the rear of the coach to claim her bags. That was the messenger's job, too. Griff waited while the two miners eased down to earth; then he shut the door and shuffled around to the back. Bill had climbed over the top of the coach and opened the boot. He didn't have to, but maybe he did it because the boss had been riding with him.

Griffin went over and caught the bags as Bill tossed them down. He set them on the edge of the boardwalk. "There you go, ma'am.

Thanks for riding with us." As if she had another choice in these mountains.

Bill scrambled back across the roof to the driver's box.

"Tell Marty I'll be over in a few minutes," Griffin called.

Bill raised his whip in salute and flicked the reins. The horses started off at a jog, knowing they were nearly home. The two miners hoofed it for the Nugget. Arthur Tinen Sr. had driven his wagon into town to meet his wife. Griffin waved to him and lifted one weary leg, setting his right boot squarely on the boardwalk.

"Bye, Mrs. Tinen." Vashti still stood on the boardwalk, waving at Jessie and Arthur and looking as pretty as a circus horse in her fancy trappings. Griffin looked her up and down.

"You want another ticket today?"

"No, sir. I came to tell you we sold two tickets while you were gone. One on yesterday's Boise coach, and the other to go to Lamar today. The money's in the tobacco tin in your desk drawer."

Griff closed one eye and considered her again. "We?"

"We, the Wells Fargo line, Fergus branch."

"Ah." He looked past her and noted for the first time that the office door was open. "Where's Marty?"

Her smile slipped for the first time. "Over to the livery, waiting to help Bill swap out the horses. I opened the office yesterday morning, like you said I might, and again today. Well, Marty unlocked for me, but I wrote the tickets and greeted the one passenger who came in yesterday afternoon and directed him to the boardinghouse. I think it's important that passengers see a friendly face when they disembark in a strange town, don't you?"

Griffin grunted.

Orissa Walker and her married daughter came out of the emporium and walked toward them. Orissa always reminded Griff of a fussy crow. The skinny, white-haired woman moved down the walk in a pause-jerk rhythm. Her arthritis must be getting worse.

"Hello, Vashti. Morning, Mr. Bane."

"Miz Walker. Ma'am." Griff touched his hat brim, groping in his mind for the daughter's married name and coming up short.

"Good day," said the daughter. Her brown dress was brightened by red trim, unlike her mother's totally drab gray fashion. "I'd like to purchase my return ticket to Portland."

"Oh, you're leaving us," Vashti said with a regretful smile. "I hope you've enjoyed your stay with your folks, Miz Hodges."

Hodges. That was it.

"Yes, thank you," the woman said with a smile. "I've had a delightful stay, but my husband wrote and told me he's lonesome, so I guess I'd better head on home tomorrow."

Orissa cackled. "I guess it didn't hurt Clay any to cook for himself this month."

"Well, step right into our office." Vashti smiled broadly and shot Griff a quick glance. "I can write up your ticket now, and you'll be all set to board the coach tomorrow."

"Why, thank you." Mrs. Hodges and her mother followed Vashti to the door.

Griffin opened his mouth and closed it again. Orissa was saying, "Vashti, I'd no idea you'd begun working on this side of the street."

Vashti's musical chuckle floated out from his office. "Yes, ma'am, Mr. Bane offered me the position a couple of days ago to free him up so's he can tend to his smithing and livery duties better. Now, let me see, you're traveling all the way through to Portland. . . ."

Griff worked his jaw back and forth a few times. He was bone tired. Seemed like he ought to tell Vashti she presumed a hair too much. On the other hand, she appeared to be handling the job well. And dealing with ladies wasn't his strong suit. He stepped a little closer to the doorway and leaned against the wall. Vashti named the price of the ticket, and he thought it sounded right. She acted as though she'd been doing this job for years. He didn't like to remember how befuddled he'd felt the first few times he'd tried to figure out the rate table. Maybe he should leave well enough alone and let her carry on. At a quarter per ticket sold, it would be a cheap way to cut down on his headaches.

"Griffin!"

He whirled around.

Maitland Dostie waved a piece of paper as he hurried across the street. "Telegram just came in for you."

Griffin stepped uncertainly to the edge of the boardwalk. He wasn't the type of person to get telegrams. That was for the sheriff or maybe the preacher or Doc Kincaid. Who would spend fifty cents a word to send a telegram to a blacksmith?

"You sure?"

"Of course I'm sure." Maitland stopped and held out the paper. "Sorry to be bringing you bad news."

"Bad news?" Griffin searched the telegrapher's face. "How bad?"

"Well, you know I have to read these things when I take them down. That is, I can't take them down without seeing what they say. And I'm sorry, Griffin."

"Wha—" Griffin quit staring and opened the folded sheet of paper. The top was a mess of letters and numbers and his name, followed by FERGUS, IDAHO, and the word CINCINNATI. Below that, set off in stark importance, were the words JACOB DIED. He stared at it for a long moment.

"Some of your kin?" Maitland frowned as if trying to look suitably sad.

Griff nodded. The only Jacob he knew in Cincinnati was his sister's husband, Jacob Frye. "My brother-in-law."

"Oh. I'm sorry." Maitland looked down at his dusty shoes. "Would you. . .er. . .like to send a reply?"

"Yeah." Griffin cleared his throat, thinking what to say to Evelyn. "You need me to come over to your office?"

"If you want to write it out, I'll take it from you here."

Orissa and her daughter and Vashti came out of the Wells Fargo office, still chattering about Mrs. Hodges's forthcoming journey.

"I'll step over with you," Griff said. He followed Maitland across the street, mulling how to word his message frugally and still offer a brother's proper support and sympathy. Evelyn was five years his elder. She'd married Jacob Frye nearly twenty years ago, and they had five children. Jacob had never earned much as a schoolmaster. How would Evelyn support those kids now? He seemed to recall that the eldest girl, Rachel, was pledged to be married soon.

He stood holding the pencil for a long time and staring down at the blank telegram form. At last he scrawled, "Very sorry. Anyway

I can help?" He hoped Maitland would let him get away with making *any* and *way* one word, though he supposed it wasn't correct usage. He scowled down at it. The deceased was a teacher, after all. His sister would likely tell her friends she'd gotten a telegram from her brother out West, and he'd used poor grammar. He erased the second sentence and replaced it with "Need anything?" There. He'd saved two words. And Evelyn couldn't complain if he only spent two dollars—she'd cut her message to the bare minimum for a dollar.

He shoved the form across the counter. "Guess that'll do. I'll write her a letter this evening."

"That'll be two dollars. I'll send this right out." Maitland set the message beside the telegraph key and reached out to take the money.

When Griffin stepped outside again, the stage was coming down the street from the livery. Apparently Marty had managed without him. The drivers and messengers weren't supposed to have to change the teams, but sometimes they had to do it, or it wouldn't get done. Griff glanced up at the sun. He was glad they hadn't waited for him, as his sister's telegram had driven all thoughts of the stage from his mind.

Across the street, Vashti stood on the boardwalk near a drummer who'd come into town yesterday. Griff decided to let her see the passenger off and go get something to eat. He'd give Augie and Bitsy a little business. And he'd worry about what to do with his new employee later.

★ CHAPTER 3 ★

A week later, Vashti met the stage from Silver City. No one got out, as Johnny Conway had made the run with an empty coach. He pulled up in front of the Wells Fargo office and touched his whip to his hat brim. He was a young man, a cowpoke turned stage driver, who thought he knew more about driving and horses than any man on earth, and more about women, too.

"No pigeons today, Miss Vashti. We'll get the box inside."

The shotgun messenger, Cecil Watson, bent to slide the treasure box out from under the seat.

"You'd best wait until Mr. Bane can come open the safe," Vashti said.

"Naw, he gets mad if we take the strongbox over to the livery. Cecil will have to stay here and guard it until Griff comes."

Vashti blew out a breath. "All right." She hurried inside and took her handbag from the hook behind the door. From its depths, she produced the pearl-handled pistol she'd bought the year before when she'd joined the Ladies' Shooting Club of Fergus.

"What's that peashooter for?" Cecil gasped out the words between breaths as he lugged the heavy wooden box to the desk.

"Thought I could help protect the box."

Cecil laughed. "Aw, go on, missy. Nothing so funny as a woman all dolled up and flashing a gun around."

Vashti scowled at him. "Oh yeah. Very funny." She turned on her high heels and strode out onto the boardwalk. Johnny was about to drive off to the livery. "Hey, Conway! Wait a second."

He froze with his whip poised. "What d'ya want?"

"I want to drive." She shoved the pistol back into her bag and grabbed the handhold on the side of the coach.

"You crazy?" Johnny asked.

"No. It's only up the street to the livery."

"No."

"Pretty please?" She hoisted herself up and plopped into the seat beside him.

Johnny's eyes narrowed. "I ain't never let no one else take the reins when I was on duty. Griff Bane would fire me."

"I'll give you two bits."

He hesitated, and she was pretty sure she had him.

"Two bits and a kiss." His blue eyes glittered.

"Four bits and you keep your lips to home."

He laughed and handed over the reins. As Vashti took them, her blood rushed eagerly through her veins. At last! She tucked one rein under each pinkie and held the other two on each side together.

"No, no. You've got to thread them through your fingers right." Johnny reached over and pried open her left hand.

"Sorry. I used to drive four."

"Six is different. A lot different. You've got to keep some tension on all of them all the time. Be ready to climb those ribbons if you have to." He fussed at the leathers until she could feel they were in place.

"Am I ready? It feels like I am."

"Hold on—"

She was afraid he would change his mind and take the reins back, but he only leaned over and took the brake off. She moved her hands forward a little to put the tiniest slack in the lines and chirruped to the horses. They took off at a trot, and Johnny grabbed the edge of the seat.

"Hey! I said wait."

"Well, we're moving now."

"Yeah. Don't let 'em put on too much speed or they'll try to take you right into the barn, coach and all. Unless you want to lose your head, that's a bad idea."

They clipped along so fast they were already passing the feed store. The leaders bent around the corner by the smithy and pounded toward home.

"Slow 'em down," Johnny yelled.

Vashti pulled back on the lines, but it seemed to have no effect.

"Lay right down on 'em!"

She put all her weight into her pull, rising up on her heels.

"Tighten the near leader's rein."

There wasn't time for her to figure out which ribbon led to the near lead horse's mouth as and they came abreast of the livery. Johnny reached over and added the strength of his muscular forearm to her tugging and gave a loud, firm "Whoa!"

The six horses stopped so fast the wheelers nearly piled up on the swing horses' tails.

"Quick," Johnny said. "Gimme the lines. Bane's coming."

As she untangled the reins from her hands, Vashti saw two men coming from the interior of the big barn.

"I'll come by for the four bits later," Johnny hissed. "Don't talk about it."

"What's going on here?" Griffin's bushy dark eyebrows met in a frown over the bridge of his nose.

Vashti felt her face flush. "Hello, Mr. Bane."

"I said, what's going on?" Griffin glared at Johnny, who refused to meet his gaze. "Conway, did you let this woman drive my stagecoach?"

Johnny's Adam's apple bobbed up and down. "Well, uh. . ."

"I've got a mind to fire you, except we're so shorthanded I can't. Get down off the box, and get out of my sight."

Johnny dropped down over the side of the coach, thrust the lines into Griffin's hands, and disappeared. Vashti craned her neck to see where he went. It appeared he was headed over to the Fennel House for some lunch—that is, if he didn't detour into the Nugget first.

"Miss Edwards."

She turned back and found Griffin had climbed up on the step and was eye-to-eye with her.

"Yes, sir?"

"What do you think you're up to?"

"Please, Mr. Bane, I told you I can drive. Let me learn to handle the six. I know I'd be the best driver you ever had." She stared into his smoldering dark eyes. For a long moment, neither of them said a word.

At last, Griffin's beard twitched, and he opened his mouth. "No." He stepped down and backed up two steps, then turned around. "Come on, Marty. Let's get the teams switched. Move!"

Vashti sighed. For a moment, she'd thought he was wavering. She gathered her skirts and climbed down on the side away from the barn door. No sense trying to get him to change his mind today. She'd walked a few yards before she remembered the treasure box. Reluctantly she turned back.

"Oh, Mr. Bane?"

He paused in unhitching the off wheeler from the whiffletree. Though he said nothing, his dark eyebrows rose in question.

"Mr. Watson's up to the office guarding the treasure box because the safe wasn't open."

Griffin frowned.

"If you don't want to give me the combination, you could go over there, and I'll help Marty switch the teams."

Griffin laughed. "First you think you can drive, and then you think you can wrangle these critters."

"Don't laugh, Griff," Marty said from the other side of the hitch. "She helped me while you were gone. She knows how to harness a team better'n Ned or Bill does."

"I doubt that." Griffin pulled out his pocket watch and scowled at it. "Time I get up there and back, we could have these horses changed." He looked at Vashti. "Just tell Cecil to stay there until I come."

"Yes, sir."

Vashti walked swiftly back to the office. When she walked in, Cecil jumped up off the edge of the desk with his shotgun in his hands. "Where's Griff? I'm hungry, and the next stage will be ready before I get anything to eat."

"He's working with Marty. Shorthanded, as usual." Vashti looked around. "Any customers wanting tickets?"

"Nope."

"All right. You stay here, and I'll run over to the Spur & Saddle and get you something."

"Mrs. Thistle feeds us."

"All right, I'll go to the boardinghouse. Maybe she'll let me bring you a plate."

Cecil nodded. "That'd be good. I don't want to head out on the next leg with an empty belly."

Vashti hung her handbag behind the door and plodded over to the Fennel House. She was no closer to becoming a driver—in fact, she may have lost ground where Griffin was concerned. Johnny would regret putting the reins in her hands, and while Marty had unexpectedly come to her defense, Griffin hadn't listened to a word he'd said. It was just as well. She didn't really want to get her dress all dirty.

By the time she got back to the Wells Fargo stop with Cecil's plate, the coach was coming around the corner by the smithy. Cecil gulped a few bites and left his dinner half eaten on Griffin's desk without so much as a thank-you. Johnny came back from his own dinner and wouldn't let Vashti catch his eye. It made her boil, but she knew he was trying to get out from under Griffin's ire. He and Cecil loaded the strongbox and climbed into their seats on the front. As the coach rumbled away, she let her shoulders droop. No tickets sold today. She'd put in more than two hours for nothing. Nothing but the feel of the lines in her hands for less than two minutes.

A heavy step made the boardwalk vibrate. She turned. Griffin stood two paces away.

"Don't you be thinking you can drive the stage again."

She gulped and looked away. "No, sir."

"Good. Because if you try, I'll fire the driver who lets you. And it'll be your fault."

Griffin dashed about his one-room home, the other half of the smithy building. He always intended to get to church in plenty of time, but sometimes he lost track. Even though he had a watch, he couldn't get used to being at the new sanctuary on the hour. For that matter, he still had trouble making sure the stagecoaches left at precisely the right time.

He wet his comb and slicked down his unruly hair. He'd have to cut it again soon. Someone had mentioned that Augie Moore would cut hair for a dime. Maybe he should get the brawny restaurateur to do it. Augie was a good friend, and he was having a hard time financially, so it would be a good arrangement all around.

By the time he got his hair to lie flat, it was soaked, with drips drenching the collar of his one good shirt. Griffin sighed and tried to pull the comb through his beard. The tangles put the brakes on that plan. He threw the comb down. No time to put on a tie. He grabbed his hat and ran out the door. Why had they built the church two blocks over, anyhow? When the congregation met in the old haberdashery on Main Street, he usually made it on time.

The bell rang out over the town as he hit the boardwalk beside the Fennel House, and he lengthened his steps. Nice thing, that bell. The ladies had campaigned for it and raised money all last winter with bake sales and a quilt raffle. The preacher took three special offerings, and the bell had arrived on one of Oscar Runnels's freight wagons a month ago. The sound of it made him feel as though he lived in a civilized town.

A few stragglers climbed the church steps as he approached. That made him feel a little better. Of course, he'd never make it to Sunday school, though the preacher encouraged everyone to come out for that an hour earlier than the worship service. Griffin puffed up the steps behind the Nash family. Peter saw him coming and held the door open.

"Thanks," Griff said.

"Morning, Griff. There's a letter for you over to the post office. Stop by my house tomorrow, why don't you?"

Griffin reared back and stared at him. "All right." Probably from his sister. It had been two or three weeks since he'd received the disturbing telegram. That must be it. She'd most likely written him the details of Jacob's demise.

He looked over the nearly filled sanctuary before sliding toward his usual pew—second from the back, on the left. In the row ahead of him, the sheriff sat on the aisle, beside his wife. Those two made quite a pair, Griff had to admit. He'd never expected Ethan to get married, but it seemed fitting that the best shot in town had won his heart. Trudy Chapman's brother, Hiram, the gunsmith, sat in the middle of the row, beside Libby Adams, the emporium's owner. No doubt they'd tie the knot soon. Romance seemed to have discovered Fergus. Griff shook his head. More and more so-called confirmed bachelors fell to the call of Cupid.

The two girls who worked at the Nugget Saloon slipped in and found seats in the back row. They wore their low-cut satins to church but covered up with their shawls. Seemed nearly everyone in town came to church these days. Griffin supposed that was a good thing.

The folks from the Spur & Saddle had claimed a pew just ahead of the sheriff and his party. That was a case where the last folks you ever expected to see in church had turned to Christ and flipped their lives head over heels. Vashti Edwards and Goldie Keller sat with Bitsy and Augie, and you'd have never thought to look at them that they'd ever been anything but respectable. Bitsy and the girls still had a heavy hand with the rouge and lip color, and they were too frugal to throw out their fancy dresses, but they'd altered them a bit. No one would think they'd been saloon girls for years.

That set Griffin's mind off on a rabbit trail. A passenger who occasionally rode the line on business had come in from Boise Friday. He'd complimented Griffin on the polite and beautiful young woman who now ran his ticket office. Griffin hadn't let on about Vashti's past. If anyone didn't know, they'd assume she'd always been decent. She didn't have a hoity-toity Eastern accent like Rose Caplinger, the milliner, but neither did she speak coarsely like the guttersnipes at the Nugget. And Goldie—why, that blond girl at the Spur & Saddle could play the piano like a professional. Last Christmas, she'd played a concert of carols at the church, and the whole town had lauded her. The reverend's wife was getting up a new collection to buy a piano for the church so they could have Goldie play the hymns every Sunday.

Susan Page Davis

The Reverend Phineas Benton rose to open the service, and Griffin focused his attention on the front of the large room. The first hymn, "Amazing Grace," helped. Griffin tended to let his mind wander when he was sitting still, listing all the things he needed to do when church was over.

Of course, he never worked at the forge on Sundays. Not since the preacher came. People would hear his hammer and know he worked on the Sabbath. But if he didn't putter around the livery on Sunday afternoon, some things would never get done. The horses needed to be fed, watered, and groomed. And Wells Fargo and Company had never heard of the no-Sunday-labor rule. The stagecoach schedules must be kept no matter what day of the week.

Everyone around him sat down, and he realized the singing was over. He sat down on his pew.

Preacher Benton gazed out over the congregation. "My fellow believers, this morning we'll look at Paul's second letter to the Corinthians and contemplate the virtue of benevolence. Gracious giving where it is perhaps not merited. Of course, if someone we love is in need, we do all we can to help them out. But what of the stranger or, even more, the person we know slightly and do not like? Can you be gracious when you don't feel like it? My friends, if you see someone unsavory in need, can you meet that need without resentment and bitterness? Ask yourself what Christ would do in this situation. Unto the least of these. . ."

Griffin tipped back his head and gazed up into the rafters. He dealt with unsavory men all the time. And the good Lord knew he'd been gracious to one of his drivers. He ought to have fired Jules Harding the first time he showed up for work drunk. But Griffin had tossed him in the watering tank behind the livery to sober him up and put him on the box of the stage dripping wet. The second time, he'd turned him away and driven the run to Dewey himself—big mistake. As experienced as he was with horses, Griffin wasn't much of a hand with a six-horse hitch. But they'd made it through. It wasn't until time number three that he'd given Jules the boot. That was benevolence, wasn't it? Giving a man three chances when old Cy Fennel would have cut him loose the first time.

"I submit to you, dear people," the reverend said, "that sometimes God would have us give our fellow man another chance. Remember the question about forgiveness?"

For some reason, Griffin's mind drifted to Vashti Edwards. Should he give her a chance at driving coaches? She was no more a stagecoach driver than he was. Less of one, if the truth be told. He'd be foolish to allow a girl who used to drive her daddy's farm wagon to climb up on the box. The passengers' lives would be at stake. No, he'd done the right thing to turn her down. And hadn't he shown grace by letting her work at the office? Of course, he paid her a pittance—and only when she sold tickets. A dim spark of guilt flickered deep in his heart.

Phineas Benton wasn't through yet. "We've all had times when we were down—when another person reached out and gave us a hand. When someone gave us a boost we needed but didn't deserve."

That was true enough. Griffin liked to think he'd built his own career. He'd been apprenticed to a blacksmith back in Pennsylvania when he was an awkward kid. His master had been tough on him, but he'd shaped Griffin into a competent farrier and ironworker. When his apprenticeship was over, Griffin had stayed on long enough to earn the money to buy his own tools. Then he'd come west. Opportunity lay in the West, he'd heard. The little town of Fergus, Idaho, had given him the chance to build his smithy and run his own business. Five years later when the livery stable owner moved on, Griffin had saved enough to buy him out, so he became one of the town's most prominent business owners.

But how much of that was due to his own hard work? To hear the preacher tell it, none. It was all God's doing, and in a way, Griff could see that viewpoint. God could have kept him from succeeding. But the Almighty had blessed him and first made it possible for him to get started and later made him able to buy the livery.

Then there was Isabel Fennel. Her father was once the richest man in town. When Cyrus died, she could have hired anyone she wanted to fulfill the Wells Fargo contract, or she could have simply told Wells Fargo they needed to find a new man to oversee the Fergus branch line. But no. She'd turned to Griffin and offered it to him. He had a lot to be thankful for. But did that mean he should turn around and put a green-as-grass girl who wasn't strong enough to control a newborn filly on the box to drive six coach horses? Griffin shuddered.

"All rise, please, for the benediction."

As they filed toward the church door, Vashti craned her neck. Griffin wasn't hard to keep track of—he stood several inches taller than anyone else in the line ahead of her.

Her friend Goldie nudged her. "Who you staring at?"

"Mr. Bane."

"You're mooning over your new boss?"

Vashti frowned at her. "No, I most certainly am not."

"What are you doing, then?"

"Trying to figure out how to make him let me drive the stage."

"You might as well forget about that. He's told you more than once he won't let you."

A lanky young man stepped into the aisle beside them. "Morning, Miss Vashti. Or should I say, 'afternoon'?" Johnny Conway cracked a broad smile at her.

"I expect it is past noon," Vashti said absently.

"You're one of the stagecoach drivers, aren't you?" Goldie asked, gazing up at Johnny with her overlarge blue eyes.

"Yes, ma'am. Have we met before?"

"Maybe." Goldie fluttered her lashes. Vashti had scolded her for continuing to flirt with men since they gave up being saloon girls, but the habit seemed ingrained in Goldie. "Ever been to the Spur & Saddle?"

"Well, sure. You're the gal who plays the pianner." Johnny's smile slipped. "I ain't been there since they changed over—well, you know."

"That's all right," Goldie said.

"You still work there?" Johnny asked.

"No, I work in the Paragon Emporium now, but I still board at the Spur & Saddle, same as Vashti."

"Oh." Johnny looked from her to Vashti and arched his eyebrows as though he expected something.

"Her name is Goldie Keller." Men were always fascinated by Goldie's china-doll looks. Vashti didn't mind, so long as they didn't get fresh with her friend. But Goldie had been around saloons long enough that she knew how to keep most fellows in line.

"I haven't seen you in church before," Goldie said, smiling up at him.

"Well, I don't usually stay over Sunday in Fergus. Most weeks I'm over to Murphy."

They had reached the door. Vashti turned her back on Johnny and Goldie and shook the pastor's hand.

"Good day, Miss Edwards." Pastor Benton always greeted the girls cheerfully, but it was his wife who soothed Vashti's heart. Though Vashti smiled at the preacher, she turned eagerly to Apphia.

"Hello, Mrs. Benton."

"Vashti, so good to see you again. You must come visit me this week, if you have a chance."

"I'd like that, thank you."

"Why don't you come Tuesday afternoon, if that won't interfere with your work? I understand you have two jobs now."

"I'm putting in a few hours at the Wells Fargo. But I could come over around two thirty."

"Wonderful. I'll have the teakettle on."

Vashti stepped out into the sunlight, feeling warm to her toes. Mrs. Benton genuinely cared about the ladies in this town, whether they were rich or poor, refined or crude. Vashti had seen her reach out to women many would consider among the least desirable residents of Fergus. She'd befriended the girls from both saloons back when there were two in town. At the time, Vashti had been jealous of the attention Apphia paid the girls from the Nugget. But now she understood. That was Apphia's nature: to love them all impartially. Even so, whenever she spent time with the pastor's wife, Vashti felt almost as if she were Apphia's only friend and certainly the one she loved best.

She went down the front steps. Griffin Bane had disappeared, probably going back to the livery or the smithy. She waited while Goldie greeted the Bentons. Johnny Conway didn't leave her friend's side. He shook the pastor's hand, too, and spoke to Apphia. He came down the steps with Goldie.

"Say, Miss Vashti, why are you so keen on learning to drive?"

Vashti bristled. "I already know how to drive."

He laughed, and it stung a little. "All right, then. Why do you want so badly to drive a stagecoach? Griff told me you've been hounding him to hire you to drive."

"So?"

"So, you're not ready."

Vashti held back her retort and gazed up at him. She liked Johnny in a way. He was boyishly handsome and had a fun-loving streak, but he'd be trouble for the woman who lost her heart to him.

"So how did *you* get ready?" What she really wanted to know was how he'd convinced Griffin Bane to hire him. Maybe it amounted to the same thing.

"When I was a kid, my pa put up a rig for me in the barn, so's I could practice handling the reins without anyone—or any horses— getting hurt."

"What kind of a rig?"

"It's just a frame with six reins attached like they are on a real hitch. You can pretend to drive for hours at a time, working those lines with your fingers until you can tighten or ease up on any one of the six without affecting the others. That's what you need to do if you're going to control all six horses 't once. You can't drive them all like you would one horse. They'd learn to take advantage of you worse than a tinhorn gambler."

Vashti scowled at him, but what he said made sense. Already her mind was groping for a place where she could have someone make a rig for her. It couldn't be at the livery—Griff would see it. Besides, she wouldn't want to be over there for hours on end, practicing.

Trudy Dooley would let her have it in her barn if she still lived with her brother. But she'd married the sheriff last summer, so she was Mrs. Chapman now and lived out on the sheriff's ranch. It wasn't far out of town, but it was too far for Vashti to trot out there every day.

Augie and Bitsy didn't have a barn. They had a woodshed, though. She wondered if there'd be room out there. They'd burned all of last winter's wood, so the shed was pretty nearly empty. But Augie would be filling it soon and ordering a ton of coal, too.

The pastor and his wife stepped outside. All of the church folks must be finished shaking their hands. The reverend closed the church door, and they turned to walk down the steps together.

Vashti smiled as another option came to mind. She hurried toward the couple.

"Mrs. Benton, Reverend—I've got a favor to ask."

Apphia paused and waited for her to reach them, a smile hovering on her lips. "What is it, Vashti? You know we'll do anything feasible for you."

Vashti wasn't quite sure what *feasible* meant, but she knew the Bentons were bighearted when it came to folks in need.

"You folks have a stable you're not using."

The minister's eyes widened. "Are you getting a horse, Miss Edwards?"

Vashti shook her head. "No, sir, that would be nice but too expensive. This is cheaper and easier to clean up after."

Mr. Benton laughed.

Apphia squeezed her hand. "Well, my dear, you have us on pins and needles. What is it you want to use the stable for?"

"For a place where I can learn to drive my imaginary stagecoach."

★ CHAPTER 4 ★

The next day as the coach came in from Reynolds, Vashti stood in front of the Wells Fargo office, ready to make sure the disembarking passengers had their needs met. Sure enough, a couple got out and turned expectantly toward her.

Too bad—it was nearly time for her to set out for the shooting club's regular practice. But Mr. Bane had made it clear that directing the passengers to food and lodging and hearing any complaints they might make was part of her job, for which he now grudgingly paid her a dime a day, plus the commission on tickets she sold.

"May I help you folks?" she asked, remembering belatedly that Griffin had also specified she smile when addressing customers. She tacked on a perfunctory curve of her lips.

"I think you might be able to." The man doffed his bowler hat, revealing his balding head. After a quick glance at his companion, Vashti catalogued them as man and wife, in their sixties, probably come to visit grandchildren.

"Do you need a place to eat lunch? Because the Spur & Saddle, over yonder, has the best food in Fergus."

"Thank you, that was to be my first question," the man said. "The second was where we might find Mrs. Elizabeth Adams."

Vashti grinned. "Well, that sure is easy. Turn around."

A couple of doors down, Libby was just coming out of the Paragon Emporium with Florence Nash, who clerked for her in the store.

"Miz Adams," Vashti called.

As usual, Libby wore a fashionable but modest dress made of good material. The powder blue gown brought out the vivid blue of her eyes, and her golden curls were topped by a matching bonnet. Florence, who was quite pretty, looked almost ordinary next to the lovely lady.

Libby advanced toward them with a smile. "Yes, Miss Edwards? May I help you?"

Her well-modulated tones inspired Vashti to speak as smoothly as the emporium's owner. "Yes, ma'am. These folks would like to see you."

Libby looked at the couple, favoring them with a hesitant smile. "Hello. Have you just arrived in Fergus?"

"Yes, ma'am." The man gestured toward his wife. "We're the Hamiltons. We've corresponded with you."

"Why, yes, of course." Libby's reserve melted, and she extended her hand, first to the lady and then to the gentleman. "Forgive me. I wasn't expecting you so soon." She turned to include Florence and Vashti in her explanation. "Ladies, this couple is interested in viewing the emporium with the prospect of buying it."

Vashti caught herself so she didn't let out an unladylike whoop. It was no secret that Libby Adams planned to marry the shy gunsmith, Hiram Dooley, but she couldn't until she sold her business. No one in Fergus could afford to buy it—with the possible exception of the schoolmarm, Isabel Fennel, who had inherited a large estate from her father. But Isabel enjoyed teaching and had no desire to run a store, thank you, so Mrs. Adams had advertised the emporium in several Eastern newspapers. Goldie had told Vashti all the details she'd learned while stocking shelves in the store.

"You must be tired." Libby addressed the lady. "Did you folks come all the way from Boise today?"

"Yes, we did," Mrs. Hamilton said. "We were anxious to get here and meet you and see the emporium."

"Of course. But you must be hungry." Libby looked to Mr. Hamilton.

"Well. . ."

"Of course you are. Please allow me to entertain you at our finest restaurant." Libby looked apologetically at Florence. "My dear, I fear I must let you go to the club without me today. Please make my excuses to Trudy. She will understand."

"Yes'm," said Florence.

"Let me give you folks a quick look at the emporium before we eat." Libby turned her head and raised her eyebrows in Vashti's direction. "Miss Edwards, could you possibly run ahead and see if the Moores can accommodate three late diners? We shall be over in ten minutes."

"I surely can." Vashti gathered her satin skirt and leaped off the boardwalk. She ran across the street.

When she charged into the dining room, Bitsy was just picking up her husband's shotgun. Dressed in her red bloomer costume, she looked the part of a sharpshooter.

"What's happened?" she asked, eyeing Vashti with trepidation.

"Nothing bad. There's a couple off the stagecoach, and they want to buy Miz Adams's store. She wants to bring them here to eat. Do you have anything left?"

"Praise the Lord," Bitsy shouted. "Augie! You hear that?"

Augie poked his shiny bald head out from the kitchen. "Hear what?"

"We've got customers coming. Is the stew still hot?"

"Yes, I've got it on the back of the stove."

"Well, heat up those leftover biscuits, too, and put the chicken pie in the warming oven." Bitsy stuck the shotgun under the serving counter. "I'll have to stay here to serve them. Tell Trudy."

"Do you want me to stay?" Vashti asked.

"No, child, you go on. But I need to get out all the luncheon things we put away. We didn't have a single customer to lunch. I thought today was the first day of our decline and bankruptcy."

"That day happened last year, when we got married and closed the bar," Augie muttered as he shuffled for the kitchen.

"Don't pay him any mind." Bitsy pulled three of the best china plates off a shelf. "Go on now, Vashti. Tell Trudy I'll be there Thursday, for sure. And you see if you can't win the prize today."

Griffin tore open the envelope as he left the post office on Mayor Peter Nash's closed-in porch. He felt bad for his sister, Evelyn. Five kids, and no grandparents nearby to help her out. He'd written to her, offering to help in a small way—he could probably send her a few dollars a month if she needed it.

He pulled the closely written sheet of paper from the envelope and stopped walking to steady it. Squinting down at her spidery writing, he immediately felt a glow of satisfaction. Offering his brotherly generosity had been just the right thing to do. It would help Evelyn and make him feel good.

My dear brother,
I cannot thank you enough for your sympathy and your
offer to help us. You cannot know how your letter affected me. I
confess, I burst into tears as I read it.

Griffin felt the sting of tears in his own eyes, just knowing the good he'd done.

Dearest Griffin, I think you are aware that Jacob's father passed
on two years ago and left my late husband his property. Since
that time, we have lived a little better than before, and I am
happy to say that I do not need financial assistance at this time.

Griffin frowned over that sentence. If she didn't need money, what did she need? Just his kind thoughts from three thousand miles away?

There is a way you can help me immeasurably, however,
and that is with my eldest boy, Justin. It grieves me to tell you
this, but he has given me great pain this past year. He's become
friends with an undesirable group of youths, and since his
father's passing I've not been able to control his behavior at all.
He comes and goes as he pleases. I don't like to mention it, but

I fear he stole some money from my reticule last week. Not only that, but he's taken up smoking. He thinks I don't know, but the odor clings to him. Dear brother, I fear the worst for my boy, and thus your letter offered a ray of hope to my grieving heart.

Griffin's chest tightened and he feared to turn the page.

I've purchased a train ticket for Justin to depart on Wednesday next. He will ride to Salt Lake City, from where he can get the stagecoach up to your territory. I expect he will arrive in Mountain Home, Idaho, about the fifth of October.

Griffin looked up in a panic. People walked along the main street as though everything was normal. A wagonload of women approached from the north. Shooting practice must be finished. Libby Adams and a middle-aged couple came out of the Spur & Saddle, chatting amicably as they headed across to the Paragon Emporium.

Sucking in a deep breath, Griffin turned and hurried back to the post office.

"Peter!" He threw the door open, but the postmaster-mayor was no longer behind the counter. He stepped to the inner door and pounded on it.

Ellie Nash, Peter's wife, opened it. "Hello, Mr. Bane. I thought you came for your mail earlier."

"I did."

"Well, Peter's out back tending the—"

"What day is it?"

"It's Monday."

"No, no, what day of the month?"

"Oh. Let's see, I believe it's the fourth."

"October fourth."

"Yes, that's right." Ellie eyed him curiously.

Griffin ran his hand through his thick beard. He still hadn't trimmed it. Why on earth hadn't Evelyn telegraphed him with this news, not to say asked permission to send the boy? He had to get to Mountain Home by tomorrow to meet his nephew, and Mountain Home wasn't even part of his branch line. He'd have to ride up to Boise and change to the main line there. That or ride a horse across country. But then what would his nephew ride back on?

"Mr. Bane? Are you all right?"

"What? Oh. Yes, thank you." He turned and staggered out the post office door and down the steps. Where would he keep the boy—Justin? He checked the letter to be sure he had the name right. His bed wouldn't hold both of them. He could give it up for Justin, he supposed. But why should he? Yet there wasn't room in his small lodging for another bed.

Could he let the boy sleep in the loft over the livery? The stage drivers slept there before the boardinghouse opened. But he'd be so far away, Griffin wouldn't hear him if he cried out in the night. How old was the lad, anyway? Evelyn hadn't said. She'd mentioned smoking. . . . He must be at least fifteen.

Griffin scrunched up his face, recalling the first and last time he'd tried smoking. His father had caught him out behind the barn and tanned his backside but good. He'd been twelve.

What was his sister doing to him?

His breath came in quick gasps, and his boots thunked loudly on the boardwalk. When he came even with the Wells Fargo office, Annie Harper had pulled her wagon over and was letting the shooting club ladies climb down. He ducked quickly inside the office and shut the door.

How could he go to Mountain Home tomorrow? He was still shorthanded. He needed to round up a shotgun messenger for tomorrow's run to Silver City, and if the man who came in on the Boise stage wouldn't do it, Griffin would have to do it himself. And what if he did go to Mountain Home? What if he got all the way over there, and Justin didn't show up? He sat down heavily. There must be a good way to handle this. It occurred to him that he didn't pray much, but now might be a good time.

Uh, heavenly Father. . .uh. . .I know I don't talk to You as much as I should. But I'm thankful for. . .for everything You do for me. And I was wondering. . .well, could You help me figure out what to do with Evelyn's boy? It's too late to tell her not to send him. Uh. . .thanks.

A soft knocking sounded on his door, and he jerked his head. "It's open."

The door creaked on its hinges. Vashti Edwards stood there in her usual crinkly finery. He guessed that was all she had to wear—satins and taffetas left over from her saloon days, but no soft cotton housedresses like the ranchers' wives wore. She was probably being frugal, wearing her old dresses until they wore out, but it was distracting.

"What do you want?" He pushed himself to his feet, not caring whether he sounded rude. He had a family crisis to deal with.

"Mr. Bane, I wondered if you'd reconsidered letting me learn to drive the coaches. I'm willing to—"

"No."

"Please, Mr. Bane? I've done a good job for you here in the office, haven't I?"

He looked her over grudgingly. "Yes, you have, but that doesn't mean you could handle a team. Besides, at the moment it's not a driver I need."

"What do you need, sir? Maybe I can help."

"I need a place for a boy to stay. And a shotgun rider for tomorrow's run to Silver City."

"A boy?"

"That's right. My nephew is coming to stay here for a while."

"That's wonderful."

"It is?"

Vashti smiled. "Of course. You have family. That's a mighty precious gift, Mr. Bane."

"Well, I suppose so." It was a long time since he'd thought deeply about family. "My sister's husband kicked off, and she doesn't know what to do with all the kids, so she's sending me her big boy."

"Does she want you to apprentice him?"

Griffin snapped his gaze to meet hers. "I didn't think of that. She wants me to keep him in line, I guess. Keep him out of trouble. She didn't say anything about teaching him a trade."

"Seems to me that would be the best thing for him."

"Well. . .it would take a lot of time."

She stepped farther into the office and stood before the desk. "Yes, it would, but you know you need someone to help with the forge work. Once you've taught him, he could maybe take that over one day. Or if he wants to move along, he'd have a skill so's he could support himself when he's grown. How big is this boy?"

"I don't know." Griffin eyed her uneasily, fearing she would berate him for neglecting his kinfolk, but she seemed deep in thought. "I don't even know for sure he's on the stage," Griffin added, "but he's supposed to come in to Mountain Home tomorrow. Guess I'll have to ride over there and fetch him."

"Where's he coming from?"

"Salt Lake. Took the train that far."

Vashti smiled. "Why don't you telegraph the Wells Fargo division manager in Salt Lake and see if he boarded the stagecoach there as scheduled? It would be worth the money the inquiry would cost you. If he's on the stage, you go get him, or else tell them to send him on to Boise. It would be easier to get him there. And if he's not on board, you won't waste the trip."

He gave that a full five seconds of consideration. "Not a bad idea. Thank you."

"You're welcome."

He rose and stepped toward the doorway, but Vashti moved into it and stood her ground. She tipped her head back so she could look up into his face. "If you write out the telegram, I could run it over to Mr. Dostie for you, and I'm sure Mrs. Thistle would have a vacant room a young man could stay in, if that suits your situation."

Griffin frowned down at her. Why was she being so helpful?

She smiled. "As to the shotgun messenger, I'd be happy to fill in for your man tomorrow. I'm a pretty good shot, if I do say so. I won the ribbon for personal best at today's shooting club meeting."

He stared down into her new-leaf-green eyes. After a long moment, he said, "I can take care of the telegram myself. And I suppose I could put him up at the boardinghouse for a few days 'til I figure out something better."

Vashti didn't move out of the way. "What about the Silver City run? I'd love to do it."

He huffed out a breath and shook his head. "You don't understand, do you? I cannot—I *will* not hire a woman on my stage line. I'd be laughed out of Idaho Territory. Besides, I have a responsibility to the U.S. Mail."

"But you're in a bind. You said so yourself. It's only for one day. One run. And I can do it. Just ask Trudy Chapman or Bitsy. They'll tell you I'm a good shot."

"I don't doubt that. It's just—"

"I know. It's because I'm a girl."

"Well, yes. I don't know any other way to put it. Do you think a gang of outlaws would hang back and say, 'Oh my, look at that! They've got a lady on the box today. I guess we'd better not rob that stagecoach'? Of course not! They'd be nudging each other and saying, 'Look, Billy. Easy pickings today, and a pretty little skirt, too.'"

Vashti's face paled, and he immediately regretted the words. "I'm sorry. Shouldn't have said that." His own face began to feel warm. "I'm just trying to make you understand why I can't let you do it."

She squared her shoulders and hiked up her chin. "And I'm telling you they would never get near that coach with me on the box."

"Sure. With your fiery hair and shiny satin gown calling out to them."

Vashti stamped her foot. "I'll put my hair up under a hat. I'll even wear *your* hat if you want. They wouldn't think a lady would be wearing *that*."

"What's wrong with my hat?"

"Just everything."

"Ha!"

"And I'd borrow a drab-colored dress from Isabel Fennel or Apphia Benton. They've got enough of them."

Griffin chuckled. Feisty little thing, she was. "Tell you what, Miss Pushy, I'm going to go send my telegram. You mosey on over to the Fennel House and see if Mrs. Thistle could put my nephew up for a few nights. If she says yes and if I get a telegram back saying Justin's on his way, I'll take what you said under consideration."

Her eyes glowed. "Really?"

"Said so, didn't I?"

"Oh! Thank you!" She squeezed his wrist and tore off across the street.

"Wait!"

She stopped and turned in a swirl of skirts. "Yes, sir?"

"*If* this happens, and I'm not saying that it will, you'll have to fill out some paperwork required by the Wells Fargo company for all employees."

She grinned. "I'll come back after I speak to Mrs. Thistle." She tore for the Fennel House.

Griffin stared after her. Was he nuts? Well, at least he hadn't promised her. Maybe he could back down later. Or maybe Justin was delayed, and he wouldn't have to go to Mountain Home, or even Boise. But if he did. . .

He shook his shaggy head. He had to be crazy to consider this. He'd actually listened to her and halfway said she could ride the stage tomorrow with Bill Stout. How could he have done that?

Must be the green eyes.

⋆ CHAPTER 5 ⋆

That evening after the supper rush of six diners, Vashti pondered long over the paper Griffin had given her. Goldie came in about six thirty, after her stint at the emporium, and found the plate Bitsy had put by for her in the kitchen. She carried it over to the rough table where Vashti was seated and plopped down across from her.

"Whatcha doing?"

Vashti sighed. "Mr. Bane has practically agreed to let me ride shotgun on the Silver City stage tomorrow, but I have to write down all kinds of information first."

Goldie frowned. "What sort of information?"

"Well, name, age, address—I can do that. But the last question is 'Next of kin.' What do I put down?"

"Don't you have any kin?"

"I'm thinking on it."

Goldie bowed her head for a moment, asking the blessing on her food. As she raised her head, Bitsy breezed in from the dining room. "Mr. Dooley and Mrs. Adams just came in wanting pie and coffee. This is turning into a good night for us."

Vashti pushed her chair back. "Want me to help?"

Bitsy waved her offer aside. "I can serve two pieces of pie and two cups of coffee with one hand tied to a bucking horse. Relax and eat."

"Did you know Vashti's riding shotgun tomorrow?" Goldie asked.

"She told me."

"What do you think?"

Bitsy took half an apple pie from the pie safe. "Not my cup of tea, but if that's what she wants to do. . ."

"I think she's very brave." Goldie dove into her roast chicken and baked potato.

Bitsy put two plates on a tray and reached into the crock of forks. "I said to her, 'That could be a step toward the job you really want.' I think it's progress."

Vashti smiled her thanks across the room. "Now, if I can just figure out who to put down as next of kin."

"What's that for?" Bitsy frowned with her knife hovering above the pie.

"In case I get killed on the job, I reckon."

"Humph."

Goldie nodded. "That's what I think, too."

Vashti looked down at the paper again. At the top, she'd written as neatly as she could, *Georgia Edwards, age 24, Fergus, Idaho.* But for "next of kin," she had few options. The one relative she could think of was the last person she'd want notified on her behalf.

Bitsy poured the customers' coffee and set the pot back on the stove. "You've lived with me for more than four years, and you're like kin to me and Augie. Why can't you just put me down on that paper?"

Vashti looked over at her. For a moment, she couldn't speak. Her breath was knocked out of her, and tears filled her eyes. The weathered old Spur & Saddle building had indeed become her home, and Bitsy was closer to her than any legal family had been since she was a small child. "I like that."

Bitsy smiled at her. "Go ahead. If Griffin makes a fuss, send him to me. I'll take care of him."

"Thanks!" Vashti quickly wrote, *Mrs. Augustus Moore, Fergus, Idaho*, and folded up the paper.

The next morning, Vashti ran along the dirt street, holding her skirt above her ankles. She turned in at the path to the pastor's house, ran up the steps, and knocked, panting for breath.

Apphia Benton opened the door. "Well, good morning, Vashti.

I didn't expect you until later."

"I can't come this afternoon. I just wanted to let you know—I'll be away."

Apphia stepped back and gestured for her to step inside. "Away? Where are you going?"

"Sorry, but I can't stop long. Mr. Bane's nephew is coming, and he has to go and get him. He's taking the Boise stage today. But he'd been planning to ride shotgun to Silver City, in the other direction, so I'm taking his place."

"What? My dear, do come sit down and explain this to me. Surely you're not—"

"Yes, ma'am. The shotgun messenger who usually has that run quit and headed for the Yukon."

"Oh, I heard they'd found gold up there."

"That's right, so Mr. Bane is short a messenger, and he can't send the coach without one today, on account of something I'm not supposed to tell you."

Apphia arched her eyebrows but said nothing. Vashti gulped. She'd almost blabbed about the treasure box coming down from one of the mines tomorrow. One of the first and most important rules Griffin had taught her when he let her tend the Wells Fargo office was to never reveal to anyone when money and other valuables would be on a stagecoach. Not that the minister's wife would tell anyone, but it was the principle. That, and if Griffin found out, he'd fire Vashti immediately.

"Anyway, he says I can do it this once, and I'm hoping that if everything goes well, he'll let me try driving."

Apphia nodded slowly. "You told me you hoped for a chance to be a driver. I still think it's a rather rough way for a young lady to earn her living, but—"

"But I love driving," Vashti said. "I've prayed it over, like you told me I should, and I still want to do it. I don't think God would put this in my heart if He didn't want me to try it, do you?"

"Well…sometimes the Lord lets us do things that aren't especially good for us. We need to be careful not to think our wants are the same as God's will."

"But I've always loved horses." Vashti eyed her friend uncertainly. "All the time I worked in saloons, I thought that if I could just be out working with horses—animals are so much kinder than people, don't you think?"

Apphia touched her shoulder gently. "Sometimes that's true, I admit. But stagecoach driving—that's a rough-and-tumble world."

"Not so bad as selling whiskey and putting up with the men drinking it."

Apphia did not answer, but her eyes held a troubled cast.

Vashti smiled at her. "If I could drive, I'd be perfectly happy. And if I show Mr. Bane I can do a good job as a messenger, that's one step closer to driving."

"Ah, Vashti. I'll continue to pray for you. For your safety, and also that God will show you clearly if He wants you to pursue this. I know you haven't always had it easy. Just please, come see me tomorrow after you come home, to let me know you're all right."

"I will." Vashti gathered her skirts. "Now I must run. Mr. Bane says I have to sign another paper at the Wells Fargo office before I leave."

"Say, did you find someone to build that driving rig you were talking about?"

"Not yet, but I will. You don't mind, do you?"

Apphia cocked her head to one side. "I'm not sure it's the best thing, but we'll let you use the barn. I'll trust to God to stop this adventure if He doesn't want you to do it."

"Hey, Griff, I see you're busy." Hiram Dooley stepped into the dim livery barn and walked over to stand beside his friend.

"I'm always busy these days." Once again Griffin had to help Marty hitch up the stagecoach team. "Got to get these horses ready, then get over to the office and sign some paperwork with Vashti Edwards, and I'm heading to Boise later today."

"What for?"

"My sister's boy's arriving. He's going to stay with me for a while."

Hiram whistled softly. "Big change for you. What's the business you're doing with Miss Edwards? Not that it's my never-mind."

"She thinks she can ride shotgun on the Silver City stage. I'm making her sign a paper that says I'm not responsible if she breaks her neck or gets shot by road agents."

"You're really letting her do it? I knew she'd been pestering you to let her drive."

"I'm not letting her do that. But I'm in a bind, and it's common knowledge she's a good shot." Griffin finished buckling a strap and snapped his fingers. "I meant to ask Libby Adams if she had some pants that would fit Vashti. I don't want her riding in one of those flashy dresses of hers, advertising to the criminal world that my shotgun messenger is a female."

"I can go over and ask Libby if you'd like."

"That'd be a big help, since time's getting short." Griffin grinned at him. "Not like you'd mind a reason to pop in and see Libby, eh?"

Hiram smiled and stuck his thumbs under his suspenders. "Don't mind a bit. Actually, she's the reason I'm here. Wondered if you'd keep an eye out for a nice, calm saddle horse for Libby."

"Your wedding present to her?"

"Something like that."

Griffin headed toward the barn wall for the next set of harnesses. "Sure, I'll look for something. You set a date yet?"

"Nope, but she's got a likely prospect to buy the store."

"That couple that's staying at the boardinghouse?"

"They're the ones. Mr. and Mrs. Hamilton." Hiram stepped back. "So what else do you need for Vashti? A pair of pants and. . . ?"

"Anything that will make her look like a man."

"You want me to *what*?" Vashti glared at Griffin, but he refused to back down and glared back.

She put her hands on her hips. "I figured out who to name as my next of kin, and I agreed to sign that ridiculous paper swearing you wouldn't get in trouble if I get killed. Bitsy loaned me this old, drab brown dress—don't ask me where she got it from. I even told you I'd wear this bowler hat of Augie's. But apparently that's not enough."

"It's just a pair of trousers," Griffin said.

She clenched her fists and mimicked his tone saucily, "Just a pair of trousers."

Griffin scowled down at her from his height. His conscience reproached him slightly, but he ignored it. So he was demanding something of her that she didn't want to do. He did that to the drivers all the time. They lived by the stage line's rules—or else. Could he help it if Vashti saw him as a shaggy Goliath who held her future in his hands? He rather liked the idea that he was the only man in town who could boss her around.

"Look, it's very simple. If you don't want to do it, all I've got to do is tell Hi Dooley I'll pay him twice the normal rate, and he'll take this run for me. The stagecoach leaves in fifteen minutes, with or without you. What do you say?" He glared steadily back into those icy green eyes. Of course, he hadn't asked Hiram if he'd do the run, but he probably would, now that he thought of it. In fact, Griff wished he *had* asked his friend this morning. It would have been worth paying a double wage to avoid this conflict, and Hi could probably use some pocket change. He'd have to remember that for next time. There was always a next time.

He kept up the stony glare, and Vashti's face squirmed into a mask of distaste.

"I ought to refuse, but that's what you want, isn't it?" She snatched the neatly folded pants and flannel shirt off Griffin's desk. "Where do I change?"

"Mrs. Adams says you can go over there and use her back room."

Vashti turned on her high-heeled shoes and strode out the door.

Griffin didn't know whether to smile or swear.

Five minutes later, Vashti opened the door of Libby's back room and cautiously peered out into the emporium. Libby waited behind the counter.

"All ready? Let's take a look."

Only when she'd flung the door wide and taken two steps did

Vashti realize Mr. Dooley was leaning on the far side of the counter. She felt a flush speed up from the collar of the huge buffalo plaid shirt.

Hiram let out a sort of gasp and turned around.

Vashti's chest hurt. She looked anxiously to Libby. "What? Is it that bad?"

"He's just surprised. Hmm." The elegant lady looked her up and down. "You need men's boots, that's for sure. Maybe a boys' size. And how about a leather vest over that shirt? It will disguise your. . .er. . . gender better." Libby swung around and hurried between the racks of merchandise toward the far corner where boots lined one set of shelves.

Hiram glanced at Vashti then away. "I, uh, need some twelve-penny nails." He all but ran toward the hardware section.

Vashti steamed as she pulled her shoes off. Did she look so shocking in trousers? Libby had found a pair in a smaller size than the voluminous ones she'd tried first, and a belt to bring in the waist. The big shirt hung down over it. Maybe she ought to tuck that in if she was going to wear a vest, too.

Libby dashed back, holding out a pair of stiff leather boots. "Try these. I'll find a vest."

As she turned away, Griffin Bane strode in. "Hey, gal, the stage is here, and we need to load the box. We're waiting on you to stand guard while we do it."

"Uh. . ." Vashti darted a glance toward Libby.

"She's ready, Griffin," Libby called. "I'm just getting her a vest to complete her ensemble."

Quickly Vashti pulled on the boots. Libby hurried over, holding a black leather vest made for a middle-sized boy. Vashti slipped her arms into it.

"There," Libby said. "Put your hat on."

Vashti grabbed the hat off the counter. Libby had replaced Augie's overlarge bowler with a smaller cowboy hat in creamy felt with a braided leather band. Vashti loved it at first sight but wondered if her first wages as a messenger would pay for all these clothes. Boots now, too, and the soft leather vest.

Griffin stood motionless, staring at her. He opened his mouth, but no words came out.

Libby chuckled. "Makes a fine-looking boy, doesn't she, Mr. Bane?"

Griff cleared his throat. "I reckon from a couple hundred yards away she'd pass. And remember, you're not letting any outlaws get that close."

"No, sir, I'm not. Thanks, Libby. I'll settle up with you when I get home tomorrow." Vashti put on a little swagger as she left the store. Griffin came along behind her—she could feel the boardwalk shake under his heavy tread.

Two passengers were already in the coach when she reached it. Bill Stout, the white-haired veteran driver, sat on the box with his whip in its stand and the lines of the team of six horses in his hands. To Vashti's surprise, the sheriff leaned against the side of the stage line office.

Ethan Chapman straightened and stepped away from the wall. "Morning."

"Hello, Sheriff."

Vashti felt a firm hand on her shoulder. She stopped and turned to look up at Griffin.

"I told Bill to call you Sam, so people wouldn't know you're a girl," he said in as soft a voice as she imagined that barrel chest could emit.

"Sam?" she hissed. She looked around quickly. The passengers and Bill didn't seem to have heard.

"What, you don't like that name?"

She considered for a moment. "I have another name, you know, if Vashti's too feminine for this outfit."

"You mean Edwards?"

"No. I mean. . ." She leaned closer and stood on tiptoe so she could get within a foot of his ear. "My Christian name was Georgia. So whyn't you all just call me George?"

His dark, bushy eyebrows rose. He blinked. "George?"

"Is that any worse than Sam?"

"No, I s'pose not."

"Good. Didn't you read that paper I signed all legal-like for you? If you look close, you'll see that's what I put. Georgia Edwards. Only I smeared the I-A a tad, so's anyone might think it said George."

He nodded slowly. "All right then. Let Bill in on it once you get going."

She nodded and winked. He jerked his head back.

"Come on inside. I've got your shotgun in there. I'll carry the strongbox out, and you look sharp, up and down the street, while I load it."

They stepped into the office, and Griffin took a gleaming shotgun with a cherry stock from a rack on the wall and placed it in her hands. Vashti held it to the light streaming in the doorway and admired the fine tracery on the lock. Any man or woman in Fergus would be proud to own this gun. She nodded and hefted it. Not too heavy.

"Thank you."

"That's on loan while you're working for me." Griffin crossed the room and stooped to open the safe. He brought out a sturdy wooden box, painted green and bound with bands of steel.

"You go out first and make sure it's clear."

Vashti stepped out onto the boardwalk. As if anyone in Fergus would hold up the stagecoach right in town. Especially with the sheriff loafing around.

She glanced at Chapman. He stood with his hands on his belt, his right hand close to his six-shooter, looking up the street toward the Nugget Saloon. Vashti looked the other way, southward along the boardwalk and the dusty street. Beyond the emporium, Oscar Runnels, the freighter, was climbing the steps to the post office.

Griffin came out and went straight to the coach. He heaved the treasure box up and settled it on the boards where the driver and messenger rested their feet. Bill helped him slide the heavy box under the seat. They fussed for a moment, making sure it was secure; then Griffin stepped back and turned to her.

"All right, George. Time for you to go."

Vashti walked over to the step at the front of the coach and climbed up. Settling onto the seat beside Bill, she smiled at him. "Morning, Mr. Stout."

"How do, Sam."

"It's George, but that's all right." She looked down at Griffin, whose head came up as high as where her feet were braced. A strange look crossed his face. Was he thinking he ought to tell Bill to take care of her, instead of the other way around? For a moment, Vashti was afraid he'd make her get down again and tell her she couldn't go.

"We'll be just fine, Mr. Bane," she said. "I hope you and your nephew have a nice trip."

"Godspeed." Griffin stepped back.

Bill lifted the reins and let the horses have an inch or two of slack. "Get up!"

They rolled out of Fergus with the wind whistling in Vashti's ears below the hat's brim. As they passed the Spur & Saddle, she glimpsed Augie and Bitsy standing at the front door. She raised the shotgun in triumph and waved.

★ CHAPTER 6 ★

Griffin paced the porch in front of the Wells Fargo office in Boise. He had another half hour before the stage was due. He could step down the street for refreshment, but he wanted to make sure he was here when Justin arrived.

After a few minutes, he went inside. The ticket agent looked up and smiled. "Cup of coffee, Mr. Bane?"

"Thanks."

The man nodded toward the potbellied stove in the corner. "I make a fresh pot before the Mountain Home stage comes in. The cups on the shelf are clean."

Griffin poured himself a serving of the boiling, dark brew. The stove's heat made the room too warm, and he stepped away from it, toward the counter. He set the hot cup down for a minute to let the grounds settle.

"How's business up to Fergus?" the agent asked.

"Tolerable. I'm having a little trouble keeping enough drivers and messengers lined up."

"We've had a big turnover here, too," the man admitted.

"Thought I might talk to your division manager to see if he had any suggestions."

The agent shook his head. "Mr. Nelson's gone to Glenn's Ferry. I don't expect he'll be back for two or three hours at least."

Griffin picked up his tin cup. The small, curved handle was hot, but not so bad he couldn't hold it. The worst part was that the curve was so tight he couldn't get his large finger through it. He managed to raise the cup to his lips and took a cautious sip. He'd had worse coffee. Once. He grimaced and set the cup down.

"Did you get the new rate table?" the agent asked.

"Yup."

The door opened. Two men came in.

"Afternoon," one of them called. "We need tickets to Mountain Home."

Griffin stepped outside, leaving his cup of brew on the counter. He paced back and forth, ignoring the passing wagons and foot traffic. If he were home, he could be shoeing Oscar Runnels's mules, or working with the bay colt, or mending harness.

And what about the Silver City run? He'd put Vashti with his steadiest driver, but maybe he'd lowered Bill's chances of a safe run by giving him a green shotgun rider. What if road agents tried to stop them and she panicked? Griffin turned and walked the length of the porch again. Best not to think about the Silver City stage when it was too late to change things.

Ten minutes later, the ticket agent came out and piled luggage and mail sacks near where the stagecoach would halt. The two men who'd come for tickets and a few other prospective passengers milled about, making small talk.

Right on time, a bugle blew. Griffin heard the pounding hooves and rattling wheels before he caught sight of the stage. His chest swelled a little, and his throat tightened as the red and gold coach flew down the street. People scattered and stood admiring the sight or cursing the driver, who popped his whip more for show than practicality. The six bay horses—nearly matched—slowed to a trot then drew up right where the pile of luggage waited.

Griffin laughed. Those horses' flanks were dark with sweat, but their breathing wasn't labored, and no foam had formed along the harness straps. The good drivers knew how to pace the team and still put on a performance when they neared each stop.

The messenger hopped down and flung the door open.

"Welcome to Boise, folks." The ticket agent offered a hand to a middle-aged woman who climbed stiffly down from the coach. She was followed by a string bean of a boy. Griffin looked no further. The gawky lad had the Bane chin and his sister, Evelyn's, dark doe eyes, with which he warily scanned the people on the boardwalk.

"Justin." Griffin stepped forward and held out his hand.

The boy snapped his head around and caught a quick breath. "Uncle Griff?"

"That's right." His hand closed over the boy's. "Glad you got here safe. Do you have a trunk?"

"No, sir. Just a satchel."

Griffin turned to the back of the coach, and they waited for the messenger to toss down the luggage.

"We'll stay in a hotel here tonight," he told Justin. "Then we'll take the stage back to Fergus in the morning."

A battered leather bag landed with a thud beside them, and the boy stooped to grab the handle. As he straightened, he flipped his overlong hair back from his forehead.

"Just so's you know, I don't want to do no smithing."

Vashti clung to the curved metal on the side of her seat. The coach swayed on its leather straps as they barreled around a corner. She was grateful that the sheer drop-off was on Bill's side, not hers, but she realized two things: If she was going to become a top-notch driver, she'd have to get used to flying along these precarious roads. And coming back downhill tomorrow, she'd be on the side edging what amounted to a cliff.

The horses slowed to a walk as the grade increased. Bill let them lumber along up the incline. He reached into the pocket of his jacket, brought out a small hunk of tobacco, and bit off a piece. Stuffing the wad back into his pocket, he glanced over at Vashti.

"I like a chaw while I'm driving."

She nodded.

"Griff says you want to learn to drive."

"I know how to drive."

"That so?"

"I can drive two and four."

"So you could drive a stage on the flat, with four horses?"

"I could."

"Huh." They rode on in silence until the horses gained more level ground. Bill snapped the reins. "Up now." The team picked up a steady jog. "We'll trade for mules at the next stop. It's a little over halfway to Silver. The last half's the worst."

Vashti clenched her teeth and nodded. She'd never been up to the mining town before, and the road was a bit rougher than she'd imagined. The hairpin turns and sheer drops gave her pause. And Bill said the worst terrain lay ahead of them.

She watched his hands as he worked the lines gently, making fine adjustments with subtle movements she could barely see. Not one horse broke stride as they clopped through a wooded area and splashed across a shallow creek.

"Pull now," he called, and the six leaned into the harness to carry the coach up the next grade without losing speed.

"How'd you learn to drive so well?" she asked.

"Oh, I been driving since I was one-sixteenth your size."

She smiled.

"Hold on."

She grabbed the metal bar again and tried not to look toward the far edge of the road as the coach careened down a dip and up the other side. The wind tugged at her sleeves and whistled past her ears.

"That gully took my hat off the first time I ran it," Bill said with a laugh.

The horses slowed to their businesslike jog for another half mile. Bill bent down and took a bugle from beneath the seat.

"Are we nearly to the swing station?" Vashti looked ahead but saw no signs of civilization.

"Around the next curve." He put the horn to his lips and blew a long blast. Lowering the shiny instrument, he smiled at Vashti. "Now Jules Harding, he could play a right smart tattoo on the horn. I just give it a lungful."

They swept into the yard of the stage stop, and Bill pulled the team up.

Two men came running from the cabin to help unharness the blowing horses. Vashti jumped down and winced as her feet hit the ground. She hadn't realized how long she'd braced her legs on the footboard. She took a few steps to get her blood flowing and opened the coach door. "Do you gentlemen want to stretch your legs? We'll leave in about ten minutes."

The two passengers climbed down. One of them eyed her keenly as he made his exit. Vashti looked away, hoping she wouldn't blush. That would surely give away her secret. As the two men ambled toward the house, the one who'd stared at her said something to the other. The second man turned around and looked at her. Vashti turned her back to them and shut the door of the coach. Bill came around from behind the coach.

"The necessary's out back. I suggest you wait until the passengers come back."

She nodded, staring at the ground. Her face was scarlet for sure.

"You want some coffee?" Bill asked.

She shook her head.

The hostler led a team of mules out of a corral, where he'd had them hitched up and waiting in their harness. In no time flat, the bay horses had been turned out and the six mules put in their place before the stagecoach. Bill came around the corner of the cabin and nodded to her. Vashti ran around the other side of the little building. Within two minutes she was back, panting as she climbed up. The passengers had boarded, and the station agent and his helper stood leaning against the corral fence.

Vashti felt their eyes on her as she climbed aboard. The rough boots made her feet feel clumsy, but she sprang as quickly as she could up to the seat beside Bill. "What are they staring at?"

"You, of course. They think you're awfully young to be riding shotgun. I told them you're a top marksman." He spit tobacco juice over the side. "Melvin said, 'Oh, that's what you call it in Fergus.'" He laughed.

"So he knows I'm a woman?"

"I'd say so. He guessed."

"I think the passengers are suspicious, too."

"Makes no difference, so long as the lawless part of the population doesn't know."

"Word will get around."

"Mebbe so." Bill gathered the reins. "Up now, you lazy mules!"

The team began the merciless uphill pull. Another eight miles of hard going.

"You ever been held up?" Vashti asked.

"Sure."

She eyed him in surprise. "Really?"

"Every driver who's been around awhile has been."

"Here? I mean, on the Fergus line?"

"Once. Before that I was down on the Wyoming run. Wild, oh, that route was wild, especially during the war."

"You mean the War Between the States?"

"That's right. It was like the Injuns knew most of the soldiers were busy elsewhere, and they attacked all up and down the line. Stole horses and food—burned everything else. Hay, grain, stations. Everything. Times were hard then, and it cost a pretty penny to keep the line running."

"Mr. Bane told me it cost a lot more then to ride the line."

"Sure it did. But most people were afraid to ride anyway, at least on certain parts. If it hadn't been for the mail contracts, the stagecoach companies would have folded."

Vashti clung tightly to her shotgun and the edge of the seat as they took a curve.

"So what was the worst scrape you were in?"

Bill spat over the side. "About twenty Injuns come after me. Old Ben Liddel was sittin' where you are. He pumped the lead, I'm telling you."

"How'd you get away? Outrun 'em?"

"Nope. A team of horses hitched to a coach can't outrun their horses. Mules even less likely. No, we drove into a piece of road between some rocks and stood 'em off for three hours. We weren't far out from Julesburg. Finally, half a dozen men came riding out to see what had happened to us. They ran the Injuns off. Good thing, because Ben and me were about out of lead."

Vashti eyed him for a long moment. "You telling it straight?"

"I sure am."

"Did you have any passengers?"

"Not that day. Had five sacks of mail, though. And we got it through, yes sirree. 'Course, I took a bullet in my hand."

Vashti stared down at his tanned, leathery hands. "Which one?"

"That one. The right."

"Did it heal up good as new?"

"Pretty good. Still bothers me some, especially in cold weather or when it's going to rain. But I was mighty glad they didn't hit me in a worse place."

The wheels hit a rut, and Vashti lurched forward, nearly flying over the footboard.

"Hold on, there, Georgie!" Bill grabbed the back of her vest and yanked her back up onto the seat.

Vashti gasped and looked up into his placid blue eyes. "Thank you, sir."

"Don't need no 'sir.' I'm just Bill."

"Thank you kindly, Bill."

He nodded. "So, you want to drive."

"I do. I surely do." For a split second, she thought he might offer to let her take the reins.

Bill spit a stream of tobacco juice off into the brush. "What'd you ever drive before?"

"My daddy's horses."

"How long ago?"

She couldn't hold his gaze. "Awhile."

"Like ten years or more?"

"Something like that."

"Hmm." They were approaching a steep incline. Bill let out a little rein and called to the mules, "Hup now. Step along, boys."

Vashti held on and kept quiet. When they got to the top of the rise, the road leveled out for a short stretch.

"Driving a farm wagon h'ain't like driving a stage," Bill said.

"No, sir, I expect you're right. My daddy had a carriage and four."

Bill's eyes narrowed, and he shot her a sidelong glance. "That true?"

"Well. . .the team of four is."

"Ha."

"Johnny Conway said when he was a nipper, somebody made him a rig to practice driving on."

"That's a passable way to learn. At first. If you can't learn on real horses."

"Well, I don't see how I can learn on real horses when I don't have any of my own and Mr. Bane won't let me drive his."

"Hmm."

Vashti watched him cautiously for a bit then cleared her throat. "Would you make me a rig, Bill? I've got a place to put it."

"Do you?"

"Yes, sir. I mean Bill."

He pursed his lips and, after a moment, shot more tobacco juice over the side. "I'll think on it."

They rode along for another hour without much talk. Vashti stared out over the valley below them and across at the distant peaks and rock formations. Some of the stone columns had fanciful shapes. She imagined one group as a quartet of trolls, watching them strain up the ribbon of road.

"Look ahead now," Bill said.

She turned forward. They approached a place where a huge boulder crowded to the edge of the road.

"Anyplace there's cover, you need to be watching."

"You think there might be outlaws hiding behind that rock?"

"You just never know. They say that back in the old days when the most ore was coming down, this was a favorite spot."

Vashti's neck prickled. The road was so steep, the mules walked slowly, leaning into their collars. She sat straighter and flicked glances at every conceivable hiding place along both sides of the road, always coming back to the base of the boulder. The only sounds were creaking leather, the mules' labored breathing and snorting, and the crunch of the wheels on the sandy ground.

When they'd passed the spot, she sighed and relaxed a little.

Bill nudged her with his elbow. "It also makes a good courting spot, on top of that boulder."

She laughed. "Did Mr. Bane tell you his nephew's coming?"

"I heard."

"He's boarding him at the Fennel House."

Bill grunted. They reached a somewhat flat spot in the road, with no trees or large rocks about, and he halted the team. "I like to let them take a breather here. More uphill ahead."

Vashti nodded. "What would you have done if bandits jumped out from behind that rock back there?"

He frowned and spit again. "It's a bad place. Can't run away from 'em, 'cause the road's so steep. Can't turn around. Reckon I'd have to stop and give 'em what they wanted—unless you shot 'em first."

She gulped. "You think I should shoot if that happens?"

"If someone jumps out, aiming a gun at us, I'd just as soon you let off a round and didn't wait to parley. If they's only one or two of 'em, that might be enough. If they's a whole gang. . .well, that's different. At a tight spot like that, it's better to give in than get killed." He shrugged. "Just be glad we don't have to worry about Injuns anymore in these parts."

By the time they reached Silver City, every muscle in Vashti's body ached. The passengers grinned at her as they left the coach.

"Thanks, young fella," one of them said.

"You're welcome." She kept her hat on as Bill drove the coach around to where the liveryman would unharness the team.

As she climbed down again, she heard the man say to Bill, "You've got a new messenger."

"That's right." Bill came around to her side of the coach. "All right, George, let's get over to the hotel."

Vashti quietly walked alongside Bill, carrying the small canvas bag she'd brought.

"I generally share a room with the shotgun rider," Bill said as they reached the steps of the Idaho Hotel.

She paused with one foot on the bottom step. "Mr. Bane said to get a separate room."

"He paying for it?"

"I reckon."

Bill shook his head. "He won't want to keep doing that."

"Well, he was in a bind today."

"So this is a onetime thing for you?"

She raised her chin and met his gaze just below her hat brim. "No, sir. I want to learn to drive and do this regular, like I told you."

"Then you need to think about your bunking arrangements. Folks will think it's odd if you have a separate room. And that Griff pays for it, or pays you enough for you to do it. People will think about that."

"What do you think I should do?"

Bill lifted his hat and scratched his head. "Don't know. There's a widow woman over on Placer Street. Maybe if you told her who you are, she'd let you board with her whenever you come up here."

"Then wouldn't folks wonder why the widow took in a boy as her boarder?"

"Maybe so." Bill spit off to the side of the steps. "You got any ideas?"

"Well, I'm not sleeping in the same room with you."

He pulled back, frowning. "Didn't mean to suggest you should."

"Then let's get in there and ask for two rooms."

He threw his hands in the air, managing to keep hold of his whip as he did so. "Fine with me, Georgie. Come on."

★ CHAPTER 7 ★

Griffin kept in his anger all the way to the hotel. What right did this upstart boy have to tell him what he was and wasn't going to do? Evelyn had sent him here to get straightened out. Well, Griffin didn't know much about parenting, and he'd be the first to admit it. But he knew about hard work. Hard labor had made a man of him, and he figured it could do the same for Justin. But what if the boy wouldn't work? He couldn't force him to do it.

He had a mind to wire Evelyn and tell her he was sending the boy back. But that wouldn't solve any of the problems that had traveled across the country with his nephew. He'd have to give it some thought. Calm down, that was it. Keep from getting mad and saying things he'd regret later.

"When did you eat last?" he asked as he pushed open the door to the Pacifica Hotel.

"I had breakfast."

"Breakfast? What about dinner?"

Justin shrugged. "Some folks bought dinner where we stopped last."

"What? You didn't have any money?" Griffin eyed him closely.

The boy shrugged and squinted his eyes.

"Well, we're going to have us a whopping big supper, I'll tell you that." Griffin tromped to the desk. "We'd like a room, my nephew and me."

"Yes, sir." The clerk turned the guest registry toward him. "Sign here, please. That'll be a dollar."

"Thank you. And we'd like supper as soon as possible."

"Our dining room opens at four thirty for early diners."

"Can't get nothing now?"

"No, sir. Unless you go into the bar, but your nephew looks a bit young for that. If the marshal came along while you were in there, I couldn't guarantee you wouldn't face charges."

Griffin looked over at Justin. "How old are you?"

Justin hesitated. "Seventeen?"

"I doubt it."

The boy hung his head and muttered, "Fifteen and a half."

"Right. We'll go down the street and find a place where we can get something to tide us over 'til supper. Let's go put our kit in the room first."

They found a boardinghouse down the street, and the proprietor was willing to heat up some leftovers for them. A bowl of beef stew and a brace of biscuits went down quickly. Griffin considered ordering a refill, but decided it would benefit the boy more to have a small meal now and another later, rather than to stuff himself.

"How about apple pandowdy?" the woman who had served them asked.

"Surely." Griffin looked over at Justin. "You could do with a dish of that, couldn't you?"

"I guess."

Griffin scowled. "That's no way to answer. You say, 'Yes, sir.'"

"All right, yes, sir. I'd like coffee with it, if it's all the same to you."

Shouldn't boys drink milk? Griff tried to remember back when he was fifteen on the farm. He'd drunk a lot of milk. But somewhere in there, he'd started drinking coffee with his father, too. "All right." He looked up at the woman. "Another cup of coffee, please."

When she'd gone, Justin said, "How far is it to Fergus?"

"About forty miles. We'll get there tomorrow afternoon."

"Ma said you've got a smithy and a livery stable."

"Yes, and this past year I've been running the branch line for the stagecoach company. Guess I didn't tell your mother about that." He ought to write to Evelyn more often, but he seldom had time to sit down and craft a letter.

Justin's chin came up a notch. "Are you rich?"

Griffin laughed heartily. "That's a good one, son."

The boy's face clouded. "You're not my pa. In case you didn't hear, my pa's dead."

"Yes, I heard. I'm sorry about that."

"Well, just so's you know, I don't plan to be your boy."

Griffin studied him for a long moment. About the time he'd decided silence was the prudent thing, the woman came back with their dessert and coffee.

Maybe he was doing his nephew a disservice by feeding him. Maybe he'd ought to invoke that Scripture verse Pastor Benton mentioned a few weeks back—the one about people who didn't work not eating. He'd give that some thought.

"I've got a few errands to do before supper." He lifted his thick china mug and sipped the coffee. It was much better than what he'd gotten at the depot. And better than what he made in the old tin pot he kept on the shelf near the forge. His always tasted a little burnt.

"I can amuse myself while you're at it," Justin said.

That didn't seem right in Griff's mind. He recalled Evelyn's words about the boy getting in with the wrong friends. *He comes and goes as he pleases. I don't like to mention it, but I fear he stole some money from my reticule last week. Not only that, but he's taken up smoking.*

Just recalling those lines made Griff's nose wrinkle. He hadn't smelled any tobacco on the boy, but then, Justin wouldn't likely smoke on the stagecoach with other passengers present. And he appeared to have arrived broke. But if he wasn't above stealing, he might get himself into trouble if Griff turned him loose in Boise. Yep, a young fellow like Justin could find a heap of trouble in this half-grown, half-tamed town.

"You stay with me." He took a gulp of coffee.

"What?" The boy obviously took the command as an insult.

"I said, you come around with me. See what I do. I'm going to do a little livestock shopping. We could use an extra team of six, and I need another riding horse or two for the livery trade. After that, I'll go around to the Wells Fargo office again and see if the division agent is back. I need to talk to him about some stagecoach business."

"I don't want to stand around while you do all that."

"What would you do?"

The line of Justin's mouth hardened. "Explore."

"Oh yes, I can just envision that. You stay with me." Griff took another sip.

Justin cautiously slurped his coffee. He didn't make a face or ask for sugar. Maybe he'd been drinking coffee for a while, though Griff couldn't imagine Evelyn allowing it. Of course, he had no idea how Jacob Frye had raised his children; didn't know Jacob at all, for that matter. Griff tackled his apple pandowdy.

"Your pa let you drink coffee all the time?" he asked when he'd scraped out the last bite.

"Nope."

Griff drained his cup and pushed his chair back. "Come on. Let's get over to the stockyard."

The ride down from Silver City went twice as fast as the long pull uphill had gone. Vashti clung to the edge of the seat at least two-thirds of the way. Sometimes Bill drove faster than she'd have thought prudent, but on some of the slopes, it would be impossible to make the mules walk. By the time the road flattened out some, her hands ached from gripping the seat and the shotgun. Despite the warm sunshine, she could feel the tang of winter in the mountain breeze.

"Hey, young George, you done all right this trip," Bill said with a lopsided grin.

"How long 'til we get home?"

"Another hour."

Vashti nodded. They had no passengers on the return trip, but the heavy treasure box was always on her mind. That cargo had to make it safely to Fergus, and someone else would take it on to Boise.

"Think Mr. Bane will let me do it again?"

"No idea. But if he asks me, I'll tell him you did good."

"Thanks." She lifted her hat and let the sun shine on her head for a moment. It was warmer down here than it had been up at Silver.

She shot a glance at Bill. "What are you laughing about?"

"Don't ever do that when there's men about. No way they'd think you was a boy when they saw that pile of red hair."

"My hair is not red," she said with precision and dignity.

"That right?"

"It's auburn."

"Ha." Bill drove on for a bit, still smiling. "How'd you come to be with Bitsy, anyhow?"

Vashti hesitated. No one in Fergus knew her story. Not even Bitsy and Goldie, her two closest friends.

After about half a minute, Bill looked over at her. "You don't need to tell me. I just thought. . .well, you know. You could have gotten some other job besides working in saloons."

"You don't know anything about it."

"That's right, I don't."

Her joy in the sunlight, the breeze, the trotting mules, and the creaking coach crumbled. Her stomach began to ache. They came to another steep hill, and Bill let the mules extend their trot but kept the reins taut so they wouldn't break into a run and go out of control. Vashti clapped her hat on. They flew down the grade, with her clenching the edge of the seat once more and bracing with her feet.

When they slowed to a businesslike trot, she said, "My folks died when I was eleven."

"Didn't know that."

She nodded.

"Didn't you have no kin?"

"I did." She didn't like thinking about those times. For a good many years, she'd tried to forget.

"Guess they didn't treat you right."

"Something like that."

They rode in silence for another mile.

"We're almost to town." Bill leaned down and reached under the seat for his horn.

"Is this where I plug my ears?"

"You'd better not. If you do, it'll mean you're not holding on to that shotgun."

Up ahead, she glimpsed the roofline of the Spur & Saddle. Beyond it, the steeple of the new church pierced the achingly blue sky.

Bill put the horn to his lips.

She'd have to go back to see Libby at the emporium. Next time, she'd have some cotton wool in her pocket to stuff in her ears when they approached a stop.

The mules broke into a canter as the blast of the horn rang out. They charged into town in a flurry of dust. Vashti wished Griffin could see them, but he wasn't due back for another four hours at least.

"How we going to open the safe?" She turned to Bill, but he didn't seem flustered.

"Miz Adams says we can put it in hers until Griff gets back."

"Oh." Vashti looked ahead to where they would stop and unload the strongbox. There on the boardwalk in front of the Wells Fargo office and stretching up the street before the emporium almost as far as the post office, waving and calling congratulations, stood the members of the Ladies' Shooting Club of Fergus.

"I thought we were going to take the stage to Fergus." Justin scowled as he eyed the mule his uncle expected him to mount.

Just like a kid. They wanted change and excitement, but when it came along as someone else's idea, they balked. Speaking of mules. . .

"We were. But I need this string, so I bought it, and I don't know another way to get 'em home. So get in the saddle and let's move."

The boy had no idea that he had it easy. Griffin rode the one horse he'd purchased—he'd considered letting Justin take it, but if anything went wrong, he had to be able to get around quickly. Besides, this was the horse he'd chosen for Hiram to give his bride as a wedding present. The ten-year-old palomino gelding looked flashy, but he was settled and well behaved. Libby could handle him with no problems.

Griffin would ride the palomino and lead along the string of three more mules he'd bought. Six new mules would have been better, but he'd settle for four. These looked healthy and strong, and the seller had guaranteed they'd pull a coach. Griffin had already strapped Justin's satchel to one of them and his own small pack to another. The sun was up, and the day was a-wasting.

"Come on," Griffin said. "Mount up."

Justin held the mule's reins and turned to face the saddle. He wiggled this way and that and finally raised his left foot to the stirrup. Griffin almost called out to him but held back. Was the boy really as green as he seemed? He'd lived in the city. Maybe he hadn't ridden much.

When he landed in the saddle with a thud, the mule stood still and blew out a breath as though resigned to a tedious day. Justin stared down at the reins in his hand as if he knew something wasn't quite right, but he couldn't pinpoint the problem. He separated the reins and put one in his right hand.

Griffin adjusted his hat and said as calmly as he could, "You need to get the off rein on the off side. Lean forward and run it under his neck. Grab it with your other hand."

Justin sat still for a moment, like an equestrian statue, but Griffin had never seen a general cast in bronze on a mule before.

After a good half minute, Justin leaned forward along the mule's neck and fumbled with the lines under the animal's throat latch. It was all Griffin could do not to ride over, grab one rein, and pass it to the correct side. Instead he looked toward the distant hills. He counted silently to ten and then looked back. Justin had dropped the off rein and now leaned over the mule's withers to the right, groping for it. But in doing that, he pulled the mule's head around to the left without meaning to.

"Let up on the near rein," Griffin said.

Justin looked over at him.

"I said, let him have some slack."

Justin dropped the other rein.

Griffin sighed. "Good thing that's not a fresh horse, or he'd be halfway to Nampa, and you'd be eating dust." He walked his new horse over, and the other three mules went with him. He angled the horse so that he could get close to Justin's mule without jostling it.

With a swoop of his long arm, he caught the near rein and held it up for the boy. "Hold on to that loosely, and bend over the other side and get the off rein."

Finally Justin had both reins again, one on each side of the mule's neck.

"All right, let's move." Griffin headed his horse toward the road. He looked over his shoulder to make certain Justin followed.

Although the boy continued to hold the reins so slack they looped down below the mule's neck, the mule seemed content to fall in with the others and keep pace. It was going to be a lengthy process to teach his nephew to ride well—but the owner of a livery stable couldn't allow his kin to be so ignorant about animals. Of course, if Justin couldn't stay in the saddle without a struggle, he'd be unlikely to ride off and get himself into trouble. Perhaps there were advantages to not teaching him to ride.

The boy's sour expression stayed in place for the first mile or two. Griff ignored it and set a steady pace, jogging along. It was as good as he could expect when leading three mules. Justin kept his seat, though he jarred up and down in the saddle. That boy was going to be sore come tomorrow.

Finally Griffin called out, "The trail gets narrow up ahead. You go ahead of me."

Justin looked ahead and then back to him. "What if there's outlaws in those rocks?"

Griffin patted his sidearm. Since he'd ridden to Boise on the stage, he hadn't packed a long gun, but he had worn his pistol. He'd had the same thought as Justin, but he wasn't about to tell the boy that.

"Reckon there won't be. If there are, I've got my Colt, and it won't be much longer until the stage comes along behind us."

Justin hesitated, his eyes squinted into slits. After a moment, he gritted his teeth and turned forward. "Come on, mule. Get up!"

Griffin smiled. That was progress.

Vashti entered the emporium, carefully holding her basket level. In it, she carried four of Augie Moore's famous cinnamon buns wrapped in clean napkins—two for Griffin and two for his nephew. They'd be hungry when they got off the stagecoach from Boise. She intended to wait at the office and greet them when the stage came in, but first she had business to tend to with Libby Adams.

"Good afternoon, Vashti," Libby called from the hardware section of the store. "Don't you look pretty!"

"Thank you, ma'am." Vashti had taken special care in her grooming after she and Bill brought the stage in from Silver City late that morning. She'd bathed and arranged her hair in feminine waves about her face. Then she'd put on her most conservative dress. Even so, when she'd mentally compared her image in the gilt-framed mirror to the way Libby and some of her other friends looked, she knew she'd still missed the bull's-eye when it came to dressing like a lady. The hem of her dress was too short, the fabric too gaudy, and the neck too low—though she'd basted a row of lace along the edge.

"I wondered if I could have a moment of your time." Vashti looked about the dim interior of the store. A couple of women shopped among the groceries; Mrs. Walker was engrossed in yard goods, assisted by Florence Nash; and it appeared that Goldie and Libby were sorting out nails and bolts.

"Of course." Libby touched Goldie's shoulder. "Just keep counting each size, dear, and write the totals down as we've been doing." She smiled and walked toward Vashti. Even her workaday outfit was a soft blue dress with black braid and buttons—a gown any lady could wear proudly to church or on a stroll about town. "How may I help you?"

"I didn't mean to interrupt your work."

"Think nothing of it. Goldie and I are taking inventory. I'm selling the emporium to the Hamiltons—that couple who came in on the stage the other day. We're counting all the merchandise so we can give them a list of what they're buying." Libby pushed back a strand of her golden hair.

"That's a big job."

"Yes, but not too bad. I've kept good records. It shouldn't take us more than a couple of days. They can't move here immediately, but we've signed the paperwork. They'll come back in the spring and take over the store." She smiled, and her teeth showed pearly white against her pink lips. Vashti was sure Libby wore discreet cosmetics—never enough to overpower her lovely features. Libby was the most beautiful woman she knew, and she hardly needed enhancements.

Vashti gulped. "Well, ma'am, I wanted to settle up with you on the bill for the clothes you provided for me yesterday, and"—she looked down the aisle toward the yard goods—"well, I wondered if you could help me pick out a pattern for a regular dress."

"A regular. . . Oh, I see." Libby smiled. "The one you have on is very becoming."

"Thank you, but I know it's too short, and the fabric isn't at all suitable for. . .well, for most occasions." Vashti pulled her shoulders back and looked Libby in the eye. "I don't serve drinks anymore, Miz Adams. I want to look like a lady. I want to *be* a lady. Just because I want to drive a stagecoach and Mr. Bane is making me wear pants to do it doesn't mean I shouldn't look nice the rest of the time."

There. She'd said it. She didn't want to look like a boy when she worked and a floozy when she didn't.

Libby stepped toward the counter. "Why don't you set your basket here? I have several patterns that would suit you, but we also have some very nice ready-made dresses. The winter fashions just came in. There's a green woolen dress with a smart overskirt that I considered keeping myself, but it was a bit too short for me. On you, however. . ." She leaned back and considered Vashti's attributes. "Yes, I think it would just skim your ankles. Very practical, if it's not too plain for your taste."

"I'd like to see it."

They walked the length of the store together. The other women looked up. Emmaline Landry, a regular member of the shooting club, called, "Afternoon, Vashti."

"Hello, Miz Landry." What a difference from the way the townspeople used to treat her. Not so long ago, Vashti and the other saloon women used to come to the emporium after hours when none of the regular customers would see them. Now Goldie worked here, and Bitsy and Vashti came to shop whenever it struck their fancy.

Florence left her customer's side and came to join them. "Vashti!

You looked so cute in that vest and hat this morning. If I hadn't known you were a girl—"

"Now, Florence," Libby said gently, "Miss Edwards wants to look at some more feminine apparel this afternoon."

"Oh, have you seen the silk and wool shawls that came in? I told Mother she and I both have to have one."

"Yes, one of those might go well with the green woolen dress." Libby paused before a rack of dresses, skirts, and coats. She pulled out the dress in question and held it up for Vashti to see.

"That's. . .that's beautiful, ma'am. How. . .how much?"

Libby flipped the little pasteboard tag that dangled from the cuff of the gathered sleeve. "Three dollars and fifteen cents."

"Try it on, Vashti," Florence said. "I'll bet it will fit you perfectly."

"Is there time before the Silver City stage comes in?" Vashti glanced anxiously toward the front window. "I want to be out front when Mr. Bane gets here with his nephew."

"Perhaps not," Libby said. "You can come back later and try it."

Vashti nodded, disappointed. She wanted to make the best possible impression on Griffin. To her way of thinking, the buns would help, and she would tell him how smoothly everything went on the Silver City run. Bill would confirm what she told him, but she wanted to be the one to tell him first. "I was hoping. . ."

"What were you hoping, my dear?" Libby's smile left no doubt of her affection and empathy for Vashti.

"The last time he saw me, I was decked out like a boy. I wanted him to see me as a woman—a neat, professional woman. But my clothes. . ."

"What about your clothes?" Florence asked.

"They're not like yours and Mrs. Adams's. Not suitable for business. Like when I sell stage tickets." She glanced across the store toward where her friend was still diligently counting screws and nails. "Even Goldie. Since she started working here, she's bought regular clothes, and she looks fine. We were always trying to catch attention in the old days, but now I just want to look *nice*."

Libby smiled and squeezed her arm. "You come back after the stagecoach comes in, and we'll talk."

"Thanks." Vashti started to leave but turned back. "Oh, and I almost forgot. I owe you for the boy clothes. I want to settle up with you for those."

Libby spread her delicate fingers. "Mr. Bane told me to put them on his account."

Vashti opened her mouth. For years she'd turned down men's offers to buy her fancy things—laces and ribbons and silk petticoats—knowing they'd want more than a pretty thank-you in return. Now a man was buying her clothes, but they were thick work boots and a leather vest.

"It's part of his business expense," Libby said quickly.

Vashti gulped and nodded. "All right. I'll come back later."

"Don't forget your basket."

"Thank you!" She grabbed the gathering basket with the buns in it and hurried outside and down the boardwalk to stand before the office door. A man walked across the street from the Fennel House.

"Ticket to Dewey."

Vashti went inside and made out his ticket. She took his money and put it in the cash box Griffin kept in his desk drawer. The man watched her, unblinking, the whole time, and she cringed as she handed him the ticket. If only she were wearing that green dress. She rose and stepped toward the door, wondering what she'd do if he didn't move.

"You're all set for your ride to Dewey, sir. Excuse me."

He stepped back, and she exhaled. She went out again to wait for the stagecoach. Peter Nash came out of the post office. He usually met the Boise coach to claim the town's sack of mail. His presence put Vashti more at ease.

"Hello, Mayor," she called. The traveling man took a few steps down the boardwalk and leaned against the office wall.

"Good afternoon, Miss Edwards. How did your run to Silver City go?"

"Just fine."

Mr. Nash smiled and chatted pleasantly with her. Soon she heard the stage coming. Johnny Conway, the regular driver on the Boise run, didn't blow a horn when he came into town. He just ran the horses like a pack of demented wolves were after them. Griffin didn't like that. Come to think of it, why was Johnny racing the team like that with the boss inside the coach? Vashti peered down the street, trying to see through the cloud of dust that approached with the stage.

Johnny pulled up with his usual showmanship—yelling to the team to whoa and stopping them on a dime—if there'd been a dime lying in the street, that is. Vashti shook her head and scowled at him. He looked down and grinned at her, touching his whip to his hat brim.

"Afternoon, Miss Edwards. Don't you look fine?"

"Where's the boss?" Vashti had already noticed that Lenny Tucker, one of the regular messengers, rode the box with Johnny, and none of the faces she could see through the coach window had her boss's exuberant beard and shaggy head of hair.

"He didn't take the stage back."

"What?" Vashti stepped closer to the coach. Lenny jumped down on the other side and hustled around to open the door. "Where is he?"

"He told the station agent in Boise he was buying some stock for the line and driving it home."

"Oh." Vashti sagged and let out a big sigh. So much for the buns and careful toilette.

"We passed him an hour out of town," Johnny said.

She straightened. "So he'll be here soon?"

"Soon enough."

"Is his nephew with him?"

"Yup."

"What's he like?"

Johnny shrugged. "He's a kid."

Lenny set a sack of mail on the walk. "There you go, Mayor."

"Thanks, Lenny." Mr. Nash hefted the sack and swung it over his shoulder. "I guess a few folks in Fergus will be getting mail today." He ambled off up the street.

Two passengers got out and headed for the Nugget.

"We've got three more sacks of mail to go on to the mining towns," Lenny said.

Vashti looked into the coach and counted the sacks. "All right, go switch out the team."

"All set, Johnny," Lenny said moments later as he climbed back up on the box.

Johnny touched his whip to his hat again and lifted the reins.

Vashti realized she might have time to try on the green dress. She started to the emporium, then remembered the cash box and the ticket money she'd put in it. She couldn't leave any money in the Wells Fargo office unattended. Griffin would skin her alive. She ran inside and took the small amount she had collected and shoved it into her pocket. Then she dashed to the emporium.

Mrs. Adams was talking to the couple who planned to buy the store, but Goldie saw her and strode over to meet her.

"Hey! Florence told me you were coming back to try on that green dress. That would look wonderful on you."

"Thanks. I'm not sure I can afford it. I mean. . .Mr. Bane hasn't paid me yet, and I feel as though I should be the one paying for the boy's clothes, not him."

"Miz Adams thinks it's all right," Goldie said.

"Well, I want to talk to her about that. Because I don't want anyone in town getting the wrong idea."

"I s'pose." Goldie smiled. "Well, I've got hinges to count. I'm trying to be extra careful so's the Hamiltons will want me to keep working for them when they're the owners."

Vashti eyed her friend closely. "I'm sorry, Goldie. I hadn't even thought about how it will affect you if Miz Adams sells the emporium. Do you think you might not have a job anymore?"

"I don't know. Miz Adams said she'll ask them to keep Florence and me on, but it's up to them."

"We can pray about it," Vashti said.

Goldie smiled. "We surely can." She tossed her head. "Isn't it funny? A year or so ago if you'd have said that, I'd have thought you were loco. But I believe that if I lose this job, God will help me find another one."

"Well, you know you won't go hungry. Bitsy and Augie will see to that." Vashti looked down the length of the store. "Think Florence can wait on me?"

"Surely. Just tell her you want to try the dress. And I want to see you in it."

Five minutes later, Vashti stepped timidly from Libby's back room, wearing the green woolen dress. Mr. Hamilton had disappeared, but Libby and Mrs. Hamilton stood near the counter, still talking.

"There you are." Libby stepped toward Vashti. "Come on out here, dear. That looks lovely on you."

"Oh my, yes." Mrs. Hamilton smiled at her as though Vashti were a special customer.

Florence and Goldie left their tasks and came near. A couple of customers browsing the shelves glanced their way, and Vashti began to feel like a sideshow exhibit.

"It is supposed to be this long?"

Libby held up a fold of the skirt. "You could stand to have two or three inches off the hem, but for the most part, that's a good fit."

Vashti liked the way the bodice buttoned up, snug but not too tight, to her throat.

"Come look in the mirror," Florence said.

The customers made no pretense of not gawking at her.

"That's a pretty dress," said a rancher's wife.

"Thank you," Vashti whispered.

Florence led her to the long mirror mounted on the wall between the yard goods and the tinware. When she saw her reflection in the glass, Vashti caught her breath.

"Oh."

"Yes." Florence beamed at her.

I look like one of the regular women. No one would think I'd worked in saloons. Tears burned her eyelids. She'd kept wearing the old dresses because she had nothing else, and she didn't like to ask Bitsy for money when she knew cash was tight at the Spur & Saddle.

"I'll have to see if Mr. Bane pays me today. If he does, I'll come back. If not, I'll just have to see if it's still here when I get some more money."

"I'll see that Mrs. Adams doesn't sell it to anyone else," Florence whispered.

"Oh, I couldn't let you do that."

"Why not? Mrs. Runnels and Mrs. Walker ask her to hold things all the time. And Mrs. Adams says big stores back East do it regularly."

Vashti gulped. She still wasn't certain about the boots, hat, and other clothes she'd received for her role as stagecoach guard.

"I'd better take it off before I muss it." She hurried to the back room, and within five minutes she was back out on the boardwalk in her old satin. She tugged at the skirt, hoping the hemline wasn't too garishly short for daytime in a decent town. The alluring fashions she'd been expected to wear in her former life had never bothered her as much as they did now.

The door to the Wells Fargo office was still closed, but far down the street at the corner by the smithy, she could see a large man riding a horse into town. As he turned the corner toward the livery, she saw plodding behind him a string of three mules, and at the tail end of the procession came another mule with a slight figure on its back.

Griffin was home. She squared her shoulders. Time to face the giant.

★ CHAPTER 8 ★

Mr. Bane?"

Griffin finished fastening the gate to the corral before turning around. He knew who called his name, and he was in no hurry to face Vashti "George" Edwards.

He swung around. "Yeah?"

"Welcome home," she said.

She stood in the back door of the livery, wearing one of those short, shiny dresses that made him feel as though he should look elsewhere. He shot a glance toward the haystack where his nephew had sprawled the moment he climbed stiffly from his saddle. Justin sat up, eyeing Vashti like a cougar watching a plump little prairie dog. Marty leaned on his shovel just inside the dim stable, ogling her, too. Griffin scowled at him, and Marty turned and ambled farther into the barn.

"Can I help you?" Griff yanked his hat off and shot another glance at Justin, who by this time had scrambled to his feet and brushed compulsively at the straw on his clothes.

"I thought you and your nephew would be hungry after your trip, so I brought you a couple of Augie's sweet buns."

Griffin wanted to chase her off, but his belly had been growling for the last two hours, and he'd tasted Augie's sticky, cinnamon-shot buns before. They were not to be turned away lightly.

"That's nice of you."

Justin edged closer.

Griffin cleared his throat. He hadn't considered the way a fifteen-year-old boy would look at Vashti and some of the other girls in town. How in the world was he supposed to steer the boy right when the kid didn't want to be steered?

"Uh…this is Justin Frye, my nephew. Justin, that's Miss Edwards, one of my employees."

Justin snatched his hat off and held it over his heart. "It's a pleasure to meet you, miss."

There, now. He could be polite if he took a notion to. But if he'd quit staring at her ankles, Griffin would be happier.

Vashti folded back the napkin that covered the basket. "Would you like these now, or should I leave them inside?"

"Uh. . .reckon we ought to wash first." Griffin thrust his hand out and collared Justin, who already had reached toward the basket. "There's a basin and a bucket of water around the corner. Come on."

He marched Justin around the side of the livery, where a battered tin basin sat on an upended barrel. A bucket of water stood on the ground beside it, and he tipped it up, pouring the basin half full.

"Be my guest."

Justin eyed him with one cocked eyebrow, then plunged his hands into the water. He took them out and accepted the grayish towel Griffin held out to him.

Griffin sloshed his hands through the water and dried them. Maybe Vashti had left the basket and disappeared while they were gone.

"Come on."

"Does she really work for you?" The boy grinned at him.

Griffin felt a knot in his stomach just behind his belt buckle. What was Justin thinking? Nothing good, from the look on his face.

"She sells tickets at the stage office." Griffin marched past him and around the corner. Vashti still stood there with the basket. Marty was forking straw around inside the barn, pretending to be busy but waiting and watching.

"It was mighty nice of you to bring that," Griff said.

"No trouble." She handed him the basket. "I didn't think to put in extra for Mr. Hoffstead."

"Who, Marty?" Griffin peeked into the basket and saw four plump, odiferous buns oozing cinnamon and sugar icing. Men like Marty would kill for something less tempting. "Guess he can have one."

"Miss Edwards, you ought to join us," Justin said with a charming smile Griffin had never seen before on his face.

"Thank you, but those are for you fellows." Vashti smiled back at the boy and cast a tentative glance Griffin's way. "I. . .uh. . .had a couple of things I hoped I could talk over with you, Mr. Bane."

He tried not to scowl when she'd just done something nice, but it seemed Vashti always had a reason beneath the obvious for doing what she did. "I need to get Justin settled at the Fennel House. Maybe you can meet me at my office later?"

"Of course. In an hour?"

"That's fine." Griffin lifted out one of the sugary buns and offered the basket to Justin. Marty stood in the barn doorway, practically drooling. "Come on, Marty. Can't have you starving while we're eating high on the hog."

Vashti laughed as Marty came out of the shadows. "I'll see you later, then."

Justin's gaze followed her every step until she'd walked through the stable and out the front door.

When Griffin entered the office, Vashti leaped up from the chair behind the desk. She moved away from it to the corner nearest the safe, suddenly aware that the boss was in the room and she'd been sitting in his place.

He stopped inside the door and looked her over. Perhaps he was waiting for his eyes to adjust to the dimmer light, but it seemed to her that they narrowed in a rather critical expression.

"All right, what do you want to talk about?"

Not ready for such an abrupt conversation, she said, "Your nephew seems like a nice young man."

"Huh." Griffin walked around the desk and sat down. "He's all right, I guess."

"Did you leave him at the boardinghouse?"

"Yes, the kid was tuckered out after riding all day. Probably sore, too. I don't think he did a lot of riding back in Pennsylvania. He'll probably sleep until suppertime."

Vashti wondered how to ease around to the topic she wanted to discuss. "I believe his father died recently."

"Yes."

"My father's dead, too. You know, taking care of a half-grown kid has its challenges."

"What am I here for?"

She winced at his gruff tone and folded her hands before her. "I wished to speak to you about the Silver City run."

"Oh. How was it?"

"Fine. Everything went fine."

He grunted.

"Bill Stout and I got along fine."

"So everything was fine."

"Yes. Absolutely. And I. . .well, I wanted to ask you about the clothing that Mrs. Adams gave me for the ride."

"What about it? It fit you."

She felt a flush climb up her neck. Why should it bother her that he'd noticed the fit of those boys' trousers, when she'd dressed for years to draw men's eyes to her figure? "Yes, but. . .am I to keep those things?"

He shrugged. "I don't care. I'll pay for them, if that's what you're getting at."

"It's not. What I mean is"—she stepped over in front of the desk—"will I be making another run?"

"Oh." His gaze slid away from her toward the door, the window, the lantern on the shelf—anything but her face. "Well, I don't know. I wasn't planning on it. On the other hand, sometimes it's hard to come up with an extra messenger."

"Or driver?"

He brought his fist down on the desktop with a *whap* that made her jump. "I told you—you can't drive a stagecoach. You're not good enough."

She frowned but managed to keep down the anger building

inside her. "I realize I have a lot to learn. An old hand like Bill could teach me a lot."

"That so?"

"Yes, it's so. And. . .well, to be honest, after making that ride up to Silver City, I know I couldn't drive that route myself. Not yet. You're right about that."

"I am?" He scowled. "I mean, I know I am, but I'm surprised you'll admit it."

Vashti picked up the ticket book she'd left on the desk that afternoon. "As I said, I know I have a lot to learn." She laid the book down and met his gaze head-on. "All I'm asking is the chance to get that knowledge."

He watched her in silence. At last, he shifted in the chair and crossed his legs at the ankles. "I'm not going to let you practice on the stage teams."

"Didn't ask you to."

"Humph."

They stared at each other for half a minute. Vashti decided it might be a good idea to let him win, and she looked away.

"I also wished to know. . ." She gulped, suddenly losing confidence. Griffin was a very large man, and sometimes men like him had hair-trigger tempers. She didn't want to vex him. Neither did she want to go back to the Spur & Saddle without her pay. "I wished to know when you would pay me for making the run."

"I pay on Fridays."

"Oh. All right. That's it, then."

"Fine."

"Yes. Fine."

"Bane, you in there?"

Vashti whirled toward the doorway. Ted Hire, the owner of the Nugget Saloon, stood there, sweat beading on his forehead.

Griffin stood. "What do you want, Ted?"

"There's a boy over to my place—says he belongs to you."

Griffin stalked into the Nugget with smoldering fire in his chest.

Justin leaned on the bar, blinking dewy-eyed at Hannah Sue, the blonde Ted had hired a few months back. She wasn't as young or as pretty as some of the saloon girls who had come through Fergus, but she wasn't homely, either, and Griffin knew from experience that she listened well.

Probably Justin was filling her full of tales of how mean his uncle had treated him, while Hannah Sue poured him a drink of—what?—out of a clear bottle.

In three steps, he stood beside Justin and clamped his huge hand over Hannah Sue's on the bottle. "What have we got here?"

Hannah Sue's eyes widened, and she jerked her chin up. Her startled expression slid into a smile. "Well, hi, Griff. I was just making the acquaintance of your nephew. Justin here tells me he arrived in town this afternoon with you. Come all the way from Pennsylvanie, he says."

As she talked, Griffin yanked the bottle away from her so he could read the label.

Sarsaparilla.

He set it down on the bar with a sigh and turned to Justin.

"This ain't no place for a kid."

Justin straightened and thrust his shoulders back. "I ain't no kid. I'm a man now. My ma said so."

"Yeah?"

"Yeah. She wouldn't have sent me all this way by myself if I was a kid."

"That right?" Griffin glared down at him. Justin was nearly a foot shorter than him and weighed about a third as much—hardly more than a sack of feed. "Tell you what, boy: If you were a real man, you'd have stayed home and taken care of your mama and the other kids, instead of worrying her sick."

Justin's jaw clenched. "Miss Hannah Sue knows I'm ready to take a man's place in the world, don't you, ma'am?" He looked at the bar girl, innocent appeal spilling out of his big brown eyes.

"Well now, Justin, I think you could do that, I surely do." Hannah Sue's honeyed drawl soothed the boy a little, and his face relaxed. "But you've got to understand that no matter how mature you are, you have to be a certain age to come into the Nugget. Mr. Hire knows that, and he also knows that if we served you liquor, the sheriff could lock him up and close down his business."

"Even in the West? I thought it was different here."

"Not so different as you might think," Ted said from behind Griffin. "Especially when we've got a sheriff who takes the law seriously."

"That's right," Hannah Sue said. "So he went to get your uncle. Now, he could have gone for the sheriff and got you tossed out and your uncle charged with child neglect or some such tomfoolery, but he's a nice man. So instead of getting you and Mr. Bane in trouble, he just fetched your uncle, and it's up to you to play the man's part. Go on home, and don't come back here until you're older."

Justin's frown had returned. He looked down at the glass on the bar. "But you poured me a drink."

"Honey, that ain't whiskey. Go ahead and drink it if you want. On the house. Then you go on home with Uncle Griff and behave yourself. In a couple of years, I'll see you back in here." She winked at Justin, a little more provocatively than Griff thought seemly, but then, nothing about the Nugget was seemly. "Go on, now."

Justin picked up the glass and sniffed it. He set it down with a thud that slopped sarsaparilla over the edge. His shoulders slumped, and he turned toward the door without another word, shrinking back as he passed Griffin.

"Thanks, Hannah Sue," Griffin said. He knew she and Ted had both stretched it a little about the law. Most folks wouldn't have cared whether or not a fifteen-year-old boy was served liquor in a frontier town. But in Fergus, people had ideas about decency and helping friends, and he figured they'd done it for him as much as for Justin.

"No trouble," Hannah Sue said.

Griffin fished in his pocket and found a lone dime. He handed it to her and nodded at Ted. "Thank you, too. If he comes here again. . ."

"He won't."

Griff allowed that was probably true. He followed Justin out into the thin autumn sunshine. The chill of winter danced in the breeze, and a drink wouldn't have been unwelcome. But with the boy around. . .

Yes, with the boy around, Griffin was going to have to consider his habits carefully.

Justin waited at the bottom of the steps with his hands shoved into his pants pockets.

"Where's your coat?"

"Over to the boardinghouse." Justin's eyes still had the sullen cast.

"Come on. Let's go get it."

"Where are we going after that?"

"You're coming with me to the smithy."

Justin's eyes were slits of brown. "Can't I just stay in my room?"

"Like you did last time I put you there? Come on, I've got four mules to shoe."

★ CHAPTER 9 ★

Dusk hovered over Fergus, reaching long, cold fingers of shadows between the buildings, as Vashti hurried down the street toward the smithy. After the feed store, where the boardwalk ended, she lifted her skirts and quickened her pace. Winter surely was on its way.

The sound of Griffin's hammer told her that he was still at work. It wasn't the loud, musical ring of his rounding hammer on the anvil, but the *tap-tap-tap* of the smaller nailing hammer he used to fasten horses' shoes onto their hooves. As she rounded the corner, he turned the hammer's head toward him and with its claws grabbed the end of a nail protruding from the side of a mule's hoof. He twisted the pointy end off and went around the hoof, repeating the motion five times, then tossed the hammer into the toolbox. Out came another tool, with which he clinched the jagged ends of the nails he'd broken off. Then came the rasp.

Vashti wasn't sure how many more tools he needed to use in the process. Shoeing a horse—or a mule—was a lot lengthier and more complicated than she'd realized. She stepped forward and cleared her throat, but the rhythmic humming of the rasp over the clinches drowned out the noise.

"He don't hear you."

Vashti whirled toward the open smithy. Inside, Justin sat on a barrel close to the forge, no doubt soaking up its warmth.

She nodded to him, and Justin spoke again.

"You got to yell when he's working."

Griffin looked up then, taking in her presence and shooting a glance toward his nephew. He lowered the mule's foot and stood slowly. "Miss Edwards."

"Good evening. Bitsy sent me to invite you and Justin to take dinner at the Spur & Saddle tonight. It's on her and Augie."

"Well, that's right nice of her." Griffin slid the rasp into a special slot on the side of the toolbox. He pulled a bandanna from his pocket and mopped his forehead. Even in this cold air, he was sweating.

"Shall I tell her you'll come?"

Griffin looked toward Justin. "What do you say?"

"Is the food any good?"

Griffin scowled at him. "That's no way to talk!"

The boy shrugged. "Sorry. I just thought the smells at the boardinghouse were pretty good."

Griffin nodded at Vashti. "Tell Bitsy we'll be there after I clean up. And you, boy." He sent Justin another glare. "Can I trust you to go and tell Mrs. Thistle you're eating with me tonight?"

Justin's mouth went pouty. "Yes, sir."

"All right, you go, then. If you're not back by full dark, I'll come after you, and this time I'll bring the sheriff."

His harsh tone took Vashti aback. Then she recalled Ted Hire coming over to fetch Griffin earlier. The episode at the Nugget must not have gone well. She managed to smile at them. "All right. We'll look for you soon at the Spur & Saddle."

Griffin carried his toolbox inside the smithy and set it down near the door, where he always left it. A glance at the forge told him the fire had burned down enough so he could safely leave it. He opened the door to his living quarters to let some of the heat in there.

Walking back through the smithy, he shut the outside door and unhitched the mule he'd shod. The mules he'd purchased looked good, if a little thin. And the palomino—he'd show the horse to Hiram next time he came around. If his friend didn't want it, Griffin could let it out as a livery horse, but he thought Hiram and Libby would both be pleased.

He led the mule around to the corral behind the livery and headed into the barn for a couple of lead ropes. To his surprise, when he came out again Justin was waiting for him.

"Did you get washed?" Griffin growled.

"No, sir."

"Wash your hands and comb your hair." He turned toward the smaller enclosure, beyond the corral where he kept the stage teams. He'd put the palomino out there, along with a colt he'd taken in trade last summer.

"I could lead that spotted horse in for you."

He looked askance at Justin, hardly knowing how to respond to an offer of help. "Whyn't you take Mrs. Adams's palomino? I'll get the colt."

"I thought that was the horse you just bought."

"It is." Griffin opened the gate to the small corral. The palomino walked placidly toward him, and the colt trotted over, swinging his head and snorting. "I bought it for a friend of mine, Hiram Dooley. He's getting married soon, and he asked me to find a nice horse for his fiancée."

"So. . .does the spotted one belong to you?"

"Yup." Griffin clipped a lead rope to the palomino's halter and placed the end in Justin's hands. "Careful, now. Don't let him step on you. Put him in the first stall on the right."

The colt tried to duck past Griffin.

"Hold it, buster." Griffin snagged his halter and pulled his head down. "There we go." He hooked the snap on the end of the rope to a ring in the halter. "All right, mind your manners." He walked on the colt's left, holding back and downward on the rope, forcing the colt to walk beside him. This one had fire.

As he stepped inside the barn, Justin called, "Now what?"

"Hook the chain that's hitched to the wall to his halter and unhook the rope." Griffin took the colt into the stall next to the palomino's. "I'll get them some feed and roll the doors shut."

Justin came out of the stall. "Want me to close the front door?"

"Thanks. That would be good."

By the time he'd fed the two horses, Justin had both big doors closed.

"All right. Now we need to clean up."

"That paint horse sure is pretty," Justin said.

Griffin grunted and eyed the boy in the dim light. "He's too young to ride yet."

"Really? He's big."

"He'll be two in the spring. I'll start training him then. And until I do, I don't want anyone messing with him, you understand?"

"Yes, sir."

Griffin relaxed a little. "Come on." He opened the rear door just far enough to squeeze through, and he and Justin went out. Darkness had fallen, and he shivered in the chilly breeze. "I thought you didn't like horses."

Justin shrugged. "I never been around them much."

"Guess you saw more of that mule than you wanted to today."

Justin let out a short laugh.

"You sore?" Griffin asked.

"Some."

"It'll be worse in the morning." They walked over to the smithy. Griffin jerked his head toward the open door. He hated to let the boy see his disorderly living quarters, but he didn't see a way around it. "Come on, we're heating the outdoors."

Griffin and the boy appeared in the dining room half an hour after Vashti had left them. Both had damp comb marks through their hair, and Griffin had changed his shirt. The hot smell of the forge lingered on him, but Vashti didn't mind it. She smiled broadly as she led them to a table in the corner near the fireplace. In chilly weather, Augie kept the heater stove ticking, but Bitsy still liked to have a fire on the grate for atmosphere. "People feel warmer when they see the logs burning," she said.

Justin stumbled a bit as he pulled out his chair. Vashti figured he wouldn't be so clumsy if he'd quit staring at her. She couldn't wear her shawl while waiting on tables.

"I'll bring you water," she said. "Would you like coffee, Mr. Bane?"

"Lots of it, and strong."

"Yes, sir." She smiled at Justin. "And you, Mr. Frye?"

Justin glanced at his uncle, then back at her. "The same."

"Very good. Our dinner special tonight is roast chicken, but we also have a venison stew simmering."

"Bring me some of both," Griffin said. "And plenty of biscuits."

Vashti tucked in her smile and turned her attention to the boy. "And you, sir?"

"I'll have the chicken, please. And some of those biscuits."

"I'll bring a basketful."

She walked briskly to the kitchen. Bitsy was picking up two full chicken plates for Oscar and Bertha Runnels.

"Mr. Bane and his nephew are here," Vashti said.

"Oh good. I can't wait to see the boy." Bitsy lifted her tray and brushed past her with her taffeta skirts swishing.

"I'll need a basketful of biscuits for those two," Vashti said to Augie. "Hope you and Bitsy don't go broke from your charitable efforts."

"Giving away samples is good for business. If the boy likes my cookin', Griff will have him over here at least once a week. Bachelors don't want to have to cook for kids."

Vashti chuckled. "That's true. But he is putting Justin up at the Fennel House."

"Oh." Augie's bald head glistened in the lamplight as he reached to stir the big iron kettle on the stove. "Well, maybe they'll still come around now and again."

"Let's hope so. Two chicken dinners and one stew."

"Who's the third person?"

"Griffin."

Augie laughed. "He always did like my venison stew."

A few more customers drifted in, and Vashti stayed busy for several minutes. When she got back to Griffin and Justin, both had cleaned their plates.

"That was good food," Griffin said.

"Yes'm." Justin looked up at her with a shy smile. "Did you cook it?"

Vashti laughed. "No, not me. That would be Mr. Moore. He's the finest cook in Fergus."

"A man?" The boy's face stretched to new lengths.

Griffin let out a bellow of laughter. "You've never seen Augie, kid, or you wouldn't say that. He could make hash out of you with one hand."

"Would you like dessert?" Vashti asked Justin. "Mr. Moore makes delicious cakes and pies, too. You had one of his cinnamon buns earlier today."

"Two," Griffin said.

She flashed him a smile. So the boss had given one to Marty and eaten one himself and let the boy have the other two. Somehow, that warmed her feelings toward Griffin.

"What have you got for pies?" Justin asked.

She pointed to the bar that Hiram Dooley had remodeled into an efficient serving counter. "Why don't you step over and see for yourself? There're several varieties." She raised her eyebrows at Griffin.

"Just bring me apple pie with a hunk of cheese," he said. "And more coffee."

Justin pushed back his chair. "Uh, will you please excuse me, Uncle Griff?"

"To pick out your pie? Why, surely."

The boy walked away, and Vashti said softly, "Well now, he's got manners."

"Yes, when he chooses to dust them off."

She hesitated a moment then said, "You know, leaving home at that age isn't easy. Chances are, he feels as though his mother didn't want him around anymore."

Griffin's bushy eyebrows drew together. "I can understand why. I had him here ten minutes and had to go pull him out of a saloon."

"I can see he was a handful for her."

"That's putting it mildly." Griffin watched Justin as he walked slowly along the counter, eyeing each confection. "Truth is, my sister was a little scared of him and of his friends, I think. The trouble they might bring on her and the other young'uns."

Vashti nodded. "You can be a good influence in his life, Griffin Bane."

Griff sighed. "I'm beginning to think he'll be a bad one on me."

She chuckled. "I'll get that pie and coffee for you."

"Wait a sec."

"Yes?"

He shot another glance at Justin. "You've mentioned before that you had a tough time of it as a youngster. Someday, maybe you'll tell me about that."

Vashti looked at him for a long moment. "You'd really want to hear?"

"I'm starting to think I should listen to people who know about kids. What it's like to be a kid." He shrugged in apology. "Seems like a long time ago, and. . .well, he's not like I was."

She nodded, though she thought, *Maybe more like you than you realize.* Justin headed back their way, carrying a plate with two pieces of pie on it. "We'll sit down sometime. But not tonight. You look exhausted, and I think you need to make sure Justin's safe for the night."

Griffin shook his head. "I can't watch him every minute."

"No, but you've gotten him banned from the worst place in town, and there's no stagecoach out until tomorrow. Unless he steals a horse, he's stuck here."

"I've thought of that, and I wouldn't put it past him."

She hurried away to get Griffin's dessert and coffee. Doc Kincaid and the Hamiltons had come in while she talked, and Bitsy threw her a glance begging for help. Vashti took Griffin a generous slice of pie with cheese on the side and refilled his coffee, and then she turned to the Hamiltons' table.

"Sorry to keep you waiting, folks. We have a delicious roast chicken dinner tonight and a savory venison stew."

"Oh, the stew sounds good," said Mr. Hamilton. "What'll you have, dear?"

Vashti glanced back at Griffin's table. His eyelids drooped as he reached for his coffee mug, but he seemed to be listening as Justin talked with more animation than she'd seen so far on the boy's face.

Mrs. Hamilton said, "I belicve I'll try that stew as well."

Vashti smiled at them. "Very good. Would you like coffee?"

"Could you bring us a pot of tea?" Mrs. Hamilton asked, cringing almost as though she were asking for something very rare and difficult to produce.

"Of course. I'll be just a moment." As she turned away, Vashti looked once more at Griffin. He was still listening to his nephew, but a tolerant smile lit his face.

That's the way you ought to look all the time, she thought. *Griffin Bane, you could be a very handsome man.*

★ CHAPTER 10 ★

Vashti stayed on her feet, serving the customers long after Griffin and Justin left the Spur & Saddle. About seven thirty, Goldie came in from the kitchen. Though she'd spent the entire day working at the emporium, she smiled at the diners and sat down before the piano. Soon lilting music filled the restaurant. Mr. Hamilton gave her fifty cents to play "Jeanie with the Light Brown Hair." Next, Dr. Kincaid requested "Silver Threads among the Gold." After several more numbers, Goldie covered the keyboard and accepted the people's applause with a becoming blush.

Vashti had taken away all the dirty dishes but the coffee cups by then, and the diners soon ambled home. As she cleared off the last table, Goldie came to help her.

"You go on up to bed," Vashti said. "I know you're tired."

"The people are so nice now." Goldie's eyes reflected the light of the lamps and the candle chandelier. "In the old days, the cowboys wanted me to play my fingers to the bone, but they never applauded like that—like they respected me, I mean."

Vashti gave her a hug. "You deserve that respect. And a good night's sleep. Go on—Bitsy and I will get these done in no time."

As Goldie drifted up the staircase, Vashti looked up in surprise to see Griffin again coming through the doorway.

"Mr. Bane!"

"I guess you're closing."

"Well. . .the coffeepot's still on the stove."

"Would you join me for a cup?"

Vashti hesitated, her pulse tripping. "Let me just take these to the kitchen. I'll be right back."

Bitsy had already washed most of the dishes, and Augie was drying them and stacking them on the shelves.

"This is the last of them." Vashti held out a pile of cups and saucers.

Bitsy took them and plunged them into her pan of sudsy water.

"Uh. . .Mr. Bane came back."

"Oh?" Bitsy frowned. "What does he want?"

"Coffee. And conversation, I guess. He asked me to sit with him. Earlier he said he'd like to talk to me about Justin."

"Can't see any harm in that." Bitsy looked over at Augie. "What do you think?"

"Well, I dunno. Has Griff got designs on our adopted daughter?"

Bitsy flicked some soapsuds at him. "The day Griffin Bane falls in love is the day somebody finds the Blue Bucket Mine."

Augie laughed at her reference to the legend of a "lost" gold mine. "Stranger things have happened."

"That's right. You finally convinced me to marry you, didn't you?"

"Yup. Mighty strange, but I'm tickled pink." Augie squeezed her.

Vashti laughed. "I'm pretty sure it's not romance Mr. Bane has in mind. The boy's giving him headaches, and he's only been here half a day."

"Go on, girl," Bitsy said. "Just don't let him stay too late."

Vashti ran a hand over her hair, wondering if it looked all stringy and scraggly. She hadn't noticed her reflection in the big mirror for hours. What if Griffin really was interested in her? Would that be so bad? More likely, he'd tell her again why she couldn't hold a man's job and ask for more advice on dealing with Justin. Her past had taught her not to count on good things happening out of the blue. She took off her apron and went back to the dining room, a bit wary.

Griffin stood by the woodstove, pouring himself a big mug full of coffee.

"Hope you don't mind."

"No, that's fine." Vashti walked over and sat down at the table nearest the stove, where Griffin and Justin had sat earlier. "We put the pies away, but I could get you a piece."

"That's all right. I ate plenty."

"Where's Justin?"

"In bed at the Fennel House. I made sure he was sleeping this time."

"First night in a strange bed. You sure?"

"Oh yeah. I tickled his foot to see if he was faking it. What you said earlier about him stealing a horse made me think. He might do that—just take one from the livery—if he doesn't like it here."

"Do you want him to like it here?"

Griffin winced. "Not sure." He sipped his coffee and set the mug down. "I guess what I really want is for him to apologize to his mama and go home and take care of her like a man should."

"What are the chances?"

"Slim to none."

Vashti nodded. "That's about the way I saw it. That boy's got a lot of growing up to do."

"Well, I'm not sure I know how to help him do it."

"Put him to work, but not too hard. Let him see that he can do things—make things. Like you do."

"I don't know as I can get him to work around the smithy."

"Did you when you were his age?"

"Yes, but I was interested in it. I'd go by the smithy in our town after school and watch old Jack Hogan shoeing horses. And when he'd put a piece of metal in the fire and bring it out all yellow-hot and glowing and hammer it into a hinge or a spoon or something else useful, well, that seemed like magic to me." He picked up his mug. "But Justin's got no such inclination."

"Does he like horses?"

"I would have said not overly—he acted a little scared of riding at first. But he did perk up when he saw that yearling colt I've got in my barn."

"Hmm."

"He rides like a sack of flour in the saddle."

"Ouch. And he rode all the way from Boise?"

"Yeah. Maybe that was a poor decision on my part. We could have stayed over at Nampa or Reynolds, or I could have sent him on in the coach. But think how much mischief he could have gotten into until I got here."

"True. He'll get over the sore muscles in a few days." She thought about Griffin's situation. "There ought to be lots of things a boy could do around your place. Lots more than a girl can. And if he likes horses. . ."

"Yeah. If I give him a few pointers and give him decent mounts, he might get to be a good rider. The thing is, he's here, and I'm responsible for him. I couldn't just turn him loose, even if I felt like it. He's too young to take care of himself."

"Didn't you take care of yourself at his age?"

"Yes, but Justin—he doesn't seem to have any common sense, and he wants to butt heads with life, not learn how to make things work for him."

Vashti smiled ruefully. "Sounds like me in some ways."

Griffin focused on her with a pensive frown. "I've been wondering about you. How you got to be on your own so young. Didn't you have anyone to take care of you?"

She shook her head. "I was eleven when my folks died."

"What'd you do then?"

"Went to live with some kinfolk—my mother's cousin. I called her Aunt Mary. But I—I couldn't stay there."

"Why not?"

She hesitated, wondering how much to spill. "Mostly because of Uncle Joshua."

Griffin was quiet for a moment, then took a sip of his coffee. He set the mug down and met her gaze. "I see."

"Do you? I told Aunt Mary when he bothered me, but she didn't believe me. Said I was a bad girl for making up such tales. I ran away after less than a year. Headed west." She gave a little chuckle. "I thought maybe I could find a place where I'd fit in and could get a job of some sort. I found out quick enough there aren't any jobs for twelve-year-old girls."

"That's awful young to be on your own, boy or girl." Griffin's voice had taken on a gentle tone, and his eyes were velvety like an elk's.

"Yes. Far too young." Vashti stood, suddenly unable to sit under his scrutiny. "I believe I'll have some coffee, too." She went to the stove and took her time pouring a cupful. When she sat down again, she took a sip. Too hot and too strong. She blew on the surface of the dark liquid.

"You want to tell me the rest? How you got here?"

She considered whether she wanted to or not. "It was a long journey. But looking back, I believe the Lord brought me here."

He nodded slowly. "I can understand that. I reckon He wanted me here, too, at a time when I didn't know I needed Him. And now the boy. . ."

"Yes." Vashti thought about the path they had all followed to Fergus. "I know Justin wasn't in the same situation I was, but I believe you can help him avoid going down a dark road."

"How? What can I do to keep him out of trouble?"

"Take care of him. Teach him to do honest work. And maybe, sooner or later, you'll learn to love him. Because he is your kin."

Griffin lowered his head. "I would have kept him with me at my place, but it's a wreck. I figured he'd be better off at the Fennel House. I mean, I've got that one little room behind the smithy, and it's hardly as big as a tobacco tin. Can't turn around without bumping something. And. . .well, it's not the cleanest, either. I admit I've never been much at housework."

"You could stay with him at the boardinghouse."

He pressed his lips together for a moment. "That'd cost a lot. Winter's coming—my slack time."

"Well, maybe you'll think of some other arrangements. But you need to show the boy that you care about him."

"So far, that's been kind of hard." Griffin squinted at her and squirmed a little in the chair.

"Hard to like a boy who's not likable?"

"I guess I thought he'd be glad to see me. That he'd want to live out here and learn what I do and. . .well, that he'd take to the West. And to me."

"He still might."

Griffin cleared his throat. "Look, it won't be long before we get snow in the mountains. The road to Silver City will close. They used to keep it broken all winter, but since the bigger mines shut down. . ."

She nodded.

"The road to Boise might stay open another month, if we're lucky. But I still can't let you drive."

"I understand, Mr. Bane. It's still a dream of mine, but I know I'm not ready."

"Look, I. . .maybe I can let you do the Boise run—as far as Nampa, that is—as a shotgun messenger for the next couple of weeks. You'd ride with Johnny Conway. I could put Ned Harmon on with Bill until the Silver City road closes."

She nodded, trying not to show her excitement. She'd rather ride with steady old Bill Stout than with Johnny Conway, but at this point, she'd take whatever run Griffin would give her.

"Thank you. I promise you I'll defend the stage as well as any man."

"All right. It's a twice-a-week run this time of year, and I can only promise you two weeks. After that, it depends on the weather, because Ned's one of my regular men, and if he can't do the run to Silver, I'll give him whatever's open to keep him working as long as I can. He's been faithful to me. But you can be ready Monday, and if nothing drastic happens, you can ride with Johnny."

Vashti scarcely heard anything after he said, "All right." The joy that welled up in her threatened to burst out in a wild laugh. She wanted to hug him and kiss him and shout to Bitsy and Augie that he'd hired her. Instead, she clamped her teeth together and smiled serenely. "Thank you."

★ CHAPTER 11 ★

Johnny Conway looked Vashti up and down as she climbed up to the box to sit beside him. When she sat down, he spat tobacco juice off the side of the stagecoach and said, "You look better in your fancy dresses, darlin'."

"Don't call me that, and don't talk about me bein' a girl."

"Oh, pardon me." Johnny looked ahead to where Griff and Marty were holding the leaders' bridles and nodded. "Get up now!"

The holders released the team, and they sprang forward, breaking into their road trot. Vashti was a little surprised that Johnny didn't make the horses canter to show off in front of the people watching from the sidewalk.

They rolled up Main Street and out of town, and she settled back, watching the road ahead and cradling the shotgun in her arms. "Mr. Bane said you might give me some driving tips."

"Ha! Why should I teach you to drive? Next you'll be wantin' my job."

"Mr. Bane says he has trouble keeping steady drivers."

"I'm steady," Johnny said.

"Didn't say you wasn't."

"Humph."

They rode in silence for a good hour. The coach swayed along. The horses' hooves clopped on the packed road. They passed the ranches to the north of Fergus and came down out of the mountains to rolling hills. Gradually the air warmed a bit, and Vashti peeled her gloves off. They passed a horseman headed toward Fergus—one of the cowboys from the Landry ranch. Vashti and Johnny waved. The cowpoke waved back then turned his head to follow Vashti with a perplexed stare.

Johnny laughed. "He's wondering who my new guard is."

"Well, you'd best keep it quiet. Don't go telling people when you unwind tonight with a whiskey or two."

"Me? I ain't no blabbermouth."

"Humph," said Vashti, and he scowled at her.

"You sure look better in a dress."

"You said that. And I said—" She broke off, catching the glint of sun on metal ahead, among the rocks to the left of the road. "What's that?"

"What?"

"In those rocks."

Johnny peered ahead. "I don't see anything."

Ten seconds later, they'd come within a hundred feet of the rocks. A man jumped from behind the biggest boulder and stood in the middle of the road, aiming a rifle at them.

"Hang on!" Johnny laid the whip on. "Yee-haw!"

The horses leaped forward, tearing toward the gunman. Vashti had to cling to the edge of the seat to keep her perch.

"How'm I supposed to aim?" she screamed against the wind of their speed.

"Just sit tight."

At the last possible moment, the man let off a round and leaped aside. Vashti's heart pounded so hard she thought it would burst. When she looked back, she couldn't see the man. Johnny drove on for another half mile at full speed, then began to talk the horses down until they fell once more into their road trot, snorting and shaking their heads.

Vashti pulled in a deep breath and eyed him askance. "You seen that fella before?"

"Uh-huh. He tried it three or four times last summer. He's so stupid, he tries to get you coming downhill. Anyone with half a brain would know to stop the coach when the horses are going uphill so they're already going slow and can't get into a run."

"Is he dim-witted?"

"Don't know. We never stuck around long enough to find out. The first time, Bill was driving. Got his hat shot off. But Bill was carrying treasure to Boise, and he told me he just made up his mind he wouldn't stop for one outlaw, not no-how. Ever since then, if we see him, we just try to run him down."

"What if he hits one of you?"

"Hasn't yet."

Vashti huffed out a breath and stared at him. "If you hadn't lashed up the horses like that, I could've got a shot off. Put an end to his nonsense."

Johnny shrugged. "Remind me next time."

"Oh sure."

He laughed. "One of these days, he won't move fast enough, and I'll roll the coach right over his weaselly little carcass."

"Who is he, anyway? Does he live around here?"

"I dunno. He just showed up one day last June, and ever since, we watch for him."

"And he always jumps you going downhill?"

"Naw, he tried it once the other way, but Ned emptied his shotgun at him and grabbed his revolver. Thought he might have got him with a couple of pellets. The robber ran into the rocks. That was the last time I've seen him until now. But it's the same fella."

Vashti puzzled over that. "Why doesn't the sheriff come out here and scour those rocks and arrest him?"

"He tried, but the popinjay wasn't there. He's showed up on a couple different stretches of road, too."

"Well, he must live somewhere."

Johnny shook his head. "We've asked the tenders at every station, and nobody around here knows who he is. Probably just some drifter who's hiding out. Once it gets real cold, he'll probably clear out."

Vashti thought about that for the next mile, while she searched the roadside for movement that didn't belong. At last she said, "One of us could have been killed."

"Yup." Johnny grinned at her. "If'n you get shot, you want to be laid out in them clothes, or in your swishy dress?"

Griffin and Justin rode side by side toward the Chapman ranch on Wednesday morning. Justin still looked ill at ease in the saddle, but he didn't complain the way he did when he'd had to ride a mule all the way from Nampa. Griff had picked a gentle little chestnut gelding for him out of his string. "Red" was a horse he could rent out to a tinhorn and not worry about the rider breaking his neck.

Of course, Justin bounced all over the saddle.

"Sit yourself down, boy," Griffin called.

"I'm trying."

Griff shook his head. "Whoa. Here, pull up for a minute. Whoa, Red."

Justin hauled back on the reins, and they stopped. Griff's horse, Pepper, stopped next to Red.

Griffin adjusted his hat and studied the boy's posture. "Look, when you trot, you've got to set yourself in that saddle like you weigh a thousand pounds."

Justin grimaced. "How do I do that?"

"Think about how heavy you are. You weigh a ton."

"I thought you said a thousand pounds. That's half a ton."

"All right, then, half a ton. You weigh a lot. And while you set there, every ounce of you is pressing down on your feet."

"My feet?" Justin frowned at him.

"That's right. Don't keep all the weight on the horse's back. Put it down on your feet. Five hundred pounds on each foot. Heavy as lead. Heavier."

Justin's brow furrowed as he scowled toward Red's ears. He rocked forward a little so that he was almost standing in the stirrups.

"That's it," Griff said. "When Red picks up his trot, you think about that. Weight pushing down into your boots. You're so heavy you'll probably break the stirrup leathers before we get to the sheriff's house."

"How come we got to help the sheriff, anyway?" Justin's petulant words made Griff want to slap him, box him up, and ship him back to Pennsylvania.

"Because he's a friend. Ethan's as good a friend as you can get, and don't you forget it."

"Never had no use for lawmen," Justin said.

"Well, that's a mistake on your part. There'll come a day when you need a lawman on your side, and when that day comes, you'll be mighty glad Ethan Chapman's your friend."

Justin muttered something.

"What'd you say?" Griffin snapped.

"Nothing."

Griff leaned toward him. "Look here, boy, I don't know what your folks tolerated, but I don't take to letting a kid sass me."

Justin's face went stony.

Griff clenched his jaw. Light into him or let it go? He inhaled slowly then shrugged, trying to relax his tight muscles. "Hey, you and me, we can get along, or we can go our separate ways. If you're going to stay here, you'd best learn to get along."

Justin watched him from slits of eyes. "So. . .what if I don't want to get along? Are you saying I can leave?"

"Well now, that depends." Griff pushed his hat up in the back and scratched his head. "You got enough money to take the stage home?"

"No, sir."

"You got other transportation, then? I don't cotton to horse thievery."

Justin's face grew longer and darker.

Griffin straightened and clucked to Pepper so that he began to walk again. Red kept pace, though Justin hadn't cued him to move.

"On the other hand," Griff said, "I've been known to let a fella work off the cost of a horse before. You think you'd like to own a nice little horse like Red?"

Justin eyed him suspiciously. "What'd I have to do? Shovel manure for three years?"

"Nope. Maybe a year, for one hour in the morning. Or half a year for two hours. Plus bookkeeping."

"Bookkeeping? What's that? You got so many books you can't keep track of them?"

Griffin smiled. "No, sir. That's keeping records of money and such. You should know that."

"Oh, that kind of bookkeeping." Justin yawned. They rode on for a minute before he asked, "What sort of work would I do for that?"

"Well, you seem to be a hand with numbers. Maybe you could help me keep track of who owes me for smithing work and keeping their horse at the livery. And maybe even for the stagecoach business if you show yourself apt and trustworthy."

"Huh." Justin frowned and flicked a piece of straw off Red's withers.

"Come on," Griffin said. "Let's practice that trot again. Remember, five hundred pounds on each foot." He waited while Justin shifted in the saddle and took on an air of concentration and then clucked to Pepper and eased up on the reins.

They clipped along for the last half mile with Justin trying to weigh more and keep his weight low. When they reached the lane leading to the ranch, Griff called, "You're doing fine."

Justin gave him a fractured smile. "It's hard."

"Sure is." Griffin grinned as they trotted up to the ranch house.

While they tied their horses to Ethan's hitching rail, Trudy and Ethan came out of the house. Trudy had on a warm coat and hood and her split riding skirt, and she had a bundle of fabric under her arm.

"You going somewheres this morning, Mrs. Chapman?" Griffin asked.

Trudy smiled at him. "Good morning, Griff. Yes, I've got business with the shooting club." She turned her gaze on Justin. "Hello, Justin. How do you like it here so far?"

Justin wrapped Red's reins around the hitching rail. "It's cold."

Trudy chuckled. "It's a little chilly. Winter's coming."

Griff scowled at his nephew. "Here, now, don't tie him up by the reins."

Justin threw him a dark look. "Why not?"

"Because if he gets scared, he'll pull back and hurt his mouth and maybe break the leather."

"What do I tie him with?"

Griff didn't like to admit he'd brought his own lead rope, as always, in his saddlebag, but hadn't thought to add an extra for Justin.

"Here." Ethan walked down the steps and lifted the end of a rope dangling from the far end of the rail. "Use this one. I leave it tied here all the time for folks who don't bring one."

Justin hesitated, then led Red over a few steps to get it. "Thank you, sir."

Griffin beamed. Maybe there was some hope for the boy yet.

"All right, ladies, we have to hurry," Bitsy called to the other six women who'd gathered in front of the smithy. "Remember, what looks like trash to us might be a treasure this man has saved for twenty years. We don't throw anything away unless it's got mold all over it."

"Are you sure it's legal for us to do this?" Annie Harper asked, swinging her broom down off her shoulder.

Bitsy looked at Trudy. "Your husband's the sheriff. What did he say about this?"

Trudy laughed. "Ethan said he'll keep Griff and Justin busy all morning, bringing the herd down from the high pasture for the winter—but I'd better be there to dish up dinner at noontime, so let's get at it. We've only got a couple of hours."

"Yes, I have to be to work at the emporium then," Goldie said. She and Vashti had come with Bitsy. Along with Annie and her daughter Myra, and the mayor's wife, Ellie Nash, they made up the cleaning brigade.

Trudy looked toward the livery stable. "We'd best get inside, or Marty will see us."

"Yeah, we don't want him to come around asking what we're up to," Vashti said.

Bitsy picked up her scrub bucket and opened the door of the smithy. The women followed her across the dim workshop, past the anvil and the forge. Vashti looked up at the big bellows overhead. She'd always been fascinated by the forge and all the tools Griffin had in this workshop and the things he made out of plain metal bars. She'd never had a chance to watch him work, though. It would be unseemly for ladies to stand around and watch a man working.

Bitsy opened the door to the room behind the smithy. She stood still on the threshold.

"Well?" Annie said. "Are we going in, or aren't we?"

Bitsy turned with a pained expression. "The question is, *can* we?"

Vashti eased between them and looked into Griffin's home. The tiny room was jammed with junk. A rumpled bunk was nailed to one wall. Wadded blankets and clothes covered the straw tick. All around the room were stacks of boxes, kegs, and cartons. A bucket half full of water stood beside a small box stove. Hanging from the rafters were bunches of corn drying on the cob with the husks peeled back and braided together, clusters of onions, a few strings of dried apples, and squash.

"Griff got a garden somewhere?" she asked.

"I think folks pay him in foodstuffs sometimes," Annie ventured, "same as they do Doc."

Trudy nodded. "Well, it's none too fresh in here. Can we open that window, Bitsy?"

"I don't know. Maybe if we wash it, I can see where the latch is."

Vashti unrolled her apron. Inside it were a bar of soap and several rags.

"All right, ladies," Bitsy said. "We all know how to work hard. Let's get started."

For the first few minutes, they straightened things enough to make a path to the window and the bunk.

Ellie pulled the covers off the bed. "I declare, there is a sheet in there, all wound about in knots. Needs a good washing, though. I'll take all this bedding over to my place and scrub it."

"It won't be dry by noon," Trudy said.

"No, I don't expect it will."

"Well, I brought a quilt." Annie went back to the doorway, where she'd left her bundle, and brought it over. "It's a shame to put it on a dirty bed, though."

Vashti pondered the problem while Annie brought out the colorful log cabin quilt.

"That's a nice one for a man." Bitsy reached out and touched the brown and green squares.

"Thank you," Annie said. "I was going to put it on my boy Tollie's bed, but I can make him another one this winter."

"Mighty generous of you," Ellie said.

Annie shrugged. "Griffin does a lot for folks in this town. Time he was blessed."

Goldie laughed. "That's what we're doing. Blessing him. I wish we could see his face when he comes home."

"Well, we'd best get to work." Bitsy gave the quilt one last pat. "I never did any quilting."

"It's easy," Annie said. "Do you want me to tell you next time I'm working on a quilt and show you how?"

Bitsy blinked rapidly. "Why, thank you. I'd like that excessively."

Vashti hauled in a breath and took courage. If Mrs. Harper could be that nice, she could do her part. "Ma'am, I could dump the old straw out of that tick and air it out, and then I could get some fresh from the livery."

"What about Marty Hoffstead?" Annie asked.

"I'll tell him I need straw for a tick, but I won't tell him whose."

Trudy held out two nickels. "This is all I've got on me, but I reckon Marty will make you pay for the straw."

"Say, maybe I should go with you," Myra said. "Can I, Ma?"

Annie frowned. "Well. . ."

"It'd be better if both of them went," Bitsy said. "Marty ain't the kind of man a gal wants to be alone with."

Annie's frown lines deepened. "That's exactly why I don't think Myra should. . ." She pressed her lips together and shrugged. "If you stick together. Vashti, you'll look after each other, won't you?"

"Of course." Vashti and Myra seized the dank straw tick and dragged it outside. "Let's dump the old straw out back of the livery on the manure pile," Vashti said.

"How we going to rip the seam?" Myra asked when they'd reached their destination.

Vashti reached into her pocket for the small, mother-of-pearl-sided pocketknife she carried.

"Ooh, that's purty," Myra said.

"Thanks." Vashti quickly slit open one end of the tick where it had been rudely stitched together. They tipped it up and shook it. The clumped, smelly straw fell out onto the manure pile.

"What are you gals doing?" Marty stood in the back door of the livery, watching them.

"We're cleaning. Thought we'd get some fresh straw from you for this mattress," Vashti said.

He studied them for a moment, and a smile slid across his face. "Surely. Help yourselves. It's yonder." He pointed over his shoulder into the livery.

Myra looked at Vashti and swallowed hard.

"Don't worry," Vashti whispered. "If he tries anything, I'll clobber him but good." She shook the tick out again.

"We ought to let it air for a while," Myra said. "Ma always washes them before she puts new straw in."

"No time," Vashti said.

She gathered the fabric and headed for the barn, trying not to show her apprehension. There were two of them, after all.

Marty watched as Vashti led Myra across the barn floor to the enclosed area where Griffin kept bedding straw. They knelt and began to stuff armfuls into the tick.

"You ladies need any help?"

Vashti spun around. Marty was two feet from her. "We're fine."

"I could—"

"Marty! Marty, you in here?" The man's voice calling from the front of the livery was unmistakably Oscar Runnels's.

Marty grimaced. "Sounds like I have a customer. If you need anything, let me know." He turned and walked toward the front of the barn.

Myra let out a long breath. "That man makes my skin crawl."

"I know," Vashti said. "For once, Oscar Runnels played the delivering angel."

"Mr. Runnels isn't bad." Myra peered around the board partition at Marty and the stocky freighter talking in the barn's doorway.

"And his son's not bad, either, eh?"

Myra's cheeks flushed, but she smiled. The ongoing flirtation between her and Oscar's son Josiah was no secret.

"Here, we just need a little more." Vashti stood and shook the straw down into the tick. "Shove more in."

"Are you going to drive the stagecoach again soon?" Myra scooped up a huge armful of straw.

"Not driving, but I'm going along as messenger tomorrow. It's my job twice a week until the snow closes the roads."

"Really? That's so exciting! And you look cute in those boy clothes."

Vashti shook her head. "I don't like pretending to be a boy, but it's easier to do the job in that outfit. I wouldn't want to climb up onto the box many times in a skirt."

"Wish I could wear pants." Myra looked at her with a little gasp and wide eyes. "Don't tell Ma I said that, will you?"

"I won't."

They shoved in a few more handfuls of straw.

"If we put in any more, we won't be able to stitch it shut," Vashti said.

"Oh dear. How are we going to get it back to Griffin's?" Myra surveyed the bulging mattress. "We can't ask Marty to help us, or he'll know what we're doing."

"We can do it," Vashti said. "Come on, while the men are still talking." They wrestled the unwieldy tick out onto the barn floor. Each picked up one end and carried the awkward burden out the back door and around to the smithy. Both were puffing and red-faced when they reached the back.

"Hey, they've got the window open," Myra said.

Vashti set down her end of the tick and strode to the window. "Goldie, come help us!"

Her friend looked out the open window. "Well, look at that. Old Marty let you have the straw."

Vashti grinned. "Yep, and he didn't charge us a penny."

★ CHAPTER 12 ★

Even though he was bone tired, Griffin brushed Pepper and made sure Justin did a good job of grooming Red. The boy didn't have to be shown twice—he seemed to take to it. In fact, he rubbed the chestnut's flanks carefully and smoothed his mane and tail. Griff watched him over Pepper's back and saw Justin actually pet Red's neck.

"Red's a good horse." Griffin put his brush back on the shelf between the studs in the barn wall.

"Yeah. He's not bad." Justin brought his brush over and stuck it on the shelf beside Griffin's. "Now what?"

"They've about finished their oats, so we'll put them out in the corral for the night."

"Don't they get hay?"

"There's a rack full in the corral, and a water trough. Marty should have filled it, but I'll check to make sure. Unhitch Red and lead him out." Griffin unhooked Pepper's lead rope and didn't look back to see how Justin did, though it was tempting. It was dark already, and colder than it had been all day. Griffin led Pepper to the corral gate, opened it, and released the gelding. Half a dozen other horses whickered a greeting.

Justin came cautiously out of the barn, holding Red's halter with one hand. Griff waited until he got right up to the gate and swung it open.

"Walk him in and turn him around. Then you get yourself out here with me and let him go so I can shut the gate."

The boy managed to follow instructions and didn't let go of the halter until he had Red completely inside the corral and turned toward the gate.

Griff shut the swinging gate and latched it. "Feels like snow."

"Sure does." Justin shivered and shook himself.

"I'll get the colt. Can you take the palomino again?"

"Sure. But why do you keep those two inside at night?"

"They're special. Until I deliver that palomino to Mr. Dooley, I need to make sure nothing happens to it. And the colt. . .well, he's special. I don't want to take a chance of him getting loose or somebody stealing him."

"When will he be old enough for you to ride him?"

"Well, someone who doesn't weigh too much will likely be able to ride him next summer—after his training. But me?" Griffin laughed. "I wouldn't want to put my weight on a two-year-old. Another year, and his back will be strong enough, but not yet."

"So how will you train him if you can't get on his back?" Justin asked.

"You'll see." Griffin hitched the colt in his stall and left him with his feed to munch. His plans for training would fall into place when the time came. He didn't want to get too optimistic—things could change in a hurry—but he thought he might have an eager helper close by. "You ready? I need to stop at my place before we go to the Fennel House."

"You eating over there with me tonight?" Justin asked.

"Reckon so." Griffin didn't like spending as much on meals as he had been lately, but he'd been gone all day, helping Ethan, and his fire would be out. He didn't think he had much to eat in the place except a few dried apples and such. He'd never cooked much, anyway. "Come on." He grabbed the lantern he'd left hanging inside the back of the livery and shut the rolling door.

They went in through the smithy. When he got to the door to his room, he paused.

"Uh, wait here. I'll just be a second."

"All right." Justin looked doubtful, but he stood there between the anvil and the forge, shivering.

So far, Griff had managed to avoid taking the boy into his private quarters. Sometime he'd get around to redding up the place, and then Justin could see it. Not until.

Shoving the door open, he held the lantern high. And stopped in his tracks.

"What—" His heart lurched. Had he been robbed? The place looked almost bare. The floor between where he stood and his bunk was clear. And his bunk! The covers were smooth and. . .not his covers. A quilt he'd never seen before lay over the mattress, and his pillow actually had a linen cover on it. That was odd. When did thieves leave things behind?

Justin touched his arm. "Uncle Griff? Something wrong?"

"I'm not sure." Griffin stepped into the room and swung the lantern around slowly. The room felt fairly warm, like someone had kept a fire in the stove today. His extra wool pants and dungarees, along with his two other shirts, hung from nails on the wall. All his boxes and kegs were neatly stacked, and the shelves, while crowded, had an orderly look. He could actually see the surface of the small plank table he'd lost sight of months ago, and sitting in the middle of that table were a covered basket and a green bottle holding a cluster of dried weeds and red berries. It was kind of pretty.

"This place isn't so bad," Justin said. "I thought you said it wasn't fit to live in."

"Well, I. . ." Griffin swallowed hard. He didn't know who'd done this, but his initial shock had faded. Now anger vied with gratitude in his heart. Insight flashed in his brain, like the sparks that flew from his hammer when he struck white-hot iron. He could get mad at the scrubbing bandit, or he could accept an anonymous friend's act with humility. The first course would be easiest. But someone had cared about him enough to spend a lot of effort making his place nicer. And he had a feeling it wasn't done for Griffin Bane alone.

He whipped around and eyed Justin suspiciously. Had the boy complained to someone that his uncle had farmed him out to the boardinghouse? Had he told other people the room behind the smithy was too filthy to take a boy into?

"You, uh, didn't say anything to anyone about not liking the

Fennel House, did you?"

Justin shrugged. "Don't think so. Why would I? It's not half bad."

Griff nodded and looked around again. He strode to the table and lifted the napkin that covered the basket. Biscuits. And a jar of jam.

"Hmm."

"Hmm, what?" Justin came over and looked down at the basket. "Say, those look mighty good. Did you make 'em?"

"Nope." Griff laid the napkin back over the tempting biscuits. "I'd say we had company while we were out to the Chapmans' ranch."

"You mean someone brought you those biscuits while you were away?"

"No, someone brought *us* those biscuits." Griffin thought he might have an idea of whom. Vashti had known they'd be gone today. But how could she have done all this by herself and still made the stagecoach after lunch? He looked cautiously at Justin. "Do you think this place is too small for the both of us?"

Justin looked around. "Well. . .there's only one bunk."

"True. But I *could* build another one over the top."

"You mean. . ." Justin cleared his throat. "You mean you'd want me to stay with you, after all?"

"If you'd like that. But if you wouldn't, you can stay over to the boarding—"

"I would!"

"Oh." Griffin nodded slowly. "All right then. Let's go over and have supper, and I'll tell Mrs. Thistle that tonight's your last night with them. And tomorrow we'll scare up some lumber and build another bunk. How does that sound?"

"Sounds good, Uncle Griff."

Griffin smiled. "Great. And for breakfast we'll have biscuits and jam."

Griffin tried to think where he could get some lumber. He didn't want to go clear out to the sawmill, but maybe he'd have to. On Thursday morning, he rose with the sun and stoked his woodstove. He'd promised Justin he'd get him from the boardinghouse and they'd build a new bunk. The basket of biscuits all but called his name as he pulled on his trousers, suspenders, and boots. But if he ate some before Justin came, the boy would know. Best wait.

A knock came at the door.

"Hey, Griff, you up?"

He clomped over to the door as he slid on his heavy wool overshirt. "Hiram Dooley, you're out early." Griffin opened the door wide and let his friend enter.

"Oh? I need to make a firing pin for Emmaline Landry's gun." Hiram looked around the small room and nodded. "Mighty spruce, Griff."

"That's what I think, too." Maybe getting a visit from a scrubbing genie wasn't so bad. Griffin chuckled. "Used to be you were always fixing the men's guns. Now the ladies are keeping you in business."

"There's truth to that," Hiram said.

"Well, I haven't fired up the forge for two days, but help yourself." Hiram held up a burlap sack and shook it. It clinked.

Griffin shook his head. "You didn't have to bring your own coal."

Hiram shrugged. "Might need a piece of steel if you've got one that's right."

"Sure. Let me just grab my gloves and hat. I've got to go over and get my nephew."

"I heard the boy was here. How's that working?"

"All right. I'm going to bring him over here to stay with me today, but I need to make him a bunk." Griff stopped and whirled around. Hiram was the perfect person to ask. "Say, you don't have any leftover boards and such from building the church or something like that?"

Hiram nodded. "Over to my old place there's lots of lumber in the barn. Look it over and take what you want. I'll swap you for the steel."

"All right. And I've got a palomino gelding in the livery that I think you'll like the looks of. I bought it in Boise, with Mrs. Adams in mind. Rode him all the way up here. He's steady and well mannered, and he doesn't look half bad, either."

"Terrific. Do you have time to show me now?"

"All right, let's go."

They walked to the back door of the livery, and Griffin rolled the door open. He went into the palomino's stall and unhooked him. When he led the horse out onto the barn floor, Hiram's eyes lit up.

"He looks fine, Griff."

"You want to try him out?"

"I'll take your word. How much do I owe you?"

Griffin named the price he'd paid in Boise.

"I'll get it to you later today," Hiram said.

"You want to keep him here or take him out to your place?"

"I might as well take him to the ranch. All right if I take him later when I'm heading home?"

"Sure." Griffin put the horse away and came out of the stall. "Say, I've got a riddle for you."

Hiram silently raised his eyebrows and waited.

Griffin pulled in a deep breath. Did he really want to spill it? Hiram was the quietest man in town. He wouldn't tell anyone.

"Come on back to my place." They walked over to the smithy and into Griffin's living quarters. He turned to face Hiram. "Yesterday a funny thing happened. Justin and I rode out to Ethan's ranch to help him all day. When we came back at suppertime, my place was. . .well, it was the way you see it now. Except the bed was made up fresh."

Hiram glanced at the rumpled bunk and nodded.

"Don't you think that's odd?" Griffin asked.

"That your bed was made? Mighty odd."

"Yes, well, somebody came in here while I was gone and cleaned the place up." Griffin looked around again at the neat supplies and the clean window and lamp chimney. "You know what else?"

Hiram shook his head.

"My blankets were gone, and my bed was all made up with linen sheets and a new quilt. That one there."

"It's not your quilt?"

"Nope. I think they even put fresh straw in my mattress."

Hiram's eyes widened, and he looked around again. "Know who did it?"

"I've got my suspicions." Griffin picked up the basket of biscuits.

"They left this. And that there posy of weeds."

Hiram peeked under the napkin and grunted.

"Biscuits," Griff said, as if he couldn't see them.

"They any good?"

"Don't know. Justin and I ate at the Fennel House last night, and I saved these for breakfast."

"Well, it's not Trudy's basket," Hiram said.

"Hmm. But she left the ranch as soon as Justin and I got there yesterday."

"I could probably tell you who made the biscuits if I tasted one," Hiram said.

"Now, that's a thought." The two single men had eaten biscuits made by nearly every woman in town at church functions and such. Griffin laid back the napkin. "Try one."

"Thank you." Hiram took one out.

Griffin reached for one and pulled his hand back. "I'd better not. Don't want the boy to think I ate a bunch without waiting for him."

Hiram took a bite and closed his eyes, chewing slowly. Then he took another bite.

"Well?" Griff asked.

"Flaky. I'd say Augie Moore's, but there's a heavy touch with the lard. He wouldn't do that." Augie was the undisputed best cook in Fergus. Hiram broke off a piece and handed it to Griffin. "Try it. I'm guessing Ellie Nash."

"Ellie?" Griffin frowned as he took the quarter biscuit. "Why would she—" He stared at Hiram. "No. Oh no."

Hiram grinned. "I think you're right."

"Not the whole shooting club."

"Why not? They helped redd up Doc Kincaid's new house and gave him a pound party. Why not you, too?"

"I don't want all the women in town talking about—" Griffin looked wildly around. How many of them had been in here and seen his...habits? He moaned.

"Eat the biscuit," Hiram said. "It's good."

"Be better with some of that strawberry jam."

"Jam? You should have said so. That clinches it. Ellie made a

Susan Page Davis

bumper batch of strawberry this year. Remember she brought some to the harvest dinner? And Annie Harper makes quilts quicker'n you can shoe a mule."

Griff looked toward the bed again. "You must be right."

Hiram laughed. "That's gotta be it. Trudy mentioned last time I saw her that you were boarding your nephew out and how it was too bad you couldn't keep him to home." He slapped Griffin on the back. "Say, I've got an idea."

"What?"

"This place is awfully small for two men."

"I'll say. It's awfully small for me by myself."

Hiram nodded. "How much are you paying to board him?"

Griff winced. "Twelve dollars a week. Way too much, but Rilla says boys eat a lot."

"Right. My old house is sitting empty since I moved out to the Fennel ranch this fall. Libby and I—well, we intend to live at the ranch." His face flushed a little as he mentioned his upcoming nuptials. "When you go to get the lumber, take a look around my house. The back door's unlocked. You and Justin could stay there, and if you think it's worth twenty dollars a month. . ."

"You mean it?"

Again Hiram nodded.

"Say, that's a good idea. And close to the boardinghouse if we want a hot meal. Close to the jail, too." At Hiram's puzzled look, Griffin added, "I think Justin took a shine to Ethan yesterday. I want to encourage him to look on Ethan as a friend."

"Sounds reasonable. Let me know what you think."

Griffin put the basket on the table. They walked out into the smithy. Hiram moseyed over to the corner where Griffin kept steel stock. "How's your new shotgun rider doing?"

"Oh, you know about that?" Griffin asked.

"Whole town knows you hired her."

"Ah. So far, so good."

Hiram selected a small scrap of bar stock and carried it and his sack to the forge. Griffin left him as he dumped his ration of coal into the firepot.

On the road to Nampa that afternoon, Vashti wore a warm jacket Libby had provided. It was made of green wool and lined with fleece, and it buttoned up snug under her chin. Vashti had insisted on paying for it herself—she didn't want to be beholden to a man again, even if Griffin had said he would pay for it. It kept her warm, though light snow fell all around them, deadening the sound of the wheels on the road.

She reminded herself many times not to watch Johnny drive. Her job was to watch the road ahead and the rocks and trees along the sides. It was tempting to sneak glances at his hands, though, especially when they came to a curve or had to cross a stream. She would drive as well as Johnny someday—better!

"What you looking at?" Johnny asked with a sly grin.

"Nothing." She turned away from him and studied the gulley beside the road.

"Yes, you was. You like looking at me?"

"Not hardly."

"Huh."

Vashti felt her face flush. If Johnny noticed, he'd think she liked him.

"The passengers know you're a girl," he said a mile later. "I heard 'em talking back at the Democrat station."

Her heart thudded. "What'd they say?"

"One of 'em asked the tender about you, if you was really a girl."

"Which tender?"

"Jake."

She scowled and turned her face away again. The swing station was owned by a man everyone said was the only Democrat in the valley. When they'd stopped to change the team, she'd noticed a man called Jake watching her and stayed away from him.

"He told the passenger you used to be a saloon girl," Johnny said.

"Oh, wonderful." She exhaled and focused on the road, but tears stung her eyes.

"I reckon you'll know how to handle him if he tries to get fresh." She glared at him. "Be quiet, Johnny."

He laughed. "What, you think you can get away from the past that easy? Everybody in these parts knows who you are. What you are."

"And just what do you mean by that?" She felt like smacking him.

"You know." He shrugged. The horses took the slight flapping of the reins as permission to break into a canter. Johnny jerked to attention. "Here, now! Whoa, boys. Slow down."

They careened toward a downhill curve. Vashti caught her breath and jammed the butt of the shotgun against her thigh, holding it tight with one hand and grabbing the edge of the seat with the other. She knew better than to say anything at that moment, though she wanted to scream at Johnny.

As they reached the curve, the leaders began to slow, but the swing team hadn't caught on yet, and they tried to keep running, nudging the leaders' tails. Johnny tried to hold them steady and work the brake lever, too. Even so, they hit the turn way too fast. As the leaders turned, the coach wheels slid and the whole framework swung wildly to one side.

Vashti gasped as she slid over and slammed against Johnny's hip.

"Whoa now! Whoa, Rolly! Sam!" He sawed at the reins.

Vashti wanted to tell him to keep his voice even, but she couldn't breathe.

"Hey!" The muffled cry came from one of the passengers inside the coach.

Before Vashti could grab another breath, the seat fell out from under her and she was falling.

★ CHAPTER 13 ★

Vashti and Johnny hit the ground in a heap.

With no time to think about injuries or indignities, Vashti sat up. The coach had tipped over on its side. The terrorized horses dragged it, with the upper wheels spinning wildly, across the snow.

"Whoa, you lummoxes!" She clawed her way to her feet and found the shotgun lying in the snow. She'd lost her hat. "Johnny! You alive?"

Johnny sat up and shook his head. "Oh man!" He was on his feet in a flash and tore off after the horses.

Vashti gulped. There wasn't a thing she could do—she'd never catch up to him, let alone the horses. She looked around and found her hat a few yards back. After brushing the snow off it, she clamped it on her head and set off. Her hip and elbow smarted where she'd landed on them. A couple of hundred yards away, the horses had come to a halt and stood steaming and shivering. By the time she'd limped to where they'd stopped, Johnny was talking to them and running his hands over their sleek sides and down their legs.

"There, boys. Calm down now. It's all right."

She walked over to the scarlet coach. "Ahoy there, passengers. You in there, gentlemen?"

The door on the top side of the coach cracked open, then swung upward, and a man's head appeared, minus his hat, with his disheveled hair hanging down about his ears.

"Yes, ma'am. Sir. Uh—" He blinked at her. "Sorry. We're shook up, but we're all right."

Vashti nodded. "Let's get you out of there, and we'll see if we can right the coach. I'm sorry you got tossed around like that."

Johnny unhitched the team and secured them to the only tree within sight. He continued to talk to them and pet them.

When the two passengers stood on firm ground, one of them asked, "What do we do?"

Vashti eyed the overturned coach. Griff wasn't going to like this. "I'll have to see what Johnny says. He has more experience than I do."

"Oh, is that right?"

Something about the amusement in the man's gaze made Vashti flush and her blood boil. She turned on her heel and walked over to Johnny. "Whatcha reckon we should do?"

"After the horses are calm, we can hitch them to the coach broadside and let them pull it up onto the wheels again."

"Sounds like you've done this before."

"What driver hasn't?"

She let that pass. "What about damage?"

"What about it?" He glared at her. "This ain't my fault."

"Oh yeah? Whose fault is it?"

"Ice. There was ice on the road, underneath the snow."

"Whatever you say, Johnny."

A few minutes later, they led the horses over to the coach, and Johnny took a coil of rope from the boot. He hitched it to the luggage rack on the top and tied the other end to the evener. Vashti held the leaders' heads while he worked, speaking softly to the horses.

"So that gal's got a nighttime job in a saloon, I hear," one of the passengers said to Johnny, but Vashti had no trouble hearing him.

Her chest tightened, and she clamped her fingers around the bridle straps.

Johnny shook his head. "I don't know what you've been hearing, but Georgie's all right."

"She's a woman, isn't she?" asked the other passenger. "Hard to tell with that coat she's wearing."

Vashti kept her face turned away from them.

"I saw her red hair after you two fell off the coach," said the first man. "She didn't get it all up under her hat."

"Bet she's a stunner in silk stockings," said his companion.

"Look, gents," Johnny said firmly, "Georgie's a girl, it's true. But she ain't that kind of girl. So just leave her alone, you hear?"

Vashti leaned her forehead against Sam's bony muzzle. "Thank You for Johnny, Lord." Her tears fell on the horse's nose, and he snorted. She wiped her face with her sleeve before the next few tears could freeze on her cheek.

Griffin walked around the stage three times, searching out every scratch and scrape. His eyes narrowed when he looked at the cracked door panel and the broken spoke on the off front wheel. They were lucky the coach hadn't been ruined. Vashti stood perfectly still, waiting for him to explode. Johnny began to fidget. Justin stood in the shadow of the livery doorway, watching in silence.

The third time around, Griff stopped in front of Johnny. He stood six inches taller than the driver and outweighed him by at least fifty pounds, most of which was muscle made by hefting iron. He gazed down at Johnny through slits of eyes.

"Want to tell me again what happened?"

Johnny cleared his throat and looked away. "It's like I told you, boss. We came up on that corner two miles out from Democrat's, and it was slippery, and the horses got het up."

"Uh-huh." Griffin nodded. "You think that road's too treacherous for us to run any more this season?"

Johnny swallowed. "No, sir, I don't."

"Then how are you going to keep this from happening next time, Conway? Answer me that."

"I...uh..."

"You recall when Cyrus Fennel was your boss."

It wasn't a question, but Johnny said, "Yes, sir."

"What do you suppose he'd do if he were here now?"

Johnny's face lost its color. He opened his mouth and closed it again.

Griff nodded again. He took two steps and squinted down into

Vashti's face. "You get hurt?"

She gulped. "No, sir."

"Good." His momentary softening was gone. "All right, Georgie-boy, let's hear your version."

Vashti's pulse raced. Surely Griffin wouldn't punish her. Or would he? She'd never seen him so dangerously quiet.

"We, uh, we left Democrat's, and everything was fine, but the horses were frisky. The snow and all, you know."

He nodded.

"We, uh. . ."

"You *what?*"

She jumped. "On that downhill, the team started running. Johnny tried to pull them in, but then the wheels slipped, and the stage overset."

Griff held her gaze for a long moment, his dark eyes simmering. He paced back to Johnny. Each word distinct, he said, "You two will sand down the side of that coach this evening and repaint it. I will do the other repairs. The cost of the materials and my time will be deducted from your wages, Conway."

Johnny winced. "Yes, boss."

"And if this happens again while you're driving, I'll suspend you for a month of Sundays." Griffin turned away.

Vashti sneaked a glance at Johnny. His mouth drooped, and he wouldn't meet her gaze.

An hour later, Vashti knelt in the straw on the barn floor, gently scrubbing at the door panel with a piece of fine sandpaper. Griffin had removed the damaged wheel and taken it over to the smithy. The axle was propped up on a chopping block.

Johnny worked on the body panel below the window. He swore softly.

Vashti cleared her throat and threw him a pointed glance.

"Sorry," he said.

"Swearing doesn't help."

Johnny made a face at her. "If you was a boy, it wouldn't matter.

I'm as bad as that passenger—can't remember when you're a girl and when you're a boy."

She clenched her fist. "Quit it, Johnny. You're a good driver. Most of the time, anyway."

"Yeah?"

"Yeah. But you got sloppy today. We both know it. The whole world knows it."

"One second. That's all it took. One second."

"Yeah, that's about right. It takes one second for a team of horses to get out of control."

"Oh, so now you know more about driving than I do."

She straightened and faced him. "I'm not saying that."

"Sure sounds like it." He stood and towered over her, scowling.

Vashti let out a deep breath. "At least the horses didn't get hurt. Come on. Let's get this done."

"You really think I'm a good driver?"

"When you're not being reckless. And it *was* slippery on that hill."

"So it wasn't entirely my fault."

She pressed her lips together and went back to rubbing the scrape on the door.

"Thanks for not telling Griff it was my fault," Johnny said. "He'd have taken your word if you had."

"I'm not out to get you in trouble."

"You're not?"

She shook her head. "You can do that easy enough yourself."

"Ha!" He smiled ruefully. "Thought you wanted my job."

"I wouldn't mind it, but I wouldn't want to do you out of your livelihood."

He began rubbing the wood again. "Thanks."

"Well, thank you for setting that passenger in his place."

"You heard what he said?"

"Every word." She rubbed harder. She had no reason to feel guilty. God had forgiven all her past transgressions. He'd sanded away every scratch and repainted her soul a pure, sparkling white.

"You still want a driving rig to practice on?" Johnny asked.

"Bill's going to make me one."

Johnny blinked at her. "He is?"

"Yes. He thinks I'm tenacious enough to master the art."

"I reckon maybe you are."

Vashti and Apphia Benton watched as Bill Stout threaded the six long reins through the wooden rack he'd constructed in the Bentons' stable. He gathered the ends and backed up, letting the leathers slide through his hands until he'd reached a wagon seat he'd mounted on two big rounds of a log.

"All right, missy, you come over here and sit on this wagon seat."

Vashti shot Apphia a smile and walked over to the seat. She eased down and smoothed her full skirt.

"Here you go." Bill handed her the lines.

She laced them between her fingers and took up the slack.

"It's got a weight hanging from each line, to keep some tension. If you let off, it will fall down a few inches." Bill stood back and cocked his head to one side.

Vashti tried to feel each weight through the lines.

"The off leader's too tight," Bill said. "Let it out just a hair." Vashti painstakingly pushed the rein for the imaginary front right horse forward with her thumb.

"Oops," Bill said. "Now the swing is too loose."

She frowned in concentration, trying to catch the rein to the middle horse on the right side of her "coach" with her third finger and inch it up.

"Better." Bill nodded. "You look fine. I should have put the seat up higher, though."

"Vashti, how did you learn to hold the reins?" Apphia asked. "I'd get confused first thing. And you only have one line for each horse. I don't see how you can keep them under control."

Vashti glanced over at her and smiled. "When my daddy was still alive, he used to let me drive his team."

"Uh-uh." Bill shook his head. "You relaxed your hands when you spoke to Miz Benton, and you let the reins go slack. Your team just ran away with you and tipped the stage over on its side."

Vashti frowned and looked down at her hands. Bill was right. She firmed up her wrists and put a light tension on each of the six lines. The one for the near wheeler had slipped, and she worked it up until the rein ran straight from her hand to the rack again, but not too tight.

"That's better," Bill said.

"How do you use your whip, if you need both hands to drive?" Apphia asked.

Vashti determined not to look at her again so Bill wouldn't scold her. "You answer that, Bill."

He chuckled. "Good stage drivers don't use the whip much. It's more for show when you're setting out or for times when the horses need to be reminded to keep the pace up. If you're driving through mud, for instance, or if you see outlaws coming up on you. Then you take the reins in one hand, loose enough so the horses can get their heads down and run, and you crack the whip with the other."

"Oh my."

Vashti figured she'd get a talking-to about outlaws later from Apphia.

Bill watched Vashti in silence for several seconds as she moved her hands and let the weights in and out slowly. "You practice for two hours every day, and by snow melt, mebbe you'll be ready to drive one of Griff's sixes."

"Two hours a day?" Apphia stared at him. "She'd get charley horses in her hands."

"When I'm driving, I'll hold the lines longer than that at a stretch," Vashti said.

Bill nodded. "Yes, ma'am. She needs strong fingers and springy wrists. Can't have those without working 'em."

Vashti smiled up at her mentor. "Thank you so much, Bill. I'll practice every day, and I promise that next spring I won't embarrass you and overset my coach."

His eyes twinkled. "I expect you'll make me proud. You've got a sight of determination, young lady."

"She can come over and practice anytime she wants," Apphia

said, "but I'm afraid she'll get cold."

"I'll be fine." In her mind, Vashti was dashing along the Nampa road behind a team of six matched bays. She moved her hands slightly as they galloped, and tucked up the near leader's rein a bit.

"I heard the boss is moving," Bill said.

"What?" She lowered her hands and swung around to stare at him.

"Your team's running away."

"Very funny. What's that you said about Mr. Bane?"

"He's going to rent the old Dooley place, next to the jailhouse."

"Really?" Vashti looked over at Apphia.

Bill gathered up his tools. "Reckon I'd better get over to the boardinghouse. If you're late for supper there, you're apt to miss out on the pudding."

When he'd left the stable, Vashti carefully wound the lines around a stick Bill had attached to her wagon seat for a brake handle. She gathered her skirts and climbed down. "Miz Benton, do you know anything about why Mr. Bane is moving?"

"I expect it's for the boy."

"Then all the work the ladies did at his little house was wasted."

"Why do you say that?" Apphia put her arm around Vashti. "My dear, what you and the other women did was a nice gesture. I understand why you didn't tell me until it was over."

Vashti hung her head. "We figured you'd say we oughtn't to do it without his permission."

"I probably would have. Griffin is a very private man, and if his room was as filthy as you say it was, then I suspect he was embarrassed to know a group of ladies had been in there."

"He never said anything to me about it afterward."

"No, but the whole plan could have gone awry. It might have made him angry."

Vashti nodded slowly.

Apphia smiled. "You should rejoice and thank the Lord that Griffin accepted your gesture for what it was—an honest effort by a group of friends to help him. And it accomplished just what you hoped—he's got the boy living with him now."

"Yes." Vashti frowned. "I suppose moving over to Mr. Dooley's would be good for them. They'd have more space."

"That's right. Justin can have his own chamber."

"And that little room behind the smithy was drafty and cold the day we were there. The nearest water is over beyond the livery, at the well where they draw it for the horses—"

Apphia pulled her toward the door. "Come, dear. I'm cold. Let's have a cup of tea together. I think what you did was admirable, and it made Griffin consider how he could better take care of Justin. That's what you hoped, isn't it?"

"Yes. I suppose they'll be much more comfortable at the Dooleys' old place." Vashti looked back at her new rack. "God is good, isn't He, Miz Benton?"

"Yes, dear. He's very good."

★ CHAPTER 14 ★

With the first heavy snow in December, Griffin quit sending the stagecoach to Silver City. Enough mines were operating that their outfits kept the road from Fergus to Nampa rolled and packed down, which made for good sleighing, and the stages kept running through to Boise. Vashti, however, was out of a job until spring.

It was just as well. Griffin spent entirely too much time fretting when she took to the road with Johnny. He told himself it was the responsibility weighing on him, not her determination or her sparkling eyes.

On Christmas Eve, he and Justin fed the horses and buttoned down the livery for the night. In the morning, they could feed the stock and ride on out to Ethan's without having to worry about keeping a stage schedule or shoeing mules.

They'd developed an evening routine where Justin measured out the oats and Griffin threw the hay down from the loft. When the snow was deep, most of the horses stayed in the barn, though Griffin had taken four stagecoach teams to Nampa and left them there with Jeremiah Gayle for the winter. Come spring, he'd bring them back up to Fergus. He'd given Marty a month off, but even so, his workload seemed a lot easier. Part of that was due to Justin's help. The boy had lost some of his sullenness, especially while working around the horses.

Ethan's invitation to the ranch for the holiday had surprised Griffin, considering Ethan and Trudy had family close by. Hiram and Libby would join them for dinner as well. In response to the gesture, he'd stopped at the emporium the day before and picked up a box of ribbon candy to take to Trudy.

"Are we picking up Mrs. Adams in the morning?" Justin asked as he shut the grain bin.

"Yes. I'll harness two of the horses to the sled."

"Can I ride Red?"

Griffin eyed him in surprise. "I guess so." He walked over to the wall where he kept brushes and hoof picks. "How'd you like to brush the colt tonight?"

"You mean it?" Justin's eyes fairly glowed in the lantern light.

"Sure. Just speak to him soft-like, and don't do anything sudden."

Justin took the brush from him and went to the colt's stall. "Hey, fella. I'm coming in." He touched the colt's flank while standing to the side, as Griffin had taught him to.

Griffin smiled to himself. That boy could make a good hand with horses by next summer. He strolled over and leaned on the divider between the colt and Red. "That's right. Everything nice and easy. And remember, I still don't want you going in the stall with him when I'm not around."

"I won't. I promise."

"You brush him all over every night, and next week I'll have you picking up his feet."

"What for?"

Griffin chuckled. "So he'll let you."

Justin looked quizzically over his shoulder.

"You have to get a colt used to everything," Griffin said. "If you rub him all over, he gets used to being touched. Then he won't jump when a rein or a piece of rope touches him. You want him to be calm. And you practice picking up his feet and putting them down easy, so he won't mind you doing it when you need to."

"Think he'll ever be calm?" Justin asked, stroking the colt's spotted withers with the soft brush. "He's always jumping around and kicking and bucking in the corral."

"That's because he's young. He needs to learn that it's all right to play around when he's out to pasture, but when it's time for work, we get down to business."

Justin paused his strokes. "I never thought about horses needing to learn to work."

"They do, just like people. They learn that when the bridle goes on, that means you don't run and jump however you feel like it. You stay quiet and do what your master tells you. And you have fun together."

Justin began brushing the colt's mane. "You think they like it when people ride them?"

"Some of them do. When I get on Pepper, I can feel him pulling, ready to go."

Justin nodded. "I think Champ will make a good saddle horse."

"Champ?" Griffin asked.

The boy swung around and faced him. "That's what I call him in my head. Does he have another name?"

"No. No, Champ's a good name."

Justin smiled.

Justin rode ahead on Red while Griffin drove the sleigh placidly down the road. Libby sat beside him, mostly covered by a woolen quilt, cradling a large basket on her lap.

"Your nephew was very polite this morning," she said.

"He's progressing," Griffin replied.

"Have you heard anything from his mother?"

"I telegraphed her when Justin arrived, to tell her he'd gotten here safe, and we had one letter after that. To be frank, she seemed relieved to have Justin off her hands."

"That's too bad." Libby threw Griffin a smile. "It might be the best thing for you, though, and I think Justin will benefit from being with you."

"I hope you're right, ma'am."

Libby had long been known as the most beautiful woman in town, and Griffin had always felt intimidated in her presence, especially since her husband died. All the single men in Fergus had watched her, but none he knew of had dared to approach her in the first two years of her widowhood. Then, all of a sudden, Hiram Dooley was courting her. How that had come about, Griffin couldn't quite fathom. Hiram spoke so little, he couldn't imagine how the two of them passed the time when they were alone. In fact, Hiram would have been the last man in Fergus he'd have put money on to win Libby's hand. Maybe Hiram knew something he didn't.

"Will you send him to school during the winter term?" Libby asked.

Griffin jerked his head up, startled. "I hadn't thought about it. He reads and ciphers better than I do."

"He might do well with more education."

"What do you mean?"

She shrugged. "Doctors and lawyers start somewhere, Mr. Bane. Many have humble beginnings. Do you know what interests your nephew?"

"Can't say as I do."

"Maybe you should ask him."

Griffin felt he'd been mildly rebuked—but she was right. Justin had been with him more than a month, and he didn't know how the boy had spent his free time back in Pennsylvania or what he aspired to do when he was grown. Griffin had worried about keeping him away from a life of crime but hadn't considered how to keep him occupied.

By the time he turned in at the lane to the Chapman ranch, Justin had far outdistanced them, and he was unsaddling Red in Ethan's barn when Griffin drew the sled up in front of the ranch house.

"Welcome," Trudy called from the porch. Ethan and Hiram stood with her.

Hiram came down the steps and offered Libby his hand. She took it and climbed out of the sled, smiling all over.

"Drive right to the barn, Griff," said Ethan. "I'll come help you unhitch."

The McDade boys were helping Justin hang up his tack and stable Red.

"Thought those boys only worked for you in summer," Griffin said to Ethan.

"I kept them on this fall. I've been running a lot more cattle since

Trudy and I got married. They're doing my chores today and going home tomorrow to have a late Christmas with their folks. I'm giving them a couple of weeks off."

"Hey, boss," Johnny McDade called, "is it all right if Justin comes over to the bunkhouse until dinnertime?"

Ethan looked at Griffin and arched his eyebrows.

"I guess so," Griffin said.

"Sure," Ethan told Johnny. "Just come when Mrs. Chapman rings the dinner bell." They put Griffin's team away and hung up the harness. As they walked back toward the house, Ethan said, "They're high-spirited boys, but they're good workers."

Griffin sat down with his hosts in the big sitting room for a few minutes. Trudy wanted all the town gossip.

"You'll have to get the news from Libby," Griffin told her. "I don't exactly hear all the rumors."

Libby and Hiram sat off to one side, talking in low tones, holding hands, and smiling a lot. Ethan and Griffin discussed Ethan's ranching and sheriffing, and Griffin's smithing and stage coaching.

After about twenty minutes, Trudy jumped up. "I'd better go see if that goose is done."

Libby rose, too, still smiling at Hiram. "Let me help you, Trudy."

The two women disappeared through an archway. The savory smells increased, and Griffin's stomach rumbled.

"You got yourself a good one there, Hi," Ethan said.

"I know it." Hiram came over and sat down where Trudy had been. "So how are you and Justin doing at the old house?"

Griffin ran a hand across his beard. "Not too bad. It's a sight better than my little place."

Hiram nodded. "Glad it's working out for you."

Griffin still couldn't believe the change that had come over Hiram these past few months. "When are you and Libby going to tie the knot?"

"As soon as Mr. and Mrs. Hamilton come back and pay her for the store."

They talked for a while longer, until Libby came and told them dinner was ready.

"Is Trudy going to ring the bell for the boys?" Ethan asked.

"I can mosey out there and tell them," Griffin offered. He was curious as to how Justin was getting along with the McDades. He'd only met the boys once or twice at church. Both were older than Justin and seemed much more mature.

"Hold on. I'll go with you." Ethan handed Griffin his coat and hat and grabbed his own from pegs near the front door.

They ambled across the barnyard, talking about the chance of more snow. Ethan opened the bunkhouse door and stepped inside.

"Well, boys, dinner's about ready."

Griffin followed him. Justin had been seated with his back to the door, but he jumped up and whirled around with as guilty a face as Griffin had ever seen.

"All right, boss," Spin McDade said, shoving his chair back and throwing down a hand of cards.

"You boys playing poker?" Ethan sounded slightly scandalized.

"Just having fun," Johnny said with a shrug. "We don't usually get someone else to take a hand with."

Griffin frowned but decided to say nothing. He didn't want to embarrass Ethan by making a fuss, and anyway, he'd played his share of poker games. Evelyn probably wouldn't approve, but she'd given Justin's care entirely over to him.

"You're not taking Justin for every penny he's got, are you?" Ethan threw Griff an apologetic glance.

"I don't have any money, sir," Justin said. "We're playing for matchsticks." His face flushed, and he had trouble meeting Ethan's gaze.

"Aha. Well, come on and get washed up."

The boys ran ahead of them to the house.

"Sorry about that," Ethan said as he and Griffin followed.

Griffin shrugged. "His mother probably wouldn't like it, but they were just passing time. How old are those boys?"

"Spin's almost twenty. Johnny's seventeen. I never thought—"

Griffin held one hand up. "If they'd been in the Nugget playing, that'd be one thing."

"I always tell them to watch themselves in town. They know I won't put up with any nonsense. I can't. I mean, I'm the sheriff."

"I know," Griffin said. "Don't worry about it."

Ethan stamped his feet to get rid of the snow before climbing the steps. "Did you get Justin a present?"

"Yup. I'm giving him a bridle for the spotted colt he's going to help me train. And a pocketknife."

"Nice gifts for a boy that age."

"What'd you get Trudy?"

"A dress from New York. I had Libby pick it out and order it. Trudy will probably say it's too fine for her to wear."

"What'll you do if she won't wear it?"

"Oh, I think she will, though she might hang it up and look at it for a while first." Ethan chuckled. "And I got her something else she'll like real well."

"What's that?"

"A sweet, tooled leather scabbard to go on her saddle."

"Oh yeah, she'll like that. I guess Hiram's giving Libby the palomino today."

"That's the plan."

Griffin half wished for a moment that he had a special lady to give things to. It would be kind of fun to order something fancy from back East for someone pretty. He had a fleeting vision of putting a sparkly chain around the neck of an auburn-haired girl with green eyes. He shook his head as they entered the house. That would only mean spending more money, and he'd had enough trouble getting Christmas gifts for Justin. Besides, he had no intention of getting tangled up with a woman anytime soon—even one as pretty and spunky as Vashti Edwards.

At the Spur & Saddle, Christmas Day overflowed with visitors. Terrence Thistle had declared it a holiday for his wife, Rilla, at the Fennel House. Consequently, all the boarders walked down the street for dinner. Dr. Kincaid and Isabel Fennel also came to enjoy Augie's lavish ham dinner, as did Charles and Orissa Walker. Vashti and Goldie helped the Moores serve ten for dinner and then sat down together at three in the afternoon to celebrate with their own small "family."

Augie came from the kitchen carrying a covered dish. "I held back a sweet potato apiece."

"Oh good!" Goldie jumped up and planted a kiss on his cheek. "I thought sure the guests had gotten them all, and I wanted one something fierce."

After the blessing, they tucked into the ham, gravy, biscuits, cranberry sauce, squash, and carrots, along with the sweet potatoes.

"I believe I'm too full to eat any pie." Vashti leaned back and patted her stomach with regret.

Augie looked over at Bitsy and winked. "Maybe we should hold the sweets until after we see what Santy Claus brought."

Goldie chuckled. "Augie, you haven't let the fire go out long enough for Santa to come down the chimney."

"'S'all you know. Santy's magic. Isn't that so, darlin'?" Augie appealed to Bitsy with such a hopeful face that she laughed and reached over to pat his cheek.

"You're just a kid in big boots. We can have the gifts now, if you want."

They took their dishes to the kitchen then slipped into the Moores' sitting room. Bitsy guarded their private quarters closer than she did her purse. Company was generally entertained in the public dining room. The sitting room remained a place where they could retreat from the turmoil of the business.

Augie had brought in a scraggly little fir tree early in December. Though Bitsy had scoffed at it, by nightfall, she'd clothed it with strings of popcorn and a few bits and baubles. Goldie had come home from work the next day with a dozen shimmery gold glass balls the size of plums, and Vashti had strung a garland of dried cranberries. The little tree stood in splendor now, with several small packages resting at its base. Each of the residents had stolen in sometime during the morning to add their gifts to the pile.

They took their time opening them, lingering to look and exclaim over each item as it was unwrapped. Vashti felt the presents she'd chosen went over well. Goldie put on her silver cross pendant at once, thanking Vashti prettily. Bitsy and Augie declared it was a right pretty necklace and suited her well. Bitsy's face flushed with pleasure when she opened a package of cosmetics that Vashti had asked Goldie to help her select at the emporium—hand cream, face cream, and two shades of rouge.

"There, now, you knew I was getting low, didn't you?" Bitsy opened the little pot of scarlet rouge. "What a pretty color."

Buying cosmetics had long been an expenditure for business in Bitsy's life, but her lower income for the past six months had made them a splurge. Vashti was satisfied that she'd chosen something Bitsy would appreciate.

"Miz Adams has ordered in some pretty new colors of lip rouge," Goldie said. "That 'poppy petals' is my favorite."

In the past, Vashti had given Augie a bag of penny candy for Christmas, but this year was different. He and Bitsy were married now, and they'd unofficially claimed Vashti as part of their family. She'd felt something more consequential was indicated, and after a great deal of thought and observation in the kitchen, she'd made her selection.

Augie's big hands fumbled with the ribbon and brown paper on her package. She almost warned him to be careful but held her tongue. She'd wrapped it carefully to prevent an accident.

"Well, there." Augie's smile spread across his face as he gazed down at the new butcher knife. "I can't wait to cut up a few chickens. This looks like a mighty fine blade. Thank you, missy."

Vashti hugged herself, pleased with the pleasure she'd brought those she loved.

"Here's what we got you. It ain't much, but I hope you like it." Bitsy placed a package in her hands.

Vashti opened it and stared down at a pair of silk stockings folded on top of a book.

"My own Bible." She fingered the black leather cover and smiled at them. "Thank you both."

"That was Augie's idea," Bitsy said. "I got the stockings."

"I needed a new pair desperately."

Goldie, who had the comfort of regular wages, pushed another parcel into her hands. "Open mine."

Vashti tore the paper off the squishy package and laughed. Inside was a boy's woolen cap with earflaps.

"That's in case you get to ride the stagecoach this winter. I didn't want you to freeze your ears. But look inside."

Vashti turned the cap over and tugged at the wad inside it. Out came a pair of kitten-soft leather gloves. "Oh! Thank you!"

She and the Moores settled back to watch Goldie open her gift from them. Vashti thought she'd never had such a cozy, contented Christmas. Not since her parents had died, anyhow.

Her thoughts drifted to Griffin and Justin. Were they having a good time today? Trudy had told her after the last shooting club meeting that she and Ethan had invited them to the ranch for the day. Would they have asked Griffin if his nephew wasn't living with him, or if Griffin wasn't renting the Dooleys' old house? How had Griffin spent his past Christmases, anyway? It made her sad to think he'd been alone in that grubby little room behind the smithy.

Things had changed for the better this year—for both of them. She sent up a silent prayer of thanks.

"Who's ready for dried apple pie?" Augie asked.

Vashti realized she'd hardly heard a word as Goldie opened her gift of a Bible and stockings like hers. She jumped up. "I'll help you, Augie."

Only one thing could make this day more perfect. That would be Griffin forgiving her part in the stagecoach upset and looking on her as a capable driver. More than ever, she determined to keep up her practice and be ready to step into a driving job in the spring. If he would only look at her with a smile in those big brown eyes.

"What are you sighing over?" Augie asked as he opened the pie safe.

"Nothing. Just Christmas. You and Bitsy are awfully good to me and Goldie."

"You've done as much for us as we have for you. We won't ever have any kids, so you girls kind of fill a gap there. For Bitsy especially." He shrugged. "She'd be terrible sad if you was to leave. That's not to say she wouldn't want you to find matrimonial happiness of your own, you understand. She'd love some grandchildren one day."

Vashti smiled and reached for her apron. "If that happens, I won't go far. I promise." *Maybe no farther than two blocks up the street.* She shoved that thought aside. Griffin was still mad at her. He'd never look at her as marriageable. With a shock, she realized she almost wished he would. But would she rather he saw her as a sweetheart or as a potential driver? That would be a difficult choice.

★ CHAPTER 15 ★

On the last Sunday in February, Griffin and Justin had an invitation to dine with the Reverend and Mrs. Phineas Benton after services. Griffin trimmed his beard and sponged the worst spots off his good shirt that morning. He eyed Justin critically as the boy combed his hair back with water.

They'd lived in Hiram's old house for two months. Griffin liked having a solid roof over their heads and space to put their stuff—though he didn't like having to heat such a big house. It took far too much coal, in his opinion. They hardly used the parlor, but they did use the kitchen, and they both had bedrooms. He'd let Justin take the downstairs chamber, which was closer to the stove. Griff slept upstairs by himself, where there were two good-sized rooms and a large landing.

He didn't suppose he would ever have enough furniture to fill the place. Trudy Chapman had given them a table for the kitchen, and Isabel Fennel, whose father used to own the stage line, boardinghouse, and various other concerns, had told him to take a bedstead and two chairs from the Fennel House. Terrence and Rilla Thistle, who ran the boardinghouse for Isabel, weren't too happy. They'd not only lost a steady-paying customer during the slack wintertime, but now they were losing furniture, too. Still, Isabel owned the stuff, so Griffin guessed she had the say-so.

Isabel wasn't so bad. The skinny schoolmarm had scared him to death last year when she'd visited him at the smithy and babbled on about marriage and such. But nothing had come of it, and now she seemed to fancy Doc Kincaid, so that was all right. Personally, Griffin preferred females a little less bookish. And ones with a little roundness to them.

A certain female with auburn hair came to mind, but he banished the notion. He'd tried not to think any more appreciative thoughts about Vashti. After all, she and Johnny Conway were the two responsible for staving up his Concord coach back before Christmas. When he reminded himself of that, it was easy to stay slightly perturbed with Vashti.

"You ready, Justin? We'd best get over to the church. Don't want to miss Sunday school."

"Aw, do we have to?"

"Yes, you have to."

"Mayor Nash is teaching my class about the forty years in the wilderness. It's more boring than dry corn bread."

"Well, just you wait until you get into Judges. Then things will perk up." Griff grabbed Justin's hat off a hook near the back door. "Put those earflaps down. It's cold this morning."

Justin had been pretty good about going to church ever since Griffin had moved him out of the boardinghouse. He didn't complain much, and he seemed to like Pastor Benton. Too bad Peter Nash's lessons fell on the dry side. The truth was, Griffin had only started attending Sunday school himself since Justin came. Prior to having a youngster in the house, he'd gone to morning worship only. But he couldn't send the boy off alone when the pastor taught a perfectly good class for grown-ups. So they went each week, and Griff had picked up quite a few tidbits from the study of Proverbs that he hadn't known before. Like the verse that said getting into someone else's fight when you shouldn't was like grabbing a dog by the ears. He liked that one. He'd picked a few fights in his day.

Someone had shoveled the sidewalk all the way from the Spur & Saddle at the south end of town to the Nugget on the north end. Snow was heaped between the walk and the street. The wind whistled cold and sharp up from the prairie, and Griffin leaned into it until they got around the corner, where several houses shielded them.

"Do you think it was wrong to put all the Indians on the reservations?" Justin asked as they trudged along.

"What put that notion into your head?"

Justin shrugged. "Pastor Benton said last week that we're supposed to be kind to folks, no matter what color they are."

All sorts of thoughts zipped through Griffin's mind—how his father had fought in the War Between the States; what the outcome of that meant to all the slaves; and the more recent Indian conflicts. Ethan Chapman had served in the Bannock War, and Griffin had gone with a group of men to help when Silver City was attacked. How could he tell Justin it was wrong to fight the Indians? Was it?

"I don't know," he said. He didn't suppose that answer would satisfy a fifteen-year-old boy.

But Justin only nodded, frowning. A few steps later, he said, "I don't know, either. Ma used to be kind to the black washerwoman that came to do laundry for us, and she let her bring her little girl with her. But them Injuns. . ."

"You didn't see any Indians on your way here, did you?" Griffin asked.

"A few at Fort Laramie. And we passed some on the road."

"Well, some folks say we ought to get rid of them all, but I can't agree with that."

"You can't?" Justin asked.

"No. They're people, same as us. Some of 'em steal. But then, some white men do, too." He really should have sent Justin to school this winter. Then Isabel could answer these prickly questions.

"You know any Injuns?" Justin asked.

Griffin nodded. "A few. And they're Indians, not Injuns. Blackfeet, Snake. . .I know several, as a matter of fact."

"Any of them good?"

"Yes. One of them used to scout for the army. Probably some other Indians think he's bad because he helped us. But I've talked to him several times, and he seems like a decent person. Doesn't believe like we do, but he actually bought a horse off me once—didn't try to steal it."

"So he was an exception."

"I didn't say that. But some folks think all Indians are thieves."

They'd reached the church, and Griffin was glad. He hoped Justin would forget the issue and not bring it up later. Did all parents go through this?

During the worship service, Justin fidgeted a lot. The boy hadn't said much about Sunday school, but he kept swiveling his head to look at other people. Across the aisle, the Nash boys sat with Tollie Harper. Ben and Silas Nash were close to Justin's age, and Tollie was a few years younger. Justin had asked once if he could sit with the boys. Griff had almost let him go, but then he envisioned the mischief he'd have gotten into at that age—and remembered why Evelyn had sent Justin out here in the first place—and he'd told him, "You stick with me."

Griffin tried to set a good example for the boy by paying close attention to the sermon. That was kind of hard, since Vashti and Goldie sat right in front of them, along with Augie and Bitsy Moore. Vashti wore a very modest green dress that came right up to her neck. He thought it must be new this winter—he wasn't sure. But she looked nice from his vantage point, with her auburn hair wound up on the back of her head, above the high collar. He could just glimpse a little white strip of skin at the nape of her neck. A tiny brown mole contrasted with the whiteness of her flesh. Did she even know it was there?

Justin stared at him, and Griffin jerked his eyes straight ahead and squared his shoulders. The pastor was talking about why Jesus had to die on the cross. Griffin determined to pay close attention in case Justin asked any questions later. Pastor Benton had a way of explaining things. Within fifteen seconds, he'd forgotten all about the little mole on the back of Vashti's neck. Almost.

That afternoon, after a delicious dinner of ham, cornpone, and carrots, Pastor Benton invited Griffin into the parlor with him. Somehow or other, Mrs. Benton had cajoled Justin into helping her wash the dishes—something he griped about at home. Griffin was glad to have a few minutes of respite from the boy's constant surveillance. Besides, as long as Apphia kept him in the kitchen, Justin couldn't bring up controversial topics.

"What did you think of the message this morning?" the pastor asked.

"Oh, you did fine, Preacher." Griffin sipped his coffee.

"No, I don't mean my delivery. I mean, what did you think of the sermon itself?"

Griffin swallowed and set his cup down on a bitty little table that sat between their chairs. "Well, I . . ."

"Yes?" The minister leaned forward eagerly.

"It's a subject I've wondered about before."

"How so?"

"Well, you said nothing we do can get us to heaven—that it was all Christ's doing."

"That's right."

Griffin shook his head. "My ma used to tell me to be good. You know, don't lie, don't steal, do my chores well. If I didn't, she said I wouldn't go to heaven."

The pastor smiled regretfully. "I'm afraid a lot of people have that misconception."

"But isn't that what real religion is? Obeying God?"

"Yes, in one sense. But you can't truly obey God if you don't believe in Him first."

Griffin squeezed up his eyes and looked that one over. "Yup. Reckon that's right."

"And you do believe in God, don't you?"

"Of course." It was almost insulting that the preacher would ask. "How could anyone not believe in God?" Even the miners who used to come to town Saturday night and shoot up the saloons believed there was a God. They just weren't acquainted with Him.

"And do you believe in Jesus Christ as your Savior? That He died for your sins?"

"Well. . .sure."

Pastor Benton looked as happy as a pup with a hock bone. "What about Justin? I'm delighted that you've been bringing your nephew to church and Sunday school. Do you think he knows the Lord?"

Griffin puzzled over that one. "Well. . ." He had no answer.

"Griffin, since you're responsible for Justin now, it's your duty to consider his spiritual education."

"Ah. . ." Griffin wasn't quite sure what that meant. "We pray before we eat."

"That's good. Have you talked to him about God and sin and right and wrong?"

"Maybe some. Right and wrong, I mean." Griffin winced and glanced toward the kitchen. "Justin was in some trouble back in Pennsylvania."

"I see. And his mother hopes he'll behave better out here?"

Griffin scratched his chin through his beard. "I'm not really sure what she hopes. Sometimes I think she just doesn't want to hear if he gets into any more scrapes."

"So she's transferred her obligations as a parent to you."

That didn't sound very complimentary of his sister. "Evelyn was having a hard time after her husband died, and she's got other young'uns to consider."

The pastor nodded gravely. "I want you to know that I'm praying for you, and I'll be here to help you in any way that I can."

"Well, Justin likes you. That's good. Oh, and if he asks you about the Indians. . ."

Phineas Benton's eyebrows rose. "Indians?"

"Yeah. Whether reservations are right or wrong and such."

"Ah. I see the boy is a thinker."

"You might say that."

"Well, as I said, I'm here to assist you anytime you need it."

"Good. I appreciate that. And if you hear about Justin sneaking into the Nugget or smoking behind the schoolhouse, or anything like that, you tell me, all right?"

"I surely will, but it's my hope that you won't have to deal with such things."

"Oh, I've already dealt with one of them."

The pastor's eyes flared, but Mrs. Benton and Justin came in from the kitchen just then.

"There, the dishes are all clean until the next meal," Apphia said with a bright smile. "Justin was a big help."

"That's wonderful," said the pastor.

The boy plopped down on a chair. "Reverend, I heard that they don't let Mormons vote in Idaho Territory. What do you think of that?"

The glance Benton threw at Griffin was near panicky. Griffin almost laughed.

★

On Monday morning, Vashti bundled up and walked over to the Bentons' house. She didn't go to the door but walked around back in the crunchy snow, to the stable behind the house. She came every morning that Bitsy didn't need her help. Augie had rigged up a little box stove so she could have some heat while she practiced her driving. She didn't like to burn much fuel, as firewood and coal were expensive. But Bitsy said it was an investment in her future and a better job, so she kept coming.

She rolled the door open and jumped back. Three figures huddled together on the board floor near the stove. Cautiously, she poked her head back inside and eyed the young men critically.

"What are you boys doing here?"

"Uh. . ." Ben Nash stared at her, clearly groping for a believable explanation.

Justin, on the other hand, just looked at her with his jaw set in a determined frown.

Will Ingram spoke up. "We're meeting here for a clubhouse, ma'am."

"A clubhouse?" Vashti focused on Will. "Shouldn't you be in school?"

"I ain't going anymore. Justin doesn't go to school, and he's my age, so I told my pa I'd had enough learning."

"Oh really." She turned her gaze on Justin. No sense blaming him. It wasn't his fault that Griffin hadn't enrolled him in school.

"How about you, Ben? Has your father let you quit school, too?"

"Uh. . .no, ma'am. I just ran over here on recess, and. . ." He trailed off, his face flushing.

"Mighty long recess." Vashti stepped forward and closed the rolling door, then held her hands to the stove. "Thanks for making my fire up for me. What are you doing?"

"Uh. . ." Ben seemed to be stuck on that syllable. It didn't matter. She'd seen them shove cards and coins into their pockets when she'd arrived.

"Well, let me tell you something," she said, looking around sternly at the three. "Mr. and Mrs. Benton are friends of mine. They let me use this stable to practice my driving." She nodded toward the rig hanging from the rafters and the reins threaded from it to her wagon seat. "I'm pretty sure they wouldn't like it if someone else came in here without their permission. Especially not if those people were doing something they would consider immoral."

"Like what?" Will asked with a smirk.

"Oh, like drinking, or smoking, or. . .gambling."

"Huh. You should talk."

Vashti glared at him. "I beg your pardon."

Justin whirled on Will. "Hey, quit that. She's a nice lady. And she works for my uncle."

Will scowled at Vashti. "Well, I've had enough for today, anyhow. You kids need to grow up." He walked to the door and let himself out.

Ben gulped and edged toward the gap. "I'd best get back to the schoolhouse."

"Yes, I'm sure Miss Fennel wonders what's keeping you," Vashti said.

Ben scooted out. She turned to face Justin.

"Well now, it's just you and me. How'd you come to be trespassing with them?"

Justin gulped. "Are you going to tell Uncle Griff?"

"Should I?"

"No, ma'am. Because it will never happen again."

"Here? Or anyplace?"

Justin was silent for a long moment, holding her gaze.

"You know your uncle cares about you, Justin. He wants to see you grow into a responsible man."

Justin's chin sank, and he lowered his gaze. "I don't want to make him mad."

Vashti considered that. Was he afraid Griffin would punish him harshly? At last she said, "Griffin treats you all right, doesn't he?"

"Yes, ma'am. And I don't want to make him sorry that he took me in."

"Then you shouldn't sneak around places you shouldn't be, doing things you know you shouldn't do."

Slowly Justin nodded. "I know that's right. And I'm sorry I did it. I'm sorry Ben got involved, too. He's a good kid, and his dad would be really upset if he found out Ben skipped school."

Vashti walked over to the wagon seat and climbed onto it. She found it very important that Griffin should succeed as a father and that Justin shouldn't go astray. But would he listen to her?

"This is a very small town, Justin. Ben's father sees most of the residents several times a week. If you don't think that one of them— or Ben's younger brother or the teacher—will tell him Ben wasn't in school this morning, then you underestimate the power of the wagging tongues in a small town."

He stood still, staring at the floor for a minute.

"Where's your uncle this morning?" Vashti asked.

"He had to drive down to the swing station to pick up a wagonload of oats. I wanted to go, but. . ."

"But what?"

He flicked a glance at her. "He told me to stay and clean up the barn."

"Did you do it?"

"Partly."

"Hmm. Do you wish you were in school with Ben and his brother?"

Justin shrugged. "I don't mind being done with it. I like helping at the livery. Didn't think I would, but I sort of do, now that I'm not afraid of the horses anymore."

She untied the reins and laced them through her fingers. "Let me ask you something. How do think Griffin will feel if he comes home this afternoon and you haven't done the work he set you?"

"Disappointed, I guess."

"Now imagine him coming home and finding the livery all

cleaned up, even neater than he asked you to make it. How would he feel then?"

Justin pressed his lips together. "Good, I guess."

"Mmm. And you'd feel good, too. Griffin's not a hard man, Justin. I thought he was at first, but I was wrong. He's got a big heart, and he's got a soft spot for you."

He took two steps toward her and looked her in the eye. "I didn't mean to do anything bad today."

"Maybe you should tell Mr. and Mrs. Benton that."

He sucked in a breath. "Do they have to know?"

"The way I see it, if you don't tell them and I don't tell them, and then their stable burns down or they find something broken or missing from here, that wouldn't be good, would it?"

"I won't come back. Honest."

"No, but Will might. If not here, then somebody else's barn where they don't go very often. Will's a kid who has a nose for trouble. You don't want to be like him, Justin." She looked him up and down. "I think you want to be a man, not a brat of a kid that folks hate to see coming."

"Is that what people think of Will?"

"I didn't say that."

Justin stood frowning for a moment, then went over near the stove and picked up his hat. "I guess that was your wood we burned."

"I'll make good use of what heat's left."

He nodded and went to the door. "If you're going to tell Uncle Griff. . ."

Vashti smiled. "Why don't you just make things so that it won't matter whether I tell him or not?"

He eyed her suspiciously, then gave a nod and went out. He rolled the door shut behind him.

Vashti laid down the reins and hurried to the entrance. She pushed the door over an inch and squinted through the crack. Justin walked to the back door of the pastor's house and knocked. Mrs. Benton opened the door and greeted him with a wide smile. Vashti pushed the door shut and went back to her imaginary stagecoach, sending up a prayer for Griffin and Justin. Even if Griffin didn't like her, she wanted to see that family turn out all right.

★ CHAPTER 16 ★

Spring came slowly to Fergus, a gradual shrinking of the snow and a hint of red on the ends of branches as buds swelled. Mud the length of Main Street heralded the thaw, and suddenly ranchers were putting their wagon boxes back on the axles and leaving the sleigh runners in the barn.

As the bare earth appeared, ground squirrels came out, and large flocks of birds winged overhead. Vashti spent more time in the Wells Fargo office, selling tickets for the stagecoaches to the flat regions and telling folks who wanted a ride up to Silver City or Delamar that they'd have to wait a little longer.

Bill Stout came in one morning, his eyes twinkling. "Well now, Miss Edwards, you been practicing your driving skills?"

"I surely have. Missed a few days during the coldest of the cold spells, but I've been out there every day this past month and more."

"Want to try driving real horseflesh?"

She caught her breath. "You mean it?"

Bill nodded. "Hiram Dooley's got a team of four we can borrow this afternoon with his wagon. Thought we'd take them out the Mountain Road, just to let you get the feel of them."

"I'd love to!" She'd rather drive a six-horse hitch and a fine Concord coach, but this would be experience driving genuine, living horses.

She and Bill bundled up in their overcoats, woolen hats, and mufflers, and she pulled on her trousers beneath her skirt. Bill borrowed two saddle horses from the livery, and they rode out to the ranch Hiram Dooley managed. The rancher met them in the dooryard to help hitch up the horses. Vashti doffed her gloves when she took the reins. Bill joined her on the wagon seat, and they set off. The exhilaration of really driving kept her warm for the first half hour on the road, but then her hands began to chill.

"How do you keep your hands warm on a cold day?" she asked.

"Sometimes you've got to wear gloves, but unless it's a flat, smooth road and a steady team, I wouldn't recommend it. What I have in my gear is a blanket with slits in it for the reins. It's not ideal, but it lets me thread the reins through and keep my hands under the blanket. It's awkward, but it's a sight better than frostbite. Short of that, in a pinch you can take all the reins in one hand for a short time and put the other hand in your pocket, but you're not really in control if you do that."

Vashti nodded. Maybe sitting out the winter driving season hadn't been such a hardship, after all.

The horses shied as a small herd of pronghorns appeared in the road ahead.

"Easy now." She kept firm pressure on the lines and talked calmly to the team. The pronghorns skipped off across the hillside, and the horses gradually fell back into their road gait.

Bill nodded. "Spring's coming, for sure."

"Seems like it took its time."

When they returned from their drive, Bill nodded toward the hitching post before the ranch house, where a buckskin mare was tied. "Looks like Miz Chapman's here to see her brother." He helped Vashti down from the wagon. "Go on into the house and visit with her. I'll put the horses away."

"Oh no," Vashti said. "You're not doing all the work."

He frowned at her flowing skirt. "But you're not wearing your boy togs."

"Well, it won't be the first time I've unhitched a team while wearing a dress."

While they worked, Hiram came into the barn. "How'd your driving go?"

"Wonderful," Vashti said. "Thank you so much for letting me use your team."

Hiram nodded and looked to Bill.

"She did fine," Bill said. "I reckon she can handle six if she gets a chance."

Vashti glowed inside. "That's nice of you."

Bill shrugged.

"Trudy's here," Hiram said. "She's putting the kettle on."

"Go on." Bill reached to unbuckle the last harness. "We'll take care of this. Scoot."

"All right, since you gentlemen insist." Vashti hurried to the back door of the house. The ranch had belonged to Cyrus Fennel, the schoolteacher's father. Mr. Fennel had owned half the town in the old days, and now Isabel did. But after her father's death, Isabel had reached some sort of arrangement with Hiram to run the ranch for her so she could live in town. Vashti wasn't sure what Hiram's duties entailed, but she knew his job made it possible for him and Libby Adams to get married soon. At one of the shooting club meetings, Libby had told the ladies of her engagement amid blushes and prompts from Trudy.

Vashti had never been to the ranch before. She couldn't tell much so far. The barn was huge, and several outbuildings circled the barnyard. A bunkhouse, she supposed, and maybe a smokehouse and a woodshed. And the house was fine. Nicer than any in town, with the possible exception of Charles and Orissa Walker's yellow frame house.

She knocked timidly on the kitchen door. Trudy opened it, grinning. A large, flower-print apron covered most of her blue wool dress, and her hair was done up in braids, wrapped on top of her head.

"Hello! Come right in. How was your drive?"

"Magnolious," Vashti said. "Not like sitting on the box of a stage, but closer than I've been all winter."

Trudy chuckled and led her to the table. A plain brown teapot sat steaming in the middle, and two ironstone mugs and a jug of cream waited for them.

"Isn't this the grandest kitchen you ever saw?" Trudy asked.

Vashti looked around. "It's almost as big as the one at the Spur & Saddle."

"Yes, and that nickel-trimmed stove cost old Cy Fennel a pretty penny, I'll wager."

"Must have taken a lot of effort for Oscar Runnels to haul it up here with a mule team," Vashti said.

Trudy sat down and poured the tea. "Isabel took the fine china with her to her new place in town, but she left a lot of dishes and things here for Hiram. Of course, Libby has her own dishes, too, and furniture and linens. I'm not sure where they'll put everything when they get married."

"I've been in Mrs. Adams's rooms," Vashti said. "She's got beautiful things."

"Yes. Hiram's going to move it all out here before the wedding. The whole shooting club can help them move."

"That will be exciting. When's the day?"

Trudy shrugged. "The Hamiltons said they'd come back in the spring and bring her the rest of the money for the emporium. When they take over, she'll be ready to marry my brother. And the Hamiltons want to buy her whole building and live in the apartment upstairs, so it's perfect."

"Say, maybe you could give some of the extra things to Griffin and Justin."

"That's a good idea."

The men came in and joined them for hot tea, but as soon as he'd downed his cupful, Bill said, "We'd best push off, Georgie. It'll be getting dark soon."

"Georgie?" Trudy eyed him askance.

"It's actually my real name," Vashti said. "Georgia. When I'm riding the stage, the fellows call me George so the passengers won't know I'm—" She broke off and felt her face warm. "I guess it's no secret. Folks hereabouts know, anyway."

"Might protect you some," Hiram said.

Vashti looked over at him. It was the first thing Hiram had said since he came in from the barn. She'd rarely heard him speak, but she guessed he'd found enough words to convince Libby Adams to accept his suit.

When she and Bill got back to the livery stable, Griffin had one of the stagecoaches on the main barn floor and was greasing the axles. Its red paint and gold trim glinted in the afternoon light. He glanced up as they led their mounts in.

"Road to Silver's open."

Bill smiled. "Well now."

"You up to taking the run tomorrow?"

"Sure."

Griffin straightened and picked up the grease bucket. "If it doesn't rain, you should be able to go all the way through. There's a couple of real soft spots, though. If we do get some weather, you might have to lay over at Sinker Creek."

"I can handle it, boss."

Griffin nodded and fixed his gaze on Vashti. "What about you? You ready to shake out your pants and boots?"

She caught her breath. "You want me to ride shotgun for Bill tomorrow?"

"No, I've got another job in mind for you." He came over and stood facing her soberly. "I'm taking over the mail run as far as Catherine. Johnny's going to drive that route for the time being. Thought I'd put you on the Reynolds-Nampa run."

Vashti almost said, "Who's driving?" but Griffin said, almost as an afterthought, "With Ned Harmon."

Her heart raced. "You mean—"

"That's right, missy. You'll drive and Ned will watch your back."

She could hardly breathe. "Oh! Oh! Thank you!" She flung herself at him and reached up to embrace him. His bushy beard tickled her cheek.

"Hey! Watch it!"

She backed away, mortified.

Griffin laughed. "I'm holding a bucket of axle grease, gal. Don't think you want that all over your pretty dress, do you?"

"No, sir." Vashti laced her fingers together and squeezed her hands tight. She was going to drive the stage. And she'd hugged

Griffin. But maybe it didn't matter. He thought her dress was pretty. Did that mean anything?

She gulped and looked over at Bill.

His eyes twinkled. "Well, there. I guess your hard work paid off."

The next morning, Vashti came down the stairs at the Spur & Saddle in her masculine attire. Augie and Bitsy were laying out clean dishes for the noon traffic, which had been dismally slow, and Augie was polishing the big mirror behind the serving counter that used to be the bar.

"Look at that, dearest," Augie said to Bitsy. "It's our little boy going out to play."

Bitsy laughed. "Don't mind him, honey." She came over to stand before Vashti and placed both hands on her shoulders. "You take care."

"I will. And they treat me nice at the home station in Nampa."

"Good."

"Who's riding shotgun for you?" Augie asked.

"Ned Harmon."

"Well, he's not so bad. Just don't let him go carousing tonight. Remind him he's got to bring you home safe tomorrow."

"She can't stop Ned if he wants to drink." Bitsy frowned. "I expect knowing Griffin will be watching him when you get back here will keep him from doing too much damage."

"I hope so." Though Vashti had never ridden with Ned before, she remembered nights when he'd come into the saloon and drunk himself under the table. But those weren't times when he had to go on duty the next morning. Cyrus Fennel ran the line then, and he wouldn't have stood it. "I'm just glad I'll finally be sitting in the driver's seat."

"Well, don't you get too cocky," Bitsy said. "There's more to life than driving stage and showing up men who don't drive as well as you."

Vashti laughed. "I'm as green as they grow, Bitsy. I know I've got a lot to learn before I'm as good as Bill, or even Johnny."

"Well, at least you've got an old hand riding shotgun. Ned's all right, and he's been riding these roads for twenty years." Bitsy pulled her close and kissed her. "We'll see you tomorrow."

Vashti arrived at the livery an hour before the stage was scheduled to leave. She inspected the coach. It had sat idle all winter, but Griffin had gone over it and touched up the paint. The glass in the side lantern gleamed, and every piece of hardware shone.

Griffin grinned at her as he came in the back door with two large mules. "You want to brush these fellows down?"

"I'd love to." Vashti stowed the bag with the few things she'd need for her overnight stay in Nampa and went into the first stall.

Griffin brought in two more mules then stopped at the opening to the stall. "That's Blackie. He'll be your off wheeler. I'm giving you mules because there's still some heavy going in places."

"I don't mind." She didn't really, though she'd always imagined driving horses. But mules were surefooted, and they ate less than horses. They pulled better in mud or sand. "What's the other wheeler's name?"

"Elijah."

She smiled and ducked under Blackie's neck to brush his other side. When she'd finished with him, she went to Elijah's stall to groom him and check his feet. By the time she'd done with him, Marty Hoffstead was grooming the swing mules, so she headed across the barn floor to where the leaders were hitched.

Bill Stout came in, looking about in the dim, warm barn. "There you are." He walked over to Vashti. "Came to wish you luck."

"Thanks, Bill. That means a lot."

He brought his left hand from behind his back and held out a coiled driver's whip.

"Brought you this."

Vashti looked down at it, her eyes filling with tears. "Aw, Bill! That's the nicest thing you could have done." She sniffed.

He held the whip away from her and cocked his head to one side. "You ain't gonna cry now, are you?"

"No, sir." She straightened her shoulders and smiled. "I'm going to drive like a man."

Bill chuckled. "Don't know as you need to go so far as that, but the passengers might lose confidence in you if you're bawling all the way to Nampa."

"I won't be. I'll be singing inside."

Griffin, who had brought Blackie out to hitch to the coach, called, "Don't sing out loud. They'd really get nervous if they knew they had a soprano driving them."

If she heard one more word of caution or advice, Vashti might just pop her cork. With effort, she kept smiling and holding in her eagerness to be on the road.

When the mules were harnessed, Griffin walked over to her. "I reckon you want to drive the rig up to the office."

"I sure do, if you don't mind."

"Not a bit. I'll ride along with you. Marty will come over to the office, too, to hold the team while the passengers load."

Bill touched her shoulder lightly. "Godspeed, Georgie. I'm heading up to Silver in a couple hours, but I'll be thinking of you."

"Thanks, Bill." She lifted the whip in salute and hurried out to mount the box.

Marty held the leaders' bridles, and Griffin stood beside the coach.

"Ordinarily I'd help you up, but. . ."

She grinned. "It'd look pretty odd if you did." With a bound she was in her seat and gathering the reins.

Griffin climbed up beside her.

"Where's Ned?"

"He'll join us at the stop."

She adjusted the leathers along her fingers and looked ahead between the leaders' twitching ears, then nodded to Marty. He let go of their heads, and she clucked and slackened the reins.

"Let's go, boys!"

The mules set off at a laconic walk. Vashti felt her cheeks warm. This was no way to start her first official drive. Stubborn mules. She passed the near reins into her right hand and grabbed the whip Bill had brought her. She shook out the coiled lash and snapped her wrist, making the lash pop. At once, Blackie and Elijah picked up a trot, and the other four mules followed their lead.

She tucked the whip behind her boots and sorted out the lines again. When she had the six reins in position and felt the slightest tension on every one, she dared to look up again. The mules were still trotting as they passed Walker's Feed Store, almost to the Wells Fargo.

"Not bad," Griffin said.

She laughed. "Thank you."

"You'll have one sack of mail going out."

"Oh." She gulped. Carrying the mail was a heavy responsibility.

"There'll be more when you come back tomorrow."

She nodded. "All right. Ned and I can handle it."

"Nothing stops the U.S. Mail. Nothing."

"Yes, sir."

"You mind that place where the rocks are on both sides of the road?"

"Yeah. Where the outlaw hides."

"That's the spot. If he's there, you're not giving up the mail."

"I'm not giving up anything, Mr. Bane."

His eyes narrowed. "That's the spirit. But you know, if it comes down to it, the mail…well, it is the U.S. Mail, but it's not worth your life or Ned's."

"I'll keep it in mind."

"You got a weapon?"

"Got my pistol in my bag."

"I'd feel better if you and Ned both had long guns. I'll let you take that rifle I keep at the office."

"If you want."

"I do."

She guided the mules ever so slightly, and they eased on over to the boardwalk in front of the stage line office nice as you please. Several people had gathered to wait for them.

"Whoa now!" They stopped in formation and stood swishing their tails. Vashti exhaled. So far so good. She wouldn't be so nervous with Ned beside her instead of the boss. She glanced up at Griffin.

His brown eyes glittered. "Nice job, George. I think you'll do."

He hopped down and she stared after him, feeling hot all over. Who'd have thought a good word from the boss would mean so much to her?

Ned was waiting near the office door, his shotgun over his shoulder, but he straightened as Griffin stepped up on the walk. He gave Vashti a nod, and she returned it. Marty came trotting up the sidewalk, went to the front of the team, and held Blackie's cheek strap as a precaution. Ned followed Griffin into the office. The mail sack went into the coach first. The mail always took priority over passengers. If there was a lot of mail, sometimes passengers had to sit on the roof. But since this batch originated in Fergus, there wasn't much. The hundred residents hadn't written more than a couple of dozen letters.

Griffin plopped the sack into the coach while Ned stood by, watching the people milling about. The boss stood back and smiled at those who waited.

"Passengers can board now."

Ralph and Laura Storey climbed into the stage, along with two miners who'd walked down from Booneville. When all were in, Griffin shut the door and went back into the office. Ned came over to the front of the coach and mounted the box beside her, holding his shotgun.

He eyed Vashti critically. "They tell me I'm s'posed to call you George."

"Right. That's my name. George Edwards."

He laughed. "Can't fool me. Take it away, George."

At that moment, Griffin emerged from the doorway carrying a Spencer rifle. He handed it up to Ned.

"Pass that to the driver."

Vashti took it and slid it into the space behind her feet, where her small bag lay.

"It's all loaded," Griffin said quietly, "and here's a box of extra cartridges."

Ned stowed the ammunition under their seat. Griffin stood back and nodded soberly.

Vashti took up her whip, gave Marty a nod, and cracked the lash in the air. "Up now!" The mules broke in a smooth trot. She shot one glance over to the boardwalk. Griffin smiled, and she smiled back before facing the road.

★ CHAPTER 17 ★

Aside from oozy mud in the low spots and a washed-out roadbed near a creek, the drive wasn't too bad. Every stream filled its banks nearly level as snowmelt thundered down from the mountains. Even as they bowled along past the rock formations with Ned keeping a sharp eye out for the bandit, Vashti's heart sang, and she noted patches of brown grass as they came down to the flat land, with hints of green beginning to show.

The river crossing on the ferry threw her heart into her throat. She'd never ventured on the water when it flowed this high and fast. Though the mules were firmly hitched, she and Ned stood at their heads and stroked them as they were pulled across the roaring, swirling flood.

They made it through to Nampa without mishap. When they pulled up at the home station and the tender came to open the door for passengers, Vashti let out a deep sigh and coiled her whip.

"Not half bad," Ned said. He climbed over the top of the coach to get the luggage out of the boot.

Vashti scrambled down. The stationmaster was handing over the mail sack to the postmaster.

Mr. and Mrs. Storey were staying with the coach all the way to Boise. Laura leaned out the window and called, "Nice driving, George."

Vashti turned and grinned at her, and Laura winked.

"Thank you kindly. I hope you folks have a pleasant journey," Vashti said.

The home station in Nampa was run by a married man, and his wife and three children helped with the animals and the meals. A hearty dinner and a bunk in the ten-year-old daughter's room awaited Vashti. Ned went off to bunk in a room they kept for the usual stage drivers and messengers. The whole Gayle family knew she was a woman, but even the youngsters were careful to keep quiet about the open secret. When Vashti retired, young Becky was already asleep in the top bunk. Vashti put on her flannel nightgown, snuffed the candle, and slid in under a pile of quilts on the lower bed.

"Thank You, Lord." She yawned, letting the warmth and her full belly and the comfort of a safe home lull her into sleep without being more specific about her gratitude.

The next morning when they set out for Fergus, four horses pulled the stage. They would change to a team of six mules again at the Democrat Station.

Vashti was confident they'd have a good trip. True, they had to cross the swollen river again, but the ferrymen knew what they were doing. They took on two bulging sacks of mail and five passengers. One of the riders was Emmaline Landry, a member of the shooting club. She rode in the coach with three miners going to Silver City and a cowboy hoping to get a job in the hill country. When Vashti climbed to the driver's seat, Emmaline was already quizzing the cowhand about where he'd previously worked.

Early in the afternoon, they approached the rock formations again. The breeze off the mountains chilled Vashti. She buttoned her fleece-lined jacket around her neck and wrapped her black knit muffler snugly beneath her chin, wishing she'd worn a knit cap instead of her cowboy hat.

They changed the team for four different horses at a swing station and headed steadily uphill toward Fergus. They breezed along on the flatter stretches. The Democrat Station was next, where they'd get a late dinner while the tenders swapped out the team. Then the road would be mostly uphill.

Ned slumped down in the seat, but his eyes continually roved the landscape. His leathery skin made him look old, but his hair still held its medium brown color. Vashti figured he had to be past forty, but nowhere near as old as Bill.

"How long you been doing this job?" she asked.

"Too long. I'm thinking of quitting after this summer."

Vashti looked over at him in surprise. "What would you do?"

"Maybe take a swing station. Griffin has trouble keeping good tenders in some spots. I think I could make a go of it and have a garden and maybe some beef."

They approached the uphill grade, heading toward where the rocks were, and Vashti urged the horses not to slacken their pace.

"Think that outlaw's out here?" she asked.

"Too early. Another month or so, when it's warm enough to sleep out and be comfortable. The ground's not even dry yet."

That was some solace. The leaders tried to slow down. One of them broke stride. She grabbed her whip and cracked it. They surged forward. She eased up on the reins, keeping the lightest touch possible, and called out to them.

"Move, you! Get along."

Ned jerked his shotgun to his shoulder.

Vashti caught some movement in her peripheral vision and shot a glance off to the left side of the road ahead, where Ned was aiming.

"It's that outlaw." She reached for the whip again.

"If it's him, he's got friends."

Vashti's chest ached. She snapped the whip, popping the lash between the lead team's heads. "Hee-yah! Up now!"

She didn't look to the side again but watched the road ahead. In the distance, a report sounded above the creaking of harness and the pounding of hooves.

"What was that?" yelled one of the passengers.

"Land sakes, are we being held up?" Emmaline called.

"Easy, folks," Ned replied. His shotgun went off and Vashti jumped. The horses sprang into a canter, outrunning the acrid smoke. Vashti's heart hammered and her hat flew off.

Above the noise, Emmaline screeched. Vashti gritted her teeth.

Emmaline belonged to the Ladies' Shooting Club. Now would be a good time for her to stay calm and produce a weapon. She wished she could use Griffin's rifle, but she'd best concentrate on keeping this stagecoach rolling. The road passed closest to the rocks about three hundred yards ahead. If they could get past that, the road was clear to the Democrat Station.

She raised her whip, tempted to let the horses feel the lash. But that wasn't the way of a stagecoach driver. She cracked it again, first on the off side, then the near side. The team tore along the road with the coach swaying behind them on its leather thoroughbraces. Several shots powed behind her, loud and close. The passengers must be firing out the windows.

"How many?" she yelled at Ned.

"Three that I can see. One was on foot, but one's riding up behind." He braced himself and rose so he could fire over the top of the coach. The blast deafened Vashti for several seconds.

As they neared the boulder closest to her route, a mounted man emerged from behind it. He planted his dark horse facing her, directly in their path.

Vashti gasped. She shot up a prayer and determined to use Johnny's strategy. *I'll run right over him!*

"Hee-yah! Hee-yah!" She half stood and cracked her whip repeatedly. What she wouldn't give for the team of six matched bays Bill was likely driving today. They held the speed record for this stretch of road. She could feel the leaders' hesitation through the reins. They were almost on top of the rider. Could she hold them steady and pull out Griffin's rifle at the same time?

The outlaw turned his horse slightly sideways and trained his rifle on them.

"Ned?" Vashti called.

Ned's shotgun went off again with a crash. Emmaline screamed.

A horseman charged up beside them and edged past the front of the coach, up next to the wheelers. The rider had a cloth tied over his mouth and a hat pulled low over his eyes. As he gained on the stagecoach team, Vashti stared at the gunman in her path straight ahead.

Another shot cracked, and Ned dropped his gun. It slid down the box and lodged next to her feet.

"Ned!" She looked over at him as he crumpled on the seat, hugging his arm to his side.

★ CHAPTER 18 ★

The horses gave up suddenly, with the leaders stopping in their tracks before the steely-eyed gunman in their path. The wheelers ran into them and stopped, too, with loud oofs and squeals. The second outlaw rode up to the leaders and grabbed the near horse's bridle. The gunman who'd sat his horse square in the path rode forward.

"Throw down your weapons." He held his rifle aimed at Vashti.

She gulped, measuring their chances.

"Do it now, Driver."

"I need to help my messenger. You've shot him." She glared at the outlaw.

"Land, Benny, she's a girl." The man holding her team laughed.

"Shut up. I got eyes in my head."

Vashti hadn't realized until that moment that after her hat flew off, her hair had tumbled down. Strands of it flew loose about her face in the breeze.

"Hand the gun down," the one called Benny ordered.

A third outlaw had walked up to the side of the coach and stood just below her. He must be the one with no horse. Even in the chilly wind, beads of sweat stood on his brow. Vashti reached down and took Ned's shotgun. She was tempted to blast one of them.

The man on the ground must have sensed her thoughts. He pointed his gun at her and snarled, "Don't even think it, darlin'."

She held the shotgun out barrel first, and the man took it. Would they find Griffin's rifle and her pistol? She tried not to give away any more by staring coldly into his eyes, but it was hard not to think of the guns behind her feet.

"Now get down," the one called Benny said.

Besides Benny, the man holding the team, and the man on foot, a fourth outlaw had dismounted and stalked over to the door of the coach. "Time to get out, folks."

Vashti half hoped one of the passengers would let loose a barrage of gunfire so she could dive for Griff's rifle. The man covering her with his weapon glared at her.

"Move."

She looped the reins around the brake handle and turned to Ned. He huddled on the box, squeezing his arm. Blood soaked the sleeve of his wool jacket.

"Ned, are you hurt bad?"

"Hurts like blazes but could be worse." His teeth never opened as he ground out the words.

"I said get down, and I meant it. Both of you."

"Best do as they say." Ned winced.

"I'll help you." Vashti went over the side backward and groped for the step, keeping her eyes on Ned. "Can you come over this way?"

He groaned and slid into her seat.

Vashti hopped down and stood, anxiously staring upward and trying to ignore the gunman at her back. She held up her hands in a futile gesture of aid. Ned's boot found the step, and he oozed over the side of the box, sliding down in a rush. As she tried to catch him, she got knocked to the ground for her trouble.

"Take it easy, folks. Just get out nice and slow," the fourth robber said.

Vashti picked herself up and crouched beside Ned. "You okay?"

He moaned and blinked up at her.

One of the horses whinnied, and she glanced over to see one of the outlaws cutting through the leaders' harness. She opened her mouth to protest, but a stern voice behind her said, "I wouldn't try anything if I were you."

A quick assessment told her that one of the outlaws guarded her and Ned while another cut the horses free of their harness and a third one terrorized the passengers on the other side of the coach. Their outraged spluttering was all she needed to hear. The outlaws were robbing them blind.

Vashti focused on Benny, the leader. She tried to memorize as much about him as she could, but he'd masked his features well.

The one who'd cut the lead team free called, "All right, Benny. These two look good. Did you check for a money box?"

"Not yet." He dismounted and came over to the coach.

On the ground beside Ned, Vashti could see his feet as he went to where the passengers stood. "We don't have a treasure box. No money today."

"Shut up," said the one standing over her.

Vashti watched him. When he shifted so he could see Benny checking the inside of the coach, she leaned close to Ned. "Can you help if I make a move?"

His eyes widened. "Don't. They'll shoot you."

"Well, this ain't worth much." Benny threw the two mail sacks out of the stage and hopped to the ground. He and one of the other outlaws cut open the sacks and turned them upside down, dumping the mail on the ground. Letters and advertisements fluttered in the breeze and skimmed over the damp earth.

Another outlaw crowed. The one who'd cut the harnesses had mounted the coach and found Griffin's rifle.

A bitter taste filled Vashti's mouth. "I should have dropped the reins and gone for the gun first thing."

"We didn't know there were four of them." Ned grimaced and closed his eyes. "Don't do anything stupid."

She gritted her teeth and watched, but the man jumped down from the box with Griffin's rifle and extra ammunition.

"Got me a nice Spencer."

The robbers gathered, showing each other their plunder. The one who'd robbed the passengers had taken two pistols, some money, and a pocket watch. The others had collected Ned's shotgun, Griffin's rifle, and the two lead horses.

"All right, let's get out of here," Benny said.

The man who had guarded Vashti and Ned backed away from

them. From behind his neckerchief mask, he said, "You know, if we leave those other two horses, they'll be at the next station in ten minutes."

"We don't need four horses," said Benny. "Two is enough."

"We could shoot the extras," another man offered.

Heat surged through Vashti. She leaped up and faced them with clenched fists. "How could you be such monsters? I understand you wanting money, and even shooting Ned, because he'd have shot you if you didn't. But to kill innocent animals?"

Benny laughed. "Little spitfire. Maybe we should take her along with us."

"She's got grit," one of his friends admitted.

"Hey, can you cook?" Benny called.

"Let's go," the fourth man said, looking up the road toward the Democrat Station. "Someone else could come along any minute."

"Come on. Bring the other nags." Benny took the rope his cohort had tied to one of the lead team and rode off with the two horses in tow.

The man with no mount ran to the tongue of the coach and unhitched the wheelers from the whiffletrees. He stood on the tongue and swung onto the near horse's back, coiling up the long rein, and rode off after his comrades with the off wheeler still hitched to his mount and keeping stride.

Vashti stood staring after them. Tears streamed down her cheeks.

"My dear, are you all right?"

She turned. Emmaline and the other passengers had come around the coach.

"I'm fine, but I'm mad. They shot Ned and stole all our horses."

Emmaline pulled her into her embrace. "We're all alive. That's what counts."

"They took my gun and my watch," one of the men said.

Another of the passengers knelt beside Ned. "Are you all right, sir?"

Ned groaned.

"Do any of you have medical experience?" Vashti asked.

None of the men spoke, but Emmaline came forward. "I've tended the sick and wounded. I can take a look."

Vashti sobbed. "I have to collect the mail."

One of the miners shook his head. "What next? Girls driving stagecoaches!"

"We'll help you, ma'am," said the cowboy. He stooped and grabbed an empty mail sack. "Come on, boys, let's get as much as we can. This little dab of a gal will probably be in trouble if we don't save the mail."

Vashti wiped the tears from her cheeks and walked over to where Emmaline was prodding Ned's arm.

"I think we should take his coat off and try to stop the bleeding."

Vashti knelt beside her. "How bad is it?"

"I'm not sure, but it's possible he could bleed out while we wait for help." Emmaline touched Ned's cheek. "Ned, can you hear me?"

He let out a groan, and his eyelids fluttered.

"Help me," Emmaline said to Vashti. The two of them struggled with Ned's coat but at last got him out of it. He began to shiver.

"It looks real bad." Vashti swallowed down her revulsion at the bloody mess.

"It must've hit the bone," Emmaline said. "We'd best wrap it tight and run to the station."

"Yes. And get his coat back on if we can. I'll see if there's a rug or a blanket in the boot of the stage."

She hurried to the back of the coach but found nothing useful. The cowboy came over with a full mail sack.

"Here's what we've got so far, ma'am. Picked up the easy piles first. The other fellows are chasing letters that blew away."

"Thank you. That's extremely good of you. I wonder if any of you have anything in your bags that we can use to keep Mr. Harmon warm?"

He tipped his hat back and looked into her eyes. "I could build a fire."

"That would be wonderful. Thank you." She hurried back to Emmaline. "The cowboy is going to try to find enough combustibles to light a fire. I think I'd better leave for the Democrat Station."

"Ned needs the doctor." Emmaline frowned down at the patient. "If he loses too much blood. . ."

Vashti nodded. "All right. I'll check to see if those outlaws found my pistol. I think it's still in my bag."

"I sure wish I'd had my gun with me. I was going to take my rifle, but Micah said we'd be fine with the stagecoach guard to protect us. Only two of the other passengers had weapons, and as far as I could see, they couldn't shoot worth beans. Of course, the stage was lurching and bumping."

Vashti went to the front of the coach. Most of the harness had gone off with the horses, but the coach itself seemed unscathed except for some splintered wood on the front corner. She hugged herself and shivered. That must have been a bullet meant for her.

"Thank You, Lord."

She climbed onto the box and rummaged under the seat. Her small canvas bag was intact. Nestled between her spare socks and pantalets and her hairbrush was the revolver she'd bought from Libby Adams last year. She tucked it in her belt and climbed down.

She walked back to Emmaline and Ned. "Guess I'd better hoof it for the next station. It'll probably take me a half hour, so don't expect anyone to come too soon."

Emmaline stood. "I'll try to keep Ned comfortable. I was thinking we should get him off the ground, but if that fella's going to light a fire. . ."

Vashti squinted up the road. "Someone will come along before dark, I'm sure, but we can't count on it. If I get to the Democrat Station, we can bring the relief team of mules to come and haul the coach in."

Emmaline nodded. "Makes sense to me. They don't have a telegraph, do they?"

"No. But they might send a rider for Sheriff Chapman—or back to Nampa for the lawman there."

"And the doctor. Don't forget to tell Ethan to bring Doc along."

"Right."

Vashti could see the cowboy on the hillside, breaking low branches off a small pine tree. The miners had scattered, chasing the mail. She was thankful for that, but Ned's condition worried her. She waved at Emmaline and set out.

When she was out of sight of the stagecoach, the vastness of the land swept over her. She quickened her steps. These hills could swallow up a woman—or a stagecoach full of people or a band of outlaws.

Years ago, she'd felt alone like this—when she'd left home. She'd set out alone then, too, but not in a desolate place like this. Her only thought then had been to escape Uncle Joshua. Aunt Mary didn't believe her when she'd told her that her uncle had grabbed her in the barn and kissed her. Vashti was Georgia then, and eleven years old. The kiss had repulsed and confused her.

Aunt Mary confronted her husband when he came in later. "What did you do to this child?"

"Nothing. Just teased her a little. What did she say?"

"Said you kissed her."

He laughed. "She doesn't like me. She'll say anything."

She'd avoided him for weeks but saw him watching her. Aunt Mary sent her out to gather eggs before school one morning. He caught her as she came from the chicken yard.

"No, no!" she screamed. As she writhed in his grip and tried to pull away, the seam of her dress tore at the waist. At last she got away and ran for the house. She burst through the back door, crying.

"Why are you running, Georgia? And where is your egg basket?"

She halted before Aunt Mary's disapproving glare.

"I. . .I dropped it."

"Oh, look, you've torn your dress."

Uncle Joshua came through the back door. "Is the little girl all right?"

"She ripped her dress." Aunt Mary looked at him questioningly.

"I told her not to climb over the fence like that." He shook his head.

Georgia stared at him.

"Go on," Aunt Mary said with a sigh. "You'll have to wear your Sunday dress today. And if you come home with a tear in it, young lady, you'll be in trouble."

"Yes, ma'am." Georgia scurried to her attic room and changed. She hoped Uncle Joshua would be gone when she went down the ladder and took the torn dress to Aunt Mary, but he was sitting by the cookstove, drinking coffee and talking about planting corn. Vashti snatched her lunch pail off the windowsill and ran out the door. But she didn't go to school that day. Instead, she took the road for Cincinnati.

Now she wasn't terrified the way she had been then, but she'd be lying if she said she wasn't afraid. Ned could die before she got back. The outlaws' brazen thievery and disregard for life angered her, but it might have been worse. They could have killed her and the passengers as easily as not.

"Thank You, Lord, for preserving us. Please keep Ned alive until we get him some help." She began to jog, but the cool wind tore her breath away. She'd heard it was harder to breathe, the higher you got in the mountains. Wolves might lurk out here, and there were outlaws, though they'd probably ridden off a good ways to divide their plunder. Was one of the four in the gang the same man who had tried unsuccessfully to rob the stagecoaches last year? Maybe Ned was right and he'd rounded up some friends to come and help him.

She reckoned she was halfway to the station when she heard footsteps behind her.

★ CHAPTER 19 ★

Griffin paced the boardwalk in front of the Wells Fargo office. He shoved his hand in his pants pocket and pulled out Cy Fennel's old watch. No getting around it. The stage was an hour late.

Micah Landry came out of the Nugget and strode across the street toward him. "No sign of them?"

Griffin shook his head and came to a decision. "I'm going for the sheriff."

Micah tailed him over to the jailhouse, next to where Griffin and Justin now lived. Ethan's paint horse was tied out front. Griffin hurried up the walk and threw the door open. Justin was seated across Ethan's desk from him, playing a game of checkers with the sheriff. The small potbellied stove kept the office toasty, and a pot of coffee steamed on top.

"Howdy, Griff." Ethan straightened and smiled at him.

"The stage is late."

"Oh?" Ethan frowned. "How late?"

"A whole hour."

Micah came in behind Ethan and shut the door. "That's right, Sheriff, and my wife is supposed to be on it."

"Let's telegraph Nampa and see if they left on time."

"Good thinking."

Ethan slapped his hat on and reached for his jacket. Justin tagged along as they left the jail. They reached the boardwalk, and Bitsy Moore met them in front of the old haberdashery. Beneath her wool coat she had on her red bloomer costume, and a jaunty red hat with a dyed pheasant feather graced her head.

"Griffin Bane! Where's Vashti?" She hurried toward them, her high-buttoned boots clomping on the walkway.

"Don't know," Griffin said.

"So I was right and the stage is late?"

"Looks that way."

Bitsy seized Ethan's wrist. "What are you going to do, Sheriff?"

"Send a telegram to Nampa. If they left on time, we'll ride out and see if we can get word of them."

Maitland Dostie's cramped office barely held them all. They waited in silence after Maitland sent Ethan's message off.

After ten minutes, Micah Landry swore. "I could have been halfway to the first stage stop by now."

"Take it easy," Ethan said.

Griffin started to speak but thought better of it. The river was high this time of year. Maybe they shouldn't have started running the stages yet. But it hadn't rained for several days, and the ferrymen didn't take foolish chances.

The telegraph clicked. "Here comes something." Maitland picked up his pencil and began to write. After a moment, he sighed and shook his head. "Not for you."

They all let out a pent-up breath.

"I've got to take this message to Ted Hire at the Nugget," Maitland said.

Griffin grabbed his arm. "You can't leave now. This is an emergency."

"I could deliver the telegram," Justin said.

Griffin had almost forgotten he was there. "To the Nugget? I don't think so."

"I'll run it down there," Micah said. "But if you hear anything while I'm gone, make sure you let me know."

Maitland held out the sheet of paper, and Micah ran out the door.

Griffin resumed pacing. Bitsy leaned against the counter and drummed her fingers, while Ethan leaned against the wall with his arms folded. Justin stood in the corner, quiet for once.

Micah came back five minutes later, and as he opened the door, Maitland's telegraph key began to click again.

"That's your message," he said after a moment. The others crowded up to the counter and watched him. After a minute, the clicking stopped, and he looked up and read: "'To Sheriff Chapman, Fergus, from Wells Fargo agent Gayle, Nampa. Confirmed stage left 9:00 a.m., crossed river safely.'"

Griffin exhaled again. "They got across the river."

Ethan nodded. "That's good news. I guess we'd better ride out and see where they are."

"I'm coming with you," Bitsy said.

Ethan frowned. "Best not, Miz Moore."

"My girl is on that stage. If something's happened, you may need a woman along."

"My Emmaline's on it, too," Micah said. He and Bitsy eyed each other.

Bitsy nodded. "I hope they're a comfort to each other. Sheriff, we're going with you."

Ethan threw his hands in the air. "All right, but hurry."

"Will you lend me a horse, Griffin?" Bitsy asked.

He nodded. "Let's not waste any more time."

"Me, too?" Justin jogged along beside him, down the street toward the livery.

Griffin shot him a glance. "You'd best stay home."

"He's nearly a man grown," Ethan said quietly.

Griffin frowned. "All right. But if there's trouble, you do what I say, you hear?"

"Yes, sir." Justin sped ahead of them to the stable.

Vashti whipped around, holding her pistol in front of her. Fifty feet behind her was the cowboy who'd gathered the fuel for a fire. He held his hands up and stopped walking, but he smiled.

"Hey, there! Didn't mean to scare you. I thought, in light of what happened, it might be good for you to have some company."

Vashti let out her breath and stuck the holster back in her belt. "Come on, then. It's not much farther."

"A gal like you shouldn't be out here alone."

"It's broad daylight," she said.

"Yes, and we was robbed in broad daylight."

She walked along, kicking at a stone now and then. When it came down to it, she was glad it wasn't dark, but she didn't say so. "Think those outlaws went far?"

The cowboy shoved his hat back a little. "I dunno. They could have a hideout somewhere close."

"There's a lot of stage lines around here," Vashti said. "Could be they'll strike again."

"They didn't get much today."

"Huh. They got four good horses. I don't know what my boss will say."

"He won't fire you or anything, will he?"

She shrugged. Her innards dragged, and she'd have turned back if Ned weren't hurt so badly. Griffin had gone white-hot angry when Johnny had tipped the coach over last fall. She could picture his face when she told him what had happened this time.

"My name's Clell," the cowboy said.

"Oh." She looked full at him for the first time. He was about thirty, medium height, and spare. "I'm George."

He laughed. "Right."

Vashti shrugged. She didn't care what he thought.

"What do you do when you're not driving the mail coach?" Clell asked.

Was he trying to flirt with her? What was he thinking, when Ned lay bleeding to death?

"Come on if you're coming." She hurried her steps as they rounded a corner. Up the slope, she saw the northernmost fence line of the Democrat's pasture.

Griffin and the others saddled their mounts quickly and added Marty to the group. Three miles out of town, they met a lone rider.

He cantered toward them and pulled up when he got close. "Hey, Sheriff!"

"What is it?" Ethan called.

Griffin recognized one of the tenders from the Democrat Station. "Where's the Nampa stage?"

"Robbed. My boss took two men and a fresh team out. It's not supposed to be far from the station, but we didn't hear any gunfire, so it must be a piece."

Griffin swallowed hard. "Where's the driver?"

The man grinned. "The boss made her stay at the station with his wife. She didn't want to, but she was wore out and cold. Boss said they'd bring in the coach and passengers and then she could drive on to Fergus. But she says they need a doctor bad."

Griffin urged Pepper into a gallop. As he rode away he heard Ethan telling Justin to ride back to town as fast as he could and find Doc Kincaid and his deputies.

At the stage stop, Griffin jumped to the ground and ran inside.

Mrs. Jordan turned from where she was tending the stove. "Mr. Bane, you scared me."

"Where's my driver? Georgie Edwards."

"She's yonder." Mrs. Jordan nodded toward a doorway. "Poor thing was plum tuckered out." She stepped to the closed door and tapped on it. "Miss Edwards? You awake, honey? Mr. Bane's here."

A moment later the door swung open. Vashti stood blinking at him, wearing her green woolen trousers and tan shirt, with the vest hanging open and her auburn hair spilling all rumpled about her shoulders. Her green eyes looked suspiciously red-rimmed.

"I'm sorry."

"For what? Getting held up?"

"Everything." Tears coursed down her cheeks. "They wouldn't let me ride back to the stage with them. I wanted to."

"Of course you did."

"She walked up here to tell us what happened," Mrs. Jordan said.

Ethan knocked at the front door and stuck his head in. "Should we go on, Griff?"

"Yeah. I'm coming. Just wanted to hear from Vashti what happened."

"Four men, in the rocks. Three of them had horses, and the other one was on foot. They shot Ned and stole all four of our horses." She raised one hand to her mouth. "He needs a doctor, Griff."

"We sent for Dr. Kincaid," Ethan said.

Griffin reached out and ran his hand over her tangled hair. "Are you all right, Georgie?"

She nodded. "And the miners that rode with me tried to save the mail. I think they got most of it."

"All right. You rest, and we'll head out there."

"Please let me come." Her eyes brimmed with tears. "I hated to leave Ned like that."

"Anyone else hurt?"

She gulped and shook her head. "They shot him in the arm, but it's an awful mess. He's bled a lot. Emmaline was tending him when I left. Please let me come with you."

Griffin looked at Ethan, and Ethan shrugged.

"The men took all the horses we had here," Mrs. Jordan said. "That fella that walked in with Georgie took one, and my husband and Buddy. We sent Hank to find you, Sheriff. That and the team of mules was all the critters we had."

"You can ride with me." Griffin wasn't sure where the words came from, but they popped out of his mouth. Vashti dashed back into the bedroom and came out hauling on her coat.

He made sure she had a hat, her muffler, and gloves before he let her swing up behind him on Pepper's back. She reached around him and hugged his middle as Pepper began to trot.

"You going to be okay?" he yelled over his shoulder.

"Yes. But loping would be better."

He loosened Pepper's reins, and Vashti clung to him like a little burr. She was warm against his back, and when the road got steep and Pepper slowed down, she leaned her head against him. Griffin wished they could keep on riding like that a ways, but the coach wasn't far. Ethan, Bitsy, Micah, and Marty reached it before he did.

From a distance, he could see Emmaline run into her husband's arms. Those two might bicker, but when it counted, their marriage was solid.

The passengers surrounded Ethan. All of them talked at once, but he held up his hands.

"Easy, folks. I want to hear from all of you, one at a time. First I want to take a look at Mr. Harmon and assess the damage. As soon as the rest of my deputies get here, I'll be going after those outlaws. Anything you can tell me about them will help.

Griffin pulled up near where Ned lay on the ground, turned, and grasped Vashti's hand. She held on to him and slid to the ground.

"How's Ned?" she asked Emmaline.

"Not very good, but the men from the station said they'd sent for a doctor."

"That's right, and a couple of my deputies, too."

Emmaline nodded. "Well, I hope Ned makes it. Mr. Jordan brought two blankets when he came with the mule team, and we've got Ned lying on one, with the other bundled around him."

Vashti knelt beside Ned, and Griffin crouched on his other side.

"Ned, can you hear me?" Vashti's tone was a wheedling plea, but Ned didn't open his eyes.

Griffin clenched his teeth. He didn't want to lose Ned, especially not this way. Vashti would never stop blaming herself, though it wasn't her fault.

"Harmon!"

Ned twitched.

"Harmon, open your eyes," Griffin barked. "I want to know what happened here."

Slowly Ned's eyelids lifted. "Sorry, boss. We tried."

"I know you did." Griffin reached out a hand to clap him on the shoulder, but stopped. It would probably hurt Ned. "I'm not blaming you or Vashti. Listen, we've got Doc Kincaid coming, and some men are hitching up a new team. Will you let me lift you into the stage?"

"Whatever you say, boss."

Griffin slid an arm under the wool cocoon, judging where Ned's knees were. His other arm he carefully snaked under Ned's back. Ned moaned, and Vashti reached from the other side to help lift him enough for Griffin to get his arms in place.

"Make sure the coach door's open," Griff said. He stood with the limp burden in his arms and walked toward the stagecoach.

★ CHAPTER 20 ★

Vashti's stomach fluttered as Griffin counted out her pay. As each bill hit her palm, the tickle rose until she felt she'd burst. She'd be able to pay Bitsy and Augie for a month's board and room and also pay what remained on her bill at the emporium.

"Twenty-eight, twenty-nine, thirty."

"Thanks, Mr. Bane."

"Griffin. And you earned it."

She ducked her head. "I still feel like I ought to help pay to replace the horses and harness."

"Unfortunately, that's part of my business expense." Griffin's eyes narrowed. "Are you sure you want to do the mail run again next week?"

"Yes, sir. I'll be ready."

"Because I could maybe find someone—"

"I want to do it."

He looked down into her eyes for a long moment. Vashti felt the tickle move toward her heart. He looked handsome today, less shaggy. Must have trimmed his beard.

"Vashti, I don't want anything to happen to you."

She nodded. "Thanks. But don't you think they'll go more for the stages carrying treasure? Some of the mines will be shipping out gold again, and payrolls will be coming through regular."

"Yes. And you'll be carrying some of them."

She gulped. "Think the outlaws know when we're carrying something valuable?"

"It'll be pretty much even odds this summer. If they hit often enough, they'll get something eventually." Griffin scrunched up his mouth. "I guess I'd better line up some more guards. If we've got to deal with an outlaw gang this year, it's going to be rough going, no matter what run you're driving."

"Sheriff Chapman didn't find any trace of them, did he?"

"No. He was able to track them until they got into the rocks."

"I'm really sorry they got your rifle and Ned's shotgun."

Griffin sat down on the edge of his desk. "Well, don't fret over it. I'll put in my claim to the government for the guns and horses, since it was a mail coach. And I'll make sure you've got a good messenger next time."

She looked up at him. "Who will ride with me now that Ned's laid up?"

"We'll see." He looked worried, and she didn't press him.

"I'm really sorry we lost the horses, but I especially regret that Ned got hurt."

"Have you seen him since we brought him in?" Griffin asked.

"Yeah, I went over to Doc's yesterday. Ned was in a lot of pain."

"I saw him this morning." Griffin's brown eyes darkened. "The doc says his arm may never be right again. And he'll need several weeks to recuperate."

"He lost a lot of blood," Vashti said softly. "I should have stayed and helped Emmaline."

"You couldn't do that and go for help, too. Besides, she had the other passengers. Doc said there wasn't much else they could have done besides what she did—making a bandage and trying to stop the bleeding."

Vashti looked down at the money in her hand. Maybe she'd spend a dollar or so on a new petticoat for Emmaline, to replace the one she used to cover Ned's wound.

On Monday morning, Vashti mounted the stage box outside the livery and prepared to drive around to the Wells Fargo office. She had a team of four sorrel horses for a mostly downhill run. Warm sunshine beat down on her. She couldn't see any snow left in town, though the mountains still wore their snowy cloaks, and the north slopes probably still held pockets of it. The horses stamped and nickered, ready to go. If not for the fresh memory of the robbery, she'd have sung a tune under her breath.

To her surprise, when the mail and nine passengers were loaded and a green wooden treasure box was lodged in the front boot, behind her feet, Griffin himself mounted the box and sat down beside her, holding two guns. He slid a Sharps rifle under their seat and held the shotgun up against his shoulder.

"Ready, Georgie?"

She swallowed hard. "*You're* riding with me?"

"Yes, I am."

Her pulse rate doubled. Could she ride twenty-five miles with Griffin Bane sitting next to her? How would she ever concentrate on the horses? It was bad enough sitting next to her boss, but lately her heart had done strange things when he was close by. She'd pondered far too much on the brief ride she'd taken on his horse with him the day of the robbery.

"What about Justin?" she asked. "What'll he do tonight?"

"Mrs. Thistle is happy to have him as a guest once more."

Vashti gathered the reins. If she put it off any longer, they'd start late, and keeping the conversation going wouldn't put a different shotgun rider at her side. She signaled Marty, and he let go of the leaders' heads. They broke into a smooth trot. This was her dream—good horses, a fine coach, and an open road. She wouldn't think about the stretch that ran through the rocks.

The first few miles flew by, and she felt Griffin's gaze on her often while they were still near town. Of course he was watching her, evaluating her performance. She tried not to let it bother her, but she couldn't help being conscious of him every moment.

After their brief stop at the Democrat Station, where Mrs. Jordan ran out to say hello to "Georgie," Griffin sat tall, constantly scanning the broken landscape. Neither of them mentioned the rocks, but as they approached the site of the robbery, Vashti felt his tension. He sat alert and tight as a bowstring, holding the shotgun at the ready.

She kept the horses moving at a swift trot. Her heart raced as they came to the spot where she'd first seen the lone outlaw six months ago.

"I think the robber who didn't have a horse last week was the one who was out here last summer," she said suddenly.

"Ned told me as much."

She looked over at him in surprise. "He did? I thought of it that day, but I paid more attention to their leader. Benny." She shivered.

The horses kept on, never once breaking stride. She wondered where the others were now—the ones that were stolen. Would their own faithful coach horses be used to attack them?

Ahead was the narrow place where rocks loomed on both sides of the road. Vashti's lungs ached, and she held her breath.

Griffin never took his eyes off the rocks as they rolled smoothly toward the danger point. Of course, if that gang were to stop them again, the outriders would likely have shown themselves by now. You just never knew. And the coach traveled downhill. Far more likely they'd be attacked going the other way, as Vashti and Ned had been. A team plodding uphill was much easier to stop than one barreling down an incline. Still, he remained vigilant, aware of the nine passengers, the mail, and the treasure box. The weight of his responsibility pressed on his broad shoulders.

All of that and Vashti.

If his small part of the Wells Fargo line suffered another holdup, who knew what would happen? He might lose the mail contract. That could ruin him financially. Already he was hard pressed, and if he wasn't reimbursed for last week's losses, he'd have a difficult time of it. But worse—people's lives were at stake. Was he foolish to run a stage here when danger lurked?

The coach rumbled through the narrow place, and he exhaled heavily. Ahead lay more rocks—the ones most of the outlaws had hidden behind. But the best place to waylay them was now behind.

He glanced over at Vashti. A drop of sweat trickled down her temple, though it wasn't overly warm.

He wanted to assure her that they were safe, but he couldn't say that for sure. Not yet. So they rode on in silence, down out of the hills and toward the river.

As the rocks fell farther behind, Vashti uncoiled. Her jaw relaxed and her shoulders fell a little. She resumed talking to the horses now and then, as she had during the first part of the ride. He admired the way she kept all the reins almost taut—but without pressure on the horses' mouths. Gentle contact, that was all. She may not have driven long, but she had a feel for the horses.

He relaxed just a hair and scanned the terrain on both sides of the road. After looking ahead for a long minute, he allowed himself another glance at her. Watching Vashti drive was like listening to rippling music with auburn hair and green eyes.

She shot a reproachful glance at him, and he looked quickly away. When had he started caring for her? He'd known her for years in a general way—had let her bring him drinks when he visited the Spur & Saddle in the old days, before Bitsy got religion. She was a bar girl, that was all. Then she became a churchgoing member of the community. A sister in Christ, according to Pastor Benton, and Griffin supposed that was right. It had taken everyone awhile to get used to thinking of Bitsy and "the girls" that way.

Now she was much more. His employee. A member of the Ladies' Shooting Club. A holdup survivor. And one tough stage driver.

His gaze strayed to her face again, and she glanced over. She bit her bottom lip as she adjusted the reins. Was she nervous because he was here? He smiled.

Her green eyes widened for an instant, and she looked forward again, frowning slightly. The ferry lay a half mile ahead. Across the river, and they'd be nearly there. Griffin almost regretted that the end of their ride together approached. But there was the return trip tomorrow. And tonight in Nampa.

Normally if he rode one of the stages, he had a couple of drinks after dinner and hit the hay early. He didn't have enough spare cash to get into a poker game. He'd always figured he shouldn't gamble unless he wouldn't miss the money if he lost. Now and then, he found a saloon where they had a singer or dancers. One time in Boise, he'd been to the theater. That was something he still thought about two years later. Colorful costumes, music, pretty ladies, and a magician who wasn't half bad.

But tonight. . .he made himself not look at Vashti, but he knew he wouldn't stray far from the home station if she stayed there tonight.

They rolled up to the ferry, and Vashti called, "Whoa now." The team halted smoothly. The ferryman and his two helpers came out of their shack.

"How many passengers?" the ferryman called.

"Nine," said Vashti.

The man looked sharply at her.

"Good afternoon," Griffin said, louder than he'd intended. At least he distracted the ferryman.

"Oh, Mr. Bane. How are you, sir?"

"Fair to middlin'." It pleased Griffin to see the man straighten his shoulders and snap orders to his men. The ferryman knew who would pay him at the end of the month for the Wells Fargo coaches, employees, and passengers he carried.

Griffin climbed down and watched Vashti scramble to earth. If one didn't know, he supposed one might think she was a young man. But how many people between Fergus and Boise didn't know? The ferryman's helpers sneaked glances her way as they prepared to load the stage onto the ferry. After the horses and coach were aboard, the passengers and a few locals who'd been waiting to cross the river got on.

"Sir," said one of the men who'd ridden the stage.

Griffin paused beside him. Vashti went forward to make sure the horses were calm.

"Can I help you?"

"Yes, sir. I want to get to Mountain Home as quickly as possible, and I wondered if I should have bought a ticket all the way through."

"When you get to Boise you can get it, but I think you'd do better to take a train from there." He looked toward Vashti.

One of the ferryman's helpers leaned on his pole, smiling at her. The ferry was pulled across the river with ropes and a team of mules on the other side, so the men didn't have to work too hard during the crossing. This one seemed to think that gave him license to bother the passengers.

"So, you got plans for tonight, honey?" The man leaned toward Vashti and arched his eyebrows coyly.

Vashti appeared to notice him for the first time and moved around to the other side of the lead horses. The man followed her.

Griffin nodded to the man who was still talking to him. "Excuse me." He cut behind the horses and came up behind Vashti. Over the swirling river, the ferry worker's sugary tones were clear.

"You shy, darlin'? 'Cause I know some fun places we could go."

Vashti, with her back to Griffin, stood boulder still. "Leave me alone."

"It'd be more fun if we was alone *together*. I heard you know how to be a fun kind of girl."

Strange, Griffin had always thought his bulk was too great to ignore, but this fellow had zeroed in on Vashti and didn't appear to see anything else.

Griffin reached out, grabbed the back of Vashti's vest, and yanked her back a step, putting her behind him. He stood in silence, glowering down at the man.

The ferryman's helper looked up at him with his mouth hanging open. "H–h—"

"You plaguing my driver?" Griffin roared.

"N–n–n—"

"Good. Because I could hurl you into the Snake with one pop."

The man gulped and edged away between the horses. Griffin watched him, not moving a muscle until the man had disappeared behind Prince's head.

He turned around. The ferryman clung to the rudder at the other end of the boat, staring at him. Every passenger stared. Vashti stood two feet from him, her lips clamped together.

"You okay?" he asked.

"I could have handled it," she said between clenched teeth.

Griffin blinked. Her face was red, and her eyes were slits of green fire.

"Uh. . ." He glanced up and saw the others still watching. He leaned toward Vashti and said quietly, "Did I do something wrong?"

"You might say that."

"I was just protecting you. You're my employee."

"I told you, I could have handled it."

"He knew—"

"That's right. He knew. And now *everybody* knows." She shook as she spat the words out in ragged whispers. "I could have put him in his place without making a three-ring circus out of it."

He glared down at her. "Fine. Next time I'll just let the womanizers and the drunks hang all over you."

The lines of her face congealed. "He didn't touch me."

"No, but he would have."

"Oh, now you're a prophet."

A man couldn't win. Nothing he could say right now would pacify her. Griffin stomped past her toward the far end of the ferry. The passengers ducked out of his way and grabbed the railing. His shifting weight actually made the ferry rock. He slowed his steps and stayed to the middle of the craft, until he was face-to-face with the ferry's owner.

"Your man was bothering my driver."

The ferryman seemed to concentrate on steering the boat, though it was guided mostly by the pulley system.

"I'll speak to him, but I expect he was just trying to see if the rumors were true."

"What rumors?"

"That you had a loose woman driving stage for you."

Griffin clenched his fists. "I could kill you for saying that."

"That's the word I heard. I saw her last week when she came through with Ned Harmon on the box. The boys didn't catch on 'til afterward, when I told 'em."

Griffin squinted down at the much smaller man, trying to make sense of that. "Why'd you tell 'em?"

The ferryman laughed. "It's a nine-days' wonder, Mr. Bane. Something curious."

"Yeah. Curious."

One of the stagecoach passengers edged in beside Griffin.

"Curious, all right. I had no idea a woman was driving us. She did a good job."

"She's a good driver," Griffin said. "And she's *not* a—" He glanced over his shoulder. Vashti had kept to the other end of the boat. "She's not what you said. I'd appreciate it if you didn't spread rumors to that effect."

"I beg your pardon. I'd heard tell her last job was in a saloon."

Griffin hesitated. "Well, that's not a lie. But there's respectable saloons, you know."

The male passengers standing nearby broke out in laughter.

Griffin gritted his teeth and decided he'd said enough. He kept his distance from Vashti as the ferryman and his helpers brought the boat to shore. Once they'd unloaded and the passengers were back in the coach, he climbed up to the box. Vashti waited until he was settled and lifted the reins. She didn't look at him or speak as she drove toward Nampa. Griffin held his shotgun and watched the edges of the road.

Finally he couldn't stand it any longer.

"Vashti, listen to me. I didn't mean to embarrass you or make things worse for you. I honestly thought you could use some help." He sighed. "You're such a little bit of a thing, and that fellow had the wrong idea about you. I just figured I'd set him to rights."

She looked over at him. "What do you think would have happened if you hadn't been there? You think I'd have gotten mauled?"

He didn't know what to say.

"I'll tell you. I told him to leave me alone. If he hadn't respected that, I'd have gone back to where there were other people, so's he couldn't keep bothering me. If that wasn't enough, I'd have appealed to his boss."

Griffin nodded slowly. "Sounds like it might have been enough."

"Well, if it wasn't, I pack a decent punch."

He chuckled. "I'll bet you do. I'm sorry. I should have let you tend to your own business."

They rode on in silence. When they were a mile out from the home station in Nampa, she looked over at him, her green eyes anxious. "Are you going to stop me from driving?"

"Why would I do that?"

She didn't answer.

His mind whirled. There would be no hiding the fact now that one of his drivers was a female. Would that make his stages more vulnerable? Would robbers throng to the Owyhee Valley to take a crack at the girl driver? He mulled that over as Vashti drove up to the stop. He supposed outlaws might think it would be easier to rob a woman than a man. Or would they find it humiliating and tease each other about how they had to pick on a girl because the men who drove were too tough for them?

He climbed down from the box wearily. He'd had some vague notion this morning of asking Vashti to see the town with him tonight. He almost laughed aloud at the thought now.

Businesslike, Vashti gathered her personal possessions and clambered down. The station agent had opened the door for the passengers, and they piled out, exclaiming about the smooth ride the "girl driver" had given them. Each of the nine men made a point of thanking Vashti before they scattered. She stood there and took it well, smiling and returning their comments.

When the last one walked away with his luggage, she sighed and turned back toward the coach. One tender was leading the team away, and another led out the new four-in-hand.

"How many of the passengers thanked you when they thought you were a man?" Griffin asked.

Vashti's lips twitched. "Nary a one. But then, they'd been terrorized and robbed, so you can't really blame them."

Was this really only her second run? Griffin stared after her as she headed for the house.

Vashti walked slowly and deliberately. She knew Griffin was watching her. She'd hardly had a moment all day when she wasn't conscious of his gaze. Well, she intended to ignore him until time to mount the stage again in the morning.

The next driver, who wasn't under Griffin's supervision, ambled out onto the porch. He nodded at Vashti.

"You George?"

"That's right." Vashti stuck out her hand. "George Edwards, of Fergus."

The other driver, a man of about forty, gripped her hand. "Buck Eastman. I heard you had a holdup last week."

"Yes."

"An' I heard Ned Harmon got shot."

"He did. Our doctor thinks he'll recover all right, but his arm's pretty stove up."

"Too bad."

"Yes, we miss him."

"Who's riding with you?" He looked toward the stage.

"Griffin Bane."

Eastman turned wide eyes on her. "Your boss?"

"That's right."

He shrugged. "I heard he's fair. Maybe doesn't run as tight a ship as old Fennel did."

"Mr. Bane's all right," Vashti said.

Buck nodded. She expected him to move on, but he just stood there.

"Well, I'm hungry, Mr. Eastman, so if you'll excuse me—"

"I heard other things, too, and I guess I heard right."

She pulled back and eyed him suspiciously. "What sort of things?"

"Heard Bane had a woman on his Fergus-to-Nampa run."

"Well?"

He looked her up and down. "I reckon you're the one."

She set down her bag and put her hands on her hips. "Mr. Eastman, I'm a driver. The rest doesn't matter. If you want to make something of it, you go right ahead. But I'd hate to see one driver make trouble for another, even if they work on different branch lines, and even if one dislikes the other."

"I didn't say I disliked you."

"Maybe I wasn't talking about you."

His eyes narrowed, and he held her gaze for a moment. Vashti wondered if she'd made a mistake. He no doubt had a friend nearby—

he must have a shotgun messenger going with him. And she'd told Griffin not to mix into her business.

About the time she'd begun to wonder if she ought to apologize, Buck threw back his head and laughed. "Ain'tchou somethin'? Wait'll I tell Jack."

"Tell anyone you want," Vashti said. "It's no secret anymore."

Buck pulled his hat off and slapped it against his thigh. "Good luck to you, missy. I reckon you're a good driver. I heard it took a whole gang of outlaws to stop you. You take care, now, y'hear?"

"I will. Thanks."

She watched him swagger down to the coach. Griffin stood next to the wheelers, watching as usual. When Eastman stopped to speak to him, Vashti turned away and went inside. Supper and a bunk sounded mighty good. For a brief moment, she wondered what Griffin would do for the evening. The sun was just going down behind the distant mountains. Would he make the rounds of the saloons in Nampa?

She walked to the dining table. "Not even going to think about it."

★ CHAPTER 21 ★

Vashti went downstairs for breakfast early the next morning, wearing her driving clothes. The station agent's wife handed her a plate full of eggs, fried potatoes, and sausage.

"You've got a full stage this morning, Georgie."

"Oh?"

"Five fellows going up to Silver City stayed at the hotel last night. They're going to look at the Poorman mines."

Vashti arched her eyebrows. "That outfit's been shut down for years."

"I know. Wouldn't it be something if they got things running again?"

"Isn't the gold all gone?"

"Oh no. Most of the mines that closed did it because of the bank trouble in California. The owners mostly moved on. Oh, they say the easy pickings are done, but if these fellows have investors, they could get the machinery going again. The money's in ore you have to crush."

Vashti nodded. She didn't know much about stamp mills and all of that, but any investment in the Owyhee Valley would be good news. It would mean more travel on the branch line and more business at places like the Spur & Saddle.

After eating quickly, she went out to the stable. She didn't like to eat when the passengers did. She couldn't politely wear her hat in the house, and if she sat at the table without it, they'd all stare. Of course, she hadn't much hope of keeping her secret any longer.

Her favorite way to spend the last half hour before they left was getting to know the horses. The tenders were harnessing the team. Vashti took a brush and a hoof pick and checked over the leaders. With a pang of regret, she thought of the horses she'd lost last week.

When the stage from Boise rolled in, she was ready. She climbed the box and waited while the tenders hitched up the team—six horses this time—and loaded the mail and the luggage. Eight passengers climbed into the coach, and two men climbed up to sit in the seat on the roof, behind her and the shotgun messenger—Griffin. He was the last to board, looking chipper this morning. He'd greeted the mining men enthusiastically. Vashti eyed him sideways and decided he hadn't been out drinking last night, or not much, anyway. That was good. He'd be alert this afternoon when they hit the stretch leading up to Democrat's. Perhaps she'd misjudged him. Come to think of it, she couldn't remember him ever drinking more than a glass or two. Why had she assumed he'd cut loose last night? Didn't she know him better than that by now?

"Ready, Georgie?"

"Yes, sir." She uncoiled her whip and cracked it. The horses sprang forward. Vashti settled into the rhythm of the stage. Good horses, plenty of paying passengers, and splendid weather. If not for the large man sitting next to her, she might have felt lighthearted. The hulk of a blacksmith had somehow become the man who occupied her thoughts and called to her heart.

Late that afternoon when the team was put away and Marty had reported on business at the livery, Griffin plodded across the street to the Fennel House. His hips and legs felt stiff from sitting so long on the box of the stage.

"Howdy, Mr. Bane," Terrence Thistle called from the front porch. "The boy's over to the jailhouse with the sheriff."

"Thank you kindly. I expect we'll eat supper here." Griffin changed course and headed for Ethan's office.

Sure enough, Justin sat across the desk from Ethan, pushing checkers. Hiram sat on a stool in the corner, whittling and watching the game.

"Well, look at the no-accounts we got here," Griffin boomed.

Justin leaped from his chair. "Uncle Griff! I didn't know you were back, or I'd have come and helped with the team."

"That right?" His statement pleased Griffin, and he smiled at the boy. "You hungry?"

"Gettin' there."

"He's whomping me at checkers," Ethan said.

Griffin touched the top of the stove. It was cold, so he sat on the edge. "Go ahead and finish the game."

Justin eyed him for a second then resumed his seat.

"Your turn," Ethan said.

"Hey, we brought a whole flock of mining men up from Nampa," Griffin said.

Ethan and Hiram looked interested.

"Five fellows from back East. They're looking into reopening the Poorman mines."

"Well, that's news." Ethan nodded, still watching the checkerboard. "I'll keep my ears open when I make my round of the saloons tonight."

Griffin pushed his hat back. "They told me they represent a syndicate in London and they've been negotiating with the owners. They'd like to start taking ore out again."

"That'd be a boon to the valley." Ethan frowned as Justin moved a checker.

"Yup, we need more paying jobs," Griffin said. "They'd put the roads back in shape, too." Of course, some of the mines were still operating, but the population of the Owyhee Valley was far below what it had been two decades earlier, and only a trickle of silver and gold found its way out these days.

Ethan picked up one of his pieces and jumped over two of Justin's checkers. "There! I guess you won't get me this time."

"Did you find out any more about those outlaws?" Griffin asked.

Ethan shook his head. "I took Hi and my two ranch hands and

spent all day yesterday looking for a place they could have holed up, but we didn't find anything. Could be they swooped in here for one job and then cleared out."

"Doubt it," Griffin said. "They'll probably show up on another one of my lines—or wait until they know we've got a payroll in the box."

"Well, if the mines open up again, we'll get some soldiers in here to escort the shipments."

"True."

Justin made his move and hopped all the way across the board. "King me, Sheriff."

Ethan moaned. "How'd I not see that coming?" He slapped a checker on top of Justin's piece.

"I talked to the deputy marshal in Nampa," Griffin said. "He says a gang that used to operate in Cheyenne may have moved up here."

"You think those are the ones who held up Vashti and Ned?" Ethan asked.

"Could be. But one of them was that fella who camped out there in the rocks last summer. Somehow, either he got some men with horses and guns to join him, or they moved in on him and took over his territory."

"Maybe they recruited him into their gang and helped him get a horse."

"Yeah, one of my stage horses."

Ethan ran a hand through his hair and studied the checkerboard. "What I'm trying to figure out is how to prevent it from happening again."

"You and me both," Griffin said.

Hiram folded his knife and tucked it in his pocket. "You two eating at the boardinghouse?"

"Thought we would," Griffin said. "But we'll cook at home tomorrow." He looked at Justin as he said it.

"Mrs. Chapman sent us a pie." Justin smiled, and Griffin thought for the first time that he looked a little like Evelyn—that is, like the Banes.

Hiram fetched the broom from the corner and swept up his

shavings. "Reckon I'll head on home. Come and visit anytime."

Justin finished the game in a matter of minutes, leaving Ethan complaining good-naturedly about getting beat again.

"It's a sort of mathematical game, Sheriff," Justin said solemnly. "You can only move so many ways, and if you think them all through, you can see what will happen."

Ethan stared at him. "You see the whole game in your mind?"

"Not the whole game, but a ways down the road."

Griffin laughed at Ethan's baffled expression. "That's why I've got this boy setting up a ledger for me. I want him to see down the road until I'm making money again." He slapped Justin on the shoulder. "Come on, champ."

They walked out into the street.

"Uncle Griff?"

"Hmm?"

"Marty showed me how to clean the horses' feet. Well, he showed me on a mule, but I learned how."

Griffin eyed him cautiously. "So, you think you like working with horses now?"

"Yes, sir. I'm getting used to them. If I do well with the bookkeeping, would you give me some more riding lessons?"

Griffin rested a hand on Justin's shoulder. "I surely will."

Vashti sat in the Wells Fargo office the next morning, selling tickets. Seemed everyone wanted to go somewhere now that spring had arrived. She'd have a day off before her next run to Nampa, and she'd enjoy the luxury of sleeping in. Having a bath last night and putting on a dress this morning had brought back all her feminine instincts.

Griffin had finally given her the combination to the safe, and when she closed the office at noon, she locked away the morning's proceeds. She stopped in at the emporium before heading home.

"Vashti! How are you doing?" Libby came from behind the counter to take her hands. "I haven't seen you since your last run. How did it go?"

"Fine. No problems."

"That's a relief. I hope that incident last week won't be repeated." Libby smiled. "Say, you should have some special passengers next time you come from Nampa."

"Oh?"

"Yes. I had a letter from Mr. and Mrs. Hamilton in the mail you brought yesterday. They expect to arrive in Boise tomorrow, and they'll ride up here with you the next day."

Vashti tingled with excitement just from watching Libby's shining face. "Oh, Miz Adams, I'm so happy for you. This means you'll be getting married soon."

Libby's cheeks went a delicate pink. "Yes, it does. I don't mind admitting that I'm delighted."

"You and Mr. Dooley have been waiting a long time."

"Not so long as some, but long enough."

"Have you set a date?" Vashti asked.

"Not for certain, but I shouldn't think we'd wait more than a few weeks, if all goes as planned."

Vashti picked up a sack of sugar for Augie and carried it, along with Libby's news, toward the Spur & Saddle. As she reached the sidewalk on the west side of Main Street, Maitland Dostie hurried out of the telegraph office. When he saw her, he pulled up short. "Is Mr. Bane at the Wells Fargo? I have a telegram for him."

"No, sir. I believe he's working at the smithy today."

Dostie frowned. "I don't suppose you'd have time to take it to him? I don't like to leave the office that long."

"Surely. Just let me give this to Augie, and I'll be right back."

Vashti hurried into the restaurant. Bitsy scurried about, serving several traveling men and a few local residents.

"Oh dear," Vashti said as she plopped the sugar sack down on the serving counter. "Today you need me, and Mr. Dostie asked me to take a telegram over to Griffin."

"Best run and do it," Bitsy said. "Goldie's in the kitchen filling glasses of cider for me. We'll be all right."

Vashti dashed back to the telegraph office.

"Here you go." Dostie handed her an envelope. "He may want to send a reply."

Vashti's curiosity prickled, but she didn't ask questions. She hurried down the street. Griffin was shoeing one of the coach horses when she rounded the corner. Justin hovered nearby, watching everything he did. She waited until Griffin stopped nailing and reached for a rasp.

"Mr. Dostie asked me to bring you a telegram."

Griffin lowered the horse's hoof to the ground and straightened. "Me? A telegram?"

"Yes, sir." She held it out, watching his wary face. Telegrams were almost never good. She recalled his last one had announced Justin's imminent arrival.

Griffin looked down at his filthy hands. "Can you open it, please?"

"Surely." She ripped open the envelope and fished out the yellow paper.

"What's it say?"

She looked down at it and froze. "Oh no."

"What?" Griffin's features went hard. "Read it."

" 'Passengers, driver, and messenger fought off outlaws in ambush Catherine Road. One passenger killed. Advise.' "

Griffin let out a deep sigh and bowed his head. Vashti waited, her heart aching. Nick Telford, an experienced driver, had that run now, on the same branch line with Johnny Conway. She sent up a prayer for him and the passengers, and for the safety of all the drivers and messengers on the road today. Though she wouldn't like to admit it, an icy stab of fear struck her.

Griffin jerked his chin up and glared at her.

"You're not driving tomorrow."

⭐ CHAPTER 22 ⭐

Griffin moved his toolbox farther from the horse and looked at Justin. "Stay here. I've got to send a telegram. If Marty comes over, tell him I'll be right back and I'll have the team ready in time." He strode toward the street.

Vashti tagged after him in a swirl of green skirts. "What do you mean, I'm not driving?"

"Just what I said." Griffin didn't look at her. If he did, those eyes would make him think twice.

"But if they're over on the Catherine Road now—"

"They could be back here tomorrow."

"Oh, come on." Vashti grabbed his arm, but he kept walking. "You don't think they'd pull another job tomorrow, do you?"

He paused and glared down at her. "I don't know what they'd do. If I did, my men wouldn't have been attacked today, would they? And a man wouldn't have been killed."

That shut her up, at least temporarily. He marched on to Dostie's office, not wanting to think about the ambush or what could have happened if it had been on Vashti's route. He'd have to scare up another driver for her run tomorrow. He couldn't go off himself again—not so soon. Justin needed him. He guessed he'd better advertise in the *Avalanche* and the Boise paper for more drivers, though he hated to. But if a lot of businessmen and geologists were going to be coming through to get to the old mines, he'd better make the stages keep their timetable. If traffic increased, they might even need a three-times-a-week schedule from Boise to Silver City and De Lamar.

He pushed into the telegraph office. Dostie sat behind his desk at the telegraph key.

"I'm sorry, Griffin. Tough luck."

"No luck about it," Griffin said. "Send back to the station agent. 'Hire extra guard and send stage on time.' Oh, and you'd best tell him I'll ride over tomorrow and catch my men at Sinker. I need to talk to them personally." He brought his fist down on the counter. Tomorrow was the day he'd hoped to take Justin for a leisurely ride to Reynolds Creek and check in with the station agent there, who stored extra feed for Griffin. That would have to wait.

A sound behind him alerted him that Vashti had followed him in. She cleared her throat delicately, but in a manner not to be ignored.

"Yes, ma'am?" Dostie asked, peering at her.

"Has the sheriff been informed?"

"I expect it's a bit out of his territory," Dostie said.

"Yes, but he'll want to know."

Griffin nodded. "You're right. He might even take some men over to help look for those scoundrels."

"I could tell him," Vashti said.

"All right. I'd go myself, but I've got two more horses to shoe."

She started for the door.

Griffin called, "Oh, wait a sec."

Vashti turned toward him.

"Would you tell Ethan we'll need extra guards tomorrow? Maybe he can help me round up a few extra men to make the run with you."

She smiled then. "Yes, sir."

As she closed the door, Griffin kicked himself mentally. Why had he said that? He'd had no intention of letting her drive to Nampa tomorrow.

"That all you want to say in the telegram?" Dostie asked.

"Reckon so."

"Eight dollars and fifty cents."

Griffin winced. "Let me see that." He studied the spare message but couldn't see how to eliminate more than one word. "All right," he said at last. "I'll have to come around later and pay you. Don't have that much on me."

Vashti put on her trousers and boy's shirt the next morning. She frowned at herself in the mirror as she braided her hair and pinned it up. What if she got to the livery and Griffin had found another driver? She clenched her teeth. After he'd had her tell Ethan he needed more guards to go with her, she'd avoided seeing Griffin for the rest of the day. That way, he hadn't had a chance to tell her that he didn't mean it.

She eyed her reflection critically. The shirt had shrunk a little in the wash. She pulled the vest on and surveyed her figure from the front and the side. Maybe she had time to run into the emporium and buy a baggier shirt. Even if everyone local knew she wasn't a man, she couldn't drive in a dress, and she didn't want to give the tenders or the passengers reason to think she was immodest. It was too warm to wear her coat.

She pulled on her boots, grabbed her hat, whip, and overnight bag, and dashed down the stairs. In the kitchen, Bitsy and Augie were peeling vegetables for the day's guests.

"I'm heading out," Vashti called. "Need me to bring you anything?"

"Just bring yourself back, honey." Bitsy smiled at her.

"You want to take my shotgun?" Augie asked.

"No, thanks. I'll be fine." She patted her canvas bag, where her pistol lay. The last thing she needed was to lose Augie's shotgun the way she'd lost Griffin's rifle.

"Take your coat," Bitsy said. "It's fixing to rain."

Vashti smiled at her. "It's nice to have someone who cares whether or not I get wet." She walked over to the dry sink and kissed Bitsy's powdered cheek. Bitsy squeezed her.

Vashti waved at Augie and hurried over to the store. Goldie was helping Libby this morning, while several customers stocked up on groceries. Vashti went to the ready-mades section and pulled a men's shirt off the rack. She sidled up to Libby, who was pouring out a quart of milk for Mrs. Walker.

"Would it be all right if I tried this on in the storeroom?"

Libby looked at her and the shirt and nodded. "Help yourself."

The new shirt hung loosely on her, but Vashti figured that was good. She tucked it in and put the vest on over it. If this one shrank, it would still fit. She stuffed the old one into her bag and went out into the store.

Goldie was totting up a large order for Terrence Thistle. She shot a sidelong glance toward Vashti. "Whatcha got today?"

"The shirt on my back."

Mr. Thistle laughed. "You should hear the men when they come in off the stagecoach, arguing over whether you're a girl or not."

"Really?"

"My, yes. Last week I was afraid they'd come to fisticuffs over it. And then Griff Bane come in with his boy, so I says, 'Fellas, here's the division agent for the stage line. Whyn't you ask him?'"

Vashti gulped. "Did they?"

"Oh yes. And Griffin says, real somber-like, 'What's that? A woman driving one of *my* coaches?' He shook his head and said, 'What next?'"

Goldie laughed. "What did the men say?"

"Not much after that. Griff's so big, I think they was afraid to say any more."

Vashti smiled, but she wondered how much ragging Griffin would take on her account. If he was stacking up reasons to fire her, he probably had quite a stockpile by now.

"All right, Mr. Thistle, you're all set." Goldie gave him a piece of paper with his total on it.

He picked up a small crate of groceries. "I'll come back for the rest."

Vashti watched him go out the door, struggling to shut it behind him. "Too bad he lost his arm in the war."

"Yeah, but he does all right. Now, let's see, one man's cotton shirt." Goldie named the price, and Vashti laid the money on the counter.

"Think this one will shrink much?"

"Oh, I wondered why you needed a new one." She eyed the cuffs that fell down over Vashti's wrists. "That one's plenty big."

"Good. Got to run." Vashti whisked out the door and down the sidewalk. To her surprise, the door to the Wells Fargo office was open, and three people were lined up outside. She slowed her steps. As she came even with the office, she stepped down off the boardwalk to avoid the customers, but she could still hear Griffin's loud voice from within the building.

"I'm telling you, Manny, it'll be safe. I'm sending two outriders with the stage, and I'm putting an extra guard on the roof."

So that was it. People had heard about the holdups and were afraid to ride the stage. She picked up speed and ran past the feed store and down the street, cutting behind the smithy to the livery. Marty was hitching up the last of the six-mule team. Vashti wished she hadn't dawdled so long at the emporium. It must be nearly time for her to drive up to the office.

"Morning, Marty." She stopped and stared at the two riders sitting astride their horses and the young woman standing near the coach. "Hello, Trudy. Mr. Dooley. Mr. Tinen."

"Howdy," Trudy said. "My brother and I and Arthur Jr. are riding along with you today. Hope you don't mind."

"I heard Mr. Bane say he was sending extra guards with me. Didn't expect you folks."

"Well, Ned's still laid up," Trudy said. "Griff asked for my husband this morning, but he's over on Catherine Creek, helping the marshal's deputies look for the outlaws. So I said I'd go."

"I'm surprised Mr. Bane agreed."

Trudy shrugged. "He said I couldn't ride point, but I could ride on the stage with you. I suggested he stop at Hiram's place and see if he felt like an adventure."

Hiram smiled and nodded, but said nothing. He and Arthur Tinen Jr. had rifles in scabbards on their saddles, and Art also wore a sidearm.

Art said, "That's about the way of it. I was over to Hiram's to see if he could fix my leather punch for me when Griff came by, and we both thought it sounded like a noble thing to do."

"Noble," Trudy scoffed. "You only came because Griffin offered you five dollars for the trip, and even then you're lucky Starr let you go."

Arthur grinned and shrugged one shoulder. "We'd best get moving. Griffin said we had to be on time."

"Right. Climb up, Trudy." Vashti mounted the box. She stowed her canvas bag under the seat and readied her whip.

Trudy climbed up cautiously and took the seat Ned usually had. She held her rifle on her knees. "So far, this is fun. Wish I had trousers, though." She smoothed down her brown divided skirt.

"All ready, Georgie," Marty called from his place at the lead mules' heads.

Vashti gathered the reins and gave him a nod. Hiram and Arthur rode out just ahead of them, and she put the mules into a trot. As they rounded the corner by the smithy, she looked over at Trudy.

"I have to admit it feels good to have two outriders...and to have the best shot in Fergus sitting beside me on the box."

Trudy smiled. "I can see why you like this job."

"Think Ethan will mind you doing it?"

"By the time he hears, I'll be home. Besides, Griffin says we've likely got the safest route in Idaho today. Those outlaws are off east of here, hiding from the law."

"I hope he's right." Vashti felt a flicker of fear but shook it off. "Will you stay at the stage stop with me tonight?"

"Yes, Griffin gave us money for our room and board."

Vashti thought about that as she guided the mules to a stop before the Wells Fargo office. The holdup had cost Griffin a lot—more than just the horses and his rifle.

He stood, grim and foreboding, on the boardwalk. "Four of your six passengers decided not to go."

Vashti gritted her teeth. "I'm sorry. I suppose you had to refund their ticket money."

He nodded. "You okay with your new messenger?"

"Oh, sure. Trudy's great."

Griffin stepped closer and looked up at them earnestly. "You know I wouldn't let the two of you go if I didn't think the road would be safe today."

Vashti nodded. "Thanks for giving us an escort."

Griffin eyed Hiram and Arthur, who sat their horses ahead of the coach, waiting for the passengers to board. "Well, I don't like putting my friends at risk, but I didn't have anyone else on hand. I can't go off and leave Justin again so soon. Guess I could have sent Marty, but. . .well, you know Marty."

"Yeah, and he can't shoot straight, either."

Griffin cracked a smile. "All right then, Georgie. I'll load the mail sacks and tuck the passengers in. Be safe."

Vashti raised her coiled whip to her hat brim.

He turned away, and Trudy said, "That man cares about you."

Vashti chuckled. "He cares about all his employees."

"That's not what I meant. He's worried about you personally."

Vashti tucked that comment away to examine later. The mail sacks thudded on the coach floor, making the stage sway; then the two hardy men who hadn't demanded refunds climbed in. Griffin waved, and Vashti turned forward. "Up now!"

Ethan rode in tired, sweaty, and chilled. He'd been in the saddle all day, in the rain. He only wanted one thing: home. Home meant a hot meal to fill his belly, hot water to wash in, a cozy, comfortable bed to sleep in—and Trudy. He smiled as Scout plodded down the lane toward the ranch house. No smoke came from the chimney. That was odd on a chilly evening like this. The sun was bedding down for the night behind the mountains, but no lights shone from the kitchen window—or any other window.

Scout would have gone on toward the barn, which meant a meal and a dry bed for him, too, but Ethan pulled back on the reins.

"Whoa!" He stared at the silent house.

Across the sodden barnyard, a lantern glowed in the window of the little bunkhouse where the McDade brothers slept. He turned Scout toward it. Dismounting, he dropped the reins. After a brief knock, he opened the door a few inches and stuck his head into the gap.

"Spin?"

"Yeah, boss." Spin jumped up from his chair near the stove and hurried toward him. "Didn't expect you tonight."

"Where's Trudy?"

"Uh. . ."

Ethan scowled at him. "What's the matter with you?"

Johnny set his tin plate down and came to stand beside Spin. "Miz Chapman's gone."

Ethan scowled even harder at Johnny, so hard it hurt. "What do you mean, gone? Did she go over to Hiram's this evening?"

"Nope. She went to Nampa."

Ethan cocked his head to one side and considered whether the young man was teasing him or not.

"That ain't funny."

"It's true," Spin said. "She went on the stagecoach. Mr. Dooley and Arthur Tinen Jr. went along on their horses."

Ethan swiveled his gaze to Spin. "Whatever for? Did somebody die in Nampa?"

"Nope, but Griff Bane needed extra guards for the stagecoach," Johnny said.

Ethan let that sink in. Very slowly, deliberately, as if the boys were still cutting their teeth and wearing short pants, he said, "Are you telling me that my wife is riding shotgun on a stagecoach?"

Spin nodded, a gleam in his eyes. "She said you wouldn't know 'til after she came home tomorrow, but if you did get home first, to tell you not to worry."

"That's right," Johnny added. "Griff said you was keeping them outlaws so busy they wouldn't come anywhere near the stage today, so they'd be safe."

Ethan narrowed his eyes. "Well, if it's so all-fired safe, why did he send Hiram and Art and *my wife* along to protect it?"

Johnny looked away.

Spin shrugged. "Word is, folks don't want to ride the stage unless they have extra guards."

Johnny perked up again. "Yeah. I wanted to go. Griff was paying five bucks a man."

"Or woman," Spin put in.

"Yeah. Only he said I was too young."

"That right?" Ethan was feeling a mite testy by this time. He glared at Spin. "Why didn't you go?"

"Well, boss, I didn't think you'd want me to. Not with the missus gone. I mean, would you want me to leave the ranch in the hands of a seventeen-year-old rapscallion?"

Ethan looked from him to his younger brother. "Guess not." He let out a long, slow breath. "You boys got any grub?"

Vashti and Trudy chattered as they neared Nampa. The rain had slacked off, but the breeze was still chilly. Trudy rubbed at her gun barrel with a handkerchief.

"I hope this rifle doesn't rust from getting wet today."

Vashti looked over at her. "Too bad we had to drive most of the way in the rain. Are you all right?"

"I'm fine. I dressed for it. What do you do when you stay over in Nampa?"

"I usually have the rest of the day free. Once I walked up the street a little and looked in the shops, but mostly I stay at the station. I get my supper and go to bed early. I'll ask if you can be in the same room with me tonight."

"That would be fun."

Vashti called out to the riders, "Mr. Dooley! Mr. Tinen!"

They turned in their saddles.

"Station's just over that rise." She uncoiled her whip and cracked it. Had to make a good showing when you came into the station. Hiram and Art pulled off to the sides and let her pass them, then fell in behind the coach. The road was a bit muddy, but the mules managed to jog into the yard at a respectable pace.

"Whoa, boys," Vashti called and laid on the reins a little. These mules needed a firmer touch than most horses.

The station agent came out. "Well, George, I see you made it."

"Yes, sir."

"Well, well, well." He looked Trudy over. "I see Mr. Bane's hired a new messenger of the distaff side."

Trudy laughed. "Ned Harmon was injured last week. My brother and I and Mr. Tinen, back there, rode along to give Mr. Bane peace of mind."

"And you had no trouble on the road?"

"Just rain and mud," Vashti said, bending down to retrieve her bag from beneath the seat.

"Good. Got a meal ready for you, but don't get too comfortable."

Vashti paused. "What do you mean?"

"Buck Eastman busted his leg."

Vashti caught her breath.

"Who's Buck Eastman?" Trudy asked.

"He's the driver on the run from here to Boise," Vashti said.

"That's right." The station agent made a sympathetic face. "Sorry, but you'll have to drive on to Boise. You've got twenty minutes to eat while we change the teams."

★ CHAPTER 23 ★

Y ou don't have a choice?" Art Tinen asked.

"I'm afraid not. The contract I signed says if the next driver up the line can't make his run and they don't have a replacement ready, I have to make it." Vashti shoveled mashed potatoes into her mouth.

Trudy frowned at her across the table. "But what if you get to Boise and the next driver's sick?"

"They can't make me do more than two runs in a row."

Trudy, Hiram, and Art watched her eat for a minute. They'd get fed, too, but they'd have plenty of time. Vashti had to be on the box and ready to roll in ten more minutes.

Hiram rested his arm on the back of his sister's chair. His eyes matched Trudy's perfectly—stormy gray blue. "Do they have an escort for you?"

Vashti gulped down a swallow of milk. "Yes, the fellow who usually rides with Buck Eastman is here. And it's fairly civilized along the road from here to Boise. I don't think we'll see any road agents."

"So. . .what should we do?" Art asked.

"Vashti, if you want us to go with you, we can," Trudy said quietly.

"Don't be silly. You don't need to do that. I'll be fine. Stay here and rest. Besides, Ethan and Starr will worry their heads off if you don't come home tomorrow afternoon."

"But won't you drive back here tomorrow and take your regular run back to Fergus?" Hiram asked.

She hadn't thought of that. Did they expect her to drive four legs in two days? Of course, the run to Boise was only twenty miles, and the road was pretty good. "I'd better speak to the station agent."

She shoved her stool back and rose. Though she was tired, she knew she could drive as far as Boise with a fresh team. A couple of more hours wouldn't kill her. She'd spend the night in the territorial capital and head back in the morning. "It's really not that far."

Outside, the tenders had the fresh team in place—four matched bays. Vashti found herself eager to drive them. She walked to where Jeremiah Gayle, the station agent, stood talking to another man.

"Here's your driver," he said as Vashti approached. "George Edwards, meet Harold Day. He's your messenger as far as Boise, and he'll go on with the next driver from there."

Vashti shook the shotgun rider's hand. "Nice to meet you, Harold. So they have someone ready to take over in Boise?"

Harold just stood looking at her with a half smile pasted on his face.

Mr. Gayle said, "Yes, they telegraphed. Sid Carver's there, rarin' to go. He's young, but he hopes to get a permanent driving job. This will be a little test for him. You'll just go as far as Boise and stay at the hotel there."

"A hotel."

"Yup. They put drivers up at a fancy place there, right, Harold?"

Harold spat on the ground. "Wouldn't call it fancy."

Vashti gulped. She wanted to ask if it was safe for women. "And will I drive back here in the morning?"

"That's right. You'll have a different messenger with you. Likely Tom McPherson. You'll come back here and take your regular drive back to Fergus. You good with that? It means double pay."

She hadn't thought of that. "Sure. And if my friends who came along from Fergus want to go, is that all right?"

"Well, we've got a full coach for you. And we wouldn't pay for the extra riders, though I understand you needed 'em to get here safely."

"I'll be right back." She turned toward the house.

"Be quick," Gayle called. "You're scheduled to leave in three minutes."

She hurried inside and explained the situation. Passengers bustled about, gathering their belongings.

Art looked at Hiram. "What do you think? We could just stay here and join Vashti again when she leaves here for Fergus tomorrow. Our room and food are all paid for here."

Hiram nodded. "To be honest, I didn't come prepared to pay for a hotel and meals in Boise."

Trudy's mouth drooped.

"How long since you've been to Boise City, Trudy?" Vashti asked.

Her friend looked at her and shrugged. "Quite a while."

"You could probably share my room with me, if you wanted to ride along. Mr. Gayle says the coach is full, but there's always room outside." She glanced toward the window. "Of course, the rain could start up again."

Trudy's eyes glittered. "Hiram, can I borrow your hat? It'll keep the rain off better than mine."

He sighed mournfully, but his lips quirked into a little smile as he handed her the old felt hat. "If you're going, maybe there's something you can check on for me. Can I talk to you for a second?"

Trudy followed him a few steps away from the others. Vashti tapped her foot. Mr. Gayle was probably looking at his watch and steaming. Hiram put something in Trudy's hand, and she shoved it quickly into her purse. She came back to Vashti smiling.

"I'm ready."

"Mind you don't let her get into trouble," Hiram said.

"I assure you, we'll be proper ladies. Well, as proper as I can be in these clothes." For the first time, Vashti regretted not bringing a dress along on her stagecoach runs.

"Come on, then." Trudy clapped the hat on. "Hiram, you boys be good."

Hiram and Arthur laughed.

When they got outside, the coach was loaded and two men were sitting on the roof.

Vashti threw Trudy an apologetic glance. "Sorry—I didn't know we had *that* many passengers."

"Don't fret." Trudy was always game to lead the shooting club into adventure, and the prospect of an uncomfortable ride among strange men didn't seem to daunt her. She climbed up to the box and smiled at the passengers. "Excuse me, gentlemen. I'll be joining you."

Harold Day already sat on the box. He caught Vashti's eye. "Your friend can sit here with us, if you don't think it'll interfere with your driving."

At once Vashti said, "Hey, Trudy, sit with me and Harold."

"Oh. All right."

Vashti climbed up and considered whether she ought to sit on the outside or in the middle for the best control of the horses. At last she settled between Harold and Trudy and took up the reins.

"You're two minutes late leaving," Mr. Gayle said from the ground.

"I'm sorry." Vashti looked ahead to the tenders and nodded. As they released the horses' heads, she flicked her whip, careful not to jab Trudy with her elbow as she did. "Up, you." The four bays broke immediately into their road trot, and the coach rolled forward.

Though the quarters were a little close, she found the ride to Boise almost as pleasant as her earlier drive with Trudy. They soon had Harold laughing with their tales of life in Fergus. Trudy drew out the messenger, looking past Vashti to question him. They learned he was a family man living in Nampa, and the father of three children. By the time they reached the swing station where the horses were changed, Trudy and Vashti had learned all the children's names and ages, and the fact that one of them had celebrated his fourth birthday the day before.

"That reminds me," Trudy said. "Libby's birthday is next week. I'd like to get her something. Nothing big. Just something she doesn't have in the emporium, you know?"

"She and Hiram will have a cause for wedding gifts soon, too." Vashti picked up her whip, ready to set out again with the new team. "The folks who are buying her business are supposed to return with us to Fergus tomorrow."

Trudy gave her a mysterious smile and bounced a little on the seat.

"Remember when Hiram asked to talk to me at the last minute?"

"Yes."

Trudy leaned closer and whispered in Vashti's ear, "He asked me to look for a wedding ring for Libby, so's he wouldn't have to buy it at her store."

"That sounds like a fun errand."

"Do you suppose the stores will still be open when we get to Boise?" Trudy looked up, but gray clouds blocked the sun.

"Should be," Harold said. "The schedule puts us there at four."

"Then let's be on time," Vashti said. The new team was swiftly put in place, and she figured they might have made up their lost two minutes. One more passenger had climbed to the roof behind them. "Next stop Boise City," she called and nodded to the tenders. The horses tried to jump into a canter, but she steadied them. No need to rush.

A raindrop plinked on her nose.

As soon as Vashti was free to leave the stagecoach stop, she and Trudy headed for the nearest cluster of shops. With the promise of double pay when she got home, Vashti splurged on a large umbrella.

"We can both fit under it," she said.

They asked the clerk at the haberdashery what stores would be open latest and planned their itinerary accordingly. Carrying their meager luggage, they visited those between the stage stop and the hotel. Vashti found a serviceable black bombazine skirt, which she wore out of the store, carrying her trousers stuffed into her canvas bag.

"All the wedding rings they have look the same," Trudy said when Vashti came out of the fitting booth at the back.

"Well, of course. They're supposed to, aren't they?"

"I guess. Hiram didn't give me much money, but I can get one."

"I've got a little extra, if you need it."

"No. . .but they have different sizes. What size do you suppose Libby wears?"

"Hmm. Her fingers are slender."

"That's what I'm thinking." Trudy perked up suddenly. "Let's try them on."

Trying to hide their laughter, they slipped ring after ring onto their fingers as the clerk watched.

"This one, I think," Trudy said at last. She held it out to the clerk and slipped her own wedding ring on again.

Vashti turned away from the counter with a sigh. That was probably as close as she'd ever get to wearing a wedding ring.

By six o'clock, they were ready to sign in at the hotel and have dinner.

The desk clerk made no comment about the extra guest Vashti was taking to the room with her, but he did eye their headgear—men's hats on both ladies' heads—with an air of disapproval. They found they could lock their possessions in their room, so they freshened up and descended to the dining room.

"I can pay for your supper," Vashti offered as they sat down at a table near the front windows.

"I have enough," Trudy said. "I wasn't sure until I got Libby's birthday gift, but it wasn't too expensive, so I have plenty left for supper and breakfast. Do you think she'll like it?"

"I certainly do. I've heard she loves to read, and you got the very latest book from New York. She can't possibly have read it yet."

"I do hope she likes poetry."

"She'll love it," Vashti said.

A woman in a dark brown dress and ecru apron came to their table. "Good evening, ladies. What may I bring you?"

They ordered two servings of chicken pie and a pot of tea.

"I wish I could have found a good wedding present for them," Vashti said.

"There's still that store down beyond the bank," Trudy said. "We could walk down there."

When the waitress came back with their plates, Vashti asked, "Would we have time to go shopping at that big store down the street?"

"Hubbard's generally stays open until nine," the woman said.

"Would it be safe for us to walk down there?" Trudy asked.

"I'd think so, if you stay together and don't loiter."

Vashti wished the men had come with them. "What do you think?"

Trudy shrugged. "I'm willing if you are."

The waitress poured tea for them. "There is one saloon on the other side of the street, shortly before you get to Hubbard's. Just be aware and keep moving."

When they'd finished the meal, they got their wraps. Trudy put her pistol in her purse. Vashti hadn't brought a handbag, but she tucked her gun into her waistband, beneath her vest and coat. She took the umbrella, but the rain had let up.

"I don't suppose we dare leave this here."

Trudy shook her head. "If we do, it will pour just when we're ready to come back."

They walked quickly down the street. Few pedestrians were out. A wagon occasionally rattled past them. As they approached the store, it was easy to pick out the saloon. On the far side of the street, a dozen or more horses were tied to a hitching rail before a low log building. Laughter and tinny music reached them. Vashti swallowed hard at the vivid reminder of her past life.

"Come on." Trudy hung on to her sleeve and steered her quickly onward, to the quiet store. "I'm glad we didn't have to walk on the same side of the street as that place."

Inside, ready-made clothing for the entire family was displayed. Vashti hadn't been in a store bigger than Libby's Paragon Emporium since she'd come to Fergus five years ago, and she suspected that for Trudy it had been longer. They walked slowly around the perimeter, stopping to look at whatever caught their fancy—a silk shawl draped over an open chest, a pair of children's overalls on a large doll, or row after row of shoes.

"This place could outfit everyone in Fergus," Trudy said.

Vashti nodded, eyeing the headless display form that vaguely resembled a woman's body. The shimmering gown it wore caught her eye, but the decapitated figure made her shiver. "They say there wasn't even a town here thirty years ago."

"It wasn't nearly so big when I last came here," Trudy said. She fingered a challis blouse in a muted pink and white print. "Sort of wish I'd brought more money. But that's silly. I have all the clothes I need."

"It's fun to get something new now and then." Vashti turned to her with a smile. "Help me pick out a nice gift for the bride and groom."

Trudy joined her quest, and fifteen minutes later they left the store with an imported china platter, hand-painted with flowers and nesting birds, wrapped with several layers of newspaper and tied up in brown paper. Vashti had spent a little more than she'd planned, but the birds were so dear she couldn't resist it.

"When Libby and Hiram have you and Ethan over at Thanksgiving, she can serve her turkey on it," she said to Trudy.

Her friend laughed and pulled on her gloves as they left the store. They walked toward the hotel.

"Know what I'm going to do with the ring tomorrow?" Trudy asked.

"What?"

"Now, mind you, I don't think we'll get held up. But just in case we do. . ." She leaned closer and whispered, "I'm tying it into my corset."

Vashti laughed.

"You think it's funny," Trudy said, "but I heard about a robbery down in California where a lady put nine hundred dollars in her bosom. All the men got robbed. She gave the outlaws her reticule with a couple of dollars in it, and they never suspected she had more."

"Right." They were even with the saloon, and Vashti flicked a glance toward it. A man came out the door. He appeared to be sober, and he headed diagonally across the street toward Hubbard's. She would have kept going without another thought, but he turned his face into the light flowing out the store's front window, and she caught her breath. Her step faltered, and she nearly dropped the platter.

★ CHAPTER 24 ★

"Are you all right?" Trudy asked, putting out a hand to steady her friend.

Vashti whipped her head around, her heart racing. "Quick," she whispered and dashed along the sidewalk, hugging her awkward burden.

Trudy raced along beside her, craning her neck to look back and then turning forward again. "What is it? That man? He went into the store."

"Good." Vashti slowed to a brisk walk, panting. "I'm sorry."

"It's all right. Do you know him?"

Vashti felt a sick knot in her stomach. "I'm not sure. He looked like someone I used to know. But not here."

"Let's get back to the hotel, and then you can tell me about it."

They hurried along, slightly uphill. The platter grew heavier, and Vashti's feet began to drag.

"Here, let me take that." Trudy reached for the package.

Vashti didn't protest. She climbed the hotel steps wearily and went to the front desk to retrieve their room key. One more flight of stairs, and she could relax. Trudy held the package and the umbrella while Vashti unlocked the door.

Their room would be their fortress. With the door closed and locked, Vashti sank down on the edge of the bed.

"I'm sorry. I shouldn't have let him scare me like that. It startled me, though."

"Are you sure it was the man you knew?"

"No. I hope it wasn't." Vashti gulped and pulled off her gloves. "The man he looks like is one I never want to see again."

Trudy laid the platter carefully on the dresser and came around to sit beside her on the quilt. She put her arm around Vashti. "I'm sorry. We were having such a good time." Her eyes filled with sympathetic tears, and Vashti felt a pang of guilt.

"I didn't mean to get you upset, either."

"I'm all right. Do you want to tell me about this fellow, so that I'll know how to act if we meet him again?"

Vashti pulled in a long, slow breath. "I thought he was Luke Hatley."

Trudy frowned. "Don't know that name."

"He was a gambler. I met him back in Independence."

"Was he good at it?"

"At gambling? Very. But not so good at winning."

Trudy snorted a laugh. "So what happened?"

"I first met him when I was thirteen, outside a bakery. I was sniffing the bread baking and wondering if I could steal some." She tugged off her coat and laid it, with her hat and gloves, on the bed. "Anyway, I was young, and I was desperate. I figured being with him was better than being with half the men in town, so to speak. He liked me, and he seemed decent. I guess that must sound funny to you—a fellow who would do to a thirteen-year-old what he did to me. But he seemed like a way out for me. A way to survive without. . ."

Trudy stroked her back gently. "And then what? Did he leave you?"

"Sort of." Vashti jumped up and turned to face her. "Look, I didn't mean to tell you all this. Haven't told anyone but Bitsy. Well, I told Griffin some, but not this part." Trudy seemed surprised, and Vashti felt she needed to explain. "He came to talk to me shortly after Justin came. I wanted him to understand how it is if you're young and alone. If you don't have a good, honest person like Griff to take care of you."

Trudy nodded. "Justin could have gotten into all sorts of trouble, I suppose."

"He'd already started to back where he came from. It wouldn't take much for him to run away from Griffin and try to make it on his own. And then what? He'd end up with some toughs like those road agents or take to gambling and drinking. But one person—one good person—can turn a kid's life around."

"I think you're right."

"I thought Luke might be that for me, but I was wrong. He took me deeper into. . .what the reverend would call lasciviousness. And then crime."

"So you left him?"

Vashti walked over to the dresser and opened her canvas bag. "No. He left me. When it was convenient, he dumped me and rode out of town, never looking back. See, he'd gotten into debt to a fellow who owned a place."

"What kind of place?"

"A saloon."

"Oh."

Vashti turned to look at her face. Would Trudy still want to be her friend if she knew everything?

"I shouldn't have told you."

"No, I want to know. It helps me to understand some things."

Vashti pulled out her bandanna and dabbed at her cheeks. "Well, Luke gave me to this fellow Ike to cancel his debt. Ike said I had to work for him. I tried to get away, but he kept a strict eye on me and the other girls he had working there."

"You mean—"

Vashti turned away, unable to meet her gaze.

Trudy cleared her throat. "Well, obviously you got away after a while."

"Yes. Thanks to Bitsy. I ran away, and she helped me. But just seeing Luke tonight—or someone who looked a lot like him—gave me a turn. I. . .Trudy, I don't want to see him again. Ever."

"That was—what? Five years ago?"

"More like eight."

"So you worked for that Ike person for three years."

The tears flowed steadily, and Vashti nodded. She mopped her face again with the bandanna, conscious that Trudy was studying her profile.

"I'm so sorry," Trudy said.

Vashti tried to shrug it off, but she couldn't stop the tears. The intensity of her dread when she thought she'd seen Luke surprised her. Still, he hadn't been mean to her during their time together. But at the end, he proved that he didn't really care for her as much as he cared about money and winning and a good hand at the poker table. "It could have been worse, I guess. At least Luke, taking me with him like he did, put off the inevitable for almost three years." She sat down again with a sob. "I thought he'd marry me someday. Was I ever wrong."

"You said Bitsy helped you."

Vashti sniffed. "Yes. My life is good now. I have a family. I have a good place to live and a real job and friends."

Trudy smiled and stood. "Let's not think about that man we saw. It probably wasn't him, anyway. A lot of men drift around the West, especially since the gold craziness."

"True."

Trudy eyed her anxiously. "Are you sleepy? You've got a long drive again tomorrow."

"Not really."

"Tell you what: I'll go downstairs and see if we can get a pot of tea and maybe some cookies."

Vashti smiled. "That sounds good." She fished in her pocket and brought out two dimes. "Take this and use it if they won't add it to my bill."

"All right. Lock the door while I'm gone. I'll be back in two shakes of a lamb's tail."

She whisked out the door. Vashti walked over and locked it. She hung up her coat and put her hat and Trudy's on hooks beside it.

The window fronted the street. She walked over and moved the curtain aside with one finger. Lamplight lit the hotel's dooryard and several other buildings down the street. At least they were a good distance from the saloon. But that man could have a room right here in this hotel. She shuddered and let the curtain fall into place.

"Dear God, I guess this is one of those times when I should call on You. Please don't let me see that fella again. Help me not to even think of him. And if he is Luke. . ." She stopped, not knowing what to say next.

Griffin dashed for the smithy, holding a mule's bridle in his hand. How on earth did Marty do it? He was always busting something. Griffin grabbed his leather punch off the wall of tools and rummaged in a crate of leather straps for one the right width. At least the mule's mouth wasn't torn up. A shadow fell across his work as he lined up the new strap with the one on the bridle.

"Anything I can do to help, Uncle Griff?"

The blacksmith paused and looked at the boy. "That's nice of you to ask, Justin. You can run up to the office and tell Josiah Runnels we've got a small delay, but the team should be ready when the stage comes in. Ten minutes. And ask him how many passengers today. We've got two sacks of mail going out."

Justin sped off without another word. Griffin punched a couple of holes in the straps and turned to his workbench for rivets. His quick fix might chafe the mule's cheek, but what else could he do? He didn't have another harness bridle on hand to fit the mule. That robbery had really cut into his assets.

At last the bridle was patched together. He'd have to stitch it tomorrow, when this harness came home to him with the stagecoach. He dashed out the door and headed for the back of the livery. Ethan was dismounting near the corral gate.

"Hey, Griff! Thought I'd turn Scout out while I wait for the stage."

"Sure, go ahead." He hoped Ethan wasn't upset with him for letting Trudy act as a shotgun messenger. "They'll be here any minute. I've got to have this team ready, or I'd stop to chew the fat."

Ethan waved. "No problem. I'll mosey on up there."

Griffin bridled the near swing mule. Done. He turned and looked for Marty. Found him sitting on a barrel of oats, chewing a straw. Griff felt like tearing into him. The man moved slower than a snake in winter.

"Uncle Griff?"

Justin stood in the open front door of the barn.

"Yeah?"

"Josiah says seven passengers to Silver City."

"Good." There'd be room for all seven inside the coach, along with the mail sacks.

At last the team was ready. Griffin pulled out his watch. The stage should arrive any minute.

"Marty, you step lively when they bring the stage in."

"Sure, boss."

Griffin tried not to let that rankle him. Pastor Benton's last sermon had included some warnings about anger. As he strode up the sidewalk to the Wells Fargo office, he tried to think about better things. Technically, Isabel still owned the building, but if his application for the mail contract came through for another year, he could buy it from her. That and a pile of new harnesses and maybe even another coach. He could hire more drivers and messengers. . . .

Ethan lolled against the wall of the office, and a few people who planned to meet passengers milled about on the walkway. Griffin went to the door. Peter Nash stood inside talking to Josiah Runnels. Two sacks of mail sat on the desk.

"Hey, Griffin," Peter said. "I'd better get back to the post office."

Griffin nodded. "We'll take care of the mail, Mayor."

"Do you need me to help with the team?" Josiah asked.

"Wouldn't hurt. Marty moves slower every day."

"I'll get over to the livery, then." Josiah put on his hat and went out.

Griffin took out his watch again. The stage was five minutes late. His stomach started doing odd things. Those outlaws—he couldn't stand another robbery. Especially not with Vashti driving. Trudy was on the stage, too, and her husband waited outside, looking relaxed but probably tied up inside. At least it wasn't raining today.

As if Griffin's thoughts had drawn him, Ethan appeared in the doorway, squinting into the dimly lit room.

"Are they late, Griff?"

Griffin snapped the watchcase shut. "Not much."

Ethan came in and leaned on the edge of the desk. "Can't help fretting. Guess that doesn't do any good, though."

"I know what you mean."

Ethan bit his lip and nodded. "Maybe I should ride out and meet them."

"They'll be fine." Griffin wished he believed it. He kept seeing that narrow place in the rocks.

"Trudy's pretty headstrong, but I didn't expect her to go off overnight like this."

"I guess that's my fault. Hiram and Arthur were going, and she was keen to go, too. I figured it wouldn't hurt to have another crack shot along. Besides, I didn't expect anything to happen. I'm sure they're all right." Griffin walked around the desk and sat down. "You like being married?"

Ethan smiled. "Shoulda done it a long time ago."

Griffin took his hat off and laid it on the desk. He ran a hand through his bushy hair. "Sometimes I think about it."

"You surprise me."

"Have to admit there's a gal I'm a little sweet on." Griffin shot a glance at his friend. "Haven't said anything to her. Yet."

"Might that be a certain person on the stagecoach?" Ethan asked.

Griffin couldn't help smiling as he thought of Vashti in her boy clothes, cracking her whip like the best of the old-time drivers. "She's got pluck. I thought she was crazy when she first asked me for a job. But she really can drive. Bill Stout came around when he knew I was hard pressed to find drivers this spring and told me I should look twice at her. She'd been practicing." He shook his head. "Didn't expect her to mean anything to me, other than a driver."

"Well, take your time, Griff. Make sure it's not just an infatuation. She's pretty, and she's independent, given her past."

"What about her past?" Griff scowled at him. How dare Ethan bring that up?

"Easy, now. I'm just saying. . . .a gal who's been forced to take care of herself most of her life can find it hard to let other folks do things for her. She might have some ideas that aren't quite like yours." Ethan strolled to the doorway. "Your nephew's running up the street."

"Justin?" Griffin jumped up. He'd forgotten all about the boy and left him at the livery.

Justin hit the sidewalk as he reached the door and Ethan stepped aside.

"Uncle Griff! The stage is coming!"

Griffin walked past him, out onto the boardwalk. Sure enough, he could hear the team's thudding hoofbeats and the sound of the wheels skimming over the road. He looked at his watch again. Nearly fifteen minutes late. But here, just the same. Passengers who planned to ride on up to Silver City, along with those there to meet folks getting off the stage, looked eagerly toward the sound. Libby Adams stood outside the emporium's door watching.

Hiram Dooley and Arthur Tinen Jr. rode around the corner by the smithy on their horses. They looked none the worse for wear. As the coach came into view, Griffin half expected to see arrows sticking out of the sides, but that was silly. Hadn't been Indian trouble in ten years. He blew out a deep breath. Ethan came and stood beside him, bouncing on his toes.

Trudy sat on the box beside Vashti. Trudy's dark blond hair hung in a braid over her shoulder, but Vashti had her hair hidden beneath her felt hat, as he'd demanded she do. Too bad. She looked much better when she let her womanly charms show.

Griffin frowned at his thoughts. He wasn't about to let her start driving in a dress, with her hair all shiny and soft around her face, like it was that night he ate at the Spur & Saddle. She would make far too tempting a picture that way, and she traveled miles and miles of isolated roads. No, she'd best keep dressing like a boy, even if everyone in the territory knew she was anything but a man.

Trudy started waving and grinning, and Griffin looked over at Ethan. His face looked about to crack, the sheriff was smiling so big.

The coach eased to a stop, and Griffin opened the door. He took out the bag of mail for Fergus and entrusted it to Josiah to take over to Peter at the post office, then let the passengers out. The couple who'd come last fall to see Libby about buying her store got out first. Libby hurried down the boardwalk to greet them.

"The stage will leave for Silver City in twenty minutes, folks,"

Griffin said. "If you're traveling on, coffee and a quick meal can be had at the Fennel House or the Spur & Saddle. If you're late getting back, the stage won't wait for you."

Four men tumbled out, and those who planned to ride on after the stop looked around and headed quickly across the street. Last out was a salesman with a large sample case.

"I'd like to stop here overnight," he said. "Is there a clean, reasonable place to stay?"

"Fennel House." Griff pointed across the street. He turned to those planning to board the coach. "Folks, we need to swap the team out. I know we're a few minutes late, and I'm sorry about that. Let the driver take the stage around to the livery. They should be back so you can climb aboard in ten minutes." He glanced up at Vashti, and she nodded at him. Trudy still sat on the box with her. Arthur and Hiram waited a few paces away on their horses. "Did you have any trouble?" Griffin asked in a low voice.

Vashti shook her head and smiled. "It was muddy in the creeks because of the rain, but not too bad. The ferry held us up. Had to wait nigh half an hour for it."

"All right. Good job, and I'll see you after the stage leaves again." He waved to Hiram and Arthur. "Come see me at the livery, boys. I'll be down there soon." Getting Vashti back in one piece—not to mention the livestock and equipment—was well worth their wages. He wished he had enough money to pay extra guards every day. If only the postmaster general would come through with that new contract. . .

He went into his office and opened the safe. He'd be very low on cash once he paid off this week's crew. Had Wells Fargo sent him money to buy new equipment? He hadn't given up hope yet that the government would reimburse him for what he'd lost on the mail run, either, but it was probably too soon to look for a bank draft in the mail.

Someone came in and stood behind him. Griffin was suddenly conscious of how vulnerable he was, bending over his open safe like that. He looked over his shoulder. Justin stood blocking the light from the doorway.

"Anything I can do, Uncle Griff?" He sounded lonesome.

Griffin took most of the cash that was in the Uneeda Biscuit box and closed the safe. "Sure. As soon as we see off the Silver City coach, you can go back to the livery with me. Vashti and the messengers will tell us about their run. I always have the drivers give me the details, so I know how the roads are and hear any news they picked up. Then we'll go over the team that just came in, check their feet, and brush 'em down real good." Tight times or not, he determined he'd find a way to pay the boy something, now that he'd started showing a will to work.

"One of the farmers brought in a great big chestnut horse after you left. Said it needs shoeing. Mr. Robinson."

"Rancher," Griffin said. "Not a farmer, a rancher."

"Yes, sir."

Griff smiled and shoved the cash into his pocket. "Come on. Let's go outside. The stage should be back soon, ready to leave for Silver."

"Uncle Griff?"

"Hmm?" He hoped this wouldn't be another philosophical question.

"Do you s'pose I could learn to drive a four-in-hand?"

"Maybe. It takes a lot of practice. A six takes even more."

"Well, then, can I learn to drive one horse at a time?"

Griffin laughed. "I'm sure you can. And when you're comfortable with that, we'll go to two. I don't s'pose you'd care to learn to make horseshoes?"

Justin winced. "If I have to."

"You don't have to."

They walked out onto the sidewalk as the coach came up the street with Bill Stout on the box.

Trudy and Vashti waited in the barn at the livery after the coach headed out with its new team and crew. Hiram and Arthur leaned on stall dividers and told Ethan about their journey. After a while, Griffin and his nephew came into the barn. Marty, who'd been sitting on a stack of hay bales listening to Arthur's tale, jumped up, grabbed a dung fork, and disappeared into the nearest stall.

"Folks, I sure do appreciate your help." Griffin pulled his wad of bills out of his pocket. He looked at Vashti first. "I'll settle with you on Friday. You need any cash right now?"

"Nope, I'm fine until my usual payday. Thanks."

He counted out five dollars and handed it to Trudy. "Thanks a lot."

"It was fun. First time I've been out and about for a long time, and I enjoyed having some time with another woman."

He turned and gave five dollars each to Hiram and Arthur.

"Much obliged," Arthur said.

"Did they take care of you at the home station?" Griffin asked as he handed over Hiram's pay.

"Very well. Of course, Trudy went to Boise with Vashti."

"Boise?" He swung around and stared at Vashti. "You drove to Boise?"

She nodded. "Buck Eastman broke his leg. Mr. Gayle told me I had to keep going, but I didn't mind. It didn't put me off schedule. And he said I'd get double pay." She looked at him hopefully.

"Yes, all right, but why didn't you wire me?"

Vashti shrugged, wondering if she'd done wrong. "I thought Mr. Gayle had. And I didn't think you'd want me to spend money like that, anyway."

Griffin sighed. "Guess I'd better ride to Nampa tomorrow. I'll need to hire more drivers and guards for sure now." He looked over at Hiram and Arthur. "You boys want extra work?"

Arthur said, "I'll have to talk to Starr. Things are getting pretty busy on the ranch, but we are a little short on cash."

"I didn't mind doing it," Hiram said, "but Art's right. We've got spring roundup and fences to fix and all kinds of chores to see to. But if you're in a bind. . ."

"I'll find somebody."

Trudy stepped toward him. "Griffin, I think I know a way you could have plenty of guards without spending too much money."

"How's that?"

"Let the members of the Ladies' Shooting Club ride free on the stagecoaches. Some of the ladies would love a chance for a free trip to Nampa or Boise to shop, and they'd surely be willing to take their weapons along and watch out for trouble."

"I don't know. Putting ladies at risk like that."

Art laughed. "If ever there were women who could take care of themselves, it's our shooting club ladies."

"That's right," Trudy said. "Give them a free seat, and I'll bet they'd be happy to buy their own meals and lodging. Some of these women haven't been out of Fergus for upwards of five years."

Griffin scratched his chin through his beard. "I'll take that under consideration."

"Good. Now, I'm heading home with my husband."

"Finally." Ethan straightened and walked over to her. "Where's Crinkles?"

"I left him out in the corral yesterday."

Ethan walked to the back door. "I'll go get him and Scout."

Justin dashed after him. "I'll help you, Sheriff."

Trudy turned to Vashti and hugged her. "Again, thank you for showing me a good time in the city."

Vashti laughed. "Maybe we'll get to do it again."

Griffin scratched his head. "Do you think that if two or three ladies rode along, they'd pay attention to the road, or would they just..."

"Just what?" Trudy glared at him.

"Yeah," Vashti said. "Are you insinuating that our women would get caught up in conversation instead of keeping watch?"

"No. I, uh..."

Trudy fairly bristled. "Griffin Bane, our women are not only the best shots in town; they also take their duty seriously."

Ethan stepped into the doorway at the rear of the barn, frowning. "Trudy? I can't find Crinkles out there."

"What?" Trudy ran past him toward the corral. A moment later she came back. "Griffin, my horse is gone."

★ CHAPTER 25 ★

Griffin frowned and pushed his hat back. "I saw that palomino gelding out there an hour ago." His mouth twitched. "Marty! Oh, Marty!"

"Yeah, boss?" Marty leaned around the stall divider and peered at him.

"Where is Mrs. Chapman's horse?"

"Uh..."

Griffin stomped over and stood before him, glaring down from his superior height. "Where is the palomino?"

"A miner came in from the Nugget, wanting a horse to take him up to De Lamar. I told him to pick one out of the corral."

Griffin stared down at him for a long, smoldering moment. "Who saddled the horse?"

"I...uh...I guess he did."

"Did he pay for it?"

"Uh—yeah." Marty shoved his hand in his pants pocket and pulled out two bits.

"That's not the overnight rate."

Marty gulped and went prospecting for another quarter. When he finally plopped it in Griffin's hand with a grimace, Griffin said in a tight, quiet tone, "Thank you. Come by my office tomorrow and get your wages. You're done here."

Marty's head jerked up. "What? Come on, Griff, you can't fire me."

"Who says I can't? You rented out a horse that wasn't ours, and you would have kept the money if I hadn't found out. Get your stuff out of the loft and hit the road."

"Griff, you can't—"

Griffin turned his back and walked out the front door of the barn.

Vashti tugged at Trudy's sleeve. "Maybe now is a good time for us to leave."

"Come on, darlin'," Ethan said. "You can ride double with me to the ranch."

Justin came in the back door. "Mrs. Chapman, the sheriff's right. Your horse is gone."

Trudy smiled at him. "I know, Justin. We just found out Marty rented him out."

Hiram said, "I reckon I can ride up to De Lamar and get your horse, Trudy."

"You're tired," she said. "Just go catch the stagecoach and ask Bill to tell that man to bring Crinkles back tomorrow."

"I'll go with you, Mr. Dooley," Justin said. He shot a glance at Griffin. "If my uncle says I can."

Marty moved out of the shadows and slunk toward the door.

"Hey, Marty," Arthur called. "Whyn't you get on Hiram's horse and I'll get on mine, and we'll go catch the stagecoach? You can ride the stage to De Lamar and bring Trudy's horse back, and I'll lead Hiram's paint back after you're on the stage."

"Oh, I don't think. . ."

Arthur, Hiram, and Ethan silently moved into position around him.

"I think that's a fine idea," Ethan said. "Because if you don't go, I might have to arrest you for horse thieving."

"What? No!"

Ethan nodded at Arthur. "Get going, boys. And that palomino better be back in my pasture by noon tomorrow, Marty."

Arthur shoved Marty toward the front of the barn, where his pinto and Hiram's horse were tied. Justin kicked at a hay bale.

"What's the matter, Justin?" Vashti asked.

"I wanted to go."

Ethan laid a hand on his shoulder. "I've got a feeling your uncle's going to need you. He just fired his only full-time employee here at the livery. It's a big job. Now, if you were to show that you could handle it—and I don't doubt you could, maybe better than Marty—why, there's no telling what kind of arrangement you could come to."

"You mean, he'd hire me regular?"

"He might. I can't speak for Griffin, but he's a fair man. You've got to start thinking like a businessman, though."

Justin's eyes gleamed. "Well, I think a good businessman would want to make his customer happy." He walked over to Trudy. "Mrs. Chapman, there's an old mare yonder that my uncle lets me ride whenever I want. Would you like to borrow her at no charge to get you home, and return her to us when it suits you?"

Trudy smiled. "That's a very nice offer, Justin. Thank you. I'll do that."

Ethan sighed. "Finally. Let's go home."

Vashti opened the door to her bedroom and leaned against the jamb. The big tin tub sat in the middle of floor, full of steaming water. Bitsy must have had the water heating and watched for the stage to pull in.

She placed her package containing the wedding platter on her bed, then walked over and stuck her hand in the water. Not too cool, though she'd lingered at the livery. She closed the door and scrambled out of her masculine clothing. On the chair near the tub was a clean towel, a dish holding a bar of soap, and a small bottle. She picked up the bottle. Bath salts. Bitsy's way of reminding her she could feel feminine, even though she'd played the role of a man for two days. She shook a little into the bath and stirred it with her hand.

As she sank down into the warm, fragrant water, she closed her eyes. Rich women probably bathed every day, but this was a luxury in Fergus, where every drop of water had to be hauled from a well or the river.

Thank You, Lord, for blessing me with friends like Bitsy and Trudy.

She smiled as she remembered Trudy's delight at seeing a town bigger than Fergus for the first time in years. Their unintended time together in Boise had strengthened their friendship. Vashti was certain now that Trudy accepted her as an equal. The trip would have been completely uplifting if not for the man from the saloon.

She slid a little lower in the tub, until the water came up to her chin. He'd looked like Luke, but older. That was what really scared her. If he'd looked the same age as the man who'd sold her years ago, she would have known at once that it couldn't really be him.

Tears coursed down her face, and she splashed them away. Why did she have to get so mixed up when she thought about Luke? She'd loved him, hadn't she? Or was that really love? She'd trusted him, certainly, and depended on him, to her regret. The man who'd seemed her angel turned out to be the one who sold her into vile slavery. Yet during their time together, he'd treated her well. Mostly. And he'd said many times that he loved her. Was it a lie?

She took the washcloth and scrubbed her face and arms, determined not to let Luke into her mind again. She would think about the soggy ride to Nampa and Boise and Trudy's invitation to visit her at the ranch this weekend. The way Trudy and her brother and Art Tinen had stepped up to help yesterday amazed Vashti. Of course, they were being paid. But they had done it for Griffin as friends, too, not just for the pay. And Trudy had gone on to Boise with her for adventure, yes, but also to keep her company and ease her mind.

She hoped Griffin would seriously consider Trudy's suggestion of filling his coaches with ladies from the shooting club. Those outlaws who'd stopped her and Ned wouldn't have had a chance if Trudy, Libby, and Bitsy had been inside the stage. Those three women could have picked them all off. Ned, on the other hand, had let off several rounds and hit nothing.

Luke's face flashed across her mind again, unbidden. Would she see him again? Why would he come to Idaho? She knew he didn't need a reason. While she was with him, they'd drifted around from town to town, wherever he saw a chance to get some money. Luke wasn't above stealing, but he preferred gambling. So long as she stayed away from Boise and kept close to her lodgings when she was on the road, she ought to be fine. Provided Luke didn't decide to hop a stagecoach to Silver City. That was entirely possible if more of the mines opened up again. Where there was gold dust, the saloons multiplied, and that brought more gamblers.

She certainly didn't want to see Luke again. She'd look twice at only one man if he came around to call, and he wasn't Luke Hatley.

What was she thinking? She stood in the tub of water and reached for her towel, telling herself sternly, "It wasn't even him."

When Vashti went downstairs, refreshed and dressed in her old red taffeta gown, several guests were already eating in the dining room. Vashti scooted to the kitchen and donned an overall apron that hid the neckline she now found embarrassing.

"Sorry I'm so late coming down. That warm water was just too heavenly. I wanted to stay there all night."

Bitsy laughed as she picked up two platefuls of the evening special—meat loaf with mashed potatoes and gravy. "You'd have frozen if you stayed there much longer."

"Yes, it was quite cool when I finally got out." Vashti smiled. "What shall I do first?"

"Put on another pot of coffee, and then I'll let you help me serve." As she headed out the door, Bitsy called, "Augie, we might need more biscuits. Two more people just came in."

When Vashti entered the dining room a few minutes later, Hiram Dooley was holding the door for Libby Adams. She smiled at them and looked around for an empty table that would be out of the traffic, so they could talk quietly. The dining room was half full of patrons, a good turnout for Thursday supper.

Bitsy hastened to the couple and led them over to a secluded corner. Perfect. Vashti poured two glasses of water. She recalled that Libby liked a glass of water with her meal.

"Good evening, Mrs. Adams. Mr. Dooley." Vashti set the water glasses before them.

"Hello, Vashti." Libby smiled up at her. "Hiram was just telling me about your uneventful trip to Nampa."

"Blessedly boring." Vashti nodded toward the chalkboard that Augie had recently hung as a way to list the daily specials. "We've got meat loaf tonight or baked chicken. Oh, and fresh dandelion greens. Augie just told me Ruth Robinson picked a mess and brought them into town this morning. He bought all she had."

"By all means, I'll have those," Libby said. "I've been hankering for fresh greens."

"How about you, Mr. Dooley?"

He gave her his shy smile. "You can call me Hiram. I'll try some, with the meat loaf."

"Yes, meat loaf sounds good," Libby said.

"I brought your party in this afternoon." Vashti watched Libby's face.

"Yes, and I appreciate it. They said that a cute boy drove them and they didn't think he could be over sixteen." Libby laughed. "We're going ahead with the sale. The Hamiltons will take over the emporium a week from Monday. They'll stay at the boardinghouse until I've moved out of my apartment."

Libby's face was the picture of joy. Vashti felt a stab of envy. It must be wonderful to have the love of a good man. She might never find that. Even though she knew some decent men, they all knew her past—or thought they knew.

She went to the kitchen, where Augie was putting a pan into the oven.

"Big crowd tonight, my darlin' tells me."

"She's right," Vashti said. "I've got two meat loaves for Mr. Dooley and Miz Adams. And they both want the dandelion greens."

"They make a right sweet couple." Augie took a china plate from the stack and ladled a mound of mashed potatoes onto it. "Good thing I made plenty of gravy."

When she took their plates out on a tray, Hiram was holding Libby's hand on the tablecloth. As Vashti approached, he let go and picked up his water glass. So cute. Vashti could see why Libby had fallen for the quiet man. He had a romantic spirit, that one.

"Here you go, folks. I hope you enjoy your meal."

Libby glanced at Hiram then smiled up at her. "Vashti, I'm bursting to tell someone my news. Mr. Dooley and I just set the date for our wedding."

"Well now." Vashti stood there holding the tray and grinning. "I'm very happy for you. When is it?"

"Two weeks. From Saturday, that is." Libby laughed and reached out to Hiram. He grabbed her hand again, beaming but saying nothing.

"Oh my," Vashti said. "That sounds like an excuse for a new hat to me."

Libby's laugh burbled out, and other diners turned to look. She covered her mouth with one hand and continued to chuckle.

"May I tell Bitsy and Augie?"

"You certainly may. Goldie, too, if you like. It's no secret."

"Or anyway, it won't be for long," Hiram said with a wink.

When Vashti reported to the livery on Monday morning, Griffin greeted her with an anxious nod.

"You've got a shotgun messenger I pulled from the Mountain Home line, but I'm also letting Zach and Annie Harper and Opal Knoff go along, provided there are enough seats, as guests of the line. All heavily armed, and they've signed a paper saying they won't sue us if they're injured."

"Terrific. I'm a little surprised Annie's going."

Griffin shrugged. "She wanted to real bad, but Zach said he wouldn't let her go without him. Zach's a fair shot, and he's packing a hundred rounds for that shotgun of his."

"And Opal?"

"Ted says if she's not back serving drinks at the Nugget by sundown tomorrow, she's fired."

"Oh, that's accommodating of him." Vashti made a face as if she'd bitten into a crabapple. "At least he gives her a day off now and then. I'll make sure she's back on time."

Griffin slapped her shoulder lightly. "That's what I told Ted. And that he can't stop his employees from doing what they want on their own time. Of course, Art Tinen's different. Starr wanted to go, and he put his foot down. He said she's not going out and mixing it up with outlaws when they've got a baby in the house."

"Can't blame him there." Vashti imagined that when it came down to it, Starr couldn't leave the nursing infant overnight, anyway. "She's probably just jealous that Art went last time and feeling a little deprived."

"Cabin fever." Griffin nodded. "Well, you stay on guard, especially near those rocks and when you're coming to bridges. They hit the stage on the Catherine road by the bridge. I've had the station agent over there hire an extra man for Johnny Conway's run tomorrow."

"I'll keep it in mind. What are we carrying today?"

Griffin looked around and leaned toward her. "Got some ore samples and a bit of gold dust coming down from Silver, and a bank deposit for Walker's Feed. Libby Adams might want to send in the check those Hamiltons are giving her, too. I told her to bring it to the office, so I can stash it in the box when I load the mail."

Vashti gritted her teeth. Her first time carrying a significant amount of valuables. "We can handle it."

"Sure you can." Griffin held her gaze for a moment then sighed. "If I could, I'd go myself. But I've got too much to do here."

She almost wished he was going. But that was crazy. "Don't worry. We'll get through just fine."

"There's something new you'll notice when you climb up to the driver's box."

"What's that?"

"I bolted the treasure box to the floor of the driver's boot. That way, if you do get stopped and they tell you to throw down the box, you tell 'em you can't. They're doing this on other lines, and sometimes it's enough to stop the outlaws, or at least slow 'em down. And with the armed passengers and your messenger, that might be enough to tip the scales your way."

Vashti gulped. What if that only angered the robbers? "My plan is to not let them stop us in the first place."

"That's the best way, all right. You want to grease your axles while Justin and I get the team hitched up?" he asked.

"Yes, sir." Bill had taught her how to do this, assuring her that any driver worth his pay would grease his own wheel fittings and do it liberally, thus ensuring that he wouldn't have a "hot box" from the friction of the axle. Vashti didn't especially like that part of the job, but she accepted it as one aspect of caring for the equipment. When she'd finished all four wheels, she handed the dope pot to Justin and wiped her hands on a rag.

"Uncle Griffin's going to hire some more men if we get the mail contract," Justin said.

"More drivers and messengers?"

"Yes'm, and more help here at the livery, too. But he says I can keep on working for him. He's paying me now."

Vashti raised her eyebrows. "That's a fine thing. Is this your first paying job?"

"Except for stacking wood for some neighbors back home."

She nodded. "Your uncle's a fair-minded man, and I'm proof of that. Work hard, do a good job, and he'll treat you right. He appreciates people who do their job well and do it on time."

"Not like Marty."

"Well, no. Marty wasn't the best at either diligence or punctuality."

Justin frowned. "I guess. Anyhow, we heard he's gone to California."

Twenty minutes later, Vashti drove the coach to the office. Griffin loaded the mail and put a small sack and an envelope in the green treasure box and locked it. Vashti shivered. If she lost the Walkers' money, would the aging couple have enough to make do? And what would they do to her? She could envision Orissa Walker screeching at her and demanding that Griffin fire her, or even have her locked up.

"That envelope has to go directly to the bank," Griffin said. "Instructions are written on it. Make sure the driver who takes over at Nampa understands."

"Yes, sir."

Griffin drew a deep breath and held her gaze. His eyebrows pulled together the way they did when he wasn't pleased. "It doesn't seem right, sending a woman off like this. Georgie, if you want to change your mind. . ."

She scowled at him. "Change my mind? What would you do if Johnny or Bill came to you and said, 'Mr. Bane, I don't want to drive today.' Hmm?"

He gave her a tight smile and looked away. "I wouldn't blame them right now, I guess. Not with this gang plaguing our lines."

"Well, I'm in this for the long haul. And we'll get through just fine." She nodded. "I'll see you tomorrow."

She looked forward. Justin was holding the leaders' heads. They were well-behaved mules, and he hardly needed to do it, but it made the boy feel important. She smiled and nodded firmly, and he let go of their bridles and jumped up on the boardwalk.

Vashti cracked her whip three times before the mules settled into a road trot. Behind her, Opal, Annie, and Zach called good-bye to their friends who'd come to see them off. It seemed like a frolic as they breezed up the street. But once they'd passed the smithy and the Nugget, Vashti hunkered down and concentrated on driving and watching. Now and then, she shot a glance at the messenger, Cecil Watson. She half wished Griffin was beside her. Cecil had to be at least forty, but she didn't hold that against him. Bill Stout was older than that, and he was still one of the best drivers in Idaho. She just hoped Watson had good eyesight—and an even better aim.

★ CHAPTER 26 ★

Three hours after leaving Fergus, Vashti stood on the steps at the home station in Nampa, waving to the folks traveling on to Boise.

"Have a good time, and be sure you get into Hubbard's if there's time this evening."

"No fear," Opal called, waving her handkerchief. "Miz Harper and I both have shopping lists to fill."

Annie waved. "I've got a lot of things to buy for the wedding party dresses, not to mention gifts for the happy couple."

Vashti ran closer to the coach and spoke to her through the window. "I got them a china platter, so don't get that, will you?"

Annie smiled. "How lovely. We'll remember, won't we, Opal?"

"Couldn't forget."

The driver cracked his whip, and Vashti leaped back as the stage jerked forward. She would never start without warning like that, and she wouldn't jump the horses into a canter, either. At least the coach was full of passengers. Several of the men on board were packing pistols. They ought to be all right. She'd heard the Boise run had been a favorite route for holdups back in the heyday of the mines. Was it coming to that again?

Lord, keep them safe. She wished for a moment that she'd traveled on with them, but she knew she needed to rest. And she didn't really want to jounce along another two hours and sleep at the hotel. The station here in Nampa was more comfortable, to her way of thinking.

Mrs. Gayle kept a small loft chamber for her and other ladies who traveled through. The male drivers and messengers slept out in the bunkhouse with the hostlers.

She climbed the steep stairs to her room. A framed mirror hung on one wall and a crewelwork sampler on another. The bottom bunk was made up with linen sheets and a woolen quilt, with an extra blanket folded at the foot of the bed. Vashti set her canvas bag on the wooden crate below the mirror.

"Home away from home." She gazed into the mirror at her dusty face. A sixteen-year-old boy? She smiled at the thought and tried to picture herself next to Justin. How could anyone mistake her for a boy, even in this getup? She frowned and turned her head at different angles, trying to see herself the way the passengers saw her. Her appearance might fool the unsuspecting and nearsighted.

A layer of dust dulled her complexion. Her eyebrows were caked with it. No leisurely scented baths here. But it was a homelike, snug place, and she felt safe. She took off her hat and pushed the pins out of her hair, letting it cascade onto her shoulders. Mrs. Gayle had left her a white china pitcher of water and a chipped washbowl with green flowers traced on it. Vashti poured the bowl half full and found a washcloth on the rough shelf in the crate. She brushed her face with the dry cloth first, to get the worst of the dust off, then wet the fabric and carefully washed her cheeks, forehead, and chin. It took several rinsings of the cloth before the image in the mirror satisfied her. She took her hairbrush from her bag. The light from the small window at the end of the room wasn't enough to show up the auburn glints in her hair, but she kept brushing vigorously for several minutes. Finally she went down to supper.

She turned in early and slept deeply for several hours. The sun was peeking between the mountains when she jerked awake, gasping. For a moment, she wondered where she was, missing her familiar room at the Spur & Saddle. As she oriented herself, she sat up slowly and swung her feet over the edge of the bunk. Her dream had already faded, but one thing she remembered vividly— Luke's face, sneering as he shoved her toward Ike Bell to settle his gambling debt.

"No trouble?" Griffin asked anxiously as he carried the mail from the stage up the boardwalk toward the post office.

Zach Harper walked beside him, puffing at a cigar. "Not a bit. That little Georgie girl is quite a Jehu."

"Oh yeah?" Griffin didn't remember Vashti pushing the horses too hard when he was along.

"We had to wait at the ferry landing, and once we were over, she made up some time, I'll tell you. And not a sign of those bandits." Zach laughed. "I think Annie was almost disappointed. But didn't she and Opal have a time in Boise."

"Big doings?" Griffin asked as he mounted the Nashes' steps.

"Big spending is more like it." Zach opened the door for him.

Griffin entered the post office and plopped the sack on the counter. "Here you go, Mayor."

"Thank you very much, sir. Sorry I didn't get down to the stage stop to get it myself."

"No trouble."

Peter nodded. "I take it the stagecoach didn't have any trouble this time?"

"Not a lick."

"Good. Maybe that gang has moved on."

"I hope so." Griffin settled his hat by way of a farewell.

For two weeks the ladies of the shooting club and a few of their husbands rode the Nampa stage for free. Once it was known they could ride that far in comfort and pay only for the short leg from Nampa to Boise, it became a favorite outing for the club members. They always took their role seriously and avoided idle chatter during the ride through the desolate territory between towns, but once they got to the city, they kicked up their heels. Micah Landry and Zach Harper laid down the law after their wives had done two runs each. They needed their women to home, in the kitchen.

Even Bitsy went once, and after Libby had given over ownership of the Paragon Emporium to the Hamiltons, she rode to the city to shop for a trousseau and stayed over an extra day. Starr Tinen gave her husband no end of grief because he wouldn't let her go, though her mother-in-law, Jessie, went along one sunny May day with Florence Nash and Apphia Benton. Not to be outdone, a few men had come in and offered their services.

With no new robberies causing him headaches, Griffin began to wonder if he was a fool to let folks ride along for nothing and pay for their room and board in Nampa. Some of them just went for the novelty, he was sure, like Ollie Pooler. He wasn't known to be a good shot, so why should he think Griffin would allow him to go along as an extra guard? Things were getting out of hand. Everyone in town seemed to think that if they carried a gun, they could get free passage.

"Uncle Griff?"

"Yeah?"

"What's the matter?" Justin asked.

"Nothing. Why do you ask?"

"You're holding your face all pinched up while you do that."

Griffin had been hammering away for an hour, making a stack of horseshoes. He hadn't realized he'd been holding his mouth in an odd position, but now that he thought about it, his cheeks were sore.

He relaxed for a moment, letting his pritchel and rounding hammer hang loosely in his hands. "Truth is, I'm wondering if I'm going to go broke running this stage line."

"You should hear about the mail contract soon, right?" Justin brushed his hair back from his forehead.

The boy needed a haircut. Griffin wondered if he could do it himself. Annie Harper would do it if he asked, but then he'd feel as though he should pay her. That was why he usually hacked away at his own when it got so long it bothered him.

"Yes, we should. And you've been a big help. So have the Nash boys. But unless we get that contract, pretty soon I won't have any money left to pay you boys for keeping the livery clean and feeding the horses and all the other chores you've been doing."

Justin eyed him solemnly. "If you go broke, I'll still help you for nothing."

Griffin smiled. "Thanks. That means a lot. And I guess if we *don't* get the contract, I won't need so much help around here, right?"

Justin nodded slowly.

"Well, I'll still need you to help me train Champ."

That brought a smile from his nephew. "Have you thought about selling the smithy?"

"Some." Griffin put down his pritchel and used his tongs to pluck a hot bar of steel from the forge. As he began shaping it with his hammer, wrapping it around the horn of the anvil, Justin watched closely.

When the metal cooled so that it was no longer malleable, Griffin stuck it back in the coals. Justin hadn't moved a muscle.

"The outlaws haven't shown themselves since the holdup on the Catherine road."

"Maybe they got enough, and they've gone away," Justin said.

"Maybe." Griffin pumped the bellows.

"Uncle Griff?"

"Yeah?"

"I'm glad I'm working in the livery, not out there with the robbers."

Griffin inhaled deeply. "Me, too."

The Dooley-Adams wedding was the talk of the town. Every woman in town with money to spend ordered a hat from Rose Caplinger. Annie Harper skipped shooting club practice because she had so much sewing to do. Apphia Benton organized a bevy of women to clean the church thoroughly the week before the ceremony, and Isabel Fennel promised to take her schoolchildren out to gather armfuls of flowers the morning of the wedding.

On Monday and Tuesday, most of the women of the Ladies' Shooting Club met upstairs over the Paragon Emporium to help Libby pack up everything she was taking to the ranch. Griffin, Ethan, and Oscar and Josiah Runnels helped Hiram carry it all down to their waiting wagons and take it to the old Fennel ranch.

"I expect it will take us awhile to unpack and settle in," Libby murmured to Vashti and Goldie as they watched a procession of wagons drive off.

"I hope that ranch house is big," Goldie said.

"It's much bigger than my apartment." Libby frowned. "Of course, Isabel left most of the Fennels' furniture there when she moved to town. Hiram said he hardly had to take anything at all from his old house."

Vashti laughed. "The way folks in this town are playing musical houses, I wouldn't be surprised to see your furniture show up at the Chapmans', or Mrs. Benton's Scripture sampler hanging in Isabel's parlor."

Goldie elbowed her sharply, and Vashti clapped a hand over her mouth. She'd forgotten Apphia Benton was stitching a sampler for Libby and Hiram as a wedding gift. She'd shown it to some of the ladies at shooting practice the week before, after Libby had left.

Goldie had walked about with a dreamy expression ever since Libby had asked her and Florence, her other clerk, to be her bridesmaids. Libby was even paying for fancy gowns for them and Trudy Chapman, who was to serve as her matron of honor. Goldie had sworn Vashti to secrecy and told her that the gowns were rose-colored silk, finer than anything Goldie had ever seen. Finer even than Bitsy's purple silk that came from Paris.

Rumor had it that Libby's wedding gown would dazzle the entire population of Fergus, but she and Annie were close-lipped about it. During the last few days before the wedding, Libby scurried about town—from the Chapmans' ranch, where she was staying her last few days as a single woman, to Annie's for dress fittings, to the Spur & Saddle to discuss the wedding cake with Augie, to the Bentons' to speak to the pastor about the vows. Hiram went about his odd jobs—building a chicken coop for the Bentons and fixing a rifle for Oscar—with a smile on his lips.

"What are you wearing to the wedding?" Goldie asked Vashti on Tuesday afternoon.

"I haven't had time to think about it." She'd just returned from the Nampa run and was preparing to bathe and help Bitsy serve the supper crowd.

"Well, come on! It's only four days away."

"Do you think my green wool would work?"

"No! That would be too hot. It's June, Vashti! You need something lighter." Goldie shook her head. "This is what comes of you wearing boys' clothes half the time. You've lost your sense of fashion."

Vashti shrugged. "I don't care so much about fashion. But you don't have to worry—I won't wear trousers to the wedding. I guess I can wear the same dress I wore to Bitsy and Augie's wedding last year."

"Don't do that. Everyone will remember that you were a bridesmaid. And you're not a bridesmaid for Miz Adams."

"So?"

"So you want to look nice, but not as nice as the bridesmaids."

Vashti laughed. "All right, so I have to look nice but not nicer than you."

"I didn't mean it that way."

"I know you didn't. Right now I'm more worried about whether Griffin's going to get the mail contract or not. He should have heard a couple of weeks ago."

"Well, you've got plenty of pay now. Why don't you come over to the Paragon tomorrow morning and look at the ready-mades? One of the last things Miz Adams did was order in some new summer dresses, and they're very attractive."

Vashti decided not to tell her that she'd told Griffin not to pay her last Friday. She did have quite a stash from her previous paydays, even though she'd paid Bitsy board every week and bought a few things. Griffin was finding it hard to meet his payrolls.

He'd put on an extra run each week to Silver City. Since the mining men had come through and dropped hints that a couple of the big mines up there might be reopened, traffic between Boise and Silver City had tripled. It was the one stage run that more than paid for itself with passenger fares these days.

Vashti looked on it with mixed feelings. If the mines got up to full production again, her job as a driver would be secure. But the output of the gold mines would also draw more bandits.

They wouldn't go after the wagons hauling ore down to the railroad head. It was too bulky and too hard to process. But bullion or gold dust from the stamp mills, now that was a different story.

The stagecoaches usually had passengers carrying pouches of gold dust and sometimes payrolls for the mines and other businesses. Robberies were so common that the territorial government wouldn't reimburse lost equipment unless someone was killed. Vashti wasn't sure she wanted to drive in those circumstances.

She set off on her Nampa trip Wednesday, still uncertain of her attire for the wedding. Rose Caplinger rode the stage as a passenger, going to Boise to purchase supplies for her millinery business, and Myra Harper and Ellie Nash were scheduled to go as extra messengers if seats were available.

As it turned out, Rose was the only paying customer that day. They reached Nampa in safety, and Rose got out to eat a hasty dinner before boarding again for the leg to Boise.

"Do you have a hat for the wedding?" she asked Vashti as they ate the stew and cornpone Mrs. Gayle provided.

"Oh no, I—"

"I can make you a fetching chapeau for three dollars and a half." Rose squinted at her then nodded. "That blue dress you wear to church sometimes—it's too short, but you could add some tatted lace edging, and I can dye feathers to match the fabric."

Vashti felt her face warm. A man sitting down the table on the other side stared at her, neglecting his bowl of stew. She realized he was listening to their conversation and trying to reconcile it with her appearance. Her cheeks burned hotter, and she lowered her voice.

"Rose, people aren't supposed to know I'm not a man. Could we talk about this when we're back in Fergus, please?"

"Oh. Of course. But you won't have time to get up a new outfit." Rose eyed her clothing and curled her lip. "How do you stand it?"

Vashti didn't deign to answer. "Have a pleasant ride to Boise, Mrs. Caplinger. I'll see you tomorrow on your return trip." She took her empty tin plate to the side table where Mrs. Gayle liked diners to leave their dirty dishes and went to her small room at the back of the house. Mrs. Gayle had made up a pallet on the floor so that Myra and Ellie could spend the night in her room. Myra had insisted that she be the one to sleep on the floor, and Vashti had given the bottom bunk over to Ellie. Both women came in a few minutes later.

"The stage just left, and Rose with it," Myra reported.

Vashti had taken down her hair and was brushing the dust out of it. "I hope she has a good time in Boise."

"Yes, and finds all sorts of notions to make hats from," Ellie said with a smile.

"Wish I could have gone to visit the capital." Myra sat down on her makeshift bed.

Vashti didn't ask why she hadn't gone on. She knew the nineteen-year-old had come along for the adventure and to earn a little pocket money. If she went on to Boise, she'd spend more than she earned for her ticket, lodging, and meals in town.

"Maybe someday, Myra." Ellie sat on her bunk and opened her small traveling bag. "We're trying to economize. Peter didn't want me to come at all. He thinks it's too dangerous. But his salary as postmaster isn't covering all the expenses we've had lately, what with the two boys growing like weeds and prices going up."

"We'll have fun here." Vashti nodded firmly. "There's a grocery store up the road and a new hotel."

Ellie raised her eyebrows. "Nampa's getting to be quite a town."

"Yes. They're thinking of digging a canal to irrigate the farmland here, and there's a doctor who's opened up a drugstore."

"That's something," Myra said. "The Paragon always carries basic health needs, but a drugstore! Wouldn't Doc Kincaid love to have one in Fergus?"

"I'll bet he would," Vashti said. "Several houses are being built, too. If we get overly bored, we can walk around and see how the construction is coming."

Myra crinkled up her face. "No, thanks. But I wouldn't mind seeing the drugstore."

Vashti almost mentioned that the drugstore sold ice cream and phosphates, but recalling the ladies' pinched budgets, she kept quiet. If they got to the store before it closed and the right moment presented itself, she'd offer to buy them both a dish of ice cream. She smiled at the thought. Having enough honestly earned money in her pocket to consider treating her friends gave her a new sense of what she could be. She could support herself without serving drinks or worse. In Fergus, she was accepted as respectable. She'd never be as refined as Libby or as wealthy as Isabel Fennel, but she called nearly every woman in town her friend and could sit anywhere she liked in church without getting snubbed.

"I could use a walk, too," Ellie said. "Is it far?"

"Not at all. Just let me change into my skirt." For the past two weeks, Vashti had carried the black skirt and a plain blouse with her when she drove. This was the third time since Trudy's trip that other ladies had ridden with her, but usually they wanted to go on to Boise. Vashti was glad for the chance to get to know Myra and Mrs. Nash better.

The only troubling aspect was that she found the more time she spent with wives and mothers—and young women from proper homes like Myra's—the more she longed for a home of her own. As grateful as she felt for what Bitsy and Augie had given her, she yearned for a true family. But that would mean a husband, and she wasn't sure she could ever trust a man enough to commit to him for the rest of her life.

She ran through a cold mist, uphill toward Fergus, but the lights of the Spur & Saddle kept sliding farther away. Behind her, footsteps pounded, and a man's labored breathing came closer and closer. She snatched a glance over her shoulder. Luke chased her through the chilly, wet darkness, carrying an impossibly huge umbrella. "Georgia! I love you, Georgia!"

"You're lying!" she screamed back. She slammed into someone. Ike Bell. He laughed and grabbed her by her arms. "Let me go," she cried, twisting and pulling against his grip. "If you lose another harness, you're fired," he said. She jerked her head back and stared up at him. Ike had turned into Griffin. Raindrops dripped off his beard and splashed on her face. "I love you, Georgie."

"Honey? Wake up. You're dreaming."

Someone shook her, and Vashti climbed slowly through the mist and confusion toward candlelight and Ellie's soft voice.

She hauled in a deep breath.

"Are you all right?" Myra asked, climbing up with her feet on the bottom bunk so she could get closer to Vashti. "You groaned."

"I was trying to scream, I think."

"Oh, honey, I'm so sorry. It's only a dream." Ellie patted her hand.

"Yes. A nightmare." Vashti tried to calm her heart's hammering. "I'm sorry I woke you both up."

"It's all right," Ellie said. "I'm glad we were here."

Myra got down and blew out the candle. Vashti rolled over.

She lay staring into the darkness. How long until sunup? She didn't want to sink back into slumber. Luke might not be in her life anymore, but he'd ruined her haven of sleep. And what was that craziness with Griffin at the end? Insanity, that's what it was. She pulled the quilt up to her chin and prayed for peace.

★ CHAPTER 27 ★

The new church was jammed with the citizens of Fergus. Folks drove into town from outlying ranches. Hardened cowpokes and old sourdoughs rode down out of the hills to see the beautiful Mrs. Adams married. Most of them wondered how Hiram Dooley had snagged her.

As he waited for the hour to strike and the parson to start the doings, Griffin monitored his pocket watch. The stage was due in from Silver City at two. After the one o'clock ceremony, the nuptial celebration would move over to the Spur & Saddle. In case they weren't done at the church by then—though Griffin couldn't in his wildest imaginings see how a wedding could last more than an hour—he'd bribed Josiah Runnels to meet the stage for him.

He wouldn't have been in this situation, but it seemed Libby had to have three bridesmaids. That in itself wasn't a problem—Trudy Chapman, Florence Nash, and Goldie Keller were tickled to serve. But someone somewhere had made a harebrained rule that said there had to be a groomsman for every bridesmaid. And Hiram had called on him.

Sheriff Chapman was his number one choice, of course. Hiram and Ethan were best friends. Ethan looked fine, wearing the suit he'd bought for his own wedding last year. Now, that wedding had been simple. One bridesmaid—Libby—and one best man—Hiram. No fuss. Where was this "got to have three bridesmaids and three groomsmen" coming from? Libby must have seen it in *Godey's Lady's*

Book or some such Eastern convention.

Anyway, here he was. He didn't have a true suit, but Libby had allowed he could wear the black jacket he wore for funerals and a pair of black pants. He'd bought a new white shirt, and Hiram had brought him a tie just like his own and Ethan's and Augie's. Augie was the other groomsman. Griffin looked over at him and almost laughed aloud. Augie was completely bald. He stood about five feet, nine inches, and he had more muscle than anyone Griffin knew—with the possible exception of himself. But that was understandable. He pounded iron. Augie, on the other hand, pounded biscuit dough. How did he keep those muscles?

Griffin scanned the crowd, looking for Justin. Finally he spotted him near the back, squished in on a bench with the Nash boys. That might spell trouble. Peter and Ellie sat farther toward the front, so they could get a good look at Florence when she came down the aisle. Griffin guessed he'd be the one to walk out of the church with Florence. That didn't bother him any. He just hoped those boys would sit still during the wedding and not cause a disturbance. A memory of his cousin Amelia's wedding twenty years ago made him squirm. Was there any way Justin could have gotten his hands on fireworks?

Music started, and Goldie came up the aisle. She was a pretty little thing, all pink and gold in her fancy dress. Her blond hair cascaded down in back, below her white straw hat. She carried pink and white flowers and smiled all the way down the aisle. Behind her came Florence Nash. With her orange-red hair up on her head underneath her hat, she didn't clash too badly with her pink dress. It was just like Goldie's, but Florence looked ganglier and less graceful than Goldie.

Trudy Chapman had come a long way from the homely tomboy who test-fired guns for her brother. She looked good in the pink dress, too. Ethan stood watching her and grinning from ear to ear. You'd have thought he was at a horse auction and they'd led in a leggy, thoroughbred filly.

But none of the bridesmaids looked as nice as Vashti, sitting in the second row on the groom's side with Bitsy. She wore a shimmery blue dress Griffin thought he might have seen before. Maybe at church—or not. But it was far too proper to be one of her made-over barmaid dresses. She looked fine, and it was a chore to take his eyes off her.

The music changed, and all of a sudden the congregation stood, startling Griffin back to the moment. In the church doorway, Libby stood, resplendent in ivory silk, clinging to Charles Walker's arm. That was fitting. Charles had been a close friend of Libby's departed first husband.

Griffin had to admit Libby eclipsed all her bridesmaids. Not many women in Idaho would get married in a dress she could never wear anyplace else. The pale silk glimmered with tiny little beads and embroidery. Way too fancy for any other kind of outing. But he guessed Libby could afford it.

As Charles walked her down the aisle, trying hard to conceal his limp, Libby smiled at the folks on both sides, then focused on the front. Griffin turned his head and saw Hiram's face. Now there was a man in love. Griffin almost wished he knew what it felt like to be that happy.

Vashti couldn't help it. Tears gushed from her eyes as the parson pronounced Libby and Hiram man and wife. Hiram stooped to kiss his magnificent bride, and Libby raised her hands to his shoulders and kissed him back. It was the most romantic thing Vashti had ever seen. The gold band glinted on Libby's finger. Did she know Trudy had transported it from Boise tied to her corset lacings?

And Griffin! Who would have thought he could look so handsome? Augie had trimmed both his and Justin's hair in the kitchen last night. Griffin had trimmed his beard, too. He looked almost like a gentleman in his church clothes. Even Augie looked solemn and presentable.

She leaned over and poked Bitsy. "Your man looks mighty fine."

"Yes, and isn't Goldie gorgeous?"

Bitsy's eyes were full of tears, too. Vashti dabbed at her face with a new lawn handkerchief.

Pastor Benton beamed at them all. "I now present to you Mr. and Mrs. Hiram Dooley."

Everyone clapped and cheered as Hiram and Libby swooped down the aisle and out the door. Trudy took Ethan's arm and walked more sedately. Behind them came Griffin with Florence. Vashti felt the tiniest twinge of envy for the girl on Griffin's arm, but Griffin didn't seem to care much which lady he escorted. Last came Goldie, in step with Augie, grinning and swishing her rose satin skirts.

"Well, I guess we'd better scoot, or the guests will all be over to the Spur before we get there." Bitsy stood and picked up her mesh reticule. "Nice wedding."

"Yes. Very nice." Vashti followed her into the aisle.

"Hey, there."

She looked up into Johnny Conway's face. "What are you doing here?"

"No stage on my run today," Johnny said. "Griff asked me to come take over from Bill when the Silver City stage comes in. I'll take it on all the way to Boise."

"They should be coming in soon."

"I figure I've got just time for a piece of wedding cake. Say, Georgie. . ."

She frowned up at him. "What?"

"You look real good today."

"Thank you."

He nodded and pressed on through the crowd.

At the Spur & Saddle, Augie had already unlocked the door, and folks crowded into the dining room. The gifts were piled on a table to one side, where the town councilors used to have their weekly poker game. Libby had requested wedding cake, lemonade, coffee, and tea, which Bitsy had set up on the bar, with baskets of candy and dainty cookies on the tables. Since folks had eaten dinner an hour before the wedding, it was plenty.

Vashti ducked into the kitchen and found an apron. She took charge of the lemonade bowl, ladling cup after cup of the stuff. Libby and Hiram sat at the central table, receiving congratulations, and the bridesmaids and groomsmen sat with them. Myra Harper and her younger sister, Phyllis, had agreed to help serve, since Augie and Goldie were occupied. Bitsy gave them instructions and circled the room with a coffeepot in her hand.

After ten minutes or so, Augie got up and made the rounds of the tables, talking to the men. Vashti had figured he wouldn't sit still long. Griffin was the next to defect. He came over and held out his empty cup.

"More lemonade, Mr. Bane?" she asked.

"Don't mind if I do, thanks."

She could feel him watching her as she poured.

"You look fine in that dress."

She felt her cheeks heat up. "Thank you." She held out the cup but couldn't quite meet his gaze. He took the lemonade but didn't walk away. Finally she glanced up at him. "Can I get you something else?"

"I was wondering. . ."

His voice sounded odd, not at all like his usual confident self. She raised her chin and looked up into his eyes. Big, chocolate brown eyes. The haircut and clothes certainly suited him. And the expression deep in those eyes. . . Not the shameful one men used to rake her with in saloons. A wistful, yearning look. It touched her heart, and her knees shook. Griffin was one of the decent men in this town. Could he ever think of her as a decent woman?

"Yes?" It came out a whisper.

The door flew open. The wedding guests stopped in mid-chatter. Josiah Runnels looked wildly around the room and homed in on the big blacksmith.

"Griff! The stage just pulled in, and Bill's been shot."

✪ CHAPTER 28 ✪

The Spur & Saddle had never emptied so fast. Doc Kincaid and Augie were the first two out the door, but the whole town poured onto Main Street in fifteen seconds flat.

Vashti ran, trying to stick to Griffin's coattails, but his long legs carried him much faster than she could go. When she got to the coach, Doc was already inside. Griffin, Johnny, Augie, and Ethan stood in a tight group before the door, keeping folks back. Pete Gilbert, who'd been Bill's messenger, still sat on the box, the reins slack in his hands and his head bowed.

Vashti scooted around Ethan and climbed up beside Pete. She put her hand on his slumped shoulder. "What happened?"

"Road agents. Bill whipped up the mules and tried to run through them, but they shot him first thing. The mules were tearing by then, and I had to drop my gun and try to slow them down, or at least keep them from flinging the coach off one of those hairpin turns."

Vashti shuddered, recalling the steep drop-offs along the road to Silver City. "Where was it?"

"This side of Sinker Creek, maybe a mile out. Uphill. They always try to get you when you're going uphill."

She nodded. Some of those grades were worse than a pitched roof.

Ethan's head and shoulders appeared on the other side of the stage. "Pete. Want to tell me about it?"

Vashti grabbed a handful of skirts and prepared to climb down.

"I'll leave, Sheriff, and you can sit up here with him."

She dropped to the street. Doc Kincaid was backing out of the stagecoach. He turned and faced Griffin.

"I'm sorry, Bane. Does he have family to notify?"

Vashti caught her breath. Her stomach wrenched. She turned away and took a few steps to the off wheeler's head.

Bill couldn't be dead. Sweet old Bill who'd built her driving rig for her and taken her out to Hiram's ranch to practice. The white-haired driver who'd treated her like a daughter. Her first run, she'd ridden with him, and he'd helped keep the secret of her disguise at least for that first trip. She clung to the sweaty mule's harness and sobbed.

How long she stood there, she didn't know. She found her handkerchief, tucked in her sleeve—the same one she'd used an hour ago at the wedding. The voices around her faded as people moved away from the coach. Unable to stop crying, she clenched her hands around the tug strap and gritted her teeth. Dear old Bill.

A large hand rested on her shoulder.

"Come on, Georgie. Let go, so's Johnny can take the team around to the livery."

Griffin. She'd never heard his voice so gentle. Her throat was hot and achy. She stared at her hands, curled around the strap so tightly that her knuckles were white. She sobbed again.

"There now." His hand stroked her hair lightly and came down on her shoulder again. "Come on." His large, warm hands closed over her stiff fingers. He gently pried her hand from the harness. "Let Pete and Johnny take the team."

Her fingers came loose, and she backed away from the mule into Griffin's solid form. She turned and looked at the front of his shirt, clean white for the wedding. Her gaze traveled slowly up to the necktie that looked so foreign around Griffin's neck, to his neatly trimmed beard, his grim mouth, and at last his compassionate eyes.

She dove toward him, a new sob racking her body. He folded her in his arms and pulled her close against his wedding shirt.

"There now."

He eased her away from the mules and the stage. A whip cracked, and Johnny Conway clucked to the mules. The wheels rolled as the mules started forward.

Griffin held her for a minute, stroking her back softly. Finally she pulled back and took a deep breath.

"Where did they take Bill?"

"Over to the boardinghouse. Mr. Thistle said they can lay him out in the parlor."

Vashti sniffed. "Not the livery?" Somehow it seemed odd that, with all the bodies they'd laid out at the livery, a stagecoach driver should be taken somewhere else.

"The sheriff's getting up a posse. The livery's going to be busy."

She pulled away from him and turned to survey the crowd. Now that Bill's body had been removed and the coach was gone, the people focused on Ethan Chapman. The sheriff stood on the boardwalk in front of the Wells Fargo office.

"If you need to change your clothes, be quick about it," he called. "I'll leave from the livery in about ten minutes. I'll take any man who's ready to ride up to Sinker Creek with me, but you have to supply your own weapons and horses."

A dozen men broke from the crowd and ran toward the livery or their homes. Vashti hauled in a deep breath and turned toward the Spur & Saddle. Before she took one step, Griffin's hand clamped on her shoulder.

"Where you going, Vashti?"

"To get changed. I'm going with Ethan."

"That's not a good idea."

"I think it's an excellent idea." She wrenched away from him and ran.

The Boise stage pulled out ten minutes late, with Johnny Conway and Pete Gilbert on the box. Pete still looked shaken, and Griffin almost replaced him. But whom could he ask? Not any of the women after this catastrophe, and not Hiram Dooley on his wedding day.

Griffin dashed about the stable, saddling every spare horse. Even though Ethan had specified that the posse supply its own horsepower, some men like Dr. Kincaid depended on him for transportation. Justin ran back and forth from the corral to the barn, fetching tack and bringing in the few available mounts.

"Uncle Griff?"

Griffin tossed his own saddle over the back of his gray gelding. "What?"

"Can I go this time?"

Griffin eyed him over Pepper's withers. Instead of showing boyish eagerness, Justin's face was troubled.

"I don't think so, son."

"I liked Bill."

"We all did. But I need you to stay here. Folks will come around wanting news, and the stock will need to be fed at sundown. You can get Ben and Silas Nash to help you. Oh, and Justin. . ."

"Yeah?" The boy—no, the young man—didn't argue, but his mouth drooped in disappointment.

"If I'm not back by eight o'clock, you go over to the Fennel House and ask Mrs. Thistle to put you up."

"I can stay by myself. I'm old enough."

Augie ran in through the front door of the livery, with his wife on his heels in her bloomer costume and Vashti wearing her dungarees and boy's shirt, vest, and hat.

"Griff, you got any extra mounts? I know folks are supposed to have—"

"Sure, Augie, but no women." Griffin looked sternly at Bitsy and Vashti.

"Please, Griff," Bitsy said. "We're good shots. We won't slow you down."

"Trudy's outside. She's riding with her husband," Vashti said.

Griffin snatched his hat off and slapped it against his thigh. "Next I'll have the bride and groom coming around, wanting to ride out on their wedding day."

"Nope." Augie shook his bald head. "The sheriff told Hiram absolutely no way would he let him go along."

Ethan's voice sounded at that moment, out front. "All right, men, let's move!"

Griffin shot a glance at Justin. "Give Augie the chestnut and Mrs. Moore the paint mare. There's two spare mules out back. You and Vashti can take them. Don't know if they'll keep up, but it's all I've got left. The team that just came in from Silver needs to rest."

He walked Pepper out of the barn and swung into the saddle. Ethan and a band of twenty or so men already cantered toward the Mountain Road. He urged Pepper to follow, half hoping Justin and Vashti wouldn't catch up. Justin wasn't even armed. Griffin had had a couple of shooting sessions with him, but his nephew was nowhere near being a marksman, even if he had a weapon.

He clamped his teeth together. What would Evelyn say if she knew he was teaching her boy to use a gun? Out here, it was a necessary skill for a man.

Hoofbeats drummed behind him on the packed road. He looked over his shoulder. Augie and Bitsy were coming already. No. A second glance made him say something he tried not to say when Justin was around. The second rider wasn't wearing the bright red suit. It was Vashti, riding the horse he'd said Bitsy could take, and she was pulling ahead of Augie's chestnut.

"Too bad we couldn't pick up their trail." Bitsy held her hands out to the campfire that evening.

"Bill deserves better than this," Vashti said.

"It could have been you."

Vashti didn't respond. She preferred not to discuss that angle.

Ethan came to the fire, carrying his tin cup.

"More coffee, Sheriff?" Bitsy asked.

"Much obliged." She rose and poured it for him.

"I still don't know how you folks managed to grab so much stuff so fast," Ethan said.

"That's why we were late. While Augie and I were getting out of our glad rags, Goldie was down in the kitchen packing supplies for us."

Ethan smiled. "Sounds like Trudy. I wasn't of a mind to let her come, but she'd ridden in for the wedding and stashed her riding skirt at the Bentons'.'."

Parnell Oxley and Micah Landry sauntered over.

"What's the plan for morning, Sheriff?" Parnell asked.

"We'll look around a little more after daybreak, but most of these men have families and businesses they should be tending to."

Vashti's spirits plummeted even lower at Ethan's words. This was for Bill! They ought to be able to do better for him.

The other men drifted over, some still chewing their meager meal of jerky and a biscuit apiece.

"We found that mask," Josiah said.

"Yes. But that was before we got into the rocks. Awfully hard trying to track anything in these mountains." Ethan sipped his coffee.

The rough cloth mask was a gray hood with eyeholes cut into it. Josiah had found it among the brush near the creek bank. It matched what Pete Gilbert had said the robbers wore.

"Think they'll hit another stage while we're up here?" Micah asked.

Ethan shook his head. "So far they've gone two or three weeks between holdups. And they got quite a bit of money off the passengers today, as well as two thousand dollars from the treasure box. That'll keep them going for a while, I expect."

Justin and Griffin stood next to each other. Their dark eyes reflected the firelight—the giant of a man next to the slender boy. Justin had grown since he'd come last fall. In six months, he'd shot up several inches. Vashti had noticed how short his trousers were and mentioned to Griffin that the boy needed new clothes.

"Hate to head back with nothing to show for it," Griffin said.

Parnell nodded. "That's right. I say we keep after 'em."

Ethan shook his head. "I know how you feel. We all want to bring these men in. But they could be halfway to Salt Lake by now. We can't stay out here for days on end looking for them."

"Then what *can* we do?" Micah asked.

Ethan turned to Griffin. "Can't you ask for military escorts for the mail coaches?"

"I put in a request a few weeks ago, but I haven't heard anything yet. Maybe if we send a telegram and put your name on it, and Peter Nash's."

"Yeah," said Augie. "The sheriff and the postmaster ought to carry some influence."

"We can try it." Ethan dumped the dregs from his cup and set it on the rocks by the fire. "I could stay out here another day or two, but we don't have supplies, and most of you men need to get back to your regular work."

"I hate to give up," Griffin said. "After what they did to Bill. But you're right. I need to be where I can contact other people along the stage line and make sure all the routes are covered for Monday."

"We should go home and open up tomorrow," Augie said, looking at Bitsy.

Vashti reached for Bitsy's hand and clasped it. The Moores would lose money for every meal they didn't serve at the Spur & Saddle. She ought to go back with them first thing in the morning and help prepare the usual Sunday chicken dinner. Would Goldie get things ready tonight?

As much as she hated to give up the chase, she knew Ethan was right.

"You all right?" Bitsy asked her. "I know Bill was special to you."

"I'll be fine." She gritted her teeth thinking of how the brave white-haired man had died. "But I'll honor Bill's memory the best way I know how—and that's to never let my stage be held up again."

Bitsy eyed her thoughtfully. "You think you can make sure of that?"

She shrugged. "I'll do whatever I can."

"Bill probably did whatever he could, too."

Vashti didn't want to think about that. If an experienced driver like Bill was vulnerable, even with a good shotgun messenger, she would be even more so.

"It's a risky business," Trudy said.

Vashti looked over at her. She hadn't realized Trudy had come near enough to hear their conversation.

"I know, but we're sworn to protect the mail. And the passengers, of course. But the federal government gets involved when you're carrying mail."

"So why isn't the federal government out here combing these hills for that gang of road agents?" Bitsy asked.

"I don't know."

Vashti shivered and leaned closer to the fire. None of them had brought bedrolls or enough food for breakfast. Bitsy and Trudy had their husbands along to nestle up to until morning. Vashti would have to make do with her horse blanket, and nights got freezing cold this high in the mountains, even in early June.

"You've got to trust in God," Trudy said firmly. "Only He can keep you and the passengers safe. Oh, and let's not forget the U.S. Mail, too."

That hurt a little bit. Vashti was used to insults, but not from Trudy.

"I didn't mean that the mail is more important than the passengers. I just meant. . ." Tears filled Vashti's eyes, and she shook her head.

Trudy sat down beside her. "I'm sorry. I know you care about the passengers, too."

"I do." Vashti put her hands to her head. "It's just that Bill— why did it have to be him? Why does it have to be anyone? First Ned, now Bill. Those robbers are killers. We need to bring them to justice."

"Only if God wants us to," Trudy said. "But I'll tell you one thing: Until you get a military escort, the Ladies' Shooting Club will be riding your coaches, whether Griffin can afford to pay us or not. If he says no, we'll buy tickets and ride anyway. And if the stages are full, we'll ride on top, or go alongside on our own horses. We're not going to lose you, Vashti."

"Your husband—"

"Ethan knows I'm right. We have to do this. You'd do it if I were the one driving."

"Yes, I would. But I don't expect other women to risk their lives for me."

Trudy nodded, her face sober in the firelight.

Griffin and Justin walked around the fire ring and stopped near where they sat.

"Are you all right, Vashti?" Griffin asked.

"I'm fine."

He nodded. "I've been talking some more to Ethan. We'll head back in the morning. You ride with me and Justin."

Trudy stood and faced him. "Griffin, I'm going to call a meeting of the Ladies' Shooting Club about this. After shooting practice on Monday, in my kitchen at the ranch. If you're able to come address us, we'd appreciate it. And we'll set up a roster of members to ride with Vashti on every single one of her runs—like we've been doing, only more shooters. We've got to put a stop to this."

"We'll be there," Bitsy said.

"Not me. I'll be in Nampa." Vashti looked up at Griffin's glowering face.

"No, you won't. I don't want you to drive anymore."

Bitsy caught her breath.

Vashti jumped to her feet. "Why are you doing this?"

"Isn't it obvious?"

"Not to me."

Griffin glared down at her. "It's too dangerous. I'll put a man in your place, and if I can't find one at short notice, I'll drive your route myself."

"You can't."

"Can't I? Let's see, last time I looked, I was the division agent for this line. But I won't be known as the one who let women get killed driving his stages."

"I've earned the right to keep my route."

"Oh, you have? Been driving six weeks, and you're a veteran?"

They stood smoldering at each other for a long moment.

Bitsy laughed. "Come on, you two. Do I have to get my husband to bust your heads together? Settle down. You can talk about this in the morning."

"That's right," Trudy said, a little shakily. "Things will look better by daylight. Vashti, come sleep over here beside me. Ethan's going to sit up awhile with the men."

Vashti wasn't ready to give up the fight, but Griffin had already turned away and was walking off with his hand on Justin's shoulder.

Slowly she unclenched her fists and let out a long breath.

"Come on," Trudy said again.

"He can't do this."

"Well, yes, he can," Bitsy said. "I'm not so sure it's a bad thing, either. Honey, lots of people care about you. And unless I'm greatly mistaken, that man is one of them."

Impossible. If he cared, he'd know how he'd hurt her. If he cared, he'd show everyone he believed in her and let her keep driving.

★ CHAPTER 29 ★

On Sunday morning after a long, difficult ride in the dawn, the posse trotted grimly into Fergus. Griffin and Justin led the procession, and the Chapmans brought up the rear.

Vashti and the Moores left their borrowed mounts at the livery and walked down the street to the Spur & Saddle. They'd have time to get cleaned up for church and, with Goldie's help, prepare the chickens for the dozens of patrons they expected for dinner. A lot of people who hadn't ridden with the posse would come, hoping for news.

Vashti hadn't slept well on the cold mountainside, and she was sure Augie and Bitsy hadn't either, but they all arrived at church on time. As Vashti followed Goldie into the pew, Hiram and Libby came in the door.

"What are you doing here this morning?" Oscar Runnels's loud voice carried throughout the sanctuary, and the newlyweds blushed scarlet.

"Good morning to you, too, Oscar." Hiram shook his hand and guided Libby into the nearest vacant pew.

Justin came in with the other boys from his Sunday school class. Griffin may not be the ideal parent, but he was doing something right with that boy.

Vashti swung around to face forward, but she heard his voice when he entered the church. Someone greeted him near the door, and Griffin's hearty "Good morning" rang off the rafters. She didn't turn around, but she could tell by the bustle and cheerful comments that accompanied him up the aisle that he was close by.

His large form moved between her and the window across the aisle. His dark shadow lingered on her, and all grew still around them. She looked up.

Griffin stood with his hat in his hands and his Bible tucked under his arm.

"Mr. Bane," she said.

"Morning. I'd like to speak to you after church."

"I'll be helping with the chicken dinner."

"Then I'll come eat some. Can I talk to you after that?"

She hesitated. He'd only hammer home his declaration that she was done driving. She wouldn't make that easy for him. "I'll likely be washing dishes until three o'clock."

"Then I'll help you."

That surprised her. She'd expected him to say he'd wait, or he'd come around later. She squinted up at him. The sunlight from the window made his hair glow around his head. He was clean shaven—the first time she'd ever seen him without a beard. She wished he wasn't standing with his back to the light that way, so she could see his face better.

Everyone in the neighboring pews waited to hear what she would say, making no pretense of disinterest.

"Fine," she said. "Augie might have an apron that will fit you."

Several people chuckled, and Griffin cracked a smile.

"All right. We'll talk then."

Griffin paid for his dinner and Justin's and turned to his nephew. "You go on home and change now. Go over and check the livery—make sure everything's quiet there. I'll be along after I wash a few dishes and settle Miss Vashti's hash."

"Can't I do dishes, too?"

Justin's brown eyes were only a couple of inches lower than his own now, Griffin realized with a start. The boy was filling out and would likely end up as big as Griffin. He grinned. "I doubt they've got two aprons in the jumbo size."

"Can I work with Champ?"

"Sure, but don't get on him until I'm there." They'd begun saddle training a couple of weeks ago, and both colt and boy seemed to enjoy it.

"All right," Justin said. "See you later."

Anyone who saw him from the back would think he was a grown man. Griffin shook his head and turned toward the kitchen door.

Bitsy came out carrying two slices of pie on small plates. Her bright red lips curved in a grin. "I hear you're helping out with the dishes today."

"That's the plan."

"Your boss is yonder." She jerked her head toward the kitchen and passed him.

"Very funny," Griffin muttered. He reached the doorway in three steps and stood there looking in. Augie bustled about between the stove and a worktable with platters and dishes spread over it. In one corner, Vashti scraped used plates, putting the leavings in a bucket. She wore her blue satin under a big white apron, and her hair was up in a bun. When it wasn't covered by her cowboy hat, her hair looked shimmery and feminine.

"Howdy, Griff." Augie lifted a chicken leg out of a big frying pan and laid it on a platter with other crisp pieces of meat.

Griffin nodded to him and strode over to Vashti.

"Well, hello. Where's Justin?"

"I sent him home. Where's my apron?"

She smiled then, just a little smile. "You don't have to do dishes."

"I don't mind."

"All right then." She took a couple of steps and opened a drawer full of folded linens. "Let's see. . ." She pulled one out and shook it to unfold it. "This one's pretty big."

It was the kind of apron that hung around the neck with a bib to cover the wearer's shirt.

"Maybe you should take your jacket off first. Hang it over there." She indicated a row of hooks near the back door.

Griffin sauntered over and shed his coat, then went back to her and reached for the apron. She held it up, holding the neck strap away from the apron. He hesitated a second then stooped a little. She popped it over his head and smoothed the strap behind his collar.

"Turn around."

He felt silly with her tying the apron strings behind his back. Silly and a little on edge. Her light touch against the back of his shirt made his skin tingle. He pulled in a quick breath.

"There you go. What did you want to talk about?"

She seemed softer than she had this morning, more ready to listen. He turned around. She had already lifted a stack of plates and plunged them into a pan of soapy water.

"About your work for the stage line."

"What about it?"

A clean towel lay on the counter beside the dry sink, and he picked it up.

"Rinse first," she said. "You have to get the soap off. There's a kettle of hot water over there."

He went to the stove and lifted the steaming teakettle.

"She putting you right to work?" Augie asked with a wink.

"Regular slave driver," Griffin said.

Vashti put the clean dishes into another pan, and he poured the boiling water over them. She was watching out of the corner of her eye, but she didn't say anything, so he guessed he'd done it right. He grabbed the towel and began drying the first plate.

He cleared his throat. "Listen, you've been doing a good job driving."

She was quiet for a moment, then squeaked out, "Thank you," as she placed another plate in his rinsing pan.

"I mean that. You're good with the horses, and you're getting better all the time with the reins. And the passengers love you. More than one has told me you gave them a mighty smooth ride."

Her hands stilled, and she sniffed. "Do you recall what Pastor Benton spoke on this morning?"

Griffin had to think for a minute. "You mean about how we shouldn't do rash things?"

"Rash—oh yes, he did mention that." She chuckled. "Paul had a whole list of things we aren't supposed to do over in Timothy, didn't he? Funny how we each picked out different ones."

"Well, yeah, I suppose so. I'd been feeling kind of guilty—like I'd acted hastily and got mad over things I shouldn't be mad about." He eyed her cautiously. "So what one did you mean? Not loving money too much?"

"No, not that, either. It was 'boastful and proud' that hit me. Right smack in the face."

He frowned. "That doesn't sound like you."

"Doesn't it, though?" She put the last plate in his pan and reached for a pile of dirty forks. "I've been strutting around like I was the finest stagecoach driver who ever cracked a whip, when we both know I'm not." She looked up at him with earnest green eyes. "Griffin, if I were to drive every day for the rest of my life, I'd never be as good a driver as Bill Stout. Never."

"Bill was born to it." Her words made him uneasy. "That doesn't mean you can't be a fine driver one day."

"That's right. One day. Not now. I'm as green as the grass along the riverbank. I'd like to think I'm an old hand at driving, but I'm not."

"You learned a lot from Bill in a short time."

"Yes, I expect I did. But I still have a long way to go. And so. . ." She pressed her lips together for a moment, then looked up at him again. "So I'm telling you I'm sorry. I don't have a right to drive for you, like I was making out I had last night. It's a privilege, and you have the final say because you're in charge. That's fittin'."

Griffin turned around and leaned against the counter and studied the planks of the floor while he considered that. She had actually come to the place where she could stand back and let him decide what was best for the stage line. And for his drivers.

Bitsy strode in from the dining room with a tray of dirty dishes and set them down beside him.

"How's the dish crew doing?"

"Fine, ma'am."

She went over to the stove to speak to Augie.

Griffin looked over at Vashti. "I came to apologize for acting rashly and telling you that you couldn't drive anymore."

She washed another fork and plinked it into his pan. "You mean you would let me?"

"Do you still want to?"

"Yes. Very much."

He nodded, noting how pretty she looked with the steam feathering the little wisps of hair that had come loose from her bun. He could see that tiny brown mole on the back of her neck, too. He inhaled sharply and picked up the teakettle. "Let me make a suggestion. The robbers have never hit the run between here and Reynolds Creek. What if you drive that far and back every day?"

"And not go on to Nampa? What's the sense in that? You'll need another driver if I just do a short run."

He poured hot water over the soapy forks and put the kettle down. "I don't want to lose you, Vashti. I don't want to lose Georgie the driver, either, but it's not just because you're a driver. Mostly. . ." He cleared his throat. "I don't think I could live with myself if you got hit like Bill did."

She was staring at him, her pink lips parted. "Thank you. But I don't think giving me a shorter route will solve your problems."

"It won't. But it might keep me from adding to the list of ones that need solving. I could switch you with Johnny—"

"Johnny's run was hit once last month."

Griffin nodded reluctantly. "But there's not so much treasure on that route as there is over here. And with all the traffic up to Silver and the Poorman opening up again—"

"It's definite, then? They're reopening the mine?"

"That's what they tell me. And if it happens, there'll be more money going back and forth."

Vashti turned back to her dishpan and washed a few more forks. "If you put me on another route, I won't be at home between my runs, and the shooting club members won't be able to give us extra protection."

"I've been thinking about that, and I wonder if it's wise to let those women—"

"Now don't start that. You know they want to help, and they're better shots than any men you could hire. The price is right, too."

Griffin dried a fistful of forks while he thought about it. "Part of me doesn't want you driving at all, though I don't know who else I'd get to do it. And part of me wants you to go on doing it because I know it means so much to you. You're a good driver. It's true you don't have a lot of experience, but you've got a good touch."

He didn't feel he'd done the best job of explaining his reasons, but she seemed satisfied. If he told the complete truth, he'd be saying wild things about the way her eyes shone when she took the reins, and how warm it made him feel inside just knowing he'd made her happy.

"I want to keep driving," she said at last.

He nodded. "All right. We'll work something out."

"What about tomorrow?"

He sighed. "You drive to Nampa. I'll put Cecil Watson on with you until Ned's healed up. Cecil's got sharp eyes, though I'm not sure he's as good a shot as you or some of the other ladies."

"I'll put the word out that we'll take extra riders, if it's all the same to you."

"So long as there are empty seats. I won't turn away any paying customers to make room for shooters."

"Done." She wiped her hands on a towel. "I think we're caught up on dishes for the moment. Thank you for helping. Oh, and I like the new look." She nodded toward his whiskerless chin and smiled.

"Vashti. . ."

She arched her eyebrows and gazed up at him, but he couldn't think of anything else he wanted to say out loud.

★ CHAPTER 30 ★

A week later, Vashti arrived at the livery early as usual, to grease her axles and check over the harness and the horses' hooves.

"You've done a great job of grooming the team," she told Justin and the Nash boys.

"Thank you," Justin said, and the Nash brothers smiled at her. Ben was about Justin's age, and Silas was thirteen. They both seemed eager to please Griffin and earn a little pocket money. Since school was out for the summer, Griffin had decided to let Ben and Silas keep working for him at the livery with Justin until the fall term began. In the meantime, he'd scout around for a man to take over then. Vashti had never told him about the gambling incident, and so far as she knew, Justin and Ben had stayed out of trouble.

Griffin came out of one of the stalls and glanced her way. "Vashti, how's it going with Cecil?" He came over to stand directly behind her.

"Not bad." This would be her third run with Watson. Their first time out, he'd made one remark that was a bit on the crude side, and Vashti had let him know at once that she wouldn't tolerate it. It hadn't hurt that four women of the Ladies' Shooting Club were riding the stage that day. Since then, he hadn't gotten out of line, but she had the impression he resented being paired with her. On nights they were in Nampa, he disappeared shortly after supper. He always showed up on time in the morning, so she didn't ask questions.

"You've got a water run today."

She nodded. A stagecoach run with no treasure in the Wells

Fargo box suited her just fine. Of course, the passengers usually had valuables on them, and the coach would carry mail, which might also contain some money or bank drafts. But she always felt easier when they weren't carrying a payroll or precious metals.

"You didn't see anyone in those rocks last week," Griffin said.

"Nary a soul." Griffin had continued to shave, and she found it hard not to stare at him. He'd turned out rather handsomer than she'd imagined, and she was still getting used to the change.

She fixed her gaze on the front of his shirt. It struck her that she'd never seen him wear that one before—a black and white plaid that looked crisp and maybe even new. Why had Griffin taken up shaving and buying new clothes? Was it because of the mine executives who'd been coming through his office lately? Or maybe he expected an inspector for the postal service. He was now one of the handsomest men in Fergus, no doubt about it.

"I heard from the territorial governor."

That startled her into meeting his gaze. "Really?"

He nodded. "Telegram. He says we'll have a military escort in two weeks. They're giving me eight troopers."

"Eight? Fantastic."

Griffin shrugged. "That's for all my line."

"Oh."

"I figure the runs to Silver City and Boise are the most vulnerable, but I want to put two men on your run and two on the Catherine run." He frowned, and his eyebrows pushed together. That made Vashti smile. He may be well groomed, but his bushy brows still formed a hedge over his dark eyes. "I wish they'd give me more."

"It may be enough to keep the robbers away."

When she drove up to the Wells Fargo office, four women decked out for travel waited eagerly on the boardwalk. Cecil stood guard while Griffin loaded the mail. He admitted three paying passengers to the stage, then allowed the four ladies to fill the coach. Vashti hummed as he gave his signal to start. Probably Ellie and Florence Nash, Jessie Tinen, and Isabel Fennel would all go on to Boise for the night, but that was all right. Just knowing they'd be on her coach today and again tomorrow gladdened Vashti's heart.

When they approached the rocky section of the road she thought of as "the gauntlet," Cecil sat tall and watched both sides of the road like an owl, swiveling his head and staring—always staring at the boulders. Vashti kept the horses moving down the slope at a quick, controlled trot.

When they were safely through it, Cecil sat back and relaxed. "They never stop you going downhill, but it doesn't hurt to be aware."

"The last holdup happened at a bridge," Vashti said.

He nodded. "Anywhere you have to slow down and there's no houses in sight."

"Well, we should be all right at least as far as the ferry now."

They rode in silence for a ways.

"Any of those women staying over with you at Nampa?" he asked.

Vashti eyed him askance. Cecil hadn't engaged in much conversation with her since she'd put him in his place that one time.

"I don't think so. Why?"

He shrugged. "They've got a minstrel show at the school building. Thought you might want to go over and see it."

"Maybe. If any of them stay in Nampa." It might be fun, especially if Florence and her mother opted to stay.

"I meant with me."

She locked her neck muscles to keep from turning and gawking at him. The man was older than Griffin—way older. And he certainly wasn't the type she'd want to step out with.

"Oh. You mean—you and me?"

"Is that so far-fetched?"

She stared at the leaders' twitching ears, trying to form a reply that would be clear but not rude. "Thank you, but I don't think so."

"You could wear them clothes, and no one would know you was my lady friend."

The idea of being Cecil Watson's lady friend made her head swim.

"We could get a drink after," he said.

"No, thank you." She should have known there was to be an

"after" to this proposed outing.

"I heard your old employer stopped serving. Too bad. The Spur & Saddle was a top-notch watering hole."

"Well, now it's a top-notch restaurant. And I don't drink, no matter where it's served."

"You're joshing me."

"Do I look like I'm teasing?" She gave him her best glare.

"Huh."

It rankled her that he assumed because she used to work in a saloon that she would go out drinking with a man she barely knew—namely himself.

"Don't you like to have a little fun now and then?" he asked, scanning the countryside.

"I'm not sure what you consider fun."

"You know. Just—" He whipped his shotgun to his shoulder.

Vashti's heart raced and she stared in the direction he was aiming, but the ground sloped down on Cecil's side of the road.

"What is it?"

He relaxed and lowered the gun. "A couple of pronghorns grazing on the hillside yonder. When I first saw movement, I wasn't sure what it was. Reflex."

"It's a good one to have in this job."

The horses had slowed to a jog. She unfurled her whip and cracked it in the air. "Move along, you." She looked over at Cecil as she stowed the whip again. "I get all the excitement I can use driving this route."

"So that's a no?"

"That's a no."

The four female passengers went on to Boise, as Vashti had anticipated. She ate her supper early, with Cecil sitting across the table from her. He wolfed down his pork roast, potatoes, and gravy, ignoring the mess of fresh greens Mrs. Gayle served with them. After that, he put back two pieces of pie and half a pot of coffee.

When he was done, he shoved his chair back. "You sure you don't want to see the show with me, George?"

"I'm sure. You go ahead, Cecil."

He slapped his hat on and shuffled out the door.

Vashti finished her pie and carried her dirty dishes and Cecil's to the kitchen.

"Bless you, child," said Mrs. Gayle. "I'll have seven sitting down in a few minutes."

"So many?"

"Three men who came this afternoon and are staying over to take your stage in the morning, along with Mr. Gayle and the tenders. And myself, of course."

"Allow me to set the table for you," Vashti said.

"I won't refuse." As Mrs. Gayle counted out the forks for her, she kept talking. "I wrote my sister's girl and asked her to come help me out here, but she said she expects she'll get married before fall. I really do need some help."

"If I hear of any likely ladies needing work, I'll tell them."

"Thank you. Decent girls only." Mrs. Gayle put the silverware in her hand, and Vashti went to the dining room and laid places for seven. Was Mrs. Gayle saying that a woman with Vashti's background wouldn't be suitable for the job? She doubted that. The hostess was kindhearted and always treated her with respect. More likely she was only saying she didn't want to take on an employee who would cause problems with the men about the place.

When she'd finished, Vashti went to her little chamber with the bunk beds. She wished one of the women had stayed. She wouldn't have thought it, but she longed for female companionship. Back in Fergus, she had Bitsy and Goldie to talk to, and sometimes Mrs. Benton. She wondered what the minstrel show was like. It might be fun to see it. If she went by herself, no one would bother her—they'd think she was a young man.

At once she knew that was a bad idea. Cecil might spot her. Besides, enough people in Nampa knew her secret by now that she couldn't count on going out alone in the evening without fear of being bothered. When the dining room quieted below and she knew the crew and guests had been fed, she went down and helped Mrs.

Gayle wash the supper dishes.

"You're such a lovely young lady," the hostess said. "Why haven't you married, child?"

Vashti hesitated. Surely this woman knew her background. "I don't expect the Lord has that in mind for me," she said at last.

"No reason why not."

Vashti turned the topic, and when they finished, she borrowed an old magazine from Mrs. Gayle and retired to her room. Why hadn't she married? The question came back to her as she sat staring at an advertisement for shoes. If only that option was open to her. If she had the chance, there was only one man she'd consider now—one she had come to trust—and she doubted he'd ever look at her with marriage in mind. Though he had looked at her a few times with a sober, wistful air.

She turned the page of the magazine and began to read an article on cooking, something she loathed. Anything to keep from thinking of Griffin.

The next morning, she rose and dressed, knowing she had a couple of hours until the Boise stage arrived for her to take over. She went to the kitchen and found Mrs. Gayle brewing the morning coffee.

"That shotgun rider of yours never came in last night," Mrs. Gayle said.

Vashti stopped in her tracks. "Are you sure?"

"Yes. My husband's gone out to look for him."

Vashti's throat went dry. "What'll happen if he doesn't find him?"

"He'll telegraph Mr. Bane. I suppose he could send one of our tenders along as a guard."

Vashti took an apron from a peg near the back door. "My friends who went to Boise yesterday should be back this morning. They can serve as my shotgun messengers."

"Those women?"

"Yes. They all belong to the Ladies' Shooting Club of Fergus."

"I heard about that club." Mrs. Gayle shook her head. "Well, chances are my husband will find Watson, but whether he'll be sober or nay, who can tell?"

When the stage rounded the corner and rolled down the street toward him, Griffin let out a great sigh. Vashti was on time, coming in from Nampa. On the box beside her sat Florence Nash, her red hair flying. Vashti kept the mules at a spanking trot to the very last second. They pulled in and stopped on a dime, with the door of the coach directly in front of him. Ben Nash ran to take the near leader's bridle.

"You help with the bags," Griffin said to his nephew. He opened the door and mustered a smile he didn't feel.

"Welcome to Fergus, folks."

Jessie Tinen, Ellie Nash, and Isabel Fennel exited first.

"Ladies, thank you so much. If you can stick around for a few minutes, I'd love to have a word with you all."

They nodded and smiled and allowed they could do that. Griffin turned to the other passengers.

"Thank you for riding with us, gentlemen. I trust you had a good trip up from Nampa."

"Couldn't have asked for a smoother ride or more congenial company," said the first man out. A dapper man with graying hair peeking from beneath his derby, he walked over to Isabel. "Miss Fennel, may I offer you lunch? I'd love to talk with you further about your fine town and the real estate you're considering selling." He carried a black case, and Griffin pegged him for a drummer.

Isabel's face went pink, and she fluttered the fan she held. "Why thank you, Mr. Madden. My boardinghouse, just across the way, offers a fine luncheon."

"Excellent. Let me fetch my suitcase."

By this time, three other men had climbed out of the coach. Justin had scrambled to the roof and was tossing luggage down to Silas. The boys were doing a first-class job, Griffin noted.

When the passengers had cleared, he took out the mail sacks. Peter had arrived by then and hugged his returning wife and daughter.

"Did you have a good time?" he asked.

"Yes, we did." Ellie's eyes glowed with satisfaction. "We got in a little shopping, and we ate in a restaurant fancier than the Spur &

Saddle, if you can believe that."

"Wait until you see what I brought you, Papa." Florence bounced on her toes.

"I shall have to," Peter said. "I need to take care of the mail first, but I'll do it with great anticipation."

"Your boys can help you take the sacks to your house," Griffin said. He looked up at Vashti. "Anything in the box?"

"Just Mrs. Tinen's handbag."

"Oh dear, I nearly forgot. I asked Vashti to put it in there so I wouldn't have to keep track of it." Jessie stepped over and accepted her leather purse from Vashti's outstretched hand.

"Well, ladies, we're very grateful that you were along on this run. As I'm sure Miss Edwards told you, our shotgun messenger disappeared on us in Nampa."

"Shocking," said Isabel. The drummer waited near her, listening avidly.

"Yes. Well, I'm happy to say that in a couple more weeks we should have a military escort for the mail coaches. Meanwhile, we appreciate your services more than I can tell you. And as a token of my gratitude, even though I said I couldn't pay you, I'd like to give you each a silver dollar, which I'm docking from Cecil Watson's wages—if he ever shows up to collect them."

"You don't need to do that, Mr. Bane," Florence said. "We had a grand time."

"Yes, we did," Jessie said.

"I'm glad that you enjoyed yourselves. Because we had no regular messenger aboard, and because you were willing to step in and fill the role of protectors for our passengers if needed, I want to do this." Griffin reached into his pocket and distributed the four silver dollars he'd put there for the purpose.

The ladies accepted gracefully and said good-bye. The Nash family headed up the street toward their house, carrying the mail sacks and the ladies' luggage. Isabel walked across to the Fennel House with the drummer, and Jessie waved to her husband, Arthur Tinen Sr., who was just rumbling into town in his buckboard.

Griffin walked around the coach and climbed up beside Vashti.

Justin had taken over the tender's place from Ben.

"Hold them long enough for Justin to jump in," Griffin said.

"Yes, sir." Vashti nodded to the young man, and he released the mule's bridle.

"Climb aboard and ride over to the livery with us," Griffin yelled.

The mules fidgeted while Justin ran to the side of the coach, scrambled in, and closed the door. Vashti eased up on the reins and clucked to the team.

When she stopped the coach a minute later in front of the livery, Griffin said, "Let the boys unhitch the team. I need to talk to you."

"All right." She eyed him uneasily.

"I just want to know what happened with Cecil."

"I don't know."

"Uncle Griff?" Justin was out of the coach and looking up at him. "You want me to take the team in?"

Griffin had forgotten the Nash boys went home with their parents. "Start unhitching. I'll be right there." He looked back into Vashti's green eyes. "Everything go all right on the way to Nampa?"

"Yes, sir. And Cecil and I ate our supper first thing when we got there."

"Then what?"

"I'm not sure. Cecil went out." She frowned. "He did say something earlier about going to see a minstrel show in town."

"Did you tell Mr. Gayle that?"

"Yes, sir. When he came back this morning and said he hadn't found Cecil at any of the saloons or. . .well, other places he'd checked, that's when I remembered. I told him, and Mr. Gayle went to see the people in charge of the show."

"But he didn't pick up Cecil's trail."

"No, sir." She gritted her teeth.

"What aren't you telling me, Vashti?" He tried to keep his voice gentle, so he wouldn't spook her, and quiet enough that Justin wouldn't hear.

"Nothing, really. Just. . .he wanted me to go to the show with him. He asked me on the way if the ladies were staying in Nampa with me. Said we might want to see the show. I thought he meant all of us at first, but it turned out he meant just me and him. He wanted to make sure the others wouldn't be there, I guess."

"That snake."

"Why do you say that? He wasn't too obnoxious about it."

"But I told him to leave you alone." How much should he tell her? He'd given Cecil the same ultimatum he'd given Marty last fall: Keep away from Vashti or be fired. Had he walked off the job to avoid being fired?

She scrunched her lips together—shapely lips no boy would ever own up to—and looked down at the whip in her hands. "I can—"

"I know. You can take care of yourself."

She glanced up. "Actually, I was going to say, I can appreciate your doing that. As an employee."

He nodded slowly. "Let me know if you think of anything else, all right?"

"Yes, sir."

"Good. Let's get these nags unhitched."

He clambered down, and Vashti unwound the reins from the brake handle.

When Vashti walked to the livery in her driving outfit on Thursday, she looked about the shadowy barn. Justin and Griffin were bringing in the coach horses. Dr. Kincaid was saddling a dun gelding in one of the stalls, and the Nash boys were filling a wheelbarrow with manure.

Vashti walked over to meet Griffin. "Who's my messenger today?"

He hitched the near leader's halter to a tie rope. "You're looking at him."

"You?"

"Me."

"Bitsy plans to ride inside," she said.

"Good. The Dooleys are riding along, too."

"Hiram and Libby are coming?"

"That's right," he said. "They're taking a little trip."

Vashti bit her lip.

"What?" Griffin asked. "You don't like it?"

"It's so soon after their wedding."

"That's the idea. It's called a honeymoon."

She glared at him.

"Well, we're not getting stopped," he said. "Right?"

"Right."

"And the lovebirds will be well armed; you can count on that."

"No doubt. So. . .no word on Cecil?"

"Nope. Maybe Jeremiah Gayle will have some news when we get to Nampa."

Vashti went to get the pot of axle grease. When the team was harnessed and she'd inspected the fittings on the coach and horses, she climbed to the box.

Griffin sprang up beside her. "The boys can ride up the street inside."

"All right." Vashti waited until Justin, Ben, and Silas were inside the stage, then set out for the Wells Fargo office. "Where will Justin stay tonight?" she asked. "At the Fennel House?"

"No, the Nashes invited him to spend the night. Ellie sent a note over with Ben saying it was all right."

"It's nice that Justin's made some good friends."

"Yes. I've had a few talks with Peter and Ellie about raising boys. They know heaps more about it than I do."

"I'm proud of you. You've made great progress with Justin." She smiled at him. "Are you starting to feel like a father?"

Griffin's lips twitched. "Maybe more like an uncle should. I admit I wasn't keen on the setup when he first arrived."

"It's obvious things are going better. You've both come a long way."

He nodded soberly. "I think we turned a corner back around Christmastime."

"I'm glad."

She pulled up at the office, and he said offhandedly, "I'll load the treasure box."

"We're carrying money today?"

"A deposit for Ted Hire and another for the Paragon."

He climbed down, and Vashti noted that the sheriff stood

near the office door. Griffin must have told him they'd be carrying treasure. The Dooleys and Bitsy waited to one side with a couple of other passengers. Justin hopped out of the stage and ran to the horses' heads. Ben and Silas approached the passengers.

"Load your luggage, ma'am?" Ben asked Bitsy.

"Thank you, but I just have this little bag, and I thought I'd keep it with me."

"You may load ours, Ben," Libby said, and he took a tapestry satchel Hiram held out to him.

Vashti wrapped the ends of the reins around the brake handle and climbed down. She walked over to her friends. "I'm glad you folks are coming along."

"Thank you, Vashti," Libby said, all smiles.

Bitsy elbowed Libby. "That's Georgie," she whispered, a bit too loudly for a secret.

Libby covered her mouth with one dainty, gloved hand, and Hiram's lips twitched.

One of the male passengers, a cowboy from the Tinens' ranch, peered at her through half-closed eyes. Vashti looked away, but he took a step closer and stared at her openly.

"You can't be that gal from the Spur & Saddle."

His comment flustered Vashti. "You're probably right," she managed.

He pulled his head back and frowned. "You ain't the one that plays the pianner."

"Right again."

Hiram and Libby laughed.

"That there is George," Bitsy said sternly. "He's one of Mr. Bane's best drivers."

"Are you folks traveling on to Boise?" Vashti asked Libby.

"Yes, we decided to spend a few days in town."

Griffin came out of the office carrying a sack, and Ethan straightened and scanned the waiting passengers and the street beyond. Peter walked toward them carrying a mail bag.

"Excuse me, folks." Griffin nudged the cowboy aside and climbed partway up to the box.

"Maybe we'd ought to pray together." Bitsy looked around at them timidly, as though expecting her suggestion to be rejected.

"Good idea." Vashti looked toward Libby and Hiram.

"I could lead us if you wish," Libby said. "My husband can join the sheriff in keeping watch."

"Thank you," Vashti said.

Hiram nodded and took a step away, cradling his Sharps rifle in his arms and gazing out over the quiet town.

Vashti bowed her head, determined not to think about the other waiting passengers and their opinions.

"Our heavenly Father," Libby said softly, "we thank Thee for this opportunity to help our friends and to travel. We ask Thy protection as we go. Bring us safely here again. In the name of Jesus we pray. Amen."

"Amen," said Vashti and Bitsy.

Vashti opened her eyes and turned around. Griffin was locking the treasure box in the driver's boot. Since he had bolted the chests to his coaches, he couldn't lift them down to load and unload them. It made the transfer of treasure a little awkward, but that was a minor inconvenience.

When he'd finished, Griffin stepped down to the boardwalk and glanced at the boys. All the luggage was loaded. He took the mail sack from Peter and placed it in the coach, then walked over to Vashti and the volunteers.

"Folks, we thank you for offering your services. Just remember, lives are the most precious thing we're carrying, then the U.S. Mail. The front box is important, but it's nothing to die for."

They nodded.

"I suggest you keep your weapons loaded and close at hand, but ride with them pointing in a safe direction. I'll be on the box, watching the road all the time, but it wouldn't hurt to have you folks paying attention, too."

"You want me to ride on the roof?" Hiram asked.

Griffin smiled. "I think you should stick with your bride. I don't anticipate trouble today, but lately things haven't been exactly predictable."

They all nodded soberly. Griffin turned and walked to the coach and opened the door. "All aboard." The men stood back to allow the ladies to enter first.

Vashti hurried to the front of the coach and climbed up. A moment later, Griffin loomed beside her and settled into his seat, holding a new shotgun. The driving box seemed much smaller with him sitting there.

Though his presence set her on edge, the feeling was not entirely unpleasant. The more she saw of him, the more she liked him. Lately, she had begun to think that she might be persuaded to love him.

The very thought sent a flood of heat to her face.

"Anytime, Georgie," he said softly.

She gathered the reins and picked up her whip.

★ CHAPTER 31 ★

A mile out of Fergus, the stagecoach passed the Dooleys' ranch, then the Chapmans'. Griffin wished Hiram sat on the box with him to talk cattle and horses. On the other hand, he didn't mind being near Vashti. She concentrated on her driving and stayed aware of what each horse did. He watched the road ahead, but there wasn't much chance of a holdup on this stretch.

They wound down out of the hills, with the horses trotting steadily.

"How's Justin doing with the bookkeeping?" Vashti asked.

"Good. He made out my monthly report for Wells Fargo at the end of May. Did a fine job."

"I'm glad to hear it. His attitude has changed since he came."

"I think the colt helps."

"You told me Justin seemed interested in him last fall." She flicked the reins to keep the horses from lagging on a slight upgrade.

"Yes, he up and named it first thing. Champ." Griffin smiled. "He took to that colt right away. I let him take care of it, and he does a fine job. Of course, I told him that if he got into trouble or tried to jump ahead of the training program, I'd take the colt away."

"And how's Champ doing?"

Griffin smiled. "He's terrific. We've started saddle training, and Justin loves it. He's still green, but he's learning as fast as the colt is."

She grinned at him. "I'd like to see Justin work with him sometime."

"All right. I'll tell him."

When they stopped at the Democrat Station, the passengers got out to use the necessary while the tenders switched teams. Griffin stayed out near the coach while the tenders unhitched the team and brought out the new horses—four well-muscled bays that matched except for their leg markings. In just twenty minutes the coach was ready, with one new passenger added.

"Hello, Rice," Griffin greeted the man as he boarded the stage. "Going to town?"

"Yeah, just a quick jaunt in and back."

Griffin shut the people in. There were six inside now, not crowded, though they did have the mail sack to contend with. He mounted the box, and Vashti took them out with a stylish flurry of whip cracking.

After they'd gone a short ways and settled into the rhythm of the road, Griffin eyed her frankly. "You're doing well, Georgie."

"Thank you."

When she smiled, her face took on decidedly feminine lines. He realized no one who looked closely would believe she was a man. Maybe she could wear a false mustache. The thought made him smile. No, a beard would be needed to disguise her dainty chin and the smooth curve of her neck.

"What?" she asked.

He snapped his gaze forward, realizing they would soon be at the rocky stretch of road where the outlaws sometimes lurked. "Nothing. Just admiring your skill." He could feel her sneaking glances at him as he scanned the terrain ahead and to the sides.

The next time he looked at the driver, her mouth was set in a determined scowl. She was watching, too. Watching and probably remembering the other holdup.

"They don't stop you going downhill," he said.

"That fellow tried once when I was with Johnny. And if he's got friends now..."

She said no more, but Griffin renewed his vigilance. No chatter could be heard from within the coach. The others must also know this was one of the most dangerous spots on the road.

When they emerged on the downhill side of the tumbled boulders, Vashti sighed. Her shoulders fell slightly, and she cast Griffin a glance.

"I appreciate the good stock you keep for the teams."

"It pays in the long run."

"Well, I'll always be sorry for the horses Ned and I lost you."

"Can't be helped." He took a broad view, swinging his head all around to inspect the vista spread below them. The desolate country lay empty for the most part. A few ranches lay farther on, but the rocky foothills remained largely unsettled. He turned the other way, and Vashti's gaze met his. Her leaf-green eyes smiled at him. He couldn't think of any other way to describe it, and his heart jolted.

She looked forward again. "This stretch of road will be pretty when the flowers come out."

Griffin inhaled deeply. Was he out of his mind, putting a beautiful woman like her in danger day after day? His hands tightened on the stock of his gun. Was this danger any worse than what she'd lived through to get this far?

"You started telling me a bit about your past once." He looked over at her, trying to judge her reaction. "I don't want to pry, but I admit I'm curious, and I'd like to know more about you. How you came here, and why. If you don't mind telling it."

Her smile was not a happy one, and he regretted broaching the topic.

"Why did you come here?" she countered without looking at him.

"Work. A chance to be my own boss."

She nodded. "Well, I've never had that. I tried being on my own when I ran away from Aunt Mary and Uncle Joshua, but I wasn't ready to take care of myself. I tried asking for work, and a man in St. Joe actually let me sweep the front stoop of his store for him and gave me some food. But his wife found out and wouldn't let me stay on. I kicked around town, first asking for work, then begging. . . then stealing."

Griffin eyed her narrowly, thinking of the desperate twelve-year-old girl, but said nothing.

"Then I stole from the wrong person."

"You got caught?"

She nodded. "I'd been swiping food, but it was getting on for fall and the cold was setting in. I needed money, so I practiced lifting things out of sacks and pockets. I did all right the first couple of times. I got a coin purse out of a lady's handbag, and I picked up the change off a store counter. But when I tried to lift a man's wallet, he grabbed my wrist and wouldn't let go. I'd surely picked the wrong mark."

"A lawman?"

"Nope. He owned a saloon."

"Oh." Griffin frowned and looked away. He'd known it had to be in there somewhere, that plunge from petty crime into hopeless, inky darkness.

"I was there near two years," she said. "He had me sweep and scrub and wash glasses. I wasn't allowed to go out in the barroom when there were men out there drinking."

"So he had some sense of morality."

Vashti shrugged. "Not much." The pace had lagged a little, and she clucked to the horses. They quickened their trot. "After a while I caught on to what the bar girls were up to when they took a fellow upstairs. I heard one of them arguing with the owner about me one day. She kept saying I was too young. I wasn't fourteen yet. He said youth was worth big money. Well, I didn't need to hear more. I lit out first chance I had. And this time I didn't take his wallet. I knew where to get some cash from a box he kept in the kitchen." She raised her chin and looked Griffin in the eye. "I could have taken fifty dollars, but I didn't. I took three dollars and fifty cents—enough to get me out of St. Joe."

"You should have taken more."

"Yeah. That's what I figured when I got to Independence. I'd been really stupid, and now I was in worse straits than I was before. Because now men were looking at me like I was more than just an orphaned little kid."

She faced forward. The breeze past his ears, the creak of leather, and the rattle of the wheels on the hard-packed road were the only sounds he heard. Griffin's heart had gone all mushy and mournful.

He shifted on the seat and watched her as she adjusted the reins. "I'm sorry."

She shrugged it off. "I didn't pay much account to God back then, but in a way, I guess He looked after me. At least, He sent along a fella who kept me with him for a long time. He took pretty good care of me. Mostly." She flicked a glance at Griffin.

He didn't buy it. A man who took advantage of a girl that young was *not* taking care of her.

"Well, he asked for favors in return," she admitted, though he hadn't asked. "But that was better than working for somebody like my next employer." She made a face, as though she'd tasted foul medicine.

Griffin drew in a deep, painful breath. "You didn't stay with him—the fellow you said took care of you."

She shook her head. "He owed someone money, and he. . .he gave me to the man he was in debt to. The wrong kind of man." She blinked rapidly and turned her face a little to the side, but he saw a tear escape and trickle down her cheek. Did she regret revealing how far she'd sunk before she came to Fergus? Surely she wasn't actually missing the fellow who'd debauched her and sold her into slavery.

"Look, I don't want to talk about this anymore, all right?"

"Sorry. I respect that. But a man who'll give over the woman he's been protecting to settle a debt—that ain't right."

"Yeah." The horses started down a gradual slope toward a creek bottom, where they would cross a wooden bridge. Vashti took in a little rein and focused on the leaders. He was surprised when she spoke again.

"I'll just say that Bitsy Shepard was my angel. I met up with her at the dry goods store in Cheyenne, and she asked me what I was doing there. I told her I was working at the Pony, and she got this look on her face. Asked me how old I was. I told her twenty, because I was, by then. I told her I'd been with Ike—he's the one who owned the Pony—for nigh on three years. Felt like a century. You know what she did?"

Griffin shook his head. Vashti lifted a shoulder and scrubbed away the errant tear with the shoulder of her vest.

"She got me out of there. She gave me five dollars and said, 'I've got a place in Idaho Territory. I'm headed back there tomorrow. If you can get out of that filthy place in the morning without anyone seeing you, come to the depot, and I'll take you with me.' I told her I thought I could, but I might not be able to get out with my things, or Ike would catch me. Or one of the other girls would see me, and they'd tell him. She said not to worry about my clothes. She'd outfit me—and I wouldn't have to. . .to. . .to entertain men." She flushed scarlet. "Anyway, that's all I needed to hear."

"Good old Bitsy." Griffin smiled, pleased that the brusque saloon keeper had come through for the desperate girl.

"She's the best. I've been here with her four years now, and she's kept her word. Augie, too. They've protected me and let me earn an honest living."

"The Spur & Saddle has always been a high-class place, even when it was a saloon."

Vashti nodded. "It's home now. And Bitsy and me, we both found God here. I'll always believe He put me in her path that day at the dry goods. Ever since I learned to pray, I've been thanking Him." She smiled at him, though tears still glittered in her eyes.

Griffin returned her smile. Somehow they'd crossed a line—dismantled a barrier between them. He glanced ahead, down the slope to the bridge. Trees overhung the road before the short span, and he looked into the shadow beneath the branches of the pines. They were nearly halfway from Democrat's to Nampa. Laughter issued from the coach behind them—Bitsy's loud guffaw. He glanced at Vashti, and she grinned with him.

Beyond Vashti's hat brim, Griffin caught a glimpse of movement in the trees. Automatically he swung his gun barrel toward it. Vashti's eyes flared and she turned, snapping the reins and clucking to the team.

The leaders were only five yards from the bridge when two men jumped from beneath the pines, one on either side of the road.

"Ye-ha!" Vashti slapped the reins on the wheelers' sides as the outlaws took aim. The horses lurched forward then stalled for a second as the leaders saw the men and the bridge.

"Up!" Vashti yelled, and the lead team plunged toward the span. If they would just charge onward, maybe they could cross the bridge and leave the outlaws behind.

Griffin fired toward the robber on his side of the road, and she knew it might be the only shot he got off. Another gun went off somewhere behind her. Wood splintered between her and Griffin. A horse screamed. On the far side of the bridge, another man stood squarely in their path.

One of the two men she'd seen first ran toward her side of the coach. Vashti unfurled her whip, jerking the tip off to the side. Beside her, Griffin half stood, bracing his feet, as she cracked her whip at the outlaw on the ground. The masked man leaped back from the stinging lash. His gun fired, but the bullet went wide.

The horses thundered toward the bridge. The outlaw on the far side of the span drew a bead and fired. The off lead horse veered left and crashed into his harness mate, throwing the near leader off balance only a few feet short of the bridge. The two horses went down in a tangle, pawing and whinnying shrilly, while the two wheelers plowed into them. The stage swayed. Griffin and Vashti flew forward.

Vashti grabbed wildly as she landed on the off wheeler's rump. Somehow she managed to keep hold of the reins and clutch the backstrap of the harness. A moment later she felt Griffin's huge hand as he clenched a fistful of her vest and yanked her up beside him. She sprawled between the seat and the footrest.

"You hurt?" he asked.

She stared up at him, gasping. "I don't think so." She still held the reins in her hands.

"Stay down." He shoved her head lower.

"They shot one of the horses."

"I know."

The horses plunged and clattered, trying to get their footing—all but the wounded one, who neighed piteously and thrashed about on the ground. Two more men had appeared out of the brush and leveled pistols at Griffin. Someone was keeping up fire from within the coach.

"Throw down your weapons," the man at the far end of the bridge yelled over the noise.

"Griffin!"

He looked down at her, and she reached a hand toward him.

"Don't give them the mail."

"We've got no choice, Georgie. There's five of them at least."

Griffin laid his gun down in the driver's boot. They'd take it, just like they had his other gun. Scowling ahead at the outlaw across the bridge, Griffin slowly raised his hands.

"Put 'em up!"

Vashti realized he meant her, and she straightened enough so that she could obey. Raising her hands over her head was the hardest thing she'd ever done. A lull in the shooting brought a stillness broken only by the horses' breathing and struggling.

"All right, you two. Throw down the box."

Vashti caught her breath and stared toward the man on the bridge. He seemed to be the leader. She rose on her knees and wrapped the reins around the brake handle, staring all the while toward the outlaw. She squinted, eyeing his tall, lanky form closely. It couldn't be—

"Hurry up!" His boots thudded on the bridge as he walked toward them. "Get that box down here." He stepped carefully around the fallen horse and off the bridge.

When she heard his voice, Vashti was sure. After eight years, she was looking into the eyes of Luke Hatley, the man she'd at one time hoped to marry. The man who'd sold her to settle his two-hundred-dollar poker debt.

★ CHAPTER 32 ★

Pain stabbed through Griffin's knee as he tried to straighten it. When he'd catapulted forward, he'd slammed into the metal rail on the footrest. Good thing, or he'd have sprawled on top of the wheel team, the way Vashti had, but he'd smashed his knee in the process.

A quick glance around told him that two outlaws stood on the near side of the stage—his side—and one on Vashti's side. One of their men must have gone down, but whether it was the one he'd shot at first, he had no idea. Maybe one of the passengers had hit a robber.

He focused on the leader, who walked deliberately toward them with his gun pointed squarely at Griffin's chest.

"We can't throw the box down," he called.

The leader stopped and stared at him through the eyeholes in his rude sack of a mask. "Why not?"

"The box is bolted to the frame of the stagecoach." Griffin waited, his hands still at shoulder level, half expecting the man to shoot him point-blank. He glanced uneasily at Vashti. She still crouched between the driver's seat and the footrest, staring at the man. "You all right?" he asked, low enough that he hoped no one else heard.

Her lips twitched, but she didn't answer.

"All right, get down," the outlaw said, gesturing with his rifle. "Nice and easy. Get over the side and stand a couple yards away from the coach. And don't try anything."

"Come on, Georgie." Griffin lowered his hands slowly and gripped her shoulder. "With one horse down, we're not going anywhere, so we may as well do this peacefully."

"But we can't let them take the mail!"

"Yes, we can," he said between clenched teeth. "Come on. I'm not letting you get shot because of your stubbornness." Her eyes snapped. That was good. She was mad at him now, and that anger would get her moving. "Climb down on my side. I don't want the coach between us so I can't see you."

He turned to get his footing. One of the outlaws, wearing a mask, stood just below him. He jerked his rifle, indicating that Griffin must get down. He looked back at Vashti. "Come this way. Stay close to me."

She nodded but kept her gaze fastened on the leader, who now stood near the wheelers.

Griffin hopped down. Another outlaw had opened the coach door and was herding the passengers out.

"Leave all weapons and belongings in the coach, folks," he said, as if this were a sightseeing trip.

Griffin looked up. Vashti was at the edge of the messenger's seat, about to lower one foot over the side.

"Get over there," the outlaw near Griffin said, nodding toward where Hiram, Libby, Bitsy, and the other three passengers huddled.

Griffin ignored him and stayed close until Vashti hopped down from the steps to the ground. "Come on, Georgie." He placed himself between her and the outlaw and walked beside her toward the others.

"That one's Benny," she hissed.

"The one behind us?"

She nodded. So she recognized one of the robbers from the earlier holdup, even though they wore masks this time. If they ever got the chance, she might be able to identify him in court.

"I'm sorry, Griff," Bitsy said when they reached the knot of passengers.

"Nothing to be sorry for," he said.

"Hiram got one of them, but—"

"Shut up!" The man guarding them lunged toward Bitsy, pointing his gun at her midsection.

Bitsy clamped her lips together and glared at him. The red feather on her hat quivered.

Griffin noted the checkering on the stock of the gun the outlaw held. That was his shotgun—the one the robbers had stolen weeks ago. He looked away.

"Keep your hands up," growled Benny.

Griffin turned slowly, his hands in the air. Vashti stood between him and Bitsy, her mouth set in a hard line. He looked down the line at the others. They stood still in the sun with the breeze fluttering the spruce boughs. Leo Rice, whom they'd picked up at the Democrat Station, had blood on his cheek. Not shot, Griffin decided. A splinter must have caught him when the outlaws peppered the coach.

The leader and the fourth outlaw climbed up to the driver's box and rummaged around. One of them lifted Griffin's shotgun and examined it. The other held up the little canvas bag Vashti carried on her trips. He pulled out a skirt and a pair of pantalets and held them up, laughing. "Well, boss, I guess you was right."

Griffin scowled. He expected them to pull out Vashti's pistol next, but he didn't see them do that. Instead, the leader used his own handgun to shoot the lock off the treasure box. Griffin winced. More repairs to the coach. The two outlaws whooped.

"Well, boys," the leader called, "we hit pay dirt this time."

"All right," said the one who'd threatened Bitsy. "If you folks have anything of interest in your pockets, now's the time to hand it over."

Griffin sighed and reached into his pocket for Cy Fennel's watch. He handed it to Benny, with a few coins and his case knife. "That's it."

"And you, young fella?" The outlaw shifted his attention to Vashti.

"I've got nothing of value," Vashti said, stony faced.

"That right?"

"Yeah, that's right."

While Benny relieved the cowboy, Hiram, and the third male passenger of their cash, his companion looked Vashti up and down. "I heard they was a girl driving stage out here, but I didn't believe it."

Vashti said nothing, but her cheeks colored.

"Leave the driver alone," Griffin said.

"I just want to know what he's got in his pockets." The outlaw reached toward Vashti's vest.

"Here! You want this? You can have it." She swiftly unbuttoned the front and wriggled out of the vest.

The shocked outlaw stared at it and then at her cream-colored shirt. "Well now."

Griffin caught his breath and made himself look away. When she'd peeled off the vest, Vashti had turned her back slightly toward him. Stuck in the back of her trousers' waistband was her Colt revolver. The outlaw crumpled the vest in his hands and then explored its pockets, pulling out a snowy cotton handkerchief. While the robber was occupied, Griffin snaked his hand out and slipped the pistol from Vashti's waistband. She never twitched, but he knew she felt him take it. Her body shielded his action as he tucked it behind him, in his own belt. He wished he had Libby's voluminous skirts to hide it in. If the robbers decided to search him, he'd had it.

The leader and his companion climbed down from the stage laden with treasure and Griffin's new shotgun.

"You got everything?" the leader called.

"There's two sacks of mail in the coach, boss," Benny replied.

"Could be some money in it," said the man holding Vashti's vest.

"Leave it," said the leader. "We've got plenty. But bring the driver."

They all stared at him.

Vashti's stomach lurched. He knew. That was why he'd attacked this stage. But she wouldn't go with Luke, not if it meant losing her life.

Libby spoke first. "You can't take Georgie."

"Can't I?" Luke strode forward, holding his rifle trained on Griffin. "Step back, mister."

Griffin hesitated.

"I'd as soon shoot you as not," Luke snarled.

Griffin took one step back. Vashti wondered if she could distract Luke and give Griffin time to bring out her pistol. But it would be one gun against four.

"Cover the others, Benny." Luke seized Vashti's wrist and yanked her toward him. "Come on, Georgia, you're coming with me."

"No. You left me in Cheyenne, Luke Hatley. I'm not going anywhere with you." She twisted her arm, but his grip clamped her wrist like a vise.

He twisted her arm and pulled her closer. "Oh yes, you are, sweetheart. You can come along peaceful, or you can watch these good people die one by one. Which is it?"

Sick dread shot through her. The Luke Hatley she'd known wasn't a violent man, but that was eight years ago. She'd changed immeasurably. Perhaps he had, too.

He pulled her arm back farther, and she gritted her teeth.

"All right."

Luke loosened his grip but kept hold of her wrist. "That's better. Come on. I've got a horse for you across the bridge." He looked at Griffin and the passengers. "Don't try to follow us, folks, or your darling little driver will wind up dead."

He pulled her toward the bridge. The other three outlaws followed, walking backward and still brandishing their guns. Vashti stared at Griffin. He stood stock still, watching, a look of pain and disbelief on his face. Would she ever see him again, or would Luke take her far away? And if he did, would Griffin even try to find her? No man she'd trusted had ever come through for her before.

"Come on now." Luke jerked her around and dragged her past the horses.

Griffin watched in shock as the outlaw leader pulled Vashti with him. Luke Hatley must be the man who had given her to a brothel owner. He wanted to kill the man, but with three others holding him at gunpoint, he was helpless. The only thing he would accomplish by drawing the pistol would be to get himself and his unarmed friends killed. Then who would help Vashti?

When Luke got to where the team still stood, with one lead horse down and moaning, he hauled Vashti around the horses, onto the span of the bridge. The other three outlaws turned and ran after them.

Griffin whipped the pistol from behind his back.

"Hiram!" Bitsy called. She bent and pulled the right leg of her bloomers up to her knee.

"Griff, wait," Hiram said.

Griffin looked over at him. Bitsy thrust her tiny, genuine Deringer pistol—made by the master gunsmith Henry Deringer himself—into Hiram's hand.

"All right, now!" Hiram ran a few steps forward.

The outlaws were still on the bridge. Hiram took cover behind the horses and aimed. The Deringer popped, and one of the outlaws fell.

The leader had reached the far end of the bridge. He looked back and saw one of his men had fallen. He raised his rifle. Vashti wrenched away from him and leaped over the side of the bridge.

Griffin fired once and ducked behind the team, near Hiram.

"They'll likely drop the rest of the horses," Hiram said.

"You got another shot left?" Griffin asked.

"Nope. Single shot."

"Then take Vashti's sixer." Griffin handed him the revolver. Hiram was a better shot than he would ever dream of being. "There should be five shots left. I'll distract them."

"How?"

"Don't know."

Griffin glanced over his shoulder. Libby, Bitsy, and the other passengers had retreated into the trees, out of sight. He peeked around the lead horse's muzzle, preparing if necessary to run into the open and draw Luke's fire.

Luke stood on the bridge, looking down over the side. The other two outlaws were scrambling for the far side.

"He's going to get Vashti." Griffin leaped into the open. "Hatley!"

As Luke swung toward him, Hiram stepped out from the shadow of the near wheeler's side and took aim, holding Vashti's Colt with both hands, and squeezed the trigger.

★ CHAPTER 33 ★

Vashti lay in the icy water, stunned. The fall was farther than she'd bargained for, and the bottom rockier. She'd had the breath knocked out of her. Both ankles and one wrist throbbed, but she didn't move. She lay with her head to one side, hauling in gulps of air and concentrating on keeping her face out of the six-inch-deep water.

Above and behind her, several shots rang out. She didn't care. She only wanted to breathe.

A closer explosion jerked her into reality. She craned her neck and looked up at the bridge. Luke was up there, still wearing the ridiculous mask. He'd spotted her in the creek. He raised his rifle to his shoulder and pointed the barrel at her.

"What's the matter, Georgia? You used to like me."

She turned her face away. Let him shoot her if he wanted. That would be better than going with him again. *Lord, if You want to take me home, I'm ready,* she thought. Then she remembered Griffin and the others. She looked around at Luke again. He was still aiming at her.

"Come on. I haven't got all day. Get up."

She closed her eyes.

Two more shots rang out. Something splashed in the water beside her. She opened one eye. A rifle was caught in the current but snagged on the rocks. It lay there in the burbling water. Had Luke dropped his gun?

A bigger splash threw gallons of freezing water over her. She raised her head. Luke lay facedown in the creek, on top of his rifle.

Vashti huddled, shivering in the stagecoach. Libby and Bitsy rubbed her hands and feet. Both had donated their shawls to keep her warm, and they'd recovered her leather vest.

"You're going to be all right," Bitsy said, wrapping Vashti in her arms. "Griff and the other men will get the team straightened out, and we'll take this coach back home."

"No," Vashti said. "We've got to get the mail through to Nampa."

"We'll go back to the Democrat Station, and they'll get a new team," Libby said. "Then we'll take you home. Someone else can drive to Nampa."

They wouldn't have an extra driver on hand, but Vashti knew it was useless to explain the quirks of the stage line.

A gunshot sounded, very close and loud. She jumped and grabbed Bitsy's hand.

"There now, honey. Griff said they'd have to put the one horse down. I'm sorry."

Vashti squeezed her eyes tightly shut. A tear escaped and ran down her cheek.

Hiram came to the door of the coach. "How are you doing, ladies?"

"We're all right." Libby's usually cheerful voice was subdued as she looked to her husband for news.

"Griff's unhitching the lead horse that wasn't hurt. He's going to send the cowboy to get the men from the Democrat Station."

"What about the outlaws?" Bitsy asked.

"Mr. Rice and the other passenger are guarding the two that Griffin captured."

Bitsy frowned. "So. . .two dead?"

"Three. That one we got first thing—" Hiram stopped and swallowed hard.

"The one you shot out the window? What about him?" Bitsy asked.

"We took all their masks off. It's Cecil Watson."

Vashti stared at him for a moment, then collapsed against the back of the seat. The man who'd run out on her in Nampa had joined the outlaws. She felt as if every ounce of energy had been drained from her.

Outside, receding hoofbeats told her the cowboy was leaving for the swing station. A moment later, Hiram stepped aside and Griffin appeared in the doorway.

"We've decided to wait until they bring another team out. One of the wheel horses has a flesh wound. He'll heal up, but I don't want to ask him to pull right now."

Vashti sat up, finding new strength. If Griffin could keep going with his knee all smashed up, she could, too. "What about the leader? The one blocking the bridge?"

Griffin winced. "We'll have to move him. I figure when Mr. Jordan and his boys get here, we'll hitch the new team to the horse and drag him off the road. Maybe we can get a crew out here this afternoon to dig a hole. Don't want to leave something dead that big so close to the road."

She nodded, thankful for that. She wouldn't have to pass the horse's carcass every time she drove this road.

Griffin leaned his big body inside so that he was half in the coach and blinked in the dimness. His gaze focused on Vashti. "How you doing?"

She nodded, frowning. "I'll be all right. I'm a little sore in places."

He reached out and touched her cheek gently. "You sure?"

"Yes."

"We'll have Doc check you over."

She nodded and on impulse grabbed his hand. "How about you? Hiram said one of the outlaws was Cecil Watson."

"That's right. He's dead. Him and Hatley and the one they called Benny. So now we know: They had an insider who knew when there would be treasure in the box."

She sucked in a breath. "Thank you, Griff. You and Hiram." Her tears let loose, and she turned her face away.

Two hours later, Griffin and Vashti rode together in the stagecoach.

Mr. Jordan had insisted he could drive a team of mules back to his station. It wasn't that far, and the injured parties needed to sit inside, in relative comfort.

Libby, Bitsy, and Hiram opted to ride on the roof with Jordan, and the other passengers rode the two healthy horses from their original team. Griffin thought they'd all gone to great lengths to put him and Vashti alone in the stage together, but he didn't mind. If his knee didn't hurt so much, he'd have been tickled.

"You'd better have Doc check out that knee," Vashti said. She hadn't protested when he sat beside her on the cushioned seat at the back of the coach, instead of one of the other seats. He took that as a good sign.

"My knee will be fine. It's you I'm worried about."

"I'm just bruised up. Nothing's broken." Her clothes were still damp, but she'd dried out considerably. She probably would heal up within a couple of weeks, but it wasn't her bumps and bruises that worried him.

"What about Luke?" he asked.

"What about him?"

Griffin drew in a deep breath. "Did you know he was in these parts?"

She was quiet for a moment; then she looked at him. "I thought I saw him in Boise, that one time I drove through. Trudy was with me. I saw a man come out of a saloon, and I thought it was Luke. Scared me something awful."

"Did you tell Trudy?"

Vashti nodded. "I decided it wasn't really him—just my imagination."

"Do you think he came here looking for you?"

"No. He probably came looking for a chance to make some easy money. When he heard about me, he probably thought it was a streak of luck."

"Folks have been talking about the female driver," Griffin said.

"Yes. And if he heard my name was George Edwards. . ."

"He knew you as Georgia?"

"Yes. I changed my name after I left Ike's." She sighed and shrank away from him, into the corner of the seat.

Griffin reached over and found her icy cold hand. He cradled it in his and stroked it with his thumb. "That's all in the past."

"I know." Her voice had gone tiny, but she didn't pull her hand away.

He inhaled deeply and let the breath out in a puff. "So why did you pick the name Vashti?"

She blinked at him. "You sure you want to chitchat now?"

"Might as well."

She looked out the coach window. They were going uphill, only half a mile or so from Democrat. She sat back with a sigh, still letting him hold her hand. "When I came here to Idaho, I wanted a new name. Somebody told me once that Vashti was the name of a queen in the Bible."

"I reckon that's right."

"Yeah. But see, after we got the parson and I started going to church, I found out the king got mad at Vashti and kicked her out. He got himself a new queen."

Griffin nodded. "Esther."

"That's the one. And Esther was the really pretty one, and she ended up being the honorable queen. Vashti was thrown out of the palace in disgrace. Esther saved her people."

"That's true, but I wouldn't be so hard on Vashti if I were you."

"You wouldn't?"

"Nope. From what Reverend Benton says, I'd say Queen Vashti was quite a lady."

"You think so?"

"Yes. Her husband wanted her to act in an unseemly manner, and she refused."

Vashti pondered that. "I thought she was bad because she wouldn't do what the king said."

"Maybe. But I think she had a reason for that. Maybe if you ask Miz Benton, she can tell you more about Queen Vashti."

"I might do that."

"Good. Because I happen to think the name suits you more than you know."

"Really?"

"Yup. You don't stand by convention, and. . .well, if anyone was to ask me, I'd say you had a regal way of moving, and you're pretty enough to show off, too."

She eyed him critically, as if she thought he was making fun of her.

"I mean it," he said softly. "I think a heap of you, Vashti Edwards."

She sucked in a breath. "Honest?"

He squeezed her hand. "Honest."

Halfway back to Fergus they met the welcoming party. Jordan had taken the stage and its paying passengers on to Nampa himself, driving the mule team and taking one of his hostlers along as shotgun messenger. He'd loaned Griffin his farm wagon. With Hiram driving, they'd headed out with the two sound horses from the stage team in harness. Libby and Bitsy sat on the seat with Hiram, and Griffin and Vashti sat in the back on a quilt.

From the road ahead, a whooping broke out with the sound of pounding hoofbeats. Vashti held on to the side of the wagon and raised herself until she could see three horses approaching at breakneck speed.

Ethan and Trudy Chapman galloped toward them, and out in front came Justin on Griffin's gelding, Pepper.

"Uncle Griff!" When Justin saw his uncle in the wagon, he halted Pepper and slid to the ground. Hiram stopped the team, and Justin climbed over the wheel into the wagon bed. He flung himself into Griffin's arms. "What happened? Mrs. Chapman and I were worried, so the sheriff telegraphed Nampa. They said you were late."

"We got waylaid." Griffin slapped the boy on the back. "We're all right, so quit fretting."

Justin looked at Vashti. "You, too, Miss Edwards?"

"I'm going to be fine, Justin," she said.

Ethan and Trudy rode up to the wagon and greeted them all. Bitsy launched into a colorful account of the day's events.

"So where are all these road agents you whipped?" Ethan asked.

"Down to Democrat's," Bitsy said. "Two living and three killed."

Ethan looked them over solemnly. "You folks all right?"

"We're fine," Hiram said. "One of the passengers was grazed, but he wanted to go on to Nampa."

"Griffin and Vashti both need to see Doc when we get home," Libby said.

Trudy rode Crinkles around the wagon. When she came close, Vashti reached out and petted the mare's nose, glad to see Trudy's mount had been returned to her.

"You sure you're all right?" Trudy asked.

"Scrapes and bruises," Vashti said. "Griffin hurt his knee, but we'll make it."

"I guess I'd better go on to Democrat's," Ethan said.

"They've got the prisoners locked in the corn crib," Hiram said. "Maybe you'd better get a few men to help you take them to Boise."

"I'll loan you a wagon, if you want to come to the livery," Griffin said.

"You're not going alone to take two prisoners in." Trudy eyed her husband sternly.

"I'll get a couple of my deputies." Ethan returned her stubborn look. "My male deputies. This isn't a job for ladies."

"For once, I'm going to agree with you," Bitsy said. "Can we go home now?"

Two nights later, Griffin walked slowly down the street to the Spur & Saddle. He still limped, but his knee didn't hurt so bad anymore. He went slowly up the steps and into the building. Bitsy was wiping off a table. Doc Kincaid and Isabel Fennel sat in one corner, chatting softly. Rose Caplinger lingered at a table across the room, sipping coffee with Maitland Dostie. Griffin looked, then looked again. He supposed it made sense—Rose had opened her millinery shop last year in the vacant storefront next to the telegraph office. The two must see each other every day.

Bitsy looked up and smiled. "Hello, Griff. Where's your shadow?"

"I left Justin over to the Nashes' playing Chinese checkers with Ben and Silas."

Bitsy nodded. "Have you eaten?"

"Yes, ma'am."

"Piece of pie, then? Coffee? Or did you just come for the company?"

Griffin smiled and glanced toward the kitchen. "I came to see one of my drivers."

"She's in the dishpan, as usual."

"Is my apron hanging by the door?" Griffin asked.

She laughed and shooed him toward the kitchen. Griffin found Vashti scrubbing Augie's saucepans.

"Evening, Griff," Augie called. He picked up a bucket of slops and went out the back door.

Vashti smiled at him but kept on scrubbing the pan. "What brings you out?"

Griffin grabbed an apron off a hook and walked toward her. "I came to see how you were doing and if you'll be ready to drive again Monday."

"You mean you'd let me?"

He smiled. "I don't think we'll see any outlaws on the Nampa run for a while." He held out the apron.

She took it and pulled up the neckband. Griffin stooped toward her. She slid it over his head, then leaned close and kissed his cheek.

He straightened, eyeing her closely. "What's that for?"

"You saved my life. I've already been to see Hiram and thanked him personally."

"Did you kiss him?"

Her face went scarlet. "No, I. . ."

Griffin laughed.

She eyed him askance and began to laugh, too. "That was just for you." She turned back to her dishwater.

"Aren't you going to tie my apron strings?"

"If you want."

"Vashti. . ."

"Yes?"

He could look into those leaf-green eyes forever. He reached for her, and she came into his arms before he even knew what he was going to do. Her kiss was sweeter than Augie's cinnamon rolls.

He held her close against his apron front and sighed. "You can drive anytime you want, sweetheart."

She reached all the way around him and squeezed him tight. Griffin held her, wanting never to let go. After a while, he dared to reach up and stroke her hair. "You know I only opposed your driving because I wanted to take care of you."

"Is that so?" Her tone held amusement.

He pulled back a little and looked down at her. "Maybe not at first. But. . .well, you're a strong woman. I didn't know how strong. But I'd still like to take care of you. For the rest of my life, if you'll have me."

Her lips curved into a smile. "What kind of talk is that? *If* I'll have you."

"I mean it."

She shook her head. "I'm the one who's got a load of baggage. Are you sure you can overlook everything?"

"It's in the past. I'll make sure it stays in the past."

She looked away, frowning, then turned back to face him. "I never. . ." Tears glistened in her eyes. She cleared her throat. "I never got close to a man except those that had bad intentions."

"Well, my intentions are honorable."

She nodded slowly. "And you won't make me quit driving?"

"No." A sudden thought came to him. "Well, not unless. . .well, you know." Blood rushed to his cheeks, and he wished he still had his beard to hide it. "If you were in a delicate way. . ."

She reached up and stroked his stubbly cheek. "I love you, Griffin Bane."

It was the one thing he'd meant to say, but hadn't been sure how—and now she'd said it first. "I love you, too. Can we go see the parson after services tomorrow?"

"That would be lovely."

He kissed her again, and the dishes would have sat unwashed for hours if Augie hadn't come in with his empty slop bucket and slammed the back door.

"Well now! Wait 'til Bitsy hears about this! She'll be some tickled."

Susan Page Davis

Vashti stood beside her bridegroom in the dining room of the Spur & Saddle, ready to cut the wedding cake. Augie had outdone himself. With help from Rose Caplinger, he'd fashioned a garden of sugar roses and topped the four-tiered masterpiece with two feathery white doves.

Ethan Chapman came over near the table and raised his hands. "Folks, if I could interrupt for just a minute, I have an announcement to make."

The murmuring quieted as everyone focused on the sheriff. Ethan looked over at Griffin, and he shrugged. Vashti took that to mean he had no idea what was going on, but he was in a mellow mood and didn't care how many announcements people made today. The vows were said, and nothing could change that. She reached for his big hand, and he squeezed hers, smiling.

"Some of you know I got back from Boise yesterday. I delivered some prisoners to the U.S. Marshal there a few days ago. Those outlaws are two of the gang we believe held up the stagecoach twice on the Nampa run and once each on the Catherine and Silver City runs. The postal service had sent notice of a reward to the marshal before Griff Bane and Hiram Dooley caught the outlaws."

"We had some help," Griffin muttered.

Ethan swung around and grinned at him. "Yes, you did. In fact, I have orders to give a share of the reward to the following people: Griffin Bane, Hiram Dooley, Leo Rice, Buck Ashley—"

Arthur Tinen Jr. let out a whoop at the mention of the name of one of his cowhands. Ethan smiled and nodded at him.

"Yes, Buck was on the stage that day, and other witnesses say he acquitted himself well. The same with the drummer who was a passenger, Mr. John Sedge. The marshal will send his part to him. Also receiving a share of the reward will be Miss Georgia Edwards, Mrs. Hiram Dooley, and Mrs. Augustus Moore."

Libby, Bitsy, and Vashti exchanged looks across the room. Hiram beamed, and Augie said, "That's my darlin' girl." He gave Bitsy a loud smack on the cheek.

Griffin let go of Vashti's hand and slid his arm around her waist. "You deserve it, Queen Vashti."

Ethan grinned. "If each of you will please see me when it's convenient, I'll give you a bank draft for your share in the ten-thousand dollar reward."

"Ten thousand!" Bitsy's jaw dropped.

"What's that make your share?" Augie asked.

"That's $1,250," yelled Justin, who had been sipping lemonade in a corner with his friends.

Ethan smiled at the boy. "That's exactly right, and spoken by Mr. Bane's accountant."

Everyone laughed.

Goldie called out, "And the newlyweds get a double share."

"That's fittin'," said Bitsy.

Vashti looked up into Griffin's brown eyes. With that and the money Wells Fargo had sent for new equipment, they wouldn't wonder where the money to keep the stage line running would come from. Griffin nodded, contentment oozing from him. She snuggled close and hugged him around the waist.

Johnny Conway stepped up beside Ethan with his driving whip in his hand. "Folks, I have an announcement, too."

The crowd quieted.

"I know it's not far to the happy couple's new home," Johnny said, "but when they've finished their cake and are inclined to leave this jolly gathering, Ned and I have a carriage waiting outside to carry them home."

Griffin's bushy eyebrows shot up. "What?"

"Take a look out the window, boss," Ned Harmon called.

Griffin seized Vashti's hand and strode to the front window. They both looked out at their transportation for the two-block ride home: the red and gold Concord coach, with roses twined all along the top luggage rack and tucked into the horses' harness.

"Anytime you're ready, just say the word, and we'll drive you home," Johnny said.

Vashti tugged the whip out of his hand. "Oh no, you won't. You can ride along as far as the house if you want, but *I'm* driving."

About the Author

SUSAN PAGE DAVIS is the author of more than thirty novels in the historical romance, mystery, romantic suspense, contemporary romance, and young adult genres. A history and genealogy buff, she lives in Kentucky with her husband, Jim. They are the parents of six terrific young adults and are the grandparents of six adorable grandchildren. Visit Susan at her Web site: www. susanpagedavis.com.

OTHER BOOKS BY
SUSAN PAGE DAVIS

The Sheriff's Surrender
The Gunsmith's Gallantry